SWALLOWING DARKNESS

LAURELL K.

HAMILTON

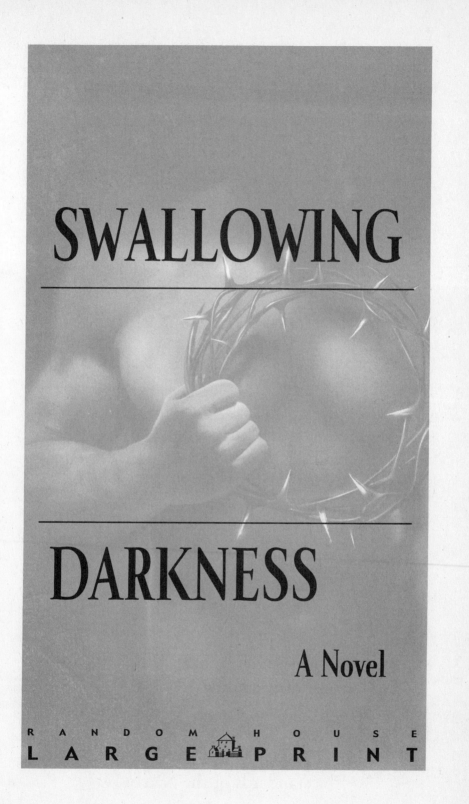

SWALLOWING

DARKNESS

A Novel

RANDOM HOUSE
LARGE PRINT

Copyright © 2008 by Laurell K. Hamilton

Published in the United States of America by Random House Large Print in association with Ballantine Books, New York.
Distributed by Random House, Inc., New York.

Cover design: David Stevenson
Cover illustration © Don Sipley

The Library of Congress has established a Cataloging-in-Publication record for this title.

ISBN: 978-0-7393-2808-8

www.randomhouse.com/largeprint

FIRST LARGE PRINT EDITION

10 9 8 7 6 5 4 3 2 1

This Large Print edition published in accord with the standards of the N.A.V.H.

I FEEL LIKE ONE,

WHO TREADS ALONE

SOME BANQUET HALL DESERTED.

WHOSE LIGHTS ARE FLED,

WHOSE GARLANDS DEAD,

AND ALL BUT HE DEPARTED!

From "Oft, in the Stilly Night"
By Thomas Moore
(National Airs, 1818)

TO JONATHAN, WHO WALKS THE EMPTY

PLACES WITH ME,

AND TURNS ON THE LIGHTS AS WE GO.

ACKNOWLEDGMENTS

Darla, who helps my good intentions become reality. Sherry, who is still fighting the fight to organize us artsy types. Merrilee, my agent, who is always ready to put on her armor and go into battle at my side. Shawn, for a friendship that is now old enough to go into a bar by itself and order its own drinks. Charles, who has taught me the joy of a little bit of chaos, and that just because I don't have a detailed plan doesn't mean it can't work out. Pili and Carri, who braved Dragon Con with us. Science fiction author and Army and Air Force veteran Michael Z. Williamson, who volunteered to help with the military bits. All mistakes in that area are mine and mine alone, but his input kept them to a minimum. My writing group, The Alternate Historians: Deborah Millitello, Mark Sumner, Marella Sands, Sharon Shinn, and Tom Drennan. Friends in the trenches.

SWALLOWING DARKNESS

CHAPTER ONE

HOSPITALS ARE WHERE PEOPLE GO TO BE saved, but the doctors can only patch you up, put you back together. They can't undo the damage. They can't make it so you didn't wake up in the bad place, or change the truth to lies. The nice doctor and the nice woman from the SART, Sexual Assault Response Team, couldn't change that I had indeed been raped. The fact that I couldn't remember it, because my uncle had used a spell for his date-rape drug, didn't change the evidence—the evidence that they'd found in my body when they did the exam and took samples.

You would think being a real live faerie princess would make your life fairy-tale-like, but fairy tales only **end** well. While the story is going on, horrible things happen. Remember Rapunzel? Her prince got his eyes scratched out by the witch, which blinded him. At the end of the story, Rapunzel's tears magically restored his sight, but that was at the end of the story. Cinderella was little better than a slave. Snow White was actually nearly killed four different times by the evil queen. All anyone remembers is the poisoned apple, but don't forget the huntsman, or the enchanted girdle and the poisoned comb. Pick any fairy tale that's based on older stories, and the heroine of the piece has a miserable, dangerous, nightmarish time of it.

I am Princess Meredith NicEssus, next in line to a high throne of faerie, and I'm in the middle of my story. The happy-ever-after ending, if it's coming at all, seems a very long way away tonight.

I was in a hospital bed, in a nice private room, in a very nice hospital. I was in the maternity ward, because I was pregnant, but not with my crazy uncle's baby. I had been pregnant before he stole me away. Pregnant with the children of men I loved. They'd risked everything to rescue me from Taranis. Now, I was safe. I had one of the greatest warriors that faerie had ever seen at my side: Doyle, once the Queen's Darkness, and now mine. He stood at the window, staring off into the night that was so ruined by the lights from the hospital parking lot that the blackness of his skin and hair was much darker than the night outside. He'd removed the wraparound sunglasses that he almost always wore outside. But his eyes were as black as the glasses that hid them. The only color in the dim light of the room was the glints from the silver rings that climbed the graceful line of one ear to the point that marked him as not pure blood, not truly high court, but mixed blood, like me. The diamonds in his earlobe sparkled in the light as he turned his head, as if he'd felt me staring at him. He probably had. He had been the queen's assassin a thousand years before I was born.

His ankle-length hair moved like a black cloak as he came toward me. He was wearing green hospital scrubs that he'd been loaned. They had replaced the blanket from the ambulance that had brought us here. He'd entered the golden court, to rescue me, in the form of a large black dog. When he shape-shifted he lost everything, clothes, weapons, but strangely never the piercings. The many earrings and the nipple piercing survived his return to human form, maybe because they were part of him.

He came to stand beside the bed, and take my hand—the one that didn't have the intravenous drip in it, which was helping hydrate me, and get me over the shock I'd been in when I had arrived. If I hadn't been with child, they'd have probably given me more medicine. For once I wouldn't have minded stronger drugs, something to make me forget. Not just what my uncle, Taranis, had done, but also the loss of Frost.

I gripped Doyle's hand, my hand so small and pale in his large, dark one. But there should have been another beside him, beside me. Frost, our Killing Frost, was gone. Not dead, not exactly, but lost to us. Doyle could shape-shift to several forms at will and come back to his true form. Frost had

had no ability to shape-shift, but when wild magic had filled the estate where we'd been living in Los Angeles, it had changed him. He had become a white stag, and run out the doors that had appeared into a piece of faerie that had never existed before the magic came.

The lands of faerie were growing, instead of shrinking, for the first time in centuries. I, a noble of the high courts, was with child, twins. I was the last child of faerie nobility to be born. We were dying as a people, but maybe not. Maybe we were going to regain our power, but what use to me was power? What use to me was the return of faerie, and wild magic? What use was any of it, if Frost was an animal with an animal's mind?

The thought that I would bear his child and he would neither know nor understand made my chest tight. I gripped Doyle's hand, but couldn't meet his eyes. I wasn't sure what he would see there. I wasn't sure what I was feeling anymore. I loved Doyle, I did, but I loved Frost, too. The thought that they would both be fathers had been a joyous one.

He spoke in his deep, deep voice, as if molasses, and other, thick, sweet things, could be words, but what he said wasn't sweet. "I will kill Taranis for you."

I shook my head. "No, you will not." I had thought about it, because I had known that Doyle would do just what he'd said. If I asked, he would try to kill Taranis, and he might succeed. But I could not allow my lover and future king to assassinate the King of Light and Illusion, the king of our enemy court. We were not at war, and even those among the Seelie Court who thought Taranis was mad or even evil would not be able to overlook an assassination. A duel, maybe, but not an assassination. Doyle was within his rights to challenge the king to a duel. I'd thought about that, too. I'd half liked that idea, but I'd seen what Taranis could do with his hand of power. His hand of light could char flesh, and had nearly killed Doyle once before.

I had let go of any thought of vengeance at Doyle's hand when I weighed it against the thought of losing him too.

"I am the captain of your guard, and I could avenge my honor and yours for that reason alone."

"You mean a duel," I said.

"Yes. He does not deserve a chance to defend himself, but if I assassinate him, it will be war between the courts, and we cannot afford that."

"No," I said, "we can't." I looked up at him then.

He touched my face with his free hand. "Your eyes glow in the dark with a light of their own, Meredith. Green and gold circles of light in your face. Your emotions betray you."

"I want him dead, yes, but I won't destroy all of faerie for it. I won't get us all kicked out of the United States for my honor. The treaty that let our people come here three hundred years ago stated only two things that would get us kicked out. The courts can't make war on American soil, and we can't allow humans to worship us as deities."

"I was at the signing of the treaty, Meredith. I know what it said."

I smiled at him, and it seemed strange that I could still smile. The thought made the smile wilt a little around the edges, but I guess it was a good sign. "You remember the Magna Carta."

"That was a human thing, and had little to do with us."

I squeezed his hand. "I was making a point, Doyle."

He smiled, and nodded. "My emotions make me slow."

"Me, too," I said.

The door behind him opened. There were two men in the doorway, one tall and one short. Sholto, King of the sluagh, Lord of that Which Passes Between, was as tall as Doyle, and had long, straight hair that fell toward his ankles, but the color was white-blond, and his skin was like mine, moonlight pale. Sholto's eyes were three colors of yellow and gold, as if autumn leaves from three different trees had been melted down to color his eyes, then everything had been edged in gold. The sidhe always have the prettiest eyes. He was as fair of face as any at the courts, except for my lost Frost. The body that showed under the t-shirt and jeans he'd worn as part of his disguise when he came to save me seemed to cling to a body as lovely as the face, but I knew that at least part of it was illusion. Starting at his upper ribs, Sholto had extra bits, tentacles, because, though his mother had been high-court nobility, his father had been one of the nightflyers, part of the sluagh, and the last wild hunt of faerie. Well, the last wild hunt until the wild magic had returned. Now, things of legend were returning, and Goddess alone knew what was real again, and what was still to return.

Until he had a coat or jacket thick enough to hide the extra bits, he would use magic, glamour, to hide the extras. No reason to scare the nurses. It was his lifetime of having to hide his differences that had made him good enough at illusion to risk coming to my rescue. You do not go lightly against the King of Light and Illusion with illusion as your only shield.

He smiled at me, and it was a smile I had never seen on Sholto's face until the moment at the ambulance when he had held my hand, and told me he knew he would be a father. The news seemed to have softened some harshness that had always been there in his handsome body. He seemed the proverbial new man, as he walked toward us.

Rhys was not smiling. At 5'6", he was the shortest full-blooded sidhe I'd ever met. His skin was moonlight pale, like Sholto's, like mine, like Frost's. Rhys had removed the fake beard and mustache he'd worn inside the faerie mound. He'd worked at the detective agency in L.A. with me, and he'd loved disguises. He was good at them, too, better than at illusion. But he'd had enough illusion to hide the fact that he only had one eye. The remaining eye was three circles of blue, as beautiful as any in the court, but where his left eye had once lain was white scar tissue. He usually wore a patch in public, but tonight his face was bare, and I liked that. I wanted to see the faces of my men with nothing hidden tonight.

Doyle moved enough so Sholto could put a chaste kiss against my cheek. Sholto wasn't one of my regular lovers. In fact, we'd only been together once, but as the old saying goes, once is enough. One of the children I carried was part his, but we were new around each other, because in effect we'd only had one date. It had been a hell of a first date, but still, we didn't really know each other yet.

Rhys came to stand at the foot of the bed. His curly white hair, which fell to his waist, was still back in the ponytail he'd worn to match his own jeans and t-shirt. His face was very solemn. It wasn't like him. Once he'd been Cromm Cruach, and before that he'd been a god of death. He wouldn't tell me who, but I had enough hints to make guesses. He'd told me that Cromm Cruach was god enough; he didn't need more titles.

"Who gets to challenge him to the duel?" Rhys asked.

"Meredith has told me no," Doyle said.

"Oh, good," Rhys said. "I get to do it."

"No," I said, "and I thought you were afraid of Taranis."

"I was, maybe I still am, but we can't let this go, Merry, we can't."

"Why? Because your pride is hurt?"

He gave me a look. "Give me more credit than that."

"I will challenge him, then," Sholto said.

"No," I said. "No one is to challenge him to a duel, or to kill him in any other way."

The three men looked at me. Doyle and Rhys knew me well enough to be speculative. They knew I had a plan. Sholto didn't know me that well yet. He was just angry.

"We can't let this insult stand, Princess. He has to pay."

"I agree," I said, "and since he brought in the human lawyers when he charged Rhys, Galen, and Abeloec with attacking one of his nobles, we use the human law. We get his DNA, and we charge him with my rape."

Sholto said, "And what, he will risk jail time? Even if he would allow himself to be put in human jail, it would not be enough punishment for what he has done to you."

"No, it's not, but it's the best we can do under the law."

"Human law," Sholto said.

"Yes, human law," I said.

"Under our laws," Doyle said, "we are within our right to challenge him and slay him."

"That works for me," Rhys said.

"I'm the one he raped. I'm the one who is about to be queen, if we can keep our enemies from killing me. I say what Taranis's punishment will be." My voice grew a little strident at the end, and I had to stop and take a breath, or two.

Doyle's face betrayed nothing. "You have thought of something, My Princess. You are already planning how this will help our cause."

"Help our court. For centuries the Unseelie Court, our court, has been painted black in the human world. If we have a public trial accusing the king of the Seelie Court of rape, we will finally convince the humans that we are not the villains of the piece," I said.

Doyle said, "Spoken like a queen."

"Like a politician," Sholto said, and not like it was a compliment.

I gave him the look he deserved. "You're a king, too, of your father's people. Would you destroy your entire kingdom for vengeance?"

He looked away, then, and there was that line to his face that showed his temper. But as moody as Sholto was, he didn't hold a candle to Frost. He had been my moody boy.

Rhys came to the bedside. He touched my hand, the one to which the IV needle was taped. "I would face the king for you, Merry. You know that."

I took my free hand and held his, and met that one blue-ringed eye. "I don't want to lose anyone else, Rhys. No more of that."

"Frost is not dead," Rhys said.

"He is a white stag, Rhys. Someone told me that he may only keep that shape for a hundred years. I am thirty-three and mortal. I will not see a hundred and thirty-three years. He may return as the Killing Frost, but it will be too late for me." My eyes burned, my throat grew tight, and my voice squeezed out, "He will never hold his baby. He will never be a father to it. His babe will be grown before he has hands to hold it with, and a human mouth to speak of love and fatherhood." I lay back against the pillows and let the tears take me. I held onto Rhys's hand and let myself cry.

Doyle came to stand beside Rhys, and laid his hand against my face. "If he had known that you would grieve him most, he would have fought it more."

I blinked back the tears, and gazed up at that dark face. "What do you mean?"

"It came to us both in a dream, Meredith. We knew that one of us would be sacrificed for the return of faerie's power. An identical dream on the same night, and we knew."

"You didn't tell me, either of you," I said, and there was accusation in my voice now. Better than tears, I supposed.

"What would you have done? When the Gods themselves choose, no one can change that. But it must be a willing sacrifice; the dream was clear on that. If Frost had known it was his heart you held most dear, he would have fought more, and I would have gone for him."

I shook my head, and moved away from his hand. "Don't you understand? If it had been you changed into another form, and lost to me, I would weep as much."

Rhys squeezed my hand. "Doyle and Frost didn't understand that they were the front-runners, together."

I jerked free of his hand, and glared up at him, happy to be angry, because it felt better than any other emotion inside me in that moment. "You're fools, all of you. Don't you understand that I would mourn you all? That there is none of my inner circle that I would lose, or risk? Do you not all understand that?" I was shouting, and it felt much better than tears.

The door to the room opened again. A nurse appeared, followed by a white-coated doctor whom I'd seen earlier. Dr. Mason was a baby doctor, and one of the best in the state, maybe in the country. This had been explained to me in detail by a lawyer whom my aunt had sent. That she had sent a mortal and not one of our court had been interesting. None of us knew what to make of it, but I felt that she was treating me as she might treat herself if our situations were reversed. She had a tendency to kill the messenger. You can always get another human lawyer, but the immortal of faerie are scarce so she sent me someone whom she could replace. But the lawyer had been very clear that the queen was thrilled at the pregnancy, and would do all she could to make my pregnancy a safe one. That included paying for Dr. Mason.

The doctor frowned at the men. "I said not to upset her, gentlemen. I meant it."

The nurse, a heavyset woman with brown hair tucked back in a ponytail, checked the monitors, and bustled around me while the doctor scolded the men.

The doctor wore a wide black headband that looked very stark against her yellow hair. It made it more clear, at least to me, that the color wasn't her natural shade. She wasn't much taller than me, but she didn't seem short as she came around the bed to face the men. She stood so that she included Rhys and Doyle by the bed, and Sholto, who was still in the corner near the chair, in her frown.

"If you persist in upsetting my patient, you will have to leave the room."

"We cannot leave her alone, Doctor," Doyle said in his deep voice.

"I remember the talk, but you seem to have forgotten mine. Did I or did I not tell you that she needed to rest, and under no circumstance be upset?"

They'd had this "talk" outside the room, because I hadn't heard it. "Is there something wrong with the babies?" I asked, and now I had fear in my voice. I'd rather have been angry.

"No, Princess Meredith, the babies seem quite"—there was the smallest hesitation—"healthy."

"You're hiding something from me," I said.

The doctor and nurse exchanged a look. It was not a good look. Dr. Mason came to the side of the bed opposite the men. "I'm simply concerned about you, as I would be for any patient carrying multiples."

"I'm pregnant, not an invalid, Dr. Mason." My pulse rate was up, and the machines showed that. I understood why I was hooked up to more machines than normal. If anything went wrong with this pregnancy there would be problems for the hospital. I was about as high profile as you got, and they were worried. Also, I'd been in shock when they brought me in, with low blood pressure, low everything, skin cold to the touch. They'd wanted to make sure my heart rate and such didn't continue to drop. Now the monitors betrayed my moods.

"Talk to me, Doctor, because the hesitation is scaring me."

She looked at Doyle, and he gave one small nod. I did not like that at all. "You told him first?" I said.

"You're not going to let this go, are you?" she asked.

"No," I said.

"Then perhaps one more ultrasound tonight."

"I've never been pregnant before, but I know from friends I had in L.A. that ultrasounds aren't that common early in pregnancy. You've done three already. Something is wrong with the babies, isn't there?"

"I swear to you that the twins are fine. As far as I can see on the ultrasound and tell from your blood workup, you're healthy and at the beginning of a normal pregnancy. Multiples can make a pregnancy more challenging for the mother and for the doctor." She smiled at that last. "But everything about the twins looks wonderful. I swear."

"Be careful swearing to me, Doctor. I am a princess of the faerie court, and swearing is too close to giving your word. You don't want to know what might happen to you if you were forsworn to me."

"Is that a threat?" she said, drawing herself up to her full height and gripping both ends of the stethoscope around her shoulders.

"No, Doctor, a caution. Magic works around me, sometimes even in the mortal world. I just want you and all the humans who are taking care of me to understand that words you might say casually may have very different consequences when you are near me."

"So you mean if I said, 'I wish,' it might be taken seriously?"

I smiled. "Fairies don't really grant wishes, Doctor, at least not the kind in this room."

She looked a little embarrassed then. "I didn't mean . . ."

"It's all right," I said, "but once upon a time giving your word and then breaking it could get you hunted by the wild hunt, or bad luck could befall you. I don't know how much magic has followed me from faerie, and I just don't want anyone else hurt by accident."

"I heard about the loss of your . . . lover. My condolences, though in all honesty I don't understand everything I was told about it."

"Even we do not understand everything that has happened," Doyle said. "Wild magic is called wild for a reason."

She nodded as if she understood that, and I think she meant to leave.

"Doctor," I said, "You wanted another ultrasound?"

She turned with a smile. "Now, would I try to get out of this room without answering your questions?"

"Apparently you would, and that wouldn't endear you to me. That you talked to Doyle before me has already put a mark against you in my mind."

"You were resting peacefully, and your aunt wanted me to talk to Captain Doyle."

"And she is paying the bills," I said.

The doctor looked flustered and a little angry. "She is also a queen, and honestly, I'm not sure how to react to her requests yet."

I smiled, but even to me the smile felt a little bitter. "If she makes anything sound like a request, Doctor, she's being very nice to you. She is queen and absolute ruler of our court. Absolute rulers don't make requests."

The doctor gripped both ends of her stethoscope again. A nervous habit, I was betting. "Well, that's as may be, but she wanted me to discuss things with your primary," she hesitated, "man in your life."

I looked up at Doyle, who was still by my bedside. "Queen Andais chose Doyle as my primary?"

"She asked who the father of the children were, and I, of course, couldn't answer that question yet. I told her that an amniocentesis would up your risk of problems right now. But Captain Doyle seems very confident that he is one of the fathers."

I nodded. "He is, and so is Rhys, and so is Lord Sholto."

She blinked at me. "Princess Meredith, you only have twins, not triplets."

I looked at her. "I know who the fathers of my children are, yes."

"But you . . ."

Doyle said, "Doctor, that is not what she means. Trust me, Doctor, each of my twins will have several genetic fathers, not just me."

"How can you be certain of something so impossible?"

"I had a vision from Goddess."

She opened her mouth as if she'd argue, then closed it.

She went to the other side of the room, where they had left the ultrasound machine after the last time they'd used it on me. She put on gloves, and so did the nurse. They got the tube of gloopy stuff that I'd already learned was really, really cold.

Dr. Mason didn't bother asking if I wanted any of the men to leave the room this time. It had taken her a little while to realize that I felt that all the men had a right to be in the room. The only one we were missing was Galen, and Doyle had sent him on an errand. I had been half asleep when I'd seen them talking, low, then Galen had left. I hadn't thought to ask where, or why. I trusted Doyle.

They lifted the gown, spread the blueish goo, again very cold, on my stomach, then the doctor got the chunky wand, and began to move it across my abdomen. I watched the monitor and its blurry picture. I'd actually seen the image enough that I could make out the two spots, the two shapes that were so small, they didn't even look real yet. The only thing that let me know what they were was the fast fluttering of their hearts in the image.

"See, they look perfectly fine."

"Then why all the extra tests?" I asked.

"Honestly?"

"Please."

"Because you are Princess Meredith NicEssus, and I'm covering my ass." She smiled and I smiled back.

"That is honest for a doctor," I said.

"I try," she said.

The nurse began to clean my stomach off with a cloth, then she cleaned the equipment as the doctor and I stared at each other.

"I've already had reporters pestering me and my staff for details. It isn't just the queen who's going to be watching me closely."

She gripped her stethoscope again.

"I am sorry that my status will make this harder for you and your staff."

"Just be a model patient, and we'll talk in the morning, Princess. Now, will you sleep, or at least rest?"

"I'll try."

She almost smiled, but her eyes had that guarded look like she wasn't certain she believed me. "Well, I think that's the best I can hope for, but," and she turned to the men, "no upsetting her." She actually shook a finger at them.

"She is a princess," Sholto said from the corner, "and our future queen. If she demands unpleasant topics, what are we to do?"

She nodded, with that grip on her stethoscope again. "I've been talking to Queen Andais, so I do see your problem. Try to get her to rest, try to keep her quiet. She's had a lot of shocks today, and I'd just like it better if she rested."

"We will do our best," Doyle said.

She smiled, but her eyes stayed worried. "I'll hold you to that. Rest." She pointed her finger at me as if it were some sort of magic to make me do it. Then she went for the door and the nurse trailed after her.

"Where did you send Galen?" I asked.

"He is fetching someone who I thought would help us."

"Who and where from? You didn't send him back into faerie alone?"

"No." Doyle cupped my face in his hands. "I would not risk our green knight. He is one of the fathers and will be a king."

"How is that going to work?" Rhys asked.

"Yes," Sholto said, "how can we all be king?"

"I think the answer is that Merry will be queen," Doyle said.

"That is no answer," Sholto said.

"It's all the answer we have now," Doyle said, and I stared into those black eyes and saw colored lights. Colors of things that were not in this room.

"You are trying to bespell me," I said.

"You need to rest, for the sake of the babies you carry. Let me help you rest."

"You want to bespell me and me to allow it," I said softly.

"Yes."

"No."

He leaned in toward me with the colors in his eyes seeming to grow brighter like rainbow stars. "Do you trust me, Meredith?"

"Yes."

"Then let me help you rest. I swear to you that you will wake refreshed, and that all the problems will still be waiting to be decided."

"You won't decide anything important without me? Promise?"

"I promise," he said, and he kissed me. He kissed me, and suddenly all I could see was color and darkness. It was like standing in a summer's night surrounded by fireflies, except these fireflies were red, green, yellow, and . . . I slept.

CHAPTER TWO

I WOKE TO SUNLIGHT, AND GALEN'S SMIL-ing face. his curls were very green in the light, haloed with it, so that even the pale white of his skin showed the green tint that usually only showed when he wore a green shirt. He was the only one of my men who had short hair. The only sop to custom was a braid of hair that now trailed over his shoulder and down past the bed. I'd mourned his hair at first, but now, it was just Galen. He had been just Galen to me since I was fourteen and had first asked my father to marry me to him. It had taken me years to understand why my father had said no. Galen, my sweet Galen, had no head for politics or subterfuge. In the high court of faerie you needed to be good at both.

But he had come into the Seelie Court to find me because he, like me, was good at subtle glamour. We could both change our appearances while someone was watching, and stand a chance of having them see only the change we wanted them to see. It had been the magic that had stayed with all of faeriekind, as other, seemingly more powerful, magics had faded.

I reached up with my hand, but the IV made me stop the motion. He leaned down and laid a soft kiss on my mouth. He was the first man who had kissed me there since I was brought into the hospital. It felt almost startling, but good. Had the others been afraid of truly kissing me? Afraid it would remind me of what my uncle had done?

"I like the smile better," Galen said.

I smiled for him. He'd been making me smile in spite of myself for decades.

He touched the line of my cheek, as delicately as a butterfly's wing. That one small touch made me shiver, but not with fear. His smile brightened, and it made me remember why I had once loved him above all others.

"Better, but I have someone here who I think will help the smile stay." He moved so I could see the much smaller figure behind him. Gran was more than a foot shorter than Galen.

She had my mother's long, wavy hair, still a deep chestnut brown even though she was several hundred years old. Her eyes were liquid and brown and traditionally lovely. The rest of her wasn't so traditional. Her face was more brownie than human, which meant she had no nose. The holes were there, but nothing else, and very little lips, so that her face seemed skeletal. Her skin was wrinkled and brown and it wasn't from age, just taking after her brownie heritage. The eyes might have been my great-grandmother's eyes, but the hair had to be my great-grandfather's. He had been a Scottish farmer, and farmers didn't have portraits painted. I had only glimpses of Gran and my mother and aunt to see what I could see of the human side of my family.

Gran came to the edge of the bed and laid her hand over mine. "Dearie, my little dear, what ha' they done to thee?" Her eyes were shiny with unshed tears.

I moved my free hand to put over hers, where it lay over the IV. "Don't cry, Gran, please."

"An' why not?" she asked.

"Because if you do, so will I."

She gave a loud sniff, and nodded briskly. "That's a good reason, Merry. If you can be this brave, so can I."

My eyes burned, and my throat was suddenly tight. It was irrational, but somehow I felt safer with this tiny woman beside me than I had with the guards. They were trained to give their life for me, and they were some of the finest warriors the court could boast, but I hadn't felt safe, not really. Now, Gran was here, and there was still something of that childhood feeling that as long as she was with me nothing truly bad could happen. If only it were true.

"The king will suffer for this outrage, Merry, my oath on that."

The tears began to fade, on a wash of pure terror. I gripped her hand tightly. "I've forbidden the men to either assassinate him or challenge him to a duel, Gran. You are to leave the Seelie Court alone, too."

"I am not your bodyguard to be bossed around, child." The look on her face was one I knew well, that stubborn set to her eyes, her thin shoulders. I didn't want to see it on this topic.

"No, but if you get yourself killed trying to defend my honor, that won't help me." I rose, grabbing at her arm. "Please, Gran, I couldn't bear to lose you and know it was my fault."

"Ach, 'twouldn't be your fault, Merry. It would be that bastard king."

I shook my head, almost sitting up with all the tubes and wires tugging at me. "Please, Gran, promise me you won't do anything foolish. You have to be around to help with the babies."

Her face softened, and she patted my hand. "So it is to be twins like my own girls."

"They say twins skip a generation. I guess it's true," I said. The door opened and the doctor and the nurse were there again.

"I told you gentlemen not to upset her," Dr. Mason said in her sternest voice.

"Ah, and it were me," Gran said. "I'm sorry, Doctor, but as her grandmother, I'm a wee bit upset at what has happened."

The doctor must have already seen Gran, because she didn't do that double take that most humans do. She just gave Gran a stern look and waved her finger at her. "I don't care who is doing it. If you can't stop sending her vitals up and down and sideways, then you are going to have to leave, all of you."

"We've explained before," Doyle said. "The princess must be under guard at all times."

"There are policemen just outside the door, and more of your guard."

"She can't be alone, Doctor." This from Rhys.

"Do you truly think the princess is still in danger? Here in the hospital?" she asked.

"Yes," Rhys said.

"I do," Doyle and Sholto said together.

"A powerful man with magic at his beck and call, who'd rape his own niece, might do anything," Gran said.

The doctor looked uncomfortable. "Until we have a piece of DNA to compare to the king's, we don't have proof that it was his. . . ." She hesitated.

"Sperm," I said for her.

She nodded, and got a death grip on her stethoscope. "Very well. His sperm that we found. We have confirmed Mr. Rhys and the missing guard Frost as two of the donors, but we can't confirm who the other two are yet."

"Other two?" Gran asked.

"It's a long story," I said. Then I thought of something. "How did you get DNA to compare for Frost?"

"Captain Doyle gave me some hair."

I looked past Gran at Doyle. "How did you just happen to have a lock of his hair with you?"

"I told you of the dream, Meredith."

"So what?"

"We exchanged locks of hair, to give to you as a token. He had mine and would have given it to you to remember me if I had been chosen. I gave a few strands of the lock to the doctors for comparison."

"Where were you hiding it, Doyle? You had no pockets as a dog."

"I gave it to another guard for safekeeping. One who did not travel into the Golden Court with us."

Just saying it that way meant he'd planned on the possibility of none of them surviving. It didn't make me feel any better to hear that. We had all survived, but the fear was still there deep inside me. The fear of loss.

"Who did you trust to hold such a token?" I asked.

"The men I trust most are in this room," he said in that dark voice that seemed to match his color. It was the kind of voice that the night itself would use, if it were male.

"Yes, and by your earlier words, you planned for failure as well as success. So you left the locks of hair with someone you didn't take inside the Golden Court."

He came to stand at the foot of the bed, not so near Gran. Doyle was aware that he had been the

Queen's Darkness, her assassin, for centuries, and many folk of the court were still nervous around him. I appreciated that he gave Gran room, and I approved of him sending Galen to fetch her. I wasn't certain there was another guard among my men whom she would have trusted. The rest had been too much like enemies for too long.

I studied his dark face, though I knew that his face sometimes didn't help me at all. In the beginning he had let his emotions show around me, but as I'd come to read his face better he'd schooled that face. I knew that, if he didn't wish it, I would gain nothing from his face but the pleasure of looking at it.

"Who?" I asked.

"I left both locks of hair with Kitto."

I stared at him, and didn't try to keep the surprise off my face. Kitto was the only man in my life who was shorter than Gran. He was four feet even, eleven inches shorter than she. But his skin was moonlight white like mine, and his body a perfect male replica of the sidhe guards, except for the line of glittering, iridescent scales down his back, the tiny fold-away fangs in his mouth, and the huge slit-pupiled eyes in their sea of blue. All that proved that his father had been, or was, a snake goblin. His curling black hair, his white skin, and the magic that sex with me had awakened were from his mother's bloodline. But Kitto had not known either parent. His sidhe mother had left him to die at the edge of the goblin mound. He'd been saved, because newborns are too small to make a good meal, and sidhe flesh is valued for food among the goblins. Kitto had been given to a female goblin to raise until he was big enough to eat, like a piglet being saved for Yule dinner. But the goblin female had come to . . . love him. Love him enough to keep him alive and treat him as another goblin, not as food on the hoof, as it were.

The other guards had not considered Kitto one of them. He was too weak, and though Doyle had insisted that he hit the gym along with the rest so there were muscles under that white skin, Kitto would never be a true warrior.

Doyle answered the question that must have been plain on my face. "Everyone I trusted more went into the faerie mound with us. Of those we left behind, who would have understood what those two locks of hair would have meant to you, our princess? Who but one of the men who had been with you since the beginning of this adventure? Only Nicca was left behind, and though a better warrior than Kitto, he is not stronger of will. Besides, our Nicca is soon to be a father, and I would not involve him in our fight."

"It is his fight, too," Rhys said.

"No," Doyle said.

"If we lose, and Merry does not take the throne, our enemies will kill Nicca and his soon-to-be bride, Biddie."

"They would nae dare harm a sidhe woman who carried a child inside her," Gran said.

"I think some of them would," Rhys said.

"I agree with Rhys," Galen said, "I think Cel would rather see all of faerie destroyed than lose his chance to follow his mother onto the throne."

Gran touched his arm. "Ya have grown cynical, boy."

He smiled at her but it left his green eyes cautious, almost hurt. "I've grown wise."

She turned to me. "I hate to think that any sidhe noble is so hateful, even that one."

"The last I heard from my aunt, my cousin, Cel, had plans to get me with child, and we'd rule together."

A look of disgust showed on Gran's face. "You'd die first."

"But now, I'm already pregnant, and it can't be his. Rhys and Galen are right; he'll kill me now if he can."

"He'll kill you before the babes are born, if he can," Sholto said.

"What concern is my Merry to ya, King Sholto of the sluagh?" Gran didn't even try to keep the suspicion out of her voice.

He moved closer to the bed, standing at the foot of it. He had let the other three men do most of the touching. I appreciated that since we were still more acquaintances than friends. "I am one of the fathers of Merry's children."

Gran looked at me. It was an unhappy, almost angry look. "I heard the rumor that the sluagh's king would be a father, but I didnae credit it."

I nodded. "It's true."

"He cannae be king of the sluagh and king of the Unseelie. He cannae sit two thrones." She sounded hostile.

Normally, I would have been more diplomatic, but the time for diplomacy was past, at least among my inner circle. I was pregnant with Gran's great-grandchildren; I might be seeing a lot of her. I did not want her and Sholto bickering for nine months, or longer.

"Why are you angry about Sholto being one of the fathers?"

It was a very blunt question, rude by any standard among the sidhe. The rules were a little less subtle among the lesser fey.

"One day of being the next queen and you would be rude to your ol' granny?"

"I'm hoping to see a lot of you while I'm pregnant, but I'm not going to mess with bad will between you and my lovers. Tell me why you don't like Sholto."

The look in her lovely brown eyes was not friendly, not at all. "Did you nae wonder who struck the blow that killed your great-grandmother, my mother?"

"She died in one of the last great wars between the courts."

"Aye, but who killed her?"

I looked at Sholto. His face was its arrogant mask, but his eyes were thinking too hard. I didn't know his face as well as Rhys's or Galen's, but I was almost certain that he was thinking furiously.

"Did you kill my great-grandmother?"

"I slew many in the wars. The brownies were on the side of the Seelie Court, and I was not. I, and my people, did kill brownies and other lesser fey of the Seelie Court in the wars, but whether one of them was your blood, I do not know."

"Worse then," Gran said. "You killed her and it meant nothin' to ya."

"I killed many. It becomes difficult after a time to separate the dead one from another."

"I saw her die at his hand, Merry. He slew her and moved on, as if she were nothing." There was such pain in her voice, a raw hurt that I had never heard from my grandmother.

"Which war was this?" Doyle asked, his deep voice falling into the sudden tension like a stone thrown down a well.

"It was the third call to arms," Gran said.

"The one that started because Andais boasted that her hounds could out-hunt Taranis's," Doyle said.

"So that's why it's called the War of Dogs," I said. He nodded.

"I do nae know why it began. The king ne'r told us why we were to fight, only that to refuse was treason and death."

"Think about why the first one is called the Marriage War," Rhys said.

"That one I know," I said. "Andais offered to marry Taranis and combine the two courts, after her king died in a duel."

"I can't remember anymore which of them took insult first," Doyle said.

"That war was more than three thousand years ago," Rhys said. "The details tend to get fuzzy after that much time."

"So all the great fey wars have been over stupid reasons?" I asked.

"Most of them," Doyle said.

"The sin of pride," Gran said.

No one argued with her. I wasn't certain that pride was a sin—we weren't Christian—but pride could be a terrible thing in a society where the rulers had absolute sway over their people. There was no way to say no, no way to say "isn't this a stupid reason to get our people killed?" Not without being imprisoned, or worse. That went for both courts, by the by, though the Seelie Court was more circumspect over the centuries, so that its reputation among the media had always been better. Andais liked her tortures and executions more public.

I looked from Gran to Sholto. His handsome face was uncertain. He tried for arrogance, but there was a flinching in his tri-yellow eyes. Was it fear? Perhaps. I think he believed in that moment that I might cast him away, because three thousand years ago he had slain my ancestor.

"He waded through our people as if they were so much meat, something to be cut down, so that he could get to the main fightin'," Gran said, with rage in her voice that I'd never heard even for the abusive bastard who had been her husband at the Seelie Court.

"Sholto is the father of one of your great-grandchildren. Sex with him awakened the wild magic. Sex with him is what has given back the dogs and faerie animals that are appearing in the courts and among the lesser fey."

She gave me a look—such bitterness in that one look. It frightened me a little. My gentle Gran, so full of hate. "Rumor said that, too, but I didnae believe it."

"I swear by the Darkness that Eats all Things that it is true."

She looked startled. "Ya did nae ha' to make that oath to me, Merry-girl. I would believe ya."

"I want this clear between us, Gran. I love you, and I am sorry that Sholto slew your mother, my great-grandmother, in front of you, but he is not only the father of one of my children, he is also the consort who helped me bring back much of the magic that has returned. He is too valuable to me and to faerie to be accidentally poisoned."

"The sidhe cannae be poisoned," she said.

"Not with anything occurring in nature, no, but you've lived in the human world for decades. You know very well that there are man-made poisons now. The sidhe are not proof against artificial creations. My father taught me that."

"Prince Essus was a very wise man, and for a sidhe royal, he was a great, great man." There was a ferociousness to her words. She meant them, for she had loved my father as a son, for he, more than my mother, had loved me, and had allowed Gran to help him raise me. But the rage in those words didn't match what she was saying, as if there were other words in her mind than those on her tongue.

"He was, but his greatness is not what is in your mind, grandmother. I see a rage in you that frightens me. The kind of rage that all the fey seem capable of, so that they will trade their lives and the lives of those who depend on them for vengeance and pride."

"Do nae compare me to the lords and ladies of the court, Merry. I have a right to my anger, and my thoughts on it."

"Until I can trust that you are more my ally and grandmother than a revenge-seeking daughter, I cannot have you around me."

She looked startled. "I will be with you and the babes as I helped raise you."

I shook my head. "Sholto is my lover and the father of one of the children. More than that, Gran, sex with him brought back the most magic to faerie. I will not risk him to your vengeance, unless you make our most sacred oath that you will not harm him in any way."

She searched my face as if thinking that I must be joking. "Merry-girl, you cannae mean this. You cannae think that this monster is more to you than me."

"Monster," I said softly.

"He has used sidhe magic to hide that he is more a monster than any a' the rest."

"What do you mean, 'the rest'?" I asked.

She motioned to Doyle. "The Darkness kills withou' mercy. His mother was a hell hound, his father a phouka who bedded the bitch when in dog form. You could ha' puppies inside ya. They act as if the high lords are perfect, but they are jus' as deformed as we are. They can just hide it behind their magic better than us lesser folk."

I looked at the woman who had helped raise me as if she were a stranger, because in a way she was. I'd known that she resented the courts—most of the lesser fey did—but I had not known that she had this prejudice inside her.

"Do you have a special grudge against Doyle too?" I asked.

"When ya came to me, Merry, you had Galen with ya, and Barinthus. Them I ha' nothin' agin', but I didnae dream you would go to the Darkness. Ya feared him as a child."

"I remember," I said.

"Do ya not understand, girl, that if the queen had had your father killed, who she would ha' sent to do the deed?"

Ah. "Doyle did not kill my father."

"How do ya know, Merry? Did he tell ya he did nae?"

"Doyle would not have acted without the queen's express orders, and Andais is not a good enough actress. She did not order my father, Andais's brother's, death. I saw her anger over it. It was real."

"She didnae love Essus."

"Maybe she loves only her son, but her brother meant something to her, and she did not like that he died at someone's hand. Maybe it was anger that she had not done the ordering of it. I do not know, but I **do** know that Andais did not order the deed done, and that Doyle would not have acted without that order."

"But he would ha' done it, if ordered. You do believe that," Gran said.

"Of course," I said, and my voice was as calm as hers was growing strident.

"He would ha' killed your father at the queen's orders. He would ha' killed you."

"He was the Queen's Darkness. I know that, Gran."

"How can ya sleep with him, then? Knowing the blood that must be on his hands."

I tried to think how to say it so she would understand. Her reaction had caught me completely off guard. I didn't like that, and not just for the normal reasons that a granddaughter might not like her grandmother hating her husband-to-be. I didn't like that she had been able to hide this level of hatred from me all these years. It made me wonder what else I'd missed, what else she'd hidden.

"I could say simply that I love him, Gran, but the look on your face says that won't do. He is my Darkness now. He would kill at my orders now. He is one of the greatest warriors to ever walk the courts, and he is mine now. He is my strong right hand, my killing blow, my general. In all the courts I could not have taken a king who would have made me stronger than Doyle."

Emotions chased across her face so quickly that I couldn't follow them all. Finally, she said, "So ya took 'im to your bed because it was good politics?"

"I took him to my bed because the Queen of Air and Darkness ordered him to my bed. I never dreamed that I could part her Darkness from her side."

"How do ya know that he is nae still her creature?"

"Gran," Galen said, "are you feeling all right?"

"Ne'r better. I just want Merry to see the truth."

"And what is the truth?" Galen asked, and his voice held a tone. I studied his face, but his eyes were all for Gran. It made me study her, too. Her eyes were a little wide, her lips parted, her pulse rate up. Was it just anger, or was it something else?

"They cannae be trusted, ana of them."

"Who, Gran?" Galen asked. "Who cannot be trusted?"

"The queen's men, girl." She addressed me now. "Ya grew up knowin' the truth of that. She must see the truth." The last was whispered, and she had lost her accent. She was upset: the accent wouldn't lessen, not on its own.

"Did you see anyone from either court when you went to her home?" Doyle asked.

Galen actually thought about it before saying, "No, I didn't **see** anyone." He put too much emphasis on "see."

"What's wrong with her?" I asked softly.

"There be nothin' wrong with me, girl," Gran said, but her eyes were a little too wild, as if the spell, for it was a spell, was growing stronger.

"Gran, you and I were buddies once," Rhys said, moving up so that Doyle could move back out of her sight.

She frowned at him, as if she were having trouble recognizing him. "Aye, you ne'r did me or mine harm. You kept to yourself in the old days, and you were on the side of gold and dreams. You were allied to us once, white knight." She grabbed his arm. "How can you be with them now?"

The accent was gone; the voice was almost not hers at all. "What's happening to her?" I asked. I reached out, and she reached for me, but Galen and Rhys stepped in the way, nearly knocking each other over in their haste.

"What is it?" I asked, and this time my voice rose. I could hear the monitors getting excited again. If I didn't calm down, we'd have doctors and nurses in here. We didn't need humans in the middle of what looked to be a magical attack. I tried to calm down, while my grandmother tried to push past Rhys and Galen. She was trying to persuade them, as well as me, that we were on the side of evil.

Doyle's voice cut through mine, "There's

something in her hair, a thread, or another hair. It glows."

"I see it," Rhys said.

"I don't," Galen said.

I couldn't see around the two of them. I had only glimpses of Gran's long brown arms trying to reach past them, almost frantically.

The door opened, and Dr. Mason and two nurses came in. "What the hell is going on in here?" she asked. And this time she sounded truly pissed.

I guess I couldn't blame her, but I also couldn't think of a way to explain. Was being pregnant making me slow to think, or was I still in shock?

"Everyone out. I mean it this time!" Dr. Mason had to shout to be heard over Gran's progressively more piercing words.

Then the glass of water on the bedside table levitated, slowly, up into the air. It hovered there about eight inches above the table-top. The bendable straw in it moved a little bit from the upward movement, but the cup was steady. Gran was really good at levitating, like all brownies. She'd served me tea in china cups like this since I was very small.

The lamp beside the cup also began to rise. Then the water pitcher bobbled upward. The lamp got to the end of its cord, and moved gently in the air like a boat moored to a dock. It was all very gentle, so why was my heart rate skyrocketing, and my pulse choking me? Because brownies don't lose control of their powers. Ever. But bogarts do.

What's a bogart? A brownie gone bad. What do I mean by that? Darth Vader is still a Jedi Knight, right? The Christians still believe that Lucifer is a fallen angel, but what most people forget is that he's still an angel.

Dr. Mason had a death grip on her stethoscope again. "I don't know what's happening here exactly, but I know it's upsetting my patient. So, it stops now, or I will call security, or the police, and have this room cleared." Her voice was only a little shaky as she watched the bobbing lamp and floating cup.

"Gran," Galen said, his voice sounding loud in the sudden silence. She had stopped yelling. In fact, the room felt too quiet, like that hush that falls upon the world just before the heavens open and a storm crushes the world.

"Gran," I said softly, and my voice held the panic of my pulse in it. "Please, Gran, please don't do this."

Galen and Rhys were still between her and me, so I couldn't see her, but I could feel her. I could feel her magic as it spread through the room. The pen lifted out of the doctor's pocket. She made a small yip.

Rhys said, "You told me once, Hettie, that Meg went bogart because she was weak, and let her anger best her. Are you weak, Hettie? Will you let your anger be your master, or will you be the master of your anger?" There was more to his words than just what I could hear. There was power to his voice that was more than just words. Power, magic of a sort, filled his words like the push of the tide fills the riffling of waves. Waves can be small, but there is always that sense that behind the easy froth that curls around your ankles, there is something much larger, much less gentle. So it was with Rhys's voice, simple words, but there was a feel to them that made you want to agree with them. Made you want to be reasonable. He would never have tried such a trick on another sidhe, but Gran wasn't sidhe. Try as she might, even to marrying one of the great sidhe, she was lesser, and magic that would not work on the great might work on her.

It was both an insult from someone she thought a friend, and a move of desperation, because if it didn't work, then Rhys might have done the proverbial sowing of the wind. I prayed to Goddess that he wouldn't reap the whirlwind.

Doyle said, "Go, Doctor, go now."

She started for the door, but said over her shoulder, "I'm getting the police."

Rhys kept talking to Gran, slow, reasonable. Doyle said, "Unless the officers can do magic, they can't help here."

Dr. Mason was at the door when the water pitcher smashed itself to pieces so close to her head that the plastic cut her cheek. She screamed, and Galen started to go to her, then hesitated at the foot of the bed. He was torn between helping the woman and staying at my side. Rhys, Doyle, and Sholto had no such conflict. They moved up to the bed. They meant to simply shield me, I think, but Gran stepped back. I could see her, now that Galen was halfway to the door.

She stepped back, hands at her sides balled into fists. Her brown eyes were too wide, showing white. Her thin chest rose and fell like she'd been running. The big chair in the corner rose into the air.

"Gran, no!" I yelled, and reached out, as if my outstretched hand could do something more that my voice alone could not. I had hands of power, but none I was willing to use on my grandmother.

All the small objects in the room rushed toward the three men around my bed. Rushed toward me. But I knew that the small objects were a ruse. Throw the small then hit them with the big.

I had time to take a breath, to warn them. Then Doyle was on top of me guarding me with his body. The world was suddenly black, not from passing out, but from the fall of his midnight hair across my face.

I heard the doctor scream again. I heard unknown voices shouting from the direction of the door. Then Rhys yelled, "Sholto, no!"

CHAPTER THREE

I PUSHED AT DOYLE'S HAIR, TRIED TO CLEAR my vision, as the screams and shouts were joined by a sound like wind rushing toward us, and the breaking of glass. I heard Gran scream as I pushed desperately at Doyle. I had to see what was happening.

"Doyle, please, what's happening?" I pushed at him, but it was like pushing at a wall. There was no moving him, unless he allowed it. I spent my life being not as strong, not as much, as those around me, but in that moment, it was brought home to me that I could be their queen, but I would never be their equal.

I finally got enough of his hair out of my face to see the ceiling. I turned my head and found Galen by the door shielding the doctor with his body. There were shards of glass and wooden debris around him. The two uniformed cops by the door were inside with their guns drawn. But it was the looks on their faces that gave me some clue to what might be happening on the other side of the room.

Horror, a soft, amazed horror, was on both their faces. They raised their guns, and aimed, as if whatever they were aiming at was moving . . . a lot, and it was bigger than anything in the room that I was aware of, because they were aiming above even the tallest of the men.

The sound of gunshots exploded in the small room. I was deafened with it for a moment, then stunned by what they were firing at. Huge tentacles reached for them. Smaller shapes flew at them, black and vaguely batlike, if bats could be as large as a small person, and have tentacles in the center of their bodies that reached and writhed.

Something screamed outside the window, as the tentacles, some wide as a man's waist, kept coming in the face of the shots. The bullets were lead, and that hurts those of faerie, but I'd seen the tentacles before, and short of cutting them off, you couldn't stop them.

They slammed the two officers against the wall hard enough to shake the room. I saw smaller tentacles with guns held in them. I was okay with the disarming, because how do you explain to human police that the tentacled nightmare is on our side? Humans still have a tendency to think that good is always pretty and that evil is always ugly. I've found that it's so often the other way around.

The nightflyers swooped in like dark flying

manta rays. They had feet for perching, but their main limbs were the tentacles in the center of their bodies. They used them now to take the guns from the larger tentacles. I watched the one nearest us cling to the wall and use a smaller tentacle to put the safety on the gun. The nightflyers had great dexterity with their tentacles, which the larger beast did not.

I felt Doyle move as he lay on top of me. He turned his head, and said, "Rhys, have you removed the spell?"

"Yes."

Doyle turned back to look at the police and the doctor, still crouched under Galen's protective charge. He moved slowly off of me. I could feel how tense his muscles were, ready to react if there was more danger. He finally stood beside the bed, his shoulders and the muscles in his arms still tense enough that I could see it.

Rhys and Sholto held Gran between them. They were having to work at it though. Brownies could harvest a field single-handed in one night, or thrash a barn full of wheat. It wasn't all their ability for telekinesis; some of it was just plain brute strength.

I knew she was giving them trouble because Sholto was using more than just his two strong hands. His father had been a nightflyer, like the manta-ray creatures that had disarmed the police. The same tentacles that graced the nightflyers had now exploded from beneath the t-shirt Sholto had worn to pass for human.

His tentacles were the white of his flesh, decorated with veins of gold and jewel colors. They were pretty, actually, once you got past the fact that they were there at all.

Gran hadn't had time to get past that fact, and she was cursing Sholto soundly. "Do nae touch me with those unclean things!" Her arms looked thin as matchsticks, but when she yanked, Rhys and Sholto both moved a little.

Sholto braced two of his thicker tentacles against the floor, and when next Gran pulled only Rhys moved. Sholto had his foundation. He could hold her, thanks to his extra bits. The tentacles weren't there just to horrify, or for decoration. They were truly limbs, and like all limbs, they were useful.

Rhys shouted to be heard above Gran's yells, the police, and everything else. "Hettie, someone put a spell on you!" He chanced removing one hand from her bony wrist. I caught a glimpse of something shiny and golden caught between finger and thumb before Gran jerked herself free of his other hand. Holding a brownie was a two-person job for most people, even the warriors of the sidhe. Especially if you didn't want to hurt the brownie.

Gran balled her fist up, and I think she would have hit Rhys in the face, but Sholto caught her arm with a tentacle, and stopped her in mid-punch.

She yelled louder, screeching, and began to fight him in earnest. Small objects began to fly at him from around the room. It was when the shards of window glass began to move that Rhys slapped her.

I think it startled us all, because Gran looked at him with wide eyes. He said her name, loud and clear, putting power into it so that it rang like some great bell, echoing in the room as no human speech ever did.

He held the shining gold thread in front of her face. "Someone wove this into your hair, Hettie. It is a spell of emotions, meant to increase whatever you feel. More anger, more hatred, more rage, more prejudice against the black court. You are one of the most reasonable fey I know, Hettie. Why would you ever pick today to lose control?" He moved the golden thread so that her eyes and head followed it. He moved her gaze so that she would look at me in the bed. "Why would you endanger your granddaughter and your great-grandchildren whom she carries inside her? That is not you, Hettie."

She looked past the golden thread to me. Tears began to shine in her eyes. "Sorry I am, Merry. Sorrier that I know who did this evil thing."

There was a sound from near the doors. Galen said, "Sholto, the tentacles are crushing the policemen."

Sholto looked at the far wall with its burden of huge tentacles and police, as if he'd forgotten they were there. "If I let them go, they will try to be heroic, for they will never believe that we are not villains. We look too much like villains to be anything else to the humans." There was a tone in his voice, something bitter.

How did we explain what had just happened so that the police didn't think exactly that? How do you explain that the giant octopus tentacles are trying to rescue us, and that the little old lady was the danger?

"You must call off your beast, Sholto," Doyle said.

"They will either try to run out the door and call for reinforcements, or they will try to draw a second gun and kill my beast. They have already wounded him with lead bullets."

Him. He'd called the thing with tentacles bigger than my body a him. Funny, even with growing up with one of the nightflyers as my bodyguard, I still wouldn't have thought of the giant tentacled thing as a "him" or "her." It was an "it," but apparently not. Apparently, it was a "him," which implied a her out there somewhere. I'd assumed that this was the same tentacled creature that Sholto had brought to Los Angeles to fetch me, but maybe that had been the girl? Maybe I was still in shock, but I just couldn't think of what I was looking at as a girl.

"I am sorry that your beast was injured when all you were doing was trying to protect the princess." Doyle walked toward the policemen, staying one side of the tentacles. He spoke to the cops as they dangled.

"Officers, I am sorry that there was a misunderstanding. The tentacles that hold you came to rescue the princess, not to harm her. When the creature saw you with guns, it assumed that you were here to harm Princess Meredith, just as you would have assumed the same if strangers rushed in with pulled guns."

One of the cops looked at the other one. It was hard to tell what expression they shared, with their faces still mottled from being held too long by the tentacles, but it was almost a "do you believe this?" look.

The other cop, a little older, managed to say, "You're saying that this . . . thing is on your side?"

"I am," Doyle said.

I spoke from the bed. "Gentlemen, it's as if you came into my room and started shooting my dog, because he scared you."

The older cop said, his hands still tugging at the tentacle at his throat, "Lady, Princess, this ain't no dog."

"The hospital wouldn't let my real dogs in," I said.

Dr. Mason spoke from the floor, where she was still crouched behind Galen. "If we let you have your dogs, will this never come inside the building again?"

Doyle nodded at Galen, and it was enough. He helped the doctor to her feet, but her wide eyes remained on the huge tentacles still pinning the policemen, or maybe it was the nightflyers clinging to the ceiling just above them. So many interesting things to look at it, it was hard to tell exactly where her gaze was.

"I will keep my people outside the princess' window," Sholto said, "until we are certain the danger is past."

"So, this, these, have been outside the window all this time?" the doctor asked in a voice that was a little shaky.

"Yes," Sholto said.

"What would attack me with these as my guards?" I asked, and let the question include as many or as few of the fey in my room as the doctor wished to include.

The older cop said, "No one told us that you'd have . . ." He seemed to search for a word, and not find one.

His partner said, "Nonhumanoid." The young officer frowned at the word, as if it sounded wrong even to him, but he didn't try to pick a different word. It wasn't a bad word, and it was strangely appropriate.

"We are not required to inform the human police of all our precautions regarding the safety of Princess Meredith," Doyle said.

"If we are on the door, we should have a list of things that are on your side," the older cop said. It was a good point. It proved that he was recovering from being attacked by giant, bodiless tentacles and flying nightmares. Tough cop, or maybe just cop. You don't last on the job if you aren't tough. The older officer looked like he was past the ten-year mark. He was tough. His partner was young, and he kept giving nervous glances to the nightfly-ers on the ceiling. But he seemed to take heart or courage from the blasé attitude of his older partner. I'd seen it before when I'd worked on cases with the police at Gray's Detective Agency. The older stead-ied the younger, if it was a good pair-up.

The younger cop asked, "Can we have our guns back?"

The older cop gave him a look that said clearly that you don't ask for your weapon back. They were probably each carrying at least one hidden gun, or the older cop would be. Regulations can say what they want, but I don't know many police officers who don't double up. Your life too often depends on being armed.

"If you promise not to shoot any of our peo-ple, yes," Doyle said.

"Is the woman all right?" the older cop asked, motioning with his head at Gran, still held by Sholto, his extra bits, and his arms, but I was pretty certain that neither officer was looking at Sholto's human-looking arms. I'd have bet nearly anything that if asked to describe him later, they would have seen only the tentacles. Cops are trained to observe, but some things are just too eye-catching even for people with a badge.

Rhys came to us, smiling. "She'll be fine. Just

a bit of magic." He did that "hail-fellow-well-met" smile, and I noticed that he was wasting glamour to hide his ruined eye. He wanted to look harmless in that moment. Scars make some people think you must have done something to earn them.

"What does that mean?" the older cop asked. He wasn't going to let it go. He stood with his partner, surrounded by what he would think were nightmares. They'd taken their guns. And you would have to be a fool to not see the physical potential in Doyle and the rest of the men in the room, let alone the extra bits that Sholto was showing. The policeman was no fool, but he also saw Gran as a little old lady, and he wasn't leaving until he knew that she was all right. I was beginning to see how he'd survived in the job for more than a decade, and maybe why he'd never gotten out of uniform. If I were him, I'd have left the room and called for backup. But then, I was a woman, which makes you more cautious around violence.

"Grandmother," I said, and it may have been one of the few times I'd used her full title. She was just Gran. But tonight I wanted the police to know that we were family.

She looked at me, and there was pain in her eyes. "Oh, Merry, child, do nae call me by a title."

"The fact that you don't approve of my choice in men doesn't give you the right to use your magic to trash my hospital room, Gran."

"It was the spell. You know that."

"Do I?" I let my voice hold coldness, because I

wasn't sure. "The spell was designed to simply magnify what you truly feel, Gran. You truly do hate Sholto, and Doyle, and they are the fathers of my children. That will not change."

"Are you saying the ol' . . . woman made the stuff float and hit everyone?" the older cop asked. He sounded doubtful.

Gran pulled at Sholto's grip. "I am meself again, Lord of Shadows. Ya can let me go."

"Swear. Swear by the Darkness that Eats all Things that you will not try and hurt me, or anyone in this room."

"I'll swear ta no hurt anyone in this room, at this moment, but I will nae promise beyond that, because ya are the murderer of my mother."

"Murderer," the older cop said.

"He killed her mother, my great-grandmother, about five hundred years ago, or am I off by a century or two?" I asked.

"You're off by about two hundred years," Rhys said. He was in front of the policemen, smiling, pleasant, but he didn't have a magic that could go with the smile. Someone else in the room did though. "Why don't you talk to the nice policemen, Galen?" Rhys said.

Galen looked puzzled, but he moved the small distance to the policemen. If it bothered him to be standing directly under a crowd of nightflyers it didn't show. Which meant it didn't bother him, because Galen was almost incapable of lying that well.

"I'm sorry that you had to see our mess," he said, and he sounded reasonable, friendly. One of his abilities was to truly be pleasant. Most people wouldn't think of that as a magical ability, but to be able to charm people wasn't a small thing. I'd begun to notice that it worked really well on humans. It also worked to a certain degree on the other sidhe and some of the lesser fey. Galen had always had a bit of this kind of charm, a kind of glamour, but since we'd all gotten our powers boosted, his "friendliness" had grown to the level of real magic.

I watched the policemen's faces smooth out. The younger one smiled, all the way to his eyes. I couldn't even hear what Galen was saying, but I didn't need to. He'd understood what Rhys had wanted him to do. With Galen's pleasant magic easing the way, we got the policemen their guns, and they left, happy with the nightflyers still hanging like bats from the ceiling, and the tentacles still writhing in the window like some sort of really good 3-D. Though Sholto letting go of Gran had been the thing that had made the older cop succumb to Galen's charm. I think if the older cop had continued to see anyone in danger, he wouldn't have been so easily won over.

Oh, and Sholto had put his tentacles away. Once he would have had to use glamour to hide them, but they would have still been there. He'd been able to hide them, even if you were touching his chest and stomach. They had felt smooth and perfect. Strong glamour, that. But when the wild magic escaped, or was called into being by Sholto and myself, he had gained a new ability. His tentacles could look like a very realistic tattoo, and it **was** a tattoo, but with a thought he could make it tentacles again. It was similar to the tattoos on Galen and myself that looked like a butterfly and a moth, respectively. I'd been grateful when they stopped being alive, but trapped in our skin. It had felt very wrong.

Several of the men had tattoos, and some of them could become real. Real vines to twine down the body. None were as real as Sholto's mark, but then it was the only mark that had begun life as part of his own body.

Galen's winning personality didn't work if the person was too afraid, or was looking directly at something too frightening, so Sholto smoothed his extra bits back into the delicate tattoo. Galen's was a mild magic by our terms, but it was very, very useful in situations where the more spectacular powers were useless.

At Rhys's suggestion Galen turned to the doctor next, and it worked even better with her, but then she was a woman and he was charming. She might get to another patient or two before she finally realized that she hadn't said everything she'd wanted to say, but by then, she might be too embarrassed to admit that a nice smile had made her forget so much. One of the real benefits of subtle magic was that most humans assumed that it wasn't magic, but just how handsome the man was, and what doctor wants to admit that they can be befuddled so easily by a pretty face?

When we were alone again, just us, we all turned to Gran. I asked the question. "You said you knew who did the spell? Who?"

Gran looked at the floor, as if she were embarrassed. "Your cousin, Cair, she comes to visit now and then. She is me granddaughter." She said the last in a defensive tone.

"I know that you have more than one grandchild, Gran."

"None so dear to me as you, Merry."

"I'm not jealous, Gran. Just tell us what happened."

"She was very affectionate, touched me several times, stroked me hair, said how lovely it was. She joked that she was glad she got something lovely out of the family genetics."

My cousin, Cair, was tall, slender, and very sidhe of body, but her face was like Gran's, very brownie, noseless, and with all her smooth pale sidhe skin, her face looked unfinished. There were human surgeons who could have given her a nose for real, but she was like most sidhe. She didn't have much faith in human science.

"Did she know you were going to visit me?"

"Yes."

"Why would she wish me harm?"

"Perhaps it is not you she wished to harm," Doyle said.

"What do you mean?" I asked.

"I would nae have harmed ye on purpose, but these two," and she jabbed her thumb back at Sholto, and forward to Doyle, "I would happily have killed these two."

"Do you still feel that way?" I asked, voice soft.

She had to think about it, but finally she said, "No, not kill. You have the King of the sluagh as your man, and the Darkness; they are powerful allies, Merry. I would nae part you from such strength."

"The fact that they are the fathers of your great-grandchildren holds no weight for you?" I asked, studying her face.

"It means everything that you are with child." She smiled, and her face was illuminated with joy. It was the smile I'd grown up seeing, and treasured my whole life. She gave that smile to me, and said, "And twins, it is too good to be true, a'most."

Her face sobered.

"What's wrong, Gran?" I asked.

"You carry brownie blood in ya, child, and now one is the child of the sluagh, and Darkness can claim a mixed bag of genes too." She looked past them all to the nightflyers still clinging inside the room.

I knew what she meant. There were some potentially interesting genetics at work inside my body right this moment. I couldn't be anything but happy about it, but the concern in her face wasn't the comfort I needed.

She shook herself, as if suddenly cold. "I am no longer privy to the Golden Court, but I know someone offered Cair something she wanted greatly for her to do this. She risked me life, putting me again' these two." Again she used her thumb to point at both of them.

I thought about it, and realized Gran was absolutely right. The chances of her injuring them was somewhat high, because they wouldn't have wanted to injure my grandmother. It might have made them hesitate, but eventually if she'd risked me, or truly injured them, they would have had no choice but to fight back.

I thought about that, my Gran up against the King of the sluagh and Doyle. It made me cold just thinking about it. It must have shown on my face, because Doyle came to the other side of the bed from where Gran stood. Rhys was still keeping her a little back from the bed, or rather he stood in her way, and she made no move to come closer to the bed. I think she understood that the guards, all the guards, would be leery of her for a time. I couldn't blame them, because I agreed. Some spells leave lingering touches, even after being removed. Until we studied Cair's spell we couldn't be certain of everything it had been designed to do.

"What would she be willing to risk her own grandmother for?" Galen asked, sounding shocked.

"I think I know," Doyle said. "I was inside the Golden Court as a dog. Even the black hounds are still treated as mere dogs. People are incautious in front of dogs."

"You heard something about this spell?" Rhys asked.

"No, but about Merry's family." Doyle came to hold my hand, and I was glad for the touch. "There are still those in the court who use Cair's physical appearance as a reason not to accept Merry as their queen." He bowed to Gran. "I do not feel this way, but the Golden Court sees your other granddaughter as a monster and Merry not much better because of how human she appears. They seem to view her height and curves almost as badly as they do Cair's face."

"They are a vain lot, the Seelie," Gran said. "I lived among them for many years, married to one of their princes, but they could ne'r forgive me for looking so brownie. I think if I looked more human, like me dad, they could have accepted me more, but brownie blood beating out the human, nay, that they could not see past."

"Your twin daughters are both lovely, and except for hair and eye color look very sidhe. They can pass," Doyle said.

"But neither of the grandchildren can," Gran said.

"True," Doyle said.

"Does anyone else find it interesting that all the fathers except me are mixed blood?" Rhys asked. He was still holding the glowing thread carefully away from his body. What were we going to do with it?

"Like calls to like," Gran said.

"Some of the Seelie nobles said that if I could help a pure-blood sidhe couple get with child more of both courts would follow me," I said. "Some of them are saying that only the mixed breeds can breed with my help, because my blood isn't pure enough."

Doyle rubbed his thumb along my knuckles. It was a nervous gesture, and it meant that he wondered the same thing. Was it what Gran said, like calls to like? Was I simply not sidhe enough to help the pure-bloods?

"Doyle," Galen said, "are you bleeding?" He moved up to the other man, and touched his back. His fingers came away with dots of crimson on them.

CHAPTER FOUR

DOYLE DIDN'T FLINCH OR OTHERWISE react. "it is a very small wound."

"But how did it happen?" Galen asked.

"I believe the glass is coated with some sort of man-made material," Doyle said.

"So because it's man-made and not natural," I said, "it was able to cut you?"

"Normal glass would have still cut me."

"But it would have healed by now," I said, "without the man-made coating?"

"It is a small cut, so yes."

"But you were covering Merry's body when you were cut," Gran said, and her voice was flat, almost without accent. She could do that when she wished, though it didn't happen often.

"Yes," he said, and looked at her.

She swallowed hard. "I do nae have the magic resistance to be near my Merry right now, do I?"

"It is sidhe magic we will be fighting," he said.

She nodded, and a look of deep sorrow came over her face. "I cannae be with ya, Merry. I cannae resist what they will make me do. It's one of the reasons I left their court. A brownie is a servant there, and when we are invisible to them we are safe, but brownies were ne'r meant to dabble in court politics."

I reached out to her. "Gran, please."

Rhys stepped between us as she moved forward. "Not a good idea yet. We need to look at the spell first."

"I would say I would n'er hurt my girl, but if the Darkness . . . if Captain Doyle had not protected her, I would have cut her 'stead of his back."

"What could they have offered to Merry's cousin?" Galen asked.

"Mayhap the thing they offered me centuries ago," Gran said.

"What was that?" Galen asked.

"A chance to bed, and if with child, marry one of their Seelie nobles. No one will touch Cair for fear that her . . . deformity will breed true. I was only half human, and I worked in the court as a brownie, but I saw the Seelie and I wished to be a part of it. I was a fool, but it earned my girls a chance to be a part of that glittering mess. But Cair is always outside of it, because she looks too much like her ol' Gran."

"Gran," I said, "it's not . . ."

"No, child, I know what face I bear, and I know that it takes a special sidhe to love it. I ne'r found that sidhe, but I was not part sidhe. I did na' have the blood of the court running in my veins. I was a brownie who got uppity, but Cair, she is one of them. It must be a thing of great pain to watch the others with their perfect faces get what she longs for."

"I know what it is like to be denied a place at court," Sholto said, "because you are not perfect enough to be bedded. The Unseelie sidhe run scared of my bed, for fear they will breed monsters."

Gran nodded, and finally looked at him. "I am sorry that I said some of the things I said, Shadow Lord. I should know better'n most what it is to be hated for bein' less than sidhe."

He nodded. "The Queen called me Her Creature. Until Merry came to me, I thought I would be doomed to live out my life until I became simply Creature, as Doyle is Darkness." He smiled at me then, with that intimate look that he hadn't quite earned yet. It was so odd to be pregnant after only one night with a man. But then, hadn't that been what had happened with my parents? One night of sex, and my mother had been trapped in a marriage she did not want. Seven years of marriage before she was allowed to divorce him.

"Aye, the courts are cruel, though I had hoped the dark court would be a little less so."

"They accept more," Doyle said, "but even the Unseelie have their limits."

"They saw me as proof that the sidhe were

failing as a people, because once they could bed anything and breed true," Sholto said.

"They saw my mortality as proof that they were dying," I said.

"And now the two they feared the most may be the saving of us all," Doyle said.

"Nicely ironic," Rhys said.

"I must go, Merry-girl," Gran said.

"Let us test the spell and remove any lingering effects on you," Doyle said.

She gave him a look that wasn't entirely friendly. "Rhys and Galen can touch you," he said. "I do not need to."

She took a long breath, her thin shoulders going up and down. Then she looked at him with a softer, more thoughtful look. "Aye, ya should look at me, for the thought of you touching me was not a good one. I think the spell lingers in me mind, and it is not good to linger on such thoughts. They grow and fester in the mind and heart."

He nodded, still holding my hand in his. "They do."

"Test the spell, Rhys," she said. "Then cure me of it. I must away, unless you can find a way for me to be proof against such sorceries."

"I'm sorry, Hettie."

She smiled at him, then turned a less-happy face to me. "Sorry I am that I will nae be able to help ya through this pregnancy, or help tend the bairns for ya."

"Me, too," I said, and meant it. The thought of her leaving hurt my heart.

Rhys held the shining thread out. "I'd like your opinion on it, Doyle."

Doyle nodded, squeezed my hand, then walked around the bed to Rhys. Neither of them seemed to want to give Gran a clear way to touch me. Was it really that strong a spell, or were they just being cautious?

If it was caution, I couldn't blame them, but I wanted to say good-bye to Gran. I wanted to touch her, especially if it was the last time I'd see her until after the babies were born. Just thinking that all the way through—when the babies were born— shocked me a little. We'd been trying to get me pregnant for so many months that the pursuit of the pregnancy had been all I'd thought about. That, and staying alive. I hadn't thought about what it would mean. I hadn't thought about babies, and children, and having them. It seemed a strange oversight.

"Your face, Merry-girl, so serious," Gran said.

I looked at her, and remembered being very small, so small that I could curl up in her lap and she had seemed large. I remembered feeling utterly safe, as if nothing in the world could harm me. I had believed that. It must have been before I was six, before the Queen of Air and Darkness, Aunt Andais, had tried to drown me. That had been a moment that had brought the realities of being mortal among the immortal home to me as a child.

It was nicely ironic that the future of the Unseelie Court was in my body, my mortal body, which Andais had thought wasn't worth keeping alive. If I could be killed by drowning, then I wasn't sidhe enough to live.

"I just realized that I'm going to be a mother."

"Aye, you are."

"I hadn't thought about anything beyond getting pregnant."

She smiled at me. "It will be a few months before ya have to worry about mothering."

"Is it ever too soon to worry?" I asked.

Sholto had come to stand on the far side of the bed from Gran. Doyle and Rhys were looking at the thread. Doyle was actually sniffing it rather than using his hands. I'd seen him do that to magic before, as if he would trace it back to its owner like a hound on a scent.

Sholto took my hand in his, and I didn't pull away, but I saw Gran's face harden. Not good. I looked at him, and what I saw in his face reassured me. I'd expected him to look arrogant or angry, and to have that directed at her. I'd expected that he took my hand to prove to Gran that she couldn't stop him from touching me. But his face was gentle, and he was gazing at me.

He gave me a smile as gentle as any I'd seen on his face. His triple yellow eyes with their individual lines of gold were soft, and he looked like a man in love. I was not in love with Sholto. I had only been alone with him twice, both times ending in violent interruptions, neither of them our doing. We didn't really know each other yet, but he looked at me as if I were the world, and it was a good, safe place.

It made me uncomfortable enough that I dropped my eyes so he would not see that my look did not match his. I could not give him love in my face, not yet. Love, for me, was made up of time and shared experience. Sholto and I had not had that yet. How strange to be with his child, and not to be in love with him.

Was this how my mother had felt? Married, bedded, but not in love, then to suddenly find herself pregnant with the child of a stranger? For the first time ever, I had some sympathy with my mother's emotional ambiguity toward me.

I had loved my father, Prince Essus, but perhaps he had been a better father than husband. I realized in that moment that I truly knew nothing of how my father and mother had interacted. Had their tastes in bed been so different that they had no middle ground? I knew their politics were opposite poles.

I held Sholto's hand, and had one of those adult moments when you realize that maybe, just maybe, your hatred of your parent is not completely justified. It was not a comfortable feeling to think of my mother as the wronged party instead of my father.

It made me look up at Sholto. His white-blond hair had begun to escape from the ponytail he'd worn to rescue me. He'd used glamour to make his hair look short, but the illusion might have been harmed if someone had become tangled in his nearly ankle-length hair. Strands of his hair trailed around a face as handsome as any in the courts. Only Frost had had a more masculine beauty. I pushed that thought away and tried to give Sholto his due. The tentacles had ripped his t-shirt apart. It clung like a lace of rags around his chest and stomach. Shreds of the cloth were still tucked into his jeans, with their belt, and the heavy collar was still intact, so it, along with the sleeves, kept it all in place, but the chest and stomach revealed were lovely, the skin pale and perfect. The tattoo that decorated him from just under the breastbone to his belt looked like someone had drawn one of those sea anemones, done in shades of gold, ivory, and crystal, with edges of blue and pink, soft colors, like the sun caressing the edge of a seashell. One thicker tentacle had been drawn so that it curled up over the right side of his chest, looking as if the tentacle had been frozen in mid-movement, so that the tip was close to the darker paleness of one nipple. I wasn't certain, but I was pretty sure that the tattoo had changed. It was almost as if the tat was literally formed by what the tentacles were doing when he froze them into art.

I knew that the slender hips, and everything else that was held inside his jeans, was lovely, and that he knew what to do with it.

He lifted my hand, and his face wasn't soft

now. It was thoughtful. "You look like you are weighing and measuring me, Princess."

"And well she should be," Gran said.

Without looking at her, I said, "He spoke to me, not to you, Gran."

"So you would take his side over mine already?"

I did look at her then. I saw the anger in her eyes, and a covetousness that wasn't her, but might be my cousin. It was as if Cair had put her desire to possess into the spell, her jealousy given magical form. Subtle, and nasty. Not unlike my cousin, come to think of it. Magic was often like that, colored by the personality of the maker.

"He is my lover, the father of my child, my future husband, my future king. I will do what all women do. I will go to his bed, and his arms, and we will be a couple. It is the way of the world."

A look of deep hatred came over her face, and it was almost as if the expression were not hers. I clung more tightly to Sholto's hand, and had to fight the urge to wiggle a little farther away in the bed from this woman, because though it was Gran, there was something in her that wasn't.

Galen moved up beside us. "The expression on your face, Gran, it doesn't look much like you."

She looked at him, and her face softened. Then that other looked out of her true-brown eyes for a moment. She looked down, as if she knew she couldn't hide it.

"And how do ya feel, Galen, that you share her with so many?"

He smiled, and true happiness was shining in his face. "I've wanted to be Merry's husband since she was a teenager. Now I will be, and we'll have a child together." He shrugged, spread his hands. "It's so much more than I ever thought I'd have. How can I be anything but happy?"

"Do ya not wanne be king in yer own right?"

"No," he said.

She looked up then, and the other was in her eyes, sharp and pure, and uncomprehending. "All of you want to be king."

"As her only king, I would be a disaster," Galen said simply. "I am not a general to lead armies, or a strategist for politics. The others are better at all that than I am."

"You mean that," she said, and the voice didn't sound very much like Gran at all.

I didn't fight the urge to wiggle closer to Sholto and Galen then, and farther away from Gran and the stranger's eyes. Something was wrong with her, in her.

That strange voice said, "We could let her keep you, let her be queen of the Unseelie. You would be no threat to us."

"No threat to whom?" Doyle asked. There was no sight of the thread now. I didn't know if they'd destroyed it, or just hidden it. I'd been too caught up in Gran's strange state to notice. It wasn't good that I hadn't noticed, but the world had narrowed to the stranger in my grandmother's eyes.

"But you, Darkness, you are a threat." There was no accent now. There were simply well-spoken words, and because it was Gran's throat saying it, the words still sounded vaguely like her, but a person's voice is made up of more than just their larynx and mouth. There is a piece of yourself in your voice, and the words she spoke now belonged in someone else's mouth.

She glanced across the bed at Sholto. "Shadowspawn and his sluagh are a threat." Shadowspawn was a nickname that even the queen rarely said to his face. A lesser fey, even my grandmother, would not have risked such an insult to the King of the sluagh.

"What have they done to her?" I asked. My voice was soft, almost a whisper, as if I were afraid that if I spoke too loudly, it would tip the tension building in the room. Tip it over, and spill it into something bloody and awful and irrevocable.

Gran turned to Doyle, one hand spread wide. It was one of those moments that seem frozen in time. It is the illusion that you have all the time in the world, when in fact you have milliseconds or less to react, to survive, to watch your life be destroyed.

He reacted in a blur of movement that I couldn't follow. He was simply a dark blur, as the power burst from Gran's hand—a power that she had never possessed. White-hot light burst forth, and for a moment the room was illuminated in eye-searing brightness. I could see Doyle caught against that light, moving her arm, her body, away from the bed, away from me. I had an almost slow-motion view of the white light cutting across the front of his body.

There was a shuddering scream from near the window as the white light hit the giant tentacles still in the opening. The bed moved. It was Galen throwing himself on top of me, as a living shield. I had time to see Sholto leap over the bed, and go to join the fight, then all I could see was Galen's shirt. All I could feel was his body above mine, tensed for a blow.

CHAPTER FIVE

THERE WAS ONE TERRIBLE SCREAM, A sound of such desolation that I pushed at Galen, tried to move him away. I had to see. Doyle had been an immovable wall; Galen moved, but not away. His body was softer, less certain of itself, but I was just as trapped. I might have forced him to move if I'd been willing to hurt him badly enough, but I was unwilling to hurt more of the people I cared for.

Galen took a breath that broke in a sob. I heard Rhys's voice. "Goddess, help us!"

I pushed harder at Galen's chest. "Move, move, damnit, let me see."

He turned back to me, pressing his face against my hair. "You don't want to see."

I'd been frightened before; now it was panic. I screamed at him. "Let me see, or I will hurt you!"

It was Rhys who said, "Let her see, Galen."

"No," he said.

"Galen, move. Merry isn't like you. She'll want to see." The tone in his voice turned the panic to ice in my veins. I was suddenly calm, but it wasn't true calm. It was what happens when terror turns to something that will let you function, for a time.

Galen moved slowly, reluctance in every muscle as he crawled off the bed on the opposite side from where he'd started. He put himself close to the very thing he hadn't wanted me to see.

I saw the nightflyer first, wrapped around Gran like a shroud. One of the spines that they could carry inside their bodies had pierced her through. I saw the spikes on the spine, and knew why he, for it was a he, had not taken the spine back out. It would cause more damage going back, but it wasn't like a blade. You couldn't cut it off, so that the injury wasn't inflicted twice. It was a piece of the nightflyer's body. Why not just take it back out and be done with it?

Gran's hand reached to empty air. She was still alive. I sat up, tried to get up, and no one stopped me. That was bad in and of itself. It meant that there was more. Sitting up, I caught a glimpse of that more.

Doyle lay on the ground, eyes blinking up at the ceiling. The front of his borrowed surgical scrubs was blackened, and part was peeled away to show the raw burned flesh underneath.

Rhys knelt beside him, holding his hand. Why wasn't he shouting for a doctor? We needed a doctor. I hit the call button beside the bed.

I half fell and half crawled out of bed. When the IV pulled, I tore it out. A trickle of blood oozed down my arm, but if there was pain, I didn't feel it.

I knelt on the floor between the two of them, and only then could I see Sholto on the far side of Doyle. He was collapsed on his side, his hair spilled across his face so that I could not see if he were awake and watching me, or beyond that. The remnants of the t-shirt that had framed the perfection of his chest now showed a black-and-red ruin. But whereas Doyle's injury was on his stomach, the bolt of power had taken Sholto over the heart.

So much had gone wrong in so short a space of time that I couldn't take it all in. I knelt on the ground, frozen in my indecision. A sound made me look at the woman who had raised me. If ever I had truly had a mother, it was she. She stared at me with those brown eyes that had shown me all the kindness I had ever known from a mother. She and my father had raised me together. Now I stared up at her from my knees, the only way she would be taller than me as she had been when I was small.

The nightflyer unfurled its fleshy wings enough that I could see that the spine had taken her just under the heart. Maybe even gone through the bottom part of it. Brownies are a tough lot, but it was a terrible wound.

She stared at me, still alive, still trying to

breathe past the daggerlike spine. I took her hand, and felt her grip, which had always been so strong, now frail, as if she could not hold my hand, but she tried.

I turned to Doyle, and took his hand in mine. He whispered, "I have failed you."

I shook my head. "Not yet," I said. "It's failure only if you die. Don't die."

Rhys went to Sholto and searched for a pulse, while I held the hands of my grandmother and the man I loved and waited for them to die.

It was one of those moments when strange things come into your mind. All I could think of was what Quasimodo says as he gazes down at the Archdeacon who raised him dead on the pavement below, and the woman he loved hung and dead. "Oh! All that I have ever loved."

I threw my head back and screamed. In that moment no baby, no crown, nothing was worth the price in both my hands.

Doctors came, and nurses. They fell upon the wounded, and they tried to pry my hands out of Gran and Doyle's hands, but I couldn't seem to let go. I was afraid to let go, as if the worst would happen if I did. I knew it was stupid, but the feel of Doyle's fingers wrapped around mine was everything to me. And Gran's fragile grip was still warm, still alive. I was afraid to let go.

Then her hand spasmed against mine. I looked into her face, and the eyes were too wide, the breath not right. They eased her off the spine, and forced the nightflyer back, and as the spine came out, her life spilled with it.

She collapsed toward me, but other arms caught her, tried to save her, pulled her hand away from mine. But I knew she was gone. There might be moments of breath, and pulse, but it was not life. It was what the body does at the end sometimes, when the mind and soul are gone, but the body doesn't understand yet that death has come, and there is no more.

I turned to the other hand still in mine. Doyle gave a shuddering breath. The doctors were pulling him away from me, sticking needles in him, putting him on a gurney. I stood, trying to hold on to his hand, his fingers, but my doctor was there, pulling me backward. She was talking, something about me needing to not upset myself. Why do doctors say such impossible things? Don't get upset; stay off your leg for six weeks; lower your stress; cut back on your work hours. Don't get upset.

They pulled Doyle's fingers out of mine, and the fact that they could pull him away from me said just how hurt he was. If he hadn't been hurt, nothing short of death would have moved him from me.

Nothing short of death.

I looked at Sholto on the floor. They had a crash cart. They were trying to restart his heart. Goddess, help me. Goddess, help us all.

The doctors were clustered around Gran. They were trying, but they had triaged the wounded. Doyle first, then Sholto, then Gran. It should have been comforting, and it was, that they took Doyle first. They thought they could save him.

Sholto's body jerked with the jolt of power they put through his body. I heard their words in snatches, but I saw a head shake. Not yet. They hit him again, with more, because his body jerked harder. His body convulsed on the floor.

Galen tried to hold me, tears streaming down his face, as they put a sheet over Gran's body. The police in the room seemed unsure what to do with the nightflyer. How do you handcuff that many tentacles? What do you do when the room is charred, and the dead woman is the one whom everyone said did it? What do you do when magic is real, and cold iron burns the flesh?

I saw the doctors shake their heads over Sholto. He was so terribly still. Consort help me, help me help them. Help me! Galen tried to press my face into his chest, to keep me from looking. I pushed him away, harder than I meant to, so that he stumbled.

I went to Sholto. The doctors tried to keep me away, or talk to me, but Rhys kept them back. He shook his head, said something I couldn't seem to hear. I knelt by Sholto's body. Body. No. No.

The nightflyers that the police weren't trying to arrest came to me, and to their king. They huddled around him, like black cloaks, if cloaks could have muscle and flesh, and pale unfinished faces.

A tentacle reached out to touch his body. I reached to the nightflyers on either side of me, as you'd reach for a hand of your fellow bereaved. The tentacles wrapped around my hands, squeezing, giving what reassurance they could. I screamed, but not wordlessly this time.

"Goddess, help me! Consort, help me!" I was filled with such rage, horrible, burning rage, as if my heart would burst with it, my skin run in sweat with the heat of my anger. I would kill Cair. I would kill her for this. But tonight, now, this moment, I wanted our king to live.

I glanced into the face of the nightflyer beside me, the black eyes, the pale lipless mouth, the razor teeth. I watched a tear glide down that pale, flattened cheek. Their anger; their rage; their king, but . . . he was my king, too, and I was his queen, their queen.

I smelled roses. The Goddess was near. I prayed for guidance, and it wasn't a voice in my head. It wasn't a vision. It was knowledge. I simply knew what to do, and how to do it. I saw the spell all the way through, and knew that if it were to work, there was no time to worry that at the end was potentially something horrible. Nothing that faerie could show me tonight would be as horrible as what I'd already seen. Nightmares could not frighten me tonight, for I was past fear. There was only purpose.

I reached out to Sholto; the nightflyers moved their tentacles back so they only held my wrists as I laid hands on their king's body. I had raised magic before, with sex and life, but that was not the only magic that ran through my veins. I was Unseelie sidhe, and there is power in death, as there is in life. There is power in that which hurts, as well as in that which saves.

I had a moment of thinking of using this magic for Doyle, but this magic was only for the sluagh. It would not work for my Darkness.

The Goddess had given me choices along the way; bring life back to faerie with life or death, with sex or blood. I had chosen life and sex over death and blood. In that moment, with Gran's blood on my gown, I chose again.

I looked for Rhys, because I knew Galen would not do what I needed, not in time. "Rhys, bring me Gran's body."

Rhys had to argue with the doctors, and Galen helped him win the argument. Rhys brought her body to me. He laid her body on top of Sholto's, as if he knew what I meant to do.

They say the dead do not bleed, but that's not true. The recently dead bleed just fine. The brain dies, the heart stops beating, but the blood still flows out, for a time. Yes, for a time the dead do bleed.

Gran looked so small lying on top of Sholto. Her blood flowed out and down his pale skin, over the blackened burns the hand of power had made.

I felt Rhys and Galen at my back. I heard, vaguely, unimportantly, Galen arguing. But it didn't matter; nothing mattered but the magic.

I put my hands with the bracelets of tentacles on top of Gran's thin chest. Tears bit at my eyes, and I had to blink them away to keep my vision clear. My skin flared to life, moonlight glow. I called my power. I called all of it. If ever I were truly queen of faerie, princess of the blood, let it be this night, this moment. Give me all of it, Goddess. I ask this in your name.

My hair glowed so brightly I could see the burning garnet of it from the corners of my eyes, see it flow down the front of my gown, like red fire. My eyes cast green and gold shadows. The nightflyers that touched me glowed white, and that glow slid around the circle of them, so that their flesh glowed like sidhe flesh, white and moonlight bright.

Sholto's body began to glow, as white and pure as our own. His hair ran with yellow and white light, like the first glow of dawn in a winter's sky. I heard his first breath, a rattling sound, the sound of death living in a gasp.

His eyes opened, wide and already full of yellow and gold fire. He stared up at me. "Merry," he whispered.

"My king," I said.

His gaze went to the nightflyers glowing around us. They burned as brightly as any sidhe had ever burned. Sholto said, "My queen."

"On the life of my grandmother, I swear vengeance this night. I call kin slayer against Cair."

He put his hand over mine, and the glowing tentacles of the nightflyers flowed over his hand

and mine, binding them together. "We hear you," the nightflyers said, almost with one voice.

"Merry," Galen yelled, "don't do this!"

But I understood something I had not before. When Sholto had called the wild hunt into being inside faerie, I had not been with him. I had already begun to run. I would not run tonight. We had called the power together with our bodies, and it was with our bodies that we would ride it.

"Get the humans out," I said, in a voice echoing with power, as if we knelt in a vast cavern instead of a small room.

Rhys didn't wait to ask questions; he forced Galen to help him. I heard Rhys say, "They will go mad if they see more. Help me get them out!"

I leaned in to Sholto, with our hands laced together by the nightflyers, glowing flesh on top of glowing flesh, so that when our lips touched, the flare of light was blinding even to me.

Out of that light, that pure, Seelie light, the far wall with its broken window began to melt. To melt in the light, but it did not melt away. Out of the white, cool light, shapes formed. Shapes with tentacles, and teeth, and more limbs than seemed necessary. But whereas the last time they had spilled out of darkness and an unlight, now they poured out of light and whiteness. Their skin was as white as any sidhe, but their forms were what the wild hunt of the sluagh was meant to be. They were formed to strike terror into the heart of any who saw them, and drive mad those who were weak.

Sholto, the nightflyers, and I turned as one being toward the spill of shining nightmares. All I could see tonight was the glow of eyes, the alabaster shine of skin, the white, sharp shine of teeth. They were a thing of terrible beauty, as hard and fine as marble brought to life, with a lace of tentacles and many legs, so that the eye tried to make of them one great shape. It was only by staring that you realized it was a mass of shapes, all different, all wondrously formed with muscles and strength enough to do their work.

The ceiling melted away, and larger forms slid down toward us. The nightflyers released my hand enough for me to touch one of the tentacles' shapes, what had been a mass of shape, so confusing, so antediluvian that even with power riding me, my mind could not make form of it. The magic protected me, or my mind might have broken, trying to see what dangled from the ceiling. But the moment I touched that first shining form, it changed.

A horse flowed out of the mass of shapes. A great white horse, with eyes that glowed with red fire, and steam puffing from its nostrils with every breath. Its great hooves struck green sparks from the floor.

Sholto sat, with the small body in his arms. Gran looked so small there, like a child. His arms, his chest, were covered with her blood as he held her out to me. There were other men in my life who would not have offered me the choice. They would have already decided what they would do, but Sholto seemed to understand that it had to be my decision.

I touched the neck of the horse, and it was real, and warm, and pulsing with life. I leaned against its shoulder, for it was too tall for me to mount without aid. It nuzzled my hair, and I felt something there. I reached my hand up and found leaves. Leaves and berries in my hair, woven in among the garnet glow.

Sholto looked at me, eyes a little wide, still holding the body of the woman I had loved above all other women. "Mistletoe," he whispered, "entwined in your hair."

I'd had it happen once before inside faerie, but never outside. I looked past the nightflyers, still glowing, and found Rhys and Galen the only ones still in the room. Galen was shielding his eyes, as the rest of us had done in that night that had brought power back to the sluagh. The night that Doyle had said, "Don't look, Merry, don't look." I had a moment to think of him, carried away from me. He was somewhere in this hospital, maybe fighting for his life. I started to lose my purpose, then I looked up at the writhing nightmares. I remembered that even a glimpse of what had boiled in the ceiling of the cavern had been madness. Tonight I could look into the center of that shining, writhing mass, and understand that it was raw magic. It was only a nightmare if that was what you thought it would be. Raw magic forms in the mind before it forms to the touch.

I stared into it, and knew that until I finished this hunt there was no way to do anything else. It was like starting an avalanche—you have to ride it to its end. Only then could I embrace my Darkness once more. I prayed the Goddess would keep him safe for me until the magic freed me of its power.

Rhys gazed at it all with wonder in his face. He saw what I saw: beauty. But then he had been a god of bloodshed and war, and before that a deity of death. Galen, my sweet Galen, would never be anything so harsh. This was not a magic for the faint of heart. My heart wasn't faint; it felt as if my heart were missing. Whatever it was that allowed me to feel was gone. I looked at Gran's body, and there was a roaring emptiness inside me. I felt nothing but vengeance, as if vengeance could be its own emotion cut free of hate, anger, or sorrow. Vengeance as if it were a force of its own, something, almost, alive.

Rhys walked to the circle of nightflyers, gazing up into the writhing mass of white light and shifting shapes. He stopped at the glowing edge of the circle. He looked at me now. "Let me go with you."

It was Sholto who answered. "She has her huntsman for tonight."

Galen spoke, still staring at the floor. "Where is Merry going?" He still didn't understand. He was too young. The thought came to me that he was older than I, by decades, but the Goddess whispered through my head, "I am older than all." I understood; in this moment I was she, and that made me old enough.

"Take care of her, Galen," I said.

He glanced up at me, and saw the horse with its flashing eyes and white skin. For a moment, he wasn't afraid, he was simply amazed. He, like me, was too young to remember when the sidhe still had their shining horses. We had only had stories before this moment.

The circle of nightflyers parted and Rhys and Galen both reached upward, as if it were planned. The white shapes above us reached out toward them. Galen's reach was longer, so the horse that formed for him was as white and pure as mine. It turned flashing eyes that glowed golden to my red. There was no smoke from this one's nostrils, and the sparks from the hooves were as golden as its eyes. Only the size and the sense of strength let me know that they were kin.

Rhys's hand also brought a white horse, but it was like an illusion, or a trick of the eye. One moment white and solid and very real, the next skeletal, like the proverbial steed of death.

Rhys spoke quietly and happily as he rubbed its nose. He spoke in Welsh, but a dialect I could barely follow. I could understand that he was happy to see the horse, and that it had been too long.

Galen touched his horse, as if he were certain that it would vanish, but it didn't. It butted him gently in the shoulder, and made a high, happy whinny. Galen smiled, because you couldn't help but smile at that sound.

Sholto held Gran's body out to Galen, and he

took her gently in his arms. His smile was gone, and there was nothing but sorrow. I let him have the sorrow, let him grieve for me, because my own grief could wait; tonight there would be blood.

A shape from above touched Sholto's shoulder, as if it could not wait for him to touch it, like an overeager lover. The moment it touched him, it formed into something white and shining, but it was not exactly a horse. It was as if the great white steed had mingled with a nightflyer, so that there were more legs than any horse would have, though one graceful head rose from strong shoulders. Its eyes were the empty black of the nightflyers that had begun to sing around us. Yes, sing, in high, almost childlike voices, as if bats could sing as they flew above your head. I knew in that moment that my power had changed what this hunt would be. I was not sluagh, nor pure Unseelie, and though we would be terrible and we would bring vengeance, we would come on the songs of the nightflyers. We would come shining from the sky, and until the vengeance was done nothing could stand against us. The mistake last time had been not giving the hunt a purpose, but that mistake would not be made tonight. I knew who we hunted, and I had spoken her crime. Until she was hunted to ground, no power in faerie or mortal lands could withstand us.

Sholto lifted me to sit on the horse with its red, glowing eyes. He mounted his own many-legged steed. The nightflyers' song became a chant of words so ancient that I could feel more of the building fall away just from the sound of it. Reality tore around us, and I spoke the words, "We ride."

Sholto said, "We hunt."

I nodded, wrapping my fingers in the horse's thick mane. "We fly," I said, and kicked my bare heels into her flanks. She leaped forward into the empty night beyond. I should have been afraid. I should have doubted that a horse without wings could fly, but I didn't. I knew she would fly. I knew what we were, and the wild hunt, hunts from the air.

The mare's hooves did not so much strike the air as simply run on it. Her hooves flared with green flame at each step, as if the empty air were a road that only she could see. Sholto rode at my side, on his many-legged stallion. The nightflyers spilled around us, still shining, still singing. But it was what followed in our wake that would make the humans turn away, and hide inside their houses. They would not know why, they would simply turn away. They would think our passing the cry of wild birds, or wind.

We rode in a shine of white and magic, and dark dreams flowed in our wake.

CHAPTER SIX

THE MARE MOVED UNDER ME, HER FIERY hooves eating up the distance. The muscles in her back and the feel of her mane in my hands were real, and solid, but the rest of it . . . the rest of it was dreamlike. I wasn't certain if the feeling of unreality was what it would have always been to ride with the hunt, if it was the shock of all that had happened, or if it was my mind's way of protecting me from sights that should have destroyed my mortal mind.

Sholto moved up beside me on his own pale horse. His hair flowed behind him like a shining cloak, all white with hints of yellow, as if bits of sunlight were held in his hair, as if that hot, yellow light could be ensnared in the pale beauty of his hair.

The February cold pressed around us, caressing my bare arms and feet, but my breath did not fog in the cold. My skin did not chill. It was as if the cold were a sensation, but it had no power over me. The smoke that flared from my mare's nostrils wasn't from the cold. I remembered tales of horses in the wild hunt with flaming eyes and hellfire spilling from their nose and mouth. We could have been riding true nightmares, black and full of fire and terror, but something about my magic had turned the hunt ever so slightly to something a little less automatically frightening.

If you saw black horses that breathed fire riding down on you, you'd be convinced of evil intent, but if you saw white horses spilling toward you, even with eyes that glowed, and a little green fire at the hooves, would you automatically assume evil, or would you pause and marvel at the beauty? We rode the sky as if the Milky Way had brightened and turned into beings that could flow and travel the darkness.

I looked behind us, and found that there were other horses, barebacked, riderless, but spilling like seafoam at our backs. There were also hounds, white with red marks, like all faerie hounds, except that these had glowing eyes, and they were bulkier than the slim ones that had come to my hand only a few weeks ago. Those had looked more like greyhounds, but not these dogs. These were huge mastiffs, except for their colors, and they glowed against the darkness like some white ghost dotted with glowing red, like spilled blood across the purity of their coats.

The name for them came to me, with a scent

of roses and herbs. Hounds of the Blood, they were hounds of the blood. Bloodhounds were named not for their bloodthirstiness, but for the fact that they were once only owned by nobles—noble blood. But the hounds that rode at our backs, that began to spill around the legs of the horses, were named blood for other reasons. They rode only for blood, and the gentleness of bloodhounds was not something that this pack would understand. That knowledge filled me with a fierce pleasure.

There were things behind the hounds and horses, shapes that writhed and boiled with bodies and limbs that were nothing you would ever see outside of the worst nightmare you can imagine. I stared into the abyss of things that I'd been told not to look at, for fear that one glance would destroy my mind. But those shapes had been black and gray, and these shone like crystal and pearls and diamonds in a radiance that burned from within and just behind them. We trailed a shining cloud of light like the tail of a comet.

I had a moment to wonder—if some telescope did pick us up, would that be what their human mind would make of us? Or would they see a falling star? Or would they see nothing? Glamour didn't always work around cameras and man-made technology. I said a prayer that we did not accidentally blast some poor astronomer's mind. I wished them well, as they gazed at the night sky. I wished everyone well, save one person tonight. I realized that I meant that. I wanted Cair dead for the death of our grandmother. The king's attack on me wasn't important to me anymore. I understood then that I was truly a part of the hunt. I was moved by the vengeance I had called down. We would hunt Cair for kin slaying, and then . . . then we would see.

It was strangely peaceful, this tunnel vision. No grief existed here. No doubts. No distractions. It was comforting, in a sociopathic sort of way. And even that thought could not frighten me. I'd heard the term "instrument of vengeance," but I had not truly understood what it meant until now.

Sholto reached out to me, across the space between our steeds. I hesitated, then I reached for him, my other hand still locked in my horse's mane. The moment our fingers touched, I remembered myself, a little. I understood the true danger of riding with the hunt then—you could forget yourself. You could forget everything but righteous vengeance, and spend a lifetime listening for the words from some mortal, or immortal, mouth. Oathbreakers, kin slayers, traitors; so much to punish. It would be a simpler life than the one I was leading. To ride forever, to exist only to destroy, and to have no other choices to make. Some saw the riders with the hunt as cursed, but I understood now that it wasn't how the riders saw themselves all those centuries ago. They'd stayed with the hunt because they wished to, because it felt better than going back.

Sholto's hand in mine reminded me that there were reasons not to let the hunt consume me. I thought of the babies I carried in my body for the first time since the ceiling and wall of the hospital had melted away. But it was a distant thought. I wasn't afraid. I wasn't afraid that I might die this night and the babes with me. Part of me felt untouchable, and part of me felt as if nothing, absolutely nothing mattered as much as vengeance. Nothing.

Sholto squeezed my hand as the rhythms of our horses made our arms rise and fall between us. He looked at me with eyes gone to yellow and gold fire, but there was worry in his face too. He was King of the sluagh, the last wild hunt of faerie. He had been the huntsman before, perhaps with less magic at his back, but still, he knew the sweetness of vengeance. He knew the simplicity of the hunt, and the almost seductive whisper of it.

His hand in mine, the look on his face, brought me back from the edge. His touch kept me me. Part of me resented it. Because with me came the first whisper of grief returned. Gran, Frost, my father, Doyle injured. So much death, so much loss, and the chance for more to come. That was the true terror of love, that you could love with your whole heart, your whole soul, and lose both.

We began to spill toward the ground, in a sweep of light that cast shadows below like that of some great, magical plane. But we did not touch the ground as the plane would have had to; we skimmed above it. We wove over treetops, and across fields. Animals scattered before us. I felt the hounds flinch, and tried to give chase, but Sholto spoke one word, and they stayed with us. We were not after rabbits tonight.

There was a flash of white, and something much bigger than a rabbit dashed across the ground. The White Stag fled before us like all the other animals. I almost called his name, but if he had not even turned that great horned head, it would have broken my heart all over again. Then he was lost in the dark, as lost to me as Gran.

The faerie mounds came into view, and we sped toward them. If there were guards out, they did not make themselves known. Did they not see us, or were they too frightened to draw attention to themselves?

The Seelie mound was before us. I had a moment to think, "How do we get inside?" But I had forgotten that a true hunt, with a true purpose, is barred by no door. We flowed toward the mound, and the horses and hounds did not even slow. They knew that the way would open, and it did. There was a moment when I felt the spell on the door, and realized that someone inside had barred the way with their strongest spells. Had they thought that our court would attack tonight? Had they feared what the queen would do for her niece's rape? The thought was a distant one, as if I thought about someone else. I watched the spell spill away from the door in that spot just behind the eyes where visions happen. One moment the spell was golden and bright, the next it fell away like the petals of some great flower opening for us. The shining doors opened in a spill of warm, yellow light, and our white shine flowed into the gold of it, and we were in.

CHAPTER SEVEN

WE SWEPT INTO THE GREAT ROOM WHERE just a few hours ago there had been reporters, cameras, and police. Now there were brownies cleaning up, levitating chairs and tables, and making the trash of paper and plastic roll like small tumbleweeds. They looked up at us, eyes wide. I had a moment of my heart squeezing so tightly that I could not breathe. Would they fight us, as Gran had? But none of them lifted a hand, or threw so much as a dust rag at us. Then we were past them, and the far door that had looked too small to let the horses through was suddenly just big enough. The faerie mound, the sithen, was shaping itself to our use.

But beyond the doors was a solid wall of roses and thorns. Thorns like daggers pointed at us, roses bloomed and filled the hallway with sweet perfume. It was a lovely way to defend, so terribly Seelie.

I thought we were stopped, but the wall to the

right widened, with a sound like rock crying. The sithen widened the hallway, not in inches, but in horse lengths, so that the lovely and deadly vines collapsed inward, like any climbing rose will do when its support is cut. That heavy mass of thorns fell inward, and into the ringing silence after the rock had stopped moving I could hear the screams of the guards underneath the painful blanket.

Fire blossomed out from the edge of the thorns rich and orange, and the heat reached us, but it was like the winter cold. I could feel it, but it did not move me. The fire spattered into wasted sparks, curling into empty air, as if the fire itself turned away rather than hit us.

We swept through rooms of colored marble, silver- and gold-edged. I had a vague memory of coming this way in Lord Hugh's arms, when he and the nobles who had wanted me to be their queen had rescued me from the king's bedchamber. Then I'd had time to see it all, admire the cold beauty of it, and think that it wasn't a place for nature deities. No matter how beautiful, the trees and flowers inside our sithens should not be formed of metal and rock. They should live.

Two lines of guards appeared ahead of us in the hallway. The last time I'd seen them, they'd been dressed in modern business suits to make the human reporters more comfortable. One of the things that Taranis had insisted on but that Andais never had was uniforms. The tunics and trousers were every color of the rainbow, with more modern colors added in, but the tabards that covered them front and back like elegant cloth sandwich boards bore a stylized flame, burning against an orange-red background. Gold thread glittered around the edge of everything. Once Taranis had been worshipped by burning people alive. Not often, but sometimes. I'd always found it interesting that Taranis chose the flame and not his lightning for his coat of arms.

They began shooting arrows, but the shafts turned away, as if some great wind had caught them, to cast them shattering on the walls long before they reached us. I saw the fear on some of their faces then, and again that fierce joy hit me.

Sholto urged his horse up beside mine, and the corridor was simply wide enough. The hounds boiled at our feet, the riderless horses seemed to push at our backs, and the formless things that pushed and writhed at the tail of our train surged forward. I felt the ceiling go away, as if there were sky above us now. Sky enough for the sluagh's shining whiteness to rise above us like a mountain of shining nightmares.

Some of the guards ran, their nerves broken. Two fell to their knees, their minds broken. The rest fired their hands of power. Silver sparkles fell far short of us. A bolt of yellow energy rolled back upon itself, like the fire before it, as if the magic simply would not touch us. Colors, shapes, illusion, reality—they threw it all at us. These were the great warriors of the Seelie Court, and they fought, but nothing could touch us. Nothing could even slow our run.

We leaped over them as if they were a fence. One of them pulled a sword that did not glow of magic. He sliced upward at the leg of a hound and got blood. Cold iron can harm all in faerie.

The wounded hound dropped away from us, and a riderless horse went with it. I might have stopped, but Sholto urged his horse forward and mine followed. When the marble of the hallway had changed to yet another color, pink with veins of gold, we had a third rider with us. The guard who had wounded the dog was now astride the horse. It had changed slightly, and its eyes were filled with yellow shine, its hooves edged in gold. Its eyes were no less yellow than its rider's hair. The gold of its hooves echoed in the gold of the Seelie's eyes. Dacey, I thought his name was, Dacey the Golden. The horse had a gold and silk bridle on it now, and a bit between its teeth. The guard was forced to join us for the crime of fighting back, but his touch had changed the horse for him. Wild magic is like water; it seeks a shape to take.

Two more guards realized that cold iron was the only thing that could harm us. They joined the hunt. One horse turned pale colors under its white skin, as if pastel rainbows moved and flowed beneath. The last horse was green, with vines laced around it as its bridle. The vines moved and waved, and began to cover the rider on its back in a suit of living green. Turloch had the pale horse, and Yolland the green.

I'd thought to find my cousin in her room, or in a back place where the poor nobles are put, those with no political power, or favor of the king. But the hounds led us to the main doors, to the main throne room. I think if we had gone anywhere else, the guards would have given up by now, but because we went for the throne room, and because the king was presumably inside, the guards thought we were here for Taranis. They might have given up for anything short of the king, but they were oath bound to protect him. When faced by the wild hunt you don't want to be an oathbreaker. You can go from defending someone else to being fresh prey if you are not careful. So I think they did not truly fight for the king, but for themselves, and their oath. But perhaps I was wrong about that. Perhaps they saw in their king things I had never seen. Things worth fighting and dying for. Perhaps.

But it wasn't the guard's abilities that stopped the hunt in the great room just outside the throne room doors. It was the room itself. Just as there was an antechamber in the Unseelie Court that held last-ditch defenses, so was there one here in the Seelie Court. The Unseelie had their living roses and thorns that would drag any unwanted visitors to their bloody death. It was a magic very similar to the wall of thorns that had tried to stop us earlier. The magic of each court is not cleanly cut, but intermingled, though both sides would deny it.

What did the Seelie have in their chamber?

A great oak spread up and up, toward a ceiling

that spilled into a distant sparkle of sky, like a piece of daylight forever stored in the limbs of the great tree. You knew you were underground, but there were glimpses of blue sky and clouds forever caught in the tree's upper limbs. It was like the things you see from the corners of your eyes. If you look directly at them, they aren't there, but yet you see them. The sky was like that, almost there. The trunk of the tree was large enough that it was quite a feat to walk around it to get to the huge jeweled doors of the throne room. But it was just a tree, so what made it the last defense?

We spilled into the great chamber at a full run, the other riders at our backs, our hounds howling, the boil of not-creatures at the end of it all pushing at us like fuel, or will. It wanted to be used, the stuff that followed in our wake.

Sunlight flared down from the leaves of the tree. Bright, hot sunlight spilled over us. For a second I thought it would burn as Taranis's hand of power could, as my cousin's hand of power had, but it was sunlight. It was real sunlight. The heat of a summer's day held forever in that room, waiting to burst into life and cover us with that life-giving warmth.

One moment we were riding over stone, the next we galloped over green grass with tall summer flowers brushing our horses' bellies. The only thing that remained was the huge oak tree spreading its branches above the meadow.

Sholto yelled, "Ride for the oak. It's real. The rest isn't."

He was so certain, so utterly certain, that it left no room for doubts in my mind. I kicked my mare forward, and rode at Sholto's shoulder. The riders in back of us came with us, with no doubts voiced. I wasn't certain whether they truly had no doubts, or whether they simply had no choice but to follow the huntsmen. In that moment, I did not care, only that we pushed forward, and Sholto knew the way.

His horse hit the far side of the oak, and it was as if a curtain peeled back. One breath we rode in a summer meadow, the next we clattered on stone, and were before the jeweled doors.

Sholto's many-legged stallion reared in front of the doors, as if he could not pass. Powerful magic indeed to stop the hunt. I'd known that the doors were old, but I hadn't realized that they were one of the ancient relics brought here from the old country. These doors had stood before the throne room of the Seelie Court when my human ancestors were still making houses out of animal skins.

I urged my mare forward slowly. The hounds whined and scratched at the door, high, eager sounds that sounded almost too puppyish to come from the thick throats of the white mastiffs. Our prey was within.

I smelled roses, and I whispered, "What would you have of me, Goddess?"

The answer came not in words, but in knowledge. I simply knew what needed doing. I turned the horse so we were sideways to the huge doors. I pressed my hand against them, a hand covered in the drying blood of my grandmother. I felt the pulse of the doors, almost a heartbeat. The truly ancient objects could have that, a semblance of life, so strong was their magic, so powerful the powers that forged them. It meant that certain objects had opinions, could make choices, all on their own; as some enchanted weapons will only fight in the hands of their choosing, so other things will listen to reason.

I pressed the blood against the door, reached for that pulse of almost life, and spoke. "By the blood of my kinswoman, by the death of the only mother I ever truly had, I call kin slayer on Cair. We are the wild hunt. Taste the blood of my loss, and let us pass."

The doors made a sound, almost a sigh, if wood and metal could make such a sound. Then the double doors began to open, revealing a slice of the glittering room beyond.

CHAPTER EIGHT

THERE WAS A CONFUSION OF COLORS: yellows, reds, and oranges, and over it all was gold. Gold like the metal of a piece of jewelry, edging everything. The air itself was full of sparkles, as if gold dust were permanently suspended in the air, so that the very air you breathed was formed of it.

The gold spilled around us, moved by the speed of our passage so that it rained around us, trailed behind us, mingling with the white glow of the magic so that we appeared in the midst of the court in a vision of silver and gold.

There was a moment when I saw the Golden Court spilled out before us. A moment to see Taranis on his huge golden and jeweled throne, with all his magic, all his illusion turning him to a thing of sunset colors and near-sunlike brilliance. His court spilled to either side in its standing lines, and the smaller chairs were like a garden of brilliant flowers formed of gold and silver and jewels. His people had hair in every color of the rainbow, their clothes chosen to complement and please the king. He liked the color of jewels and fire, so as Andais's court looked as if it were always ready for a funeral, Taranis's court looked like a bright version of hell.

I had a moment to see fear on my uncle's handsome face, then his guards poured around the throne. There were cries of, "He is forsworn! To the King! To the King!" Some of that glorious court poured toward the throne and prepared to aid the guards, but some got farther away from the throne, and what they thought would be the center of the fight.

I glimpsed my grandfather, Uar the Cruel, standing head and shoulders above most of the people as they fled. He was like a tree in the midst of their shining river. Looking at him as he stood, tall and every inch a war god, I realized that I had my grandfather's hair. I saw him so seldom, I hadn't realized it until that moment.

Magic flared around us in a deadly rainbow of color, fire, ice, and storm. The guards were defending their king, for whom else would I have been able to call down the wild hunt upon? So many crimes, so many traitors; I felt again that call to be at the head of the hunt forever. So simple, so painless, to ride every night and find our prey. So much simpler than the life I was trying to lead.

A hand gripped my arm, and the touch was enough. I turned to see Sholto, his face serious, his yellow and gold eyes searching my face. His touch kept bringing me back from the thought, but the fact that he knew to keep bringing me back from the brink told me that he'd had his own temptations at the head of the hunt. You can best protect others from temptation if you are, yourself, tempted.

We stood in the center of a magical storm, formed of different spells colliding. Small twisters whirled around the room, formed when powers of heat hit powers of cold. There were screams, and outside the glow of our own magic, I could see people running. Some ran toward the throne to protect their king, others fled to save themselves, and still others huddled near the walls and under the heavy tables. We watched it all through the frosted "glass" of the magic that surrounded us.

The dogs never hesitated, were never distracted by the spells of others. They had but one purpose, one prey. The hail of spells, and the storms that they themselves were causing, began to die down. The guards had finally realized that we had no interest in the throne. We moved inexorably toward the side of the room. The huge dogs shouldered their way under the tables, and spilled around a figure that was huddled against the wall.

I felt my mare's muscles bunch under me, and I had time to shift my weight forward and get a better grip on her mane before she leaped the wide table in one powerful jump.

The mare danced on the stones, her hooves raising green sparks, little licks of green and red flame coming with the smoke from her nostrils. The red glow in her eyes became small red flames that licked the edges of her eye sockets.

The dogs had trapped my cousin against the stone wall. She pressed that tall, thin sidhe frame as tightly as she could, as if the stone would give way and she would be able to escape that way. Her orange dress was very bright against the white marble wall. There would be nothing that easy for her this night. Again, that spurt of rage and deeply satisfying vengeance came to me. Her face was lovely and pale, and if she had only had a nose and enough skin to cover her mouth with lips, she'd have been as attractive as any in court. There had been a time when I had thought Cair truly beautiful, because I had not seen what she lacked as a mark of ugliness. I loved Gran's face, so her face combined with the face of a sidhe, who were all so lovely, well, Cair could be nothing but beautiful to me. But she had not felt that way, and she had let me know with the back of her hand when no one was looking, with small petty cruelties, that she hated me. I realized as I grew older that the reason was that she would have traded her tall, lithe body for my face. She made me think that being short and curved was a crime, but my face with its more-sidhe features was what she wanted. As a child, I had simply thought that I was ugly.

Now I saw her pressed against the wall, the brown eyes of our grandmother in her face, with its so-similar bone structure, and I wanted her to be afraid. I wanted her to know what she'd done and regret it, then I wanted her to die in terror. Was that petty? Did I care? No, I did not.

Cair looked up at me with my grandmother's eyes—eyes filled with terror, and behind the fear, knowledge. She knew why we were here.

I urged my horse forward, through the growling pack of hounds. I reached out to her with the dried blood on my hands.

She screamed and tried to move, but the huge white and red dogs moved closer. The threat was there in the bass rumble of their growls, the drawn lips showing fangs that were meant for rending flesh.

She closed her eyes, and I leaned forward, my hand reaching for that perfect white cheek. My hand touched her, gently. She winced as if I'd struck her. One moment the blood was dried and beginning to cake on my skin, the next it was wet and fresh. I left a crimson print of my small hand against her perfect bone structure. All the blood on my hands and gown was liquid and running again. The old wives' tale that a murder victim will bleed afresh if its murderer lays hands on it is based on truth.

I held my bloody hand up so the sidhe could see it, and cried out, "Kin slayer I name her. By the blood of her victim, she is accused."

It was my Aunt Eluned, Cair's mother, who came to the edge of the dogs, and held her white hands out to me. "Niece, Meredith, I am your mother's sister, and Cair is my daughter. What kin did she slay to bring you here like this?"

I turned to look at her, so lovely. She was my mother's twin, but they weren't identical. Eluned was just a little more sidhe than my mother, a little less human. She wore gold from head to toe. Her red hair like my own and her father's sparkled against her dress. Her eyes were the many-petaled eyes of Taranis, except that my aunt's were shades of gold and green intermingled. I stared into those eyes and had a memory so sharp that it stabbed through me from stomach to head. I saw eyes like these except only shades of green—Taranis's eyes above me, as if in a dream, but I knew it wasn't a dream.

Sholto touched my arm, lightly this time. "Meredith."

I shook my head at him, then held my bloody hand out toward my aunt. "This is your mother's blood, our grandmother's blood, Hettie's blood."

"Are you saying that . . . our mother is dead?"

"She died in my arms."

"But how?"

I pointed at my cousin. "She used a spell to make Gran into her instrument, to give her Cair's hand of power. She forced Gran to attack us with fire. My Darkness is still in the hospital with injuries that Gran gave him with a hand of power she never owned."

"You lie," my cousin said.

The dogs growled.

"If I lied I could not have called the hunt, and pronounced you kin slayer. The hunt will not come if the vengeance is not righteous."

"The blood of her victim marks her," Sholto said.

Aunt Eluned drew herself up to her full sidhe height and said, "You have no voice here, Shadow-spawn."

"I am a king, and you are not," he said, in a voice as haughty and arrogant as her own.

"King of nightmares," Eluned said.

Sholto laughed. His laughter made light play in his hair, as if laughter could be yellow light to spill in the whiteness of his hair. "Let me show you nightmares," he said, and his voice held that anger that has passed heat and become a cold thing. Heated anger is about passion; cold anger is about hate.

I didn't think he hated my aunt specifically, but all the sidhe who had ever treated him as less. A few short weeks ago a sidhe woman had lured him to a bit of tie-me-up sex. But instead of sex, sidhe warriors had come and cut off his tentacles, skinned all the extra bits away. The woman had told Sholto that when he healed, and was free of taint, she might actually sleep with him.

The magic of the hunt changed slightly, felt . . . angrier. It was my turn to reach out and warn him. I'd always known that to be drafted to ride in the hunt could mean being trapped, but I hadn't realized that calling it could also trap the huntsman. The hunt wanted a permanent huntsman, or huntswoman. It wanted to be led now that it was back. And strong emotions could give it the key to your soul. I'd felt it, and now I saw Sholto begin to be incautious.

I gripped his arm until he looked at me. The blood that had left a mark so bright and fresh on Cair's face left no mark on his arm. I stared into his eyes until I saw him look back, not in anger, but with that wisdom that had let the sluagh keep their independence when most of the other lesser kingdoms had been swallowed up.

He smiled at me, that gentler version that I had only seen since he found out that he was to be a father. "Shall I show them that they did not unman me?"

I knew what he meant. I smiled back, and nodded. The smiles saved us, I think. We shared a moment that had nothing to do with the hunt's purpose. A moment of hope, of shared intimacy, of friendship as well as love.

He'd meant to show Aunt Eluned what nightmares could truly be. To show his extra bits in anger to horrify. Now he would reveal himself to prove that the nobles who had hurt him had failed to mutilate him. He was whole. More than whole, he was perfect.

One moment it was a tattoo that decorated his stomach and upper chest, the next it was the reality. Light and color played on the pale skin, gold and pale pink. Shades of pastel light shone and moved under the skin of the many moving parts. They waved like some graceful sea creature, moved by some warm tropical current. When last he'd come to this court, he'd been ashamed of this part of himself. Now he was not, and it showed.

There were screams from some of the ladies, and my aunt, though a little pale, said, "You are a nightmare yourself, Shadowspawn."

Yolland of the black hair and vine-covered horse said, "She seeks to distract you from her daughter's guilt."

My aunt looked at him and said, in a shocked voice, "Yolland, how can you help them?"

"I did my duty to king and land, but the hunt has me now, Eluned, and I see things differently. I know that Cair used her own grandmother as a stalking horse and a trap. Why would anyone do that? Have we become so heartless that the murder of your own mother means nothing to you, Eluned?"

"She is my only child," she said, in a voice that was not so sure of itself.

"And she has killed your only mother," he said.

She turned and looked at her daughter, who was still pressed against the wall in a circle of the white mastiffs, with our horses at the front of the circle.

"Why, Cair?" Not "how could you?" but simply "why?"

Cair's face showed a different kind of fear now. It wasn't fear of the dogs pressing so closely. She looked at her mother's face, almost desperately. "Mother."

"Why?" her mother said.

"I have heard you deny her in this court day after day. You called her a useless brownie who had deserted her own court."

"That was talk for the other nobles, Cair."

"You never said differently in private with me, Mother. Aunt Besaba says the same. She is a traitor to this court for leaving, first to live with the Unseelie, then to live among the humans. I have heard you agree with such words all my life. You said you took me to visit her because it was duty. Once I was old enough to have a choice, we stopped going."

"I visited her in private, Cair."

"Why did you not tell me?"

"Because your heart is as cold as my sister's, and your ambition as hot. You would have seen my care for our mother as a weakness."

"It **was** a weakness," she said.

Eluned shook her head, a look of deep sorrow on her face. She stepped back from the line of dogs, back from her daughter. She looked up at us. "Did she die knowing that Cair had betrayed her?"

"Yes."

"Knowing that her own granddaughter betrayed her would have broken her heart."

"She did not have the knowledge long," I said. It was cold comfort, but it was all I had to give her. I rode with the wild hunt, and truth, harsh or kind, was the only thing I could speak this night.

"I will not stand in your way, niece."

"Mother!" Cair reached out. The dogs closed in around her, giving that low bass growl that seemed to tiptoe up the spine and hit something low in the brain. If you heard that sound, you knew that it was bad.

Cair yelled again. "Mother, please!"

Eluned yelled back, "She was my mother!"

"I'm your daughter."

Eluned moved backward in her long golden dress. "I have no daughter." She walked away, and she did not look back. The nobles who had clustered by the door moved apart to let her pass. She did not stop until the far jeweled doors closed behind her. She would not fight us for her daughter's life, but she would not watch us take it either. I could not blame her.

Cair looked around frantically. "Lord Finbar, help me!" she cried.

Most of the eyes in the room went to the far table, where the king was completely hidden behind a wall of guards and sparkling courtiers. One of those was Lord Finbar, tall and handsome with his yellow, almost human-colored hair. Only the feeling of power from him and the otherworldly handsome face marked him as more. Uar was still standing to one side watching the show, but not shielding his brother. Lord Finbar was planted in front of his monarch. He was an intimate of the king's, but no friend to my aunt or my cousin, last I knew. Why would she appeal to him now?

The king was completely hidden behind the glittering, bejeweled throng that included Finbar. Maybe he was no longer even in the room, and the nobles were only using themselves as a stalking horse. But tonight, that did not matter. What did matter was why Cair would appeal to the tall blond noble who had never been her friend.

His high, sculpted-cheekboned face was set in arrogant lines, as cold as any I'd seen. It made me think of my lost Frost, when he was either at his most afraid, or most embarrassed. It was a face to hide behind, that arrogance.

Cair called out to him again, more frantically. "Lord Finbar, you promised."

He spoke then. "The girl is clearly deranged. The killing of her own matriarch is proof of that." His voice was as cold and clear as the pale line of his cheek. The words dripped surety and an arrogance bred from centuries, not of his ancestors' ruling, but of he himself ruling. Immortal and noble; it was a recipe for arrogance, and stupidity.

Cair cried out, "Finbar, what are you saying? You promised you would protect me. You swore."

"She is deranged," he repeated.

Sholto looked at me, and I understood. I spoke, and my voice carried, echoing. Tonight I held more than my own magic. "Lord Finbar, give us your oath that you did not promise my cousin your protection, and we will believe you. She is deranged."

"I do not answer to you, Meredith, not yet."

"It is not I, Meredith, who asks for your oath. Tonight I ride at the head of a different court. It is with that power that I ask a second time, Finbar. Give your oath that she lies about your protection, and no more need be said."

"I do not owe the perverse creature at your side my oath."

He had used Queen Andais's nickname for Sholto. She had called him her Perverse Creature, sometimes simply Creature. Bring me my Creature. Sholto had hated the nickname, but you did not correct a queen.

Sholto urged his many-legged horse forward, with his own extras echoing the theme. I thought he'd lose his temper, but his voice was as calm and arrogant as Finbar's had been. "How does a lord of the Seelie know the Dark Queen's nicknames for her guards?"

"We have spies, as you do."

Sholto nodded, his hair catching the yellow light, except that there was no light in the room quite the color that was sparkling in his hair. "But tonight I am not her creature. I am the King of the sluagh, and the Huntsman, this night. Would you refuse your oath to the Huntsman?"

"You are not **the** Huntsman," Finbar said.

It was the blond-haired noble who rode with us who said, "We attacked the hunt, now we ride with it. They are the huntsmen for this night."

"You are bespelled, Dacey," Finbar said.

"If the Great Hunt is a spell, then I am under it."

One of the other nobles said, "Finbar, simply give your oath that the madwoman lies, and this will be done."

Finbar said nothing to that. He just looked handsome and arrogant. In the end, it was the last defense of the sidhe, beauty and pride. I'd never had enough of either to learn the trick of it.

"He cannot give oath," Cair said, "for he would be forsworn with the wild hunt standing in front of him. It would be his doom." She sounded angry now. She, like me, had never been beautiful enough to earn the arrogance that the true sidhe had. We could have been friends, she and I, if she hadn't resented me so.

"Tell us what he promised you, Cair," I said.

"He knew I could get close enough to her to place the spell upon her."

"She lies." This came not from Finbar, but from his son, Barris.

Finbar said, "Barris, no!"

Some of the hounds had turned toward Barris where he stood at the end of the far side of the room. He had not joined his father in protecting the king. The huge dogs began to creep toward him, growling that low, threatening sound. "Liars were once the prey of the hunt," Sholto said, and he was smiling, a very satisfied smile.

I touched his arm again, to remind him not to enjoy the power too much. The hunt was a trap, and the longer we rode in it, the harder it would become to remember that.

He reached back, and took my hand in his. He nodded and said, "Think carefully, Barris. Is Cair a liar, or does she tell the truth?"

Cair spoke. "I am telling the truth. Finbar told me what to do, and promised that if I did it, he would let Barris and me be a couple. And that if I became with child, we would marry."

"Is that true, Barris?" I asked.

Barris was staring in horror at the huge white hounds as they crept forward. There was something in the way they moved that reminded me of images of lions stalking on a savannah. Barris didn't look as if he enjoyed playing the part of the gazelle.

"Father," he said, and looked at Finbar.

Finbar's face was no longer arrogant. If he'd been human, I'd have said that he looked tired, but there weren't enough lines and circles under those pretty eyes for that.

The hounds began to herd Barris with snaps of teeth and presses of huge bodies. He made a small frightened noise.

"You always were an idiot," Finbar said. I was pretty sure he wasn't talking to us.

"I know what you hoped to gain, Cair, but what did Finbar hope to gain by the deaths of my men?"

"He wanted to strip you of your most dangerous consorts."

"Why?" I asked, and I felt strangely calm.

"So that the Seelie nobles could control you once you were queen."

"You thought that if Doyle and I were dead you could control Meredith?" Sholto asked.

"Of course," she said.

Sholto laughed, and it was both a good laugh and a bad one, the kind of laugh that you might describe as evil. "They do not know you, Meredith."

"They never did," I said.

"Did you really think that Rhys, Galen, and Mistral would let you control Meredith?"

"Rhys and Galen, yes, but not the Storm Lord," she said.

"Quiet, girl," Finbar said at last. It wasn't a lie or an oath. He could order her about or insult her in safety.

"You have betrayed me, Finbar, and proved your word as worthless. I owe you nothing." She turned to me, those long, graceful hands reaching out to me, past the crowding dogs. "I will tell you all, please, Meredith, please. Faerie itself has taken care of the Killing Frost, but the Darkness and the Lord of Shadows needed to go."

"Why did you spare Rhys, Galen, and Mistral?" I asked.

"Rhys was once a lord of this court. He was reasonable, and we thought he would be reasonable again if he could come back to the Golden Court."

It wasn't just me that they didn't understand. "How long has it been since Rhys was a member of this court?"

Cair looked at Rhys. "Eight hundred years, maybe a little more."

"Did it occur to you that he might have changed in that many years?" I asked.

The look on her face was enough; it hadn't. "Everyone wants to be a noble in the Golden Court," she said, and she believed it. The proof was in her eyes, her face, so earnest.

"And Galen?" I asked.

"He is not a threat, and we cannot deprive you of all your mates."

"Glad to hear it," I said. I don't think she picked up on the sarcasm. I'd found that many of the nobles missed it.

"What of Mistral?" Sholto asked.

There was a flicker of eyes, as Cair and Barris looked at each other, then at Finbar. He did not look at anyone. He kept his face and every inch of himself to himself.

"Have you set a trap for him too?" Sholto asked.

The younger ones did the nervous look. Finbar remained impassive. I didn't like either reaction. I urged the mare forward until she nudged my cousin and Barris with the width of her chest. The dogs had herded him to stand beside his would-be bride.

"Have you sent someone to kill Mistral?"

"You are going to kill me either way," Cair said.

"You are right, but we are not here for Barris tonight. I called kin slayer, and he is not our kin." I looked at the young lord. "Do you want to survive this night, Barris?"

He looked up at me, and I saw in his blue eyes the weakness that must have made a political animal like Finbar despair. He wasn't just weak, he also wasn't bright. I'd offered him a chance to survive tonight, but there would be other nights. That I vowed.

Finbar said, "Do not speak."

"The king will save you, Father, but he has no use for me."

"The Darkness is injured badly enough that he is not at her side. It must be grave. We have missed the Shadow Lord, but if the Storm Lord dies this night, then we will be rewarded."

"If Mistral dies this night, Barris, you will follow him, and soon. This I promise you." The mare shifted underneath me, uneasy.

"Even you, Barris, must know what a promise like that means when the princess sits a horse of the wild hunt," Sholto said.

Barris swallowed hard, then said, "If she breaks the promise, the hunt will destroy her."

"Yes," Sholto said, "so you had better talk while there is still time to save the Storm Lord."

His eyes with their circles of blue showed too much white like a frightened horse. One of the hounds nudged his leg, and he made a small sound that in anyone else would have been a scream. But the nobles of the Seelie Court did not scream just because a dog nudged them.

Finbar said, "Remember who you are, Barris."

He looked back at his father. "I remember

who I am, Father, but you taught me that all are equal before the hunt. Did you not call it the great leveler?" Barris's voice held sorrow, or perhaps disappointment. The fear was beginning to fade under the weight of years. Years of never quite being what his father wanted in a son. Years of knowing that though he looked every inch a Seelie noble, he was pretending as hard as he could.

I looked at Barris, who had always seemed as perfectly arrogant as all the rest. I had never seen beyond that perfect, handsome mask. Was it the magic of the hunt that was giving me clear vision, or had I simply assumed that if you looked perfectly sidhe—tall, thin, and so perfect—you would be happy and secure? Had I truly still believed that beauty was security? That if I had only been taller, thinner, less human-looking and more sidhe my life would have been . . . perfect?

I looked into Barris's face, saw all that disappointment, all that failure, because his beauty hadn't been enough to win him his father's heart.

I felt something I hadn't expected: pity.

"Help us save Mistral and you may yet keep your life. Keep silent, let him die, and I cannot help you, Barris."

Sholto looked at me, his face careful not to show surprise, but I think he'd heard that note of pity in my voice, and found it unexpected. I couldn't blame him. Barris had helped kill my grandmother, and tried to kill my lovers, my future kings, but it hadn't been him. He had been trying to please his father, and had bargained with the only asset he had, his pure sidhe blood and all that tall, unnaturally slender beauty.

Finbar had had nothing to bargain with with Cair except his son's pale beauty. To be accepted in the court, to have a pure-blooded sidhe lover and perhaps husband, that had been the price for Gran's life. It was the same price for which Gran had agreed to marry Uar the Cruel all those centuries ago. A chance to marry into the Golden Court—for a half human, half brownie, a once-in-a-millennium chance.

"Tell us, Barris, or you will die another night."

"Tell them," Cair said, her voice thin with fear. Which said that she didn't know what their plan was for Mistral, only that there was one.

"We found a traitor to lure him out into the open. Our archers will use cold iron arrowheads."

"Where is it to take place?" Sholto asked.

Barris told us. He confessed everything while some of the king's guards held Finbar. The King was indeed gone. He'd vanished to safety. The guards didn't hold Finbar for what he'd tried to do to me, but because his actions could be seen as acts of war against the Unseelie Court. That was a killing offense at both courts, to act without the express orders of your king or queen in such a way that it could cause war. Though part of me was certain that Taranis had agreed to the plan, although not outright. He was of a flavor of kingship to ask, "Who will rid me of this inconvenient man?" Deniability that he could take oath on. But Taranis was prey for another court, and another day.

I tried to turn my mare toward the doors and the saving of Mistral, but it shook its head. It pranced nervously, but would not move.

"We must finish here, or the hunt will not move on," Sholto said.

It took me a moment to understand, then I turned to Cair, where she stood pressed to the wall, surrounded on all sides by the great hounds. I could have used them as my weapon. They would have torn her apart for me, but I wasn't certain if I could sit through that, and it would take longer. We needed something quicker, for Mistral's sake and for my own peace of mind.

Sholto held out a spear formed of bone. Did it appear out of the air? It was one of the marks of kingship among the sluagh, but it had been lost centuries ago, long before he took the throne. It and the dagger of bone in his hand had returned with the wild magic when we had first made love.

I took the spear.

Cair began to scream, "No, Meredith, no!"

I moved the long pole until I had the weight of it. I would not throw it; there was no room and no need. "She died in my arms, Cair."

She reached out to someone behind me. "Grandfather, help me!"

His voice came, and he said what I thought he'd say, "The wild hunt cannot be stopped. And I have no time for weaklings."

Cair turned back to me. "Look what she did to you and me, Meredith! She made us into things that could never be accepted by our own people."

"The wild hunt comes to my vengeance, the Goddess moves through me, the Consort comes to me in visions; I am sidhe!" I used both hands to plunge the spear downward through her thin chest. I felt the tip grate on bone, and pushed that last inch to feel the tip break out of her body, and hit empty air on her other side. With more meat on her bones it would have been harder, but there wasn't enough to her to stop that weapon and the strength of my sorrow.

Cair stared up at me, her hands grabbing at the spear, but she couldn't seem to make her hands work quite right. Her brown eyes stared up at me, as if she couldn't quite believe what was happening. I looked into those eyes, a mirror of Gran's eyes, and watched the fear fade, to leave puzzlement. Blood trickled from her lipless mouth. She tried to speak, but no words came. Her hands fell to her side. I watched her eyes begin to fade. People say that it's light that fades when humans die, but it's not; it's them. The look in their eyes that makes them who they are, that is what fades.

I jerked the spear backward, twisting it, not to cause more damage, but simply to loosen it from its sheath of flesh and bone. When the spear had come far enough back through her body, she began to fall to the floor. I just had to hold on, and the weight of her body and gravity pulled her free of it.

I looked at the bloody spear and tried to feel something, anything. I used the hem of my gown to clean the blood away, then I handed the spear back to Sholto. I would need both hands to ride.

He took the spear from me, but leaned in and gave me a gentle kiss, the tentacles brushing me gently, like hands trying to comfort me. I could not afford that comfort yet. There was work to do, and the night would fade.

I drew back from all the comfort he offered and said, "We ride."

"To save your Storm Lord," he said.

"To save the future of faerie." I turned the mare, and this time she came easily to my hand. I set my heels in her flanks, and she bounded forward in a flare of green flame and smoke. The others spilled behind me, and the glow was as white and pure as the full moon, but here and there the gold of the Seelie banquet room seemed to have absorbed into the white, so we kept that silver and gold glow. My grandfather saluted me as I rode past. I did not return the gesture. The jeweled doors opened for us.

I whispered, "Goddess, Consort, help me, help us be in time."

We rode past the great oak, and again there was that sensation of movement, but there was no summer meadow, no illusion. One moment we rode on stone, in the halls of the Seelie, the next our horses were on grass, in the night outside the faerie mounds.

Lightning cut the darkness ahead of us. Lightning not from the sky to the ground, but from the ground to the sky. I called, "Mistral!"

We rode toward the fight, rising above the grass, gaining the sky, and rushing like wind and stars toward my Storm Lord.

CHAPTER NINE

LIGHTNING CUT ALONG THE GROUND, IL-luminating the dark scene below. It was like seeing the fight through strobe flashes—bits and pieces, frozen, but nothing whole.

Mistral on his knees, one hand outstretched; arrows flying, their heads glinting dully in the hot, white light. Dark figures in the trees. Something smaller moving on the ground behind Mistral.

I tracked the flight of arrows not by sight but by the reaction of Mistral's body as they hit him. He staggered, if you could stagger when you were already on your knees. His body hunched forward, then fell to one side, only his arm keeping him from the ground. He shot another bolt of lightning from his other hand, but it fell far from the trees, scorching the ground but not reaching his attackers.

I leaned low over the mare's white shoulders. Down there was one of the fathers of the children inside me. I would not lose another of them. I would not.

Sholto seemed to understand, because he called to me, "We will take the attackers. You see to the Storm Lord."

I didn't argue. Mistral was shot full of cold metal. If he was to be saved, it would have to be soon. I didn't want vengeance in that moment. I wanted him alive.

Mistral fell on his side in the winter-ruined grass. The wind of our passage blew his hair around his body, tugged at the cloak that spilled around him. He didn't seem to notice. He pointed his hand at the trees. Lightning flared, and we were close enough that my night vision was torn; when the light left, I was blind in the dark.

There was an art to sitting a horse when it went from flying to being on the ground again. I did not have that art complete, so it was jarring as the horse's hooves crunched on the frosted grass. I had to sit on the horse in the dark while I waited for my vision to clear. It was spotted sight that returned, but it was enough to show me Mistral's body terribly still on the white and black of the ground.

The only light was the green of the flames from the mare's hooves. It was a glow that reminded me of the fire Doyle could call to his hands. I had left him hurt. If he was conscious he must be wild with worry, but one disaster at a time. Doyle had doctors, while Mistral had only me in that moment. I slipped off the mare, and the thickly frosted grass was cold under my bare feet. The night was suddenly cold. The mare pulled away from my hand, and ran after the others. I realized in that moment that I was alone. My vengeance was done; Cair was dead. I was at Mistral's side, and the magic that had sustained me this night was leaving. It was running at Sholto's side with the men we'd shanghaied from the Seelie Court. I could hear the hounds baying in the distance. They glowed against the trees, and gave enough light that I could see three figures, firing up into the hunt before the hounds spilled down upon them. I didn't think Sholto would have my squeamishness. He would use the hounds.

I went to my knees on the hard winter grass. Mistral's blood had melted the hard frost, so the ground was softer from the spill of his blood. His face was hidden by the fall of all that gray hair, not gray with age, for he would never age, but the gray of storm clouds. His hair was warm to the touch as I moved it away so I could search for the big pulse in his neck. I was never good at finding it in the wrist, and without the magic of the hunt, I was very aware that I wore only a thin gown. I was starting to shiver even as I searched for his pulse.

At first, I was afraid we were too late, but then, under my shaking fingers, I felt it. He was alive. Until I felt the pulse I hadn't wanted to look at how badly he was hurt. It was as if I were trying to pretend, but now I had to look. I had to see what was there.

His broad shoulders, his whole strong body, was pierced with arrows. I counted five. Strangely, none of them were a heart shot. The only thing I could think was that the lightning had ruined their vision as it had ruined mine. I wasn't certain if his hand of power had taken out a single attacker, but it had spoiled their aim, and saved his life. If I could get him medical help maybe he would not bleed to death, or die from the touch of so much cold iron plunged into the meat of his body. That alone was poisonous to the creatures of faerie.

The hunt was still busy, and they were still lost in the magic of it. Only I had woken from the spell. I had seen Mistral, and saving him had meant more to me than anyone else's death. Maybe that was why most of the legends of the wild hunt had male huntsmen. To be female was a more practical thing. Life meant more to us than death.

I knelt in the strangely warm grass, warmed by the spill of Mistral's life, melting the hard frost. There was a shaft in the ground. I pulled it from the winter-hardened ground carefully, because I didn't want it to break off in the ground. The shaft was wood, so the archers could handle them safely, but when I could finally see the arrowhead, my worst fears were confirmed. They hadn't even used modern metal. It was cold forged iron—the very worst thing you could use on faerie folk.

My human blood made iron no more deadly to me than any other metal. I could touch the arrowhead with no harm done, but a wooden spear could have killed me, and Mistral would have ignored it.

If the arrows had been ordinary ones, it would have been bad to remove them without medical help, but the arrowheads themselves were poisoning him. Every moment they stayed inside his body was another moment of death leaching into his system. But if I drew the arrows out, they'd widen the wounds. Damnit, I didn't know what to do. Some queen I was. I couldn't even decide this one thing.

I laid the arrow that I'd pulled from the ground beside my knees, and put my hands on his side, laid my forehead on his shoulder, and prayed. "Goddess guide me. What do I do to save him?"

"Isn't this touching?" a male voice said.

I jerked up, and Onilwyn was there, in the dark. He'd been one of my guards for a few months, but when last we left faerie he'd remained behind. Admittedly, he'd been helping wrestle my insane cousin Cel into submission at the time, but he hadn't asked to return to my service. He had always been Cel's friend, never mine, and I had found excuses not to bed him.

"The problem with the magic of the wild hunt," he said, "is that it makes you lose track of important things, like leaving your princess alone in the night with no guards. I would never be so careless, Princess Meredith."

He gave a low bow, sweeping his cloak aside, letting the thick waves of his hair fall forward. It was hard to see in the darkness, but his hair was a deep green, and his eyes were a grass green with a starburst of liquid gold around the pupil. He was a little short and wide, built more like a square than the usual lithe guards, but that wasn't what had kept him out of my bed. I simply did not like him, nor he me. He wanted to bed me only because it was the only way to ease his enforced abstinence. Oh, and a chance to be king to my queen. Mustn't forget that. Onilwyn was far too ambitious to have forgotten it.

"I applaud your sense of duty, Onilwyn. Contact the Unseelie mound, have them send healers, and help move Mistral someplace warm."

"Why would I do that?" he asked. He loomed over us in his thick winter cloak, a stray lock of hair blowing across his cheek, as the cold wind began to play along our skin. I looked up into his face, and the clouds parted in that wind, so that I had enough moonlight to see his face clearly, and what I saw put my pulse into my throat.

I shivered, but it wasn't just from the cold. I saw death on Onilwyn's face, death and deep satisfaction, almost happiness.

"Onilwyn," I said, "do as I command." But my voice betrayed my fear.

He laughed softly. "I think not." He swept back the heavy cloak, his hand seeking the sword revealed at his side.

I reached into the grass for the only weapon I had, the arrow. I used Mistral's body to shield the movement. But I had to stab Onilwyn before he drew his sword. It was one of those moments when time seems to freeze, and you have both too much time to see the disaster unfolding, and not enough time to act.

I slapped at him with my left hand, and he batted it away, almost gently. He was looking at my empty hand as I stabbed upward with the arrow. I felt the arrow cut into flesh. I shoved, and he jerked back, away from me. The arrow stayed in his leg. I had sunk it deeply enough to make him back up.

It took everything I had not to look behind me toward the glow of the hunt. The screams of the men were distant, fading, but they were miles away. They were visible in the flat farmland, but distance is hard to judge on flat land. Things can seem so much closer than they are. I could not look behind me for help.

Onilwyn jerked the arrow out of his leg. "You bitch!"

"You swore an oath to protect me, Onilwyn. Is this really the night you want to be a breaker of oaths?"

He threw the arrow to the ground, and drew his sword. "Call the hunt; even flying, they will not get here in time to save you."

I spoke the words. "I call you oathbreaker, Onilwyn. I call you traitor, and I call the wild hunt to hear me."

I heard the scream of the horses, and screams of other things, as if the shapeless things had voices now. They would turn, they would come, and

Sholto would lead them, but Onilwyn was striding across the grass, sword in hand. They would be too late unless I fought back.

The only magic I had that worked from a distance came at a price of pain. I wasn't sure what it would do to the babies, but if I died, we all died.

I called the hand of blood. It wasn't like most hands of power; there was no bolt of energy, no fire, no shining anything. I simply called it into the palm of my left hand, or maybe opened some invisible door in my hand, though my hand was solid to the eye and touch, but it was the doorway for the hand of blood for me.

I called my magic and prayed to the Goddess that what I was doing to save us wouldn't kill two of us. It was as if the blood in my veins turned to molten metal, so hot, so much pain, as if my blood would boil until it melted my skin and poured out of me. But I'd learned what to do with the pain.

I screamed, and faced the palm of my left hand toward the now-running Onilwyn. He was sidhe, he would feel the magic, or maybe he just ran to make sure I died before the hunt arrived.

I thrust that burning, boiling pain into him. He staggered for a moment, then kept coming. I shrieked, "Bleed!"

The wound that I had made in his thigh burst open. His skin split, and blood fountained. The original wound had missed the femoral artery—it was too far under the skin that low in the thigh—but my power could take a small wound and make it bigger. Nick someone even close to a major artery, and I had a chance to open it.

Onilwyn hesitated, putting a hand to his wound, his sword pointing downward. He looked past me, at the sky, and I knew what he saw. I fought not to look, because where I looked sometimes the hand of blood bled. I wanted Onilwyn to bleed, and no one else.

He raised his hand, shining dark in the moonlight with his own blood. He looked at me with deep hatred, then he raised his sword two-handed and ran at me, screaming a war cry.

I screamed my own cry of, "Bleed for me!"

The hunt was coming, but the man with the sword was too close. The only question was whether I could bleed him to death faster than he could cross that piece of ground.

CHAPTER TEN

I POINTED MY LEFT HAND AT HIM, AND screamed for blood. I pushed my power into the wound, and tore it wider. Onilwyn stumbled, but kept coming at a limping run. He was almost to me. I prayed to the Goddess and the Consort. I prayed for strength. Strength to save myself and my babies.

Onilwyn fell to his knees on the dark winter ground. He tried to stand, but his wounded leg betrayed him, and he ended on all fours, blood gushing out onto the frosted grass. The white of the frost vanished in the warm rush of his blood.

He started crawling toward me, dragging his injured leg behind him like a broken tail. He kept his sword in one fist, the point raised a little above the ground so it didn't catch on anything. The look on his face was implacable. His eyes held only certainty and hatred.

I wanted to ask what I had ever done to him

for such hatred to grow, but I had to concentrate on bleeding him to death before he could put that sword through me and my unborn children.

I wasn't even frightened anymore. All the emotion that was in me was concentrated in my left hand. Concentrated into one thought: die. I could pretend that all I wanted was his blood, but that wasn't enough. I needed death. I needed Onilwyn's death.

He was close enough that I could see the sheen of sweat on his face, even by moonlight. I kept my hand pointed at him, and I cried out, "Die! Die for me!"

Onilwyn rose to his knees, swaying like a thin tree caught in a strong wind, but he rose above Mistral's quiet body. The sword also rose.

I kept my hand pointed at him, but crawled backward from that shining metal. His hand fell, the sword striking the ground where I had been. He didn't seem to realize at first that he'd missed me. He drove the sword home viciously, as if he were cutting flesh.

I got to my feet, still bleeding him, still killing him.

Onilwyn frowned at the ground, where he was cutting nothing. He leaned on Mistral's body, one hand holding on to the other man. The other hand, with its sword, was thrust into the ground, but it was almost as if he'd forgotten it was there.

He frowned up at me, as if he couldn't quite focus. "Cel said you were weak."

"Die for me, Onilwyn. Die for me, and keep your oath."

His sword fell from his fingers. "If you can bleed me, you can save me."

"You would kill me and my unborn children. Why should I save you?"

"For pity," he said, his eyes beginning to look slightly to the side of where I stood.

I smelled roses, and the words that came from my mouth were not my words. "I am the dark goddess. I am the destroyer of worlds. I am the face of the moon when all light is gone. I could have come to you, Onilwyn, in the shape of light and spring and life, but you have called the winter down upon yourself, and there is no pity in the snow. There is only death."

"You are with child," he said, as he began to slump toward the cold ground. "You are full of life."

I touched my stomach with my right hand; the left never stopped pointing at him. "The Goddess is all things at all times. There is never life without death, never light without darkness, never pain without hope. I am the Goddess, I am creation and destruction. I am the cradle of life, and the end of the world. You would destroy me, Ash Lord, but you cannot."

He stared up at me with unfocused eyes. He reached out toward me, not with magic, but as if he would touch me, or was trying to touch something. I wasn't certain he was reaching for me, but he saw something in that moment. He saw something that made him reach for it.

"Forgive me," he whispered.

"I am the face of the goddess that you called into being this night, Ash Lord. Is there forgiveness in the face you see?"

"No," he whispered. He slumped until the side of his face touched the ground, and the rest of him was draped across Mistral's body. He shuddered, and gave a last, long breath. Onilwyn, Lord of the Ash Grove, died as he had lived, surrounded by enemies.

CHAPTER ELEVEN

I SAW THE WHITE GLOW OF THE HUNT behind me like a second moon in the sky before I heard the wind of its coming. But I kept my eyes on the fallen sidhe lord. Onilwyn looked unconscious, maybe even dead, but until it was certain, I would not turn and give him a second chance to kill me.

I heard the horses and other things land on the frozen ground. I heard running feet, and Sholto was beside me. He put himself between me and the slumped forms. The bone spear was pointed up, the bone dagger naked in his hand.

I leaned against his back, feeling the strength of him through the remnants of his t-shirt. He, like me, hadn't dressed for the cold. Magic can make you forget practicalities, until the magic recedes and you realize that you are mortal once more. Oh, I guess that was just me. Some of the sidhe never felt the cold.

"Are you hurt?" he asked.

"No, just feeling the cold." Saying it out loud seemed to give me permission to shiver. I pressed myself more tightly against the warmth of his back, and reached around to encircle his waist. I found more in the front of his body than just waist. The tentacles petted and caressed my hands and arms. He was touching me, holding me, just as he would have with his hands if they weren't full of weapons. But Sholto had enough "hands" to hold me **and** fight. There had been a time when the extra bits had disturbed me to the point that I wasn't sure I could get past them, but such petty concerns seemed ages ago. The tentacles were warm, as if they had blood close to the surface. They reached around his body to hold more of me, stretching as only things with no bones can. Tonight it wasn't disturbing, it was warm.

Yolland moved past us in his court finery, his iron sword bare in his hand. I couldn't see what he did, but he said, "The green-haired guard has only the faintest pulse."

"What about Mistral?" Sholto asked.

"The same."

"We have to get Mistral to a healer," I said, still wrapped in the warmth of Sholto's back, and other things.

"What of Onilwyn?" Sholto asked. I was pressed so close to his back that his words vibrated against my cheek.

I thought of the look on Onilwyn's face, the

hatred. He meant my death, and sparing his life wouldn't change that determination in his eyes. He would see it as weakness. "He must die."

I felt Sholto startle; even the tentacles reacted like a hand that almost draws back from yours. "We should ask the queen first, Meredith."

"Are there healers at the sluagh?" I asked.

"Yes," he said.

"Then take Mistral and me there. I must get out of the cold, and he needs the killing metal out of his body."

"Let us take you to the Seelie Court," Yolland said.

I laughed, and it wasn't a pleasant sound. "Without the power of the wild hunt, I would not enter there like this."

"Then the Unseelie Court," Sholto said.

"The men you killed were lords of that court, weren't they?"

"Yes," he said.

"Then it is not safe. Take me to your kingdom, Sholto."

"The sidhe are more fragile than the people of the sluagh. I am not certain our healers are the best for the Storm Lord."

"He needs the metal out of him, and warmth; beyond that, we will see. But time is not his friend, or ours. Kill Onilwyn. When we have survived this night, we will seek an audience with the queen."

"You cannot mean to end the life of one of the sidhe," Turloch said.

"My enemies are many, my friends are few. I must prove to the first that to come against me is death, and to the second that I am strong enough to rule here." Then I hugged Sholto and told the truth. "I saw my death and the deaths of my unborn children in Onilwyn's face. If I spare him, he will see it as weakness, not mercy. I do not want him at my back with that hot determination in his eyes. I am pregnant with twins. Would you risk the first royal babies since I was born to squeamishness?"

"It is not squeamishness, my lady," Turloch said.

"Princess," Sholto said. "She is Princess Meredith."

"Fine. Princess Meredith, it is not squeamishness, but the thought of losing another lord of the sidhe. We are so few now, Princess. Even those who are twisted and Unseelie are precious to some of us, for many of them once walked the golden corridors of our court before they fell from favor."

"I am aware that many of our lords and ladies were once yours, Lord Turloch. But that does not change Onilwyn's fate."

"You are not my queen yet, and this I will not do," he said.

Sholto started to speak, but I squeezed him tightly, and he took the hint. He let me speak instead. "I would think long, Lord Turloch, on the fact that I brought a sidhe lord down single-handedly with no weapon."

"Is that a threat?" he asked.

"It is truth," I said, and let him take it any way he wished.

"Do as she commands," Sholto said. "You are still part of the hunt, and I am still the huntsman."

"Only until dawn breaks," he said.

"We will be free at dawn, but whether you are free or condemned to ride forever with the hunt remains to be seen," I said.

"What?" he said.

"She is right," Lord Dacey said, "for we attacked the hunt. Punishment can be to ride forever."

"Only the huntsman can free you," Sholto said, "so I would prove myself a good solider, Turloch, if I were you." His voice was cold, and he was very certain of himself. Only I was close enough to feel his heartbeat speed up. Was he not certain of his words, or not certain what the sidhe would do? Or did he agree with the other men that Onilwyn should be spared? The prospect of being trapped in the hunt was a fate that might make them fight us. The magic of the hunt was beginning to fade; I could feel it. It wouldn't be dawn that broke it. We could end up with a second fight on our hands.

We needed more allies who were ours by choice, not by threat. Mistral's life was dripping away. I would not lose him because we hesitated.

I started to step back from Sholto. He held me close for a second, then let me move away from him. The tentacles caressed me reluctantly, like fingertips trailing down my arms.

The ground was colder as I walked away from Sholto. His magic had been keeping me warm. As I moved across the frozen ground, the three sidhe lords watched me, as if I were something to be cautious of, almost as if they were afraid of me. It wasn't a look I was used to seeing on the faces of the noble sidhe. I wasn't sure I liked it, but I knew I needed it. People only follow you for two reasons, love and fear. Money didn't mean anything in faerie. I preferred love, but tonight my enemies had proven that there were more of them than I had known and that there were too many plots to reason with them all. When love and sweet reason will not work, you are left with fear and ruthlessness.

I put my hand over my stomach, still barely different, but I'd heard their heartbeats, saw them moving like some magical, almost unreal shapes on the ultrasound. They were inside me, and I had to protect them. I'd honestly believed that once I was with child the sidhe would value that life, not mine but the children's. I knew I was wrong now, and I could not afford to be soft. Flinching was no longer an option. They say that being pregnant makes women softer, gentler, but in that moment I understood why so many religions have goddesses who are both creators and destroyers. I was barely pregnant, and I was already willing to do things that once would have made me hesitate. The time for hesitation was past.

Yolland had moved Onilwyn off Mistral, so that the Ash Lord lay on his back in the frosted grass. I picked up Onilwyn's dropped sword. "It is cold iron, sidhe lords. He meant to sheath it inside my body. I will give him back his blade."

I raised it two-handed, and I prayed for strength, the strength to protect myself and my children. The strength to protect the fathers of my children, and the people I loved. I prayed, and drove the blade down into his body. The blade pierced his chest just under the sternum. I drove it up through the softer tissue under the ribs. I drove it up into his heart, and left it there, as he'd meant to do to me.

I stood up with blood on my hands and arms, spattering my white gown. "Tell the other lords and ladies that I am with child. I am remade, reborn, and threats to my children and my kings will be met with the utmost severity."

I looked at them, and held out my bloody hands. My skin began to glow through the blood. The power came over me, and I was warm once more. The scent of roses filled the air, and petals began to fall from the sky like pink rain.

A golden cup appeared in the air in front of me. The chalice that had been lost from the Seelie Court centuries before hovered before me. The chalice was to me as the spear and dagger were to Sholto. It appeared and disappeared at whim. It came to my bloody hands, and it was as bright and shining a magic as it had ever been. Blood and death were not evil, but just another part of life.

The petals filled the chalice, and the Goddess moved in my mind. I knelt beside Mistral's still form, and dipped my fingers into the petals, but when my fingers came out they dripped with liquid, and I smelled wine. I touched it to his lips, and he groaned.

"Take the arrows out of him," I said.

It was the dark-haired lord, Yolland, who knelt and began to obey. Turloch said, "It cannot be the chalice."

"Do not trust your eyes; trust your skin, your bones," Lord Dacey said. "Can you not feel the thrum of its magic?"

Dacey joined Yolland. Mistral moaned as they jerked the arrows free. His hands convulsed with the pain, but at least he was still mostly unconscious. As the arrows came out, I touched the liquid from the chalice to each wound. They did not heal completely, for they were made by cold iron, but they did close partially, as if they had had days of healing. The two sidhe lords knelt in the cold, and watched the chalice work its magic. When I had touched every wound on Mistral's body, I turned to the kneeling lords. Sholto had stood and watched, because the chalice was not his magic but mine.

I offered the cup with its flower petals to the lords, and they drank from it. Their lips came away touched with a different color of liquid each time. One smelled of ale, another of beer. Turloch knelt at last, tears shining on his face.

"Goddess save us."

"She's trying to," I said, and let him drink.

The scent of something sweet and unknown to me flowed up.

The petals had begun to sprout small thorny vines, roses growing in the winter cold. We knelt surrounded by the beginnings of a thicket, as green and real as any summer day, as snow began to fall from the cold sky.

"Go back to the sidhe and tell them the wild rose has returned."

Lord Yolland said, "I would bear your mark, my goddess."

"So be it," I said.

A thin vine wrapped around one of his wrists. He flinched, and I knew the thorns cut him, then the living vine was a tattoo around his wrist, as perfect and delicate as the tendril it had been but a moment before. Yolland stared at the mark, wiping away the blood that was still on his white skin.

"The king will not be pleased," Turloch said.

"I have a mark of power from one of our royals," Yolland said. "Turloch, don't you understand what that means?"

"It means the king will see her dead."

"He thinks I bear his children," I said. "He will want me alive."

"How can that be?"

I held the chalice above my head, and let it go. It hovered for a moment, then vanished in a shower of roses and vines. "Magic," I said.

"Is the chalice gone?" Dacey asked, fear in his voice.

"No," I said, and Lord Yolland echoed me. "No, once it simply belonged to its chosen bearer. It has chosen Meredith, and that is good enough for me, Dacey." He touched his new tattoo. "I am yours when you need me. Only call and I will answer."

"You will have no choice but to answer now," Turloch said.

"That you did not ask for a mark is to your shame," Yolland said.

"I want to live," Turloch said.

"I want to serve," Yolland said.

"Go, tell what you have seen. It is time to stop hiding. The Goddess has returned to us, and her power is abroad once more," Yolland said.

"They will not believe us," Dacey said.

"They will believe this." Yolland held up his tattoo.

"The king will kill you," Dacey said.

"If he tries, then I will knock upon the sluaghs' gates and join King Sholto and his queen," Yolland said.

"You would ride with the sluagh?" Dacey asked.

"Oh, yes," Yolland said.

Sholto picked Mistral up in his arms. "Dawn approaches. Go back to your courts, and tell them what the Goddess bids. We will tend the Storm Lord."

I laid one hand on Sholto's bare arm, and put my other hand on Mistral's leg. The chalice had helped heal his wounds, but cold iron could be like poison to us. Just because you closed the wounds didn't mean that the poison had stopped doing its deadly work.

Sholto echoed my thoughts, leaning in close to me and whispering, "You have done a miracle with the chalice and stopped his blood loss, but cold iron is a tricky thing, Meredith."

"We must get him to your healers," I said.

"I can get inside my kingdom almost instantly, but I do not know if you are strong enough for the way I would choose."

I felt the strength in Mistral's body under my hand; even unconscious, there was muscle and strength. "Save him, Sholto."

"I am the King of the sluagh, the King of That Which Passes Between. Part of the wild hunt has not chosen its form. I can use it to simply step into the sluaghs' mound."

"Do it," I said.

"You are no longer part of the magic of the hunt, Meredith."

I looked back at what was left of the hunt in the meadow. The Seelie had gotten their horses and ridden away toward their faerie mound. The mare that I had ridden and Sholto's many-legged steed were nowhere to be seen. What remained was the writhing tail of the comet we had traveled on. What was there was white and shining, as if the full moon could be turned into tentacles, limbs, and eyes, pieces and parts that formed nothing that the eye could see, or rather nothing that the mind could make sense of. I'd been told that it would blast my mind to see the unformed hunt, and once it had been true. I remembered the terror of that first time weeks ago. Now I stared into it, and knew, simply knew, that I could form what I saw into anything. It was the raw stuff of chaos, and that is the beginning of all things. I could bring order to it, and form it into the things of faerie. The power of the Goddess still rode with me, and with that, I did not fear.

"I see nothing to fear. Bring it, but know that the Goddess still rides me, and she will bring order out of its chaos."

"As long as you are protected, I am content with whatever happens," he said. Then he called, not with words, but I heard the call, not with my ears, but with my body, as if my skin vibrated with some sweet word.

The glowing remnants of the wild hunt flowed around us. It was like being surrounded by flesh that ran like water, and even that was not exactly true. I had no words, no experience to match to the sensations of being carried by raw magic, raw form. My father had made certain that I was well versed in the major religions of the human world. I remembered reading about creation in the Bible. It seemed an orderly thing, as if God said "giraffe" and a giraffe appeared fully formed as we know it. But standing in the midst of the raw chaos, I knew that creation was like any birth, messy and never quite what you expected.

A tentacle touched me, and it suddenly glowed more brightly, then, with a cry, a white horse fell away from the circle that surrounded us.

Something that was almost a hand reached for me, and I took that almost hand. I stared into eyes, and I felt this formless shape ask, "What shall I be?"

What would you do, if something asked you what should it be? What form would come into your mind? If only I had had time to think, but there was no time. This was the moment of forming, and gods do not doubt. I was Goddess's vessel, but there was enough of me to know that I would never be a goddess. I had too many doubts.

The almost hand in mine became a claw. The eyes that I stared into changed to something like the head of a hawk, but it was all white and shining, and too reptilian to be a bird, and yet. . . . The claw cut my hand as it pulled away, and my blood fell like rubies, catching the white, white light. The drops of blood spun through the chaos, and where they touched, they formed shapes. All the oldest magics come down to blood, or earth. I had no earth to offer as we spun inside the whirlwind of flesh, bone, and magic, but blood, that I had.

I thanked the . . . dragon for reminding me what blood was for. Fantastic shapes formed; some of them had existed in faerie before, but some were new. Some had only ever existed in books, in fairy tales, not truth, but I was part human, and I had been educated in human schools. I had never seen many of the creatures of legend, so I could not wish them into being. It was as if my imagination was being mined for shapes. Some of the forms were beautiful, some were horrific. Never had I regretted more some of the horror-movie marathons that I'd had with friends in college, because they were there too. But some of the darkest shapes gave me eyes filled with compassion before they spilled away into the night. Some of the most heartrendingly beautiful shapes gave me eyes that were pitiless, like the eyes of a tiger that you'd hand-reared until the day you realize that it was never tame, and you are just food.

Then we were inside the sluaghs' mound with the last shining remnants of the wild magic, and the sluagh themselves turning to fight us.

Sholto yelled, "We need a healer!"

Most of them hesitated, staring at us as if struck deaf and dumb. Nightflyers peeled themselves from the ceiling and flew down one of the dark tunnels. I hoped they had gone to do as their king bid, but the rest of the surprised sluagh still seemed uncertain what to do.

The shining circle around us knelt if they had legs to kneel with, and I knew what they wanted. They wanted guidance. Guidance to pick what they would be.

I realized that we were in the great central hall. There was the throne of bones and silk at the center of the main table. This was where the court ate, and when there was an audience or important visitors the big tables were moved away. Throne rooms often doubled as the formal eating area in castles, in or outside faerie.

I spoke to the assembled sluagh. "This is wild

magic; it waits to be given form. Come and touch them, and they will become what you need, or want."

A tall hooded figure said, "The wild magic only forms to the touch of the sidhe."

"Once magic was for all of faerie. Some of you remember that time."

It was a nightflyer clinging to the wall who spoke, in their slightly hissing manner. "You are not old enough to remember what you speak of."

Sholto said, "The Goddess moves in her, Dervil." And the name let me know that it was a female nightflyer, though a glance could not have told me.

The shining, kneeling circle was beginning to fade. "Would you lose this chance to show the sidhe that the oldest magic knows the hand of the sluagh?" I asked. "Come, touch it before it fades. Call back what you have lost. I was the dark Goddess this night." I raised my still-bleeding hand. "The wild magic tasted my blood. It shines with white light, but so does the moon, and is that not the light in all your night skies?"

Someone stepped forward. It was Gethin, in a loud Hawaiian shirt and shorts, though he'd left his hat behind somewhere, so that his long, donkeylike ears draped bare to his shoulders. He smiled at me, showing that his humanlike face was full of sharp, pointy teeth. He had been one of the ones who had come to Los Angeles when Sholto first approached me. He was not one of the most powerful of the sluagh, but he was bold, and we needed bold tonight.

He put his small hand on one of the shining forms, and it was as if his touch were black ink poured into shining water. As the dark color hit the shining light, the form began to change. The light and darkness mingled, and for a moment I couldn't see, as if some magical veil had come down to hide part of the process. When it was clear to the eye again, it was a small black pony.

Gethin gave a cackling, delighted laugh. He threw his arms around the shaky neck, and the pony nickered happily at him. The happy noise showed that the pony had teeth as sharp as Gethin's, but bigger. The pony rolled its eyes up at me, and there was a flash of red.

"Kelpie," I whispered.

Gethin heard me, because, smiling, he said, "Nay, Princess, 'tis an Each Uisge. It's the water horse of the Highlands, and nothin' is meaner than the Highland folk, unless maybe the Border folk." He hugged the pony again, and it nickered at him again like a long-lost pet.

Others came forward then, with eager hands. There were hairy brown creatures that were not quite horses, but not quite anything else. They looked unfinished, but the sluagh cried gladly at the sight of them. There was a huge black boar with tentacles on either side of its snout. There were black hounds, huge and fierce, with eyes that were too large for their faces, like the hounds in the old

Hans Christian Andersen story about dogs with eyes as big as plates. Their huge round eyes were red and glowing, and their mouths were too wide, and seemed unable to close, so that their tongues lolled out around pointed teeth.

A huge tentacle the width of a man dangled from the ceiling. I looked up to find that it covered the ceiling. I'd seen the tentacles at the hospital and in Los Angeles, but I'd never seen more than the tentacles. Now I gazed up at the entire creature. It took up the entire upper dome of the huge ceiling. It clung to the surface much as the nightflyers did, but its tentacles didn't help it cling. They were turned outward, and dangled like fleshy stalactites. Two huge eyes gazed down at us, and the moment I saw the eyes I thought, "It's like some kind of humongous octopus," but no octopus ever had so many arms, so much flesh.

That long tentacle touched the last glowing shreds of the magic, and suddenly there was a man-sized version of the tentacled creature. All the other things that had formed from the magic had been animals: dogs, horses, pigs. But this was obviously a baby of what clung to the ceiling.

The tentacles on the ceiling gave a glad cry, which echoed in the hall and made some flinch, but most smile. The huge tentacle picked up the smaller version, and lifted it to the ceiling. The tentacled creature that I had no name for clung to the larger tentacle and made small happy sounds.

Sholto turned a tearstained face to me. "She has been alone so very long. The Goddess does still love us."

I put an arm around him, a hand on Mistral. "The Goddess loves us all, Sholto."

"The Queen has been the face of the Goddess for so long, Meredith, and she has no love of anyone."

In my head, I thought, "She loves Cel, her son." Out loud I said only, "I love."

He kissed me on the forehead, ever so gently. "I'd forgotten what it was to be loved."

I did the only thing I could. I went up on tiptoe and kissed him. "I will remind you." I gave him all that he needed to see in my face as I gazed up at him, but part of me was wondering where the healer was. I was going to be queen, and that meant that no one person was so dear as all of them. I was having one of those moments now. I was happy that Sholto was happy, and happier for his people and the return of so much, but I wanted Mistral to live. Where was the healer while the miracles of the Goddess were happening?

The nightflyers poured back from the far tunnel. "They will have the healer with them," Sholto said, as if he'd read my doubts in my face. There was a sadness around the edges of his happiness. He knew that he would never be my one and only. I was queen, and even more than most, my loyalties were divided among my people.

CHAPTER TWELVE

I EXPECTED TO SEE ONE OF THE SLUAGH with the nightflyers, but it was a man. He looked human, though he had a large hump on his back. He was handsome, with short brown hair, and a smiling face. He had a black doctor's bag with him.

I looked at Sholto.

"He is human, but he has been with us too long to set foot on mortal soil."

Humans could come to faerie and never age, but if they ever went back, all the years they'd cheated would come upon them all at once. Once you stayed in faerie any length of time, you could never go back, not and be truly human.

"He was a doctor before he came, but he has studied long in faerie. He will heal your Storm Lord if anyone here can."

I realized that I'd touched Mistral's body only through his clothes for a time. I moved so I could see his face, and what I saw was not a comfort. His normally shining white skin was almost as gray as his hair. Some of the sidhe, myself included, could change their skin color with glamour, but this pasty gray was not that.

Had the Goddess distracted me with magic, only to let me lose one of my kings? Surely not.

The healer said, "King Sholto and Princess Meredith, I am honored to serve." But it was a cursory greeting. His brown eyes were already looking more at the patient than at us. That was fine with me. He felt for Mistral's pulse with one well-groomed hand. His handsome face was very serious, and his eyes had that distant listening quality.

He touched one of the partially healed wounds. "My king, some magic has healed his wounds, but he is still very ill. What made these wounds?"

"Arrows tipped with cold iron," Sholto said.

The healer pursed his lips, and ran his hands quickly over Mistral. "Let us find a room where I can tend him properly."

"We will take him to my room," Sholto said.

The healer looked startled for a moment, then simply said, "As my king wills it." He began to walk back toward the tunnel from which he'd entered.

Sholto said, "Meredith, follow the doctor."

I started to argue that I wanted to be able to see Mistral, but something in Sholto's face made me simply nod. I followed the doctor and only glanced behind to see that Sholto was following with Mistral still in his arms.

Sholto was right. There was no guarantee that

I did not have enemies here in the sluagh. We thought I was safer here, but I'd had people from this faerie mound try to kill me too. It had simply been for a different motive. The hags, as in night hags, who had once been Sholto's personal guard had tried to kill me out of jealousy. They were more than just bodyguards, as were my own guards, and the hags had thought that Sholto would forget them once he had his first taste of sidhe flesh. But the hags who had meant my death were dead themselves now. Two I had killed in self-defense. One had died at Sholto's own hand, to keep me safe. There were still some among his court who feared that me being with their king would change them forever and take away what made them sluagh. That my magic would make them into a pale version of the Seelie. It was the same fear my aunt Andais, the Queen of Air and Darkness, felt among her own court.

So I walked behind the doctor with Sholto behind me. Even with Mistral's life in our hands my safety was to be worried about. Would it always be that way? Would there never be safety inside or out of faerie for me now?

I prayed to the Goddess for safety, for guidance, and for Mistral. The scent of roses came gently to me. Then the scent of herbs followed. Thyme, mint, and basil, as if we walked upon strewn herbs, but a glance down showed that the floor was bare. In fact, it was the most cavelike of all the courts, all bare stone that looked more water-carved than hand-hewn.

"I smell herbs and roses," Sholto said from behind me.

"As do I," I said.

The corridor opened wider, and there were two cloaked figures before a pair of double doors. For a moment I thought they were night hags as his guard had been once before, but then they turned and looked at us, and the figures inside the cloaks were male. They were almost as tall as Sholto himself, pale and muscular, but there was some smoothness to their faces, lipless cuts for mouths, and oval, slitted eyes that held darkness like a cave.

"My cousins," Sholto said. "Chattan and Iomhair." The last time I'd seen his guard he'd added two uncles, but both had died defending him. I wondered if these two were the sons of those lost uncles, but I did not ask. It isn't always good to remind someone that you (meaning I) were there when their fathers died. People tended to start blaming you if you were always around when people died. That one hadn't been my fault, but if you can't blame your cousin and king, I wouldn't make a bad target for blame.

I greeted them, and they said, very formally, "Princess Meredith, you honor our sithen with your presence." It was way too polite for sluagh society.

I answered automatically in a formal tone. Years of being at court had made it habit. "It is I who is honored to be among the sluagh, for you are the strong left hand of the Unseelie Court."

They exchanged a look as we went through the doors. One of them, and they looked so alike I couldn't be sure which, said, "It has been long since that title was given to the sluagh by an Unseelie royal."

Sholto carried Mistral to the large bed on the far side of the room. I turned to answer the guard. "Then it has been too long since the sluagh were given their due by the Unseelie Court. I come here tonight seeking shelter and safety among the sluagh, not among the Unseelie or the Seelie. I come with your king's unborn child in my body, and I seek safety here among his people."

"Then the rumor is true? You bear Sholto's child?"

"I do," I said.

"Leave them, Chattan," said the other guard, Iomhair. "They have wounded to tend."

Chattan bowed, and closed the doors, but he watched me as he did it, as if it were important. I stood there and held his gaze, because there was weight to it. There were moments when I could feel not just magic, but also fate weave around me. I knew that Chattan was important, or that the small conversation we'd just had was. I could feel it, and it wasn't until the doors closed that I felt free to go to the bed to see to Mistral.

Sholto and the doctor were stripping him of the last of his clothes. I remembered him as so strong, so very alive. He lay on the bed as immovable as the dead. His chest rose and fell, but his breaths were shallow. His skin still had that unhealthy gray pallor to it. Without the clothes in the way you could see how many wounds marred his body. I counted seven separate ones before Sholto came to me. He grabbed my arm and turned me from the bed.

"You look pale, My Princess. Sit down."

I shook my head. "It's Mistral who's hurt."

Sholto took both my hands in his, and looked into my face. He seemed to be studying me. He let go of one hand so he could touch my forehead. "You feel cool to the touch."

"I've been out in the winter cold, Sholto." I tried to see around his body to the bed.

"Meredith, if it comes to a choice between having the healer look at you and the babes you carry or saving Mistral, I will choose you and the babies. So sit down and prove to me that you are not going back into shock. Riding with the wild hunt is not often an occupation for women, and I have never heard of a pregnant woman or goddess doing it at all."

I heard his words, but all I could think of was that Mistral might be dying.

He squeezed my hand hard. The pain was enough to make me frown up at him and try to pull away. "You're hurting me," I said.

"I would shake you, but I don't know what that would do to the babies. Meredith, I need you to take care of yourself so we can take care of Mistral. Do you understand that?"

He let go of my hand, and led me gently by the elbow to a chair that must have been there all along. It was as if I hadn't seen the room until that moment, as if all I could see was Mistral, Sholto, and, vaguely, the healer. Was I in shock? Had I gone back into shock as the magic receded? Or were all the events of the evening simply catching up with me?

The chair Sholto sat me in was large. The arms under my hands were carved wood, smooth from years of other hands caressing it. The cushions underneath me were soft, and the draperies that were curled over the back of the chair were silk, a deep purple like ripe grapes or the darker color of wine. I looked around the room and found that most of the room was done in shades of purple and burgundy. I think I'd expected black and gray the way the Queen's room was done. Sholto spent so much time in the Unseelie Court trying to be as good as, and fit in with, the Unseelie nobles that I'd just assumed that the black he wore at court was what he would have done his home in, but now I was here, and it was nothing like I'd imagined.

Among the burgundy and purple there were hints of red and lavender, gold and yellow here and there, interwoven with the darker colors. My apartment in Los Angeles had been mostly burgundy and pink. It hadn't occurred to me until that moment that whoever I married would have a say in the decor of our home. I was pregnant with their children, but I didn't really know their favorite colors, except for Galen. I'd known that Galen liked green since I was small. But the rest of the men, even Doyle and my lost Frost, hadn't had time to tell me their likes and dislikes of small things. Colors, cushions, rugs, or bare wood; what did they prefer? I had no idea. We'd gone from emergency to emergency for so long, or been working to make ends meet, that there hadn't been time to worry about the typical things couples discuss.

I'd spent my early life with my father out among the humans, American humans, so I knew how to be a couple, but I had the same problem that all royals had. We could try to be ordinary, but in the end, it wasn't truly possible. What we were would always overwhelm who we were.

Sholto appeared in front of me with a cup in his hand. Steam rose from it, and it smelled thick, warm, sweet. I could identify some of the spices in it, but not all.

"Mulled wine, but I can't drink, not while I'm pregnant."

The healer spoke from the bed. "Did you see the servant bring in the wine?"

I blinked at him, past Sholto's shoulder. "No," I said.

"You must have something to help you, Princess Meredith. I believe you are going into shock again, and how many shocks can you take in one night while pregnant with twins? It's a hard thing on a body, and although the fact that you are descended from fertility deities is a help to you, you are also part human, and part brownie. Neither of them is free from complications."

"What do you know of brownies?" I asked, as Sholto wrapped my hands around the cup. I needed both hands for the smooth wood.

"Henry has treated many of the lesser fey while he has been with us," Sholto said. "One of the reasons he came to our court was his curiosity about our many forms. He thought he could learn more here."

"So you've helped brownies birth babies?" I asked.

Sholto used one hand to start the cup toward my mouth. My hands stayed around the cup, but didn't help him. I felt strangely passive, as if nothing mattered that much. They were right. I needed something.

"I have," the doctor said, "and I promise you, Princess, that one cup of mulled wine will not harm you or your children. It will help you think more clearly, and warm you from the terrible things you have seen this night." He sounded very kind, and his brown eyes were full of sincerity.

"You're a witch," I said.

"A good one, I promise, but I did train as a doctor, and I am a healer. But, yes, I am what the humans call a psychic now. Back in my mortal day I was a witch, and that, along with the hump on my back, put me in grave danger of being killed for dealing with the devil."

"The old king of the sluagh," I said.

He nodded. "I was seen with some of the sluagh one night, and that sealed my fate among the humans. Now drink. Drink and be well." There was more to his words than just kindness. There was power. Drink and be well. I knew there was magic and will in his words, and more than just spices in the wine.

Sholto helped me drink it, and from the first touch of the warm, spicy liquid on my tongue I felt a little more alert. Swallowing it spread warmth through my entire body, in a rush of comfort. It was like being wrapped in a favorite blanket on a winter's night, with a cup of hot tea in one hand, a favorite book in the other, and your beloved lying with his head in your lap. It was all that in one cup of warm wine.

I drank, and by the end of the cup Sholto was no longer having to guide my hands.

"Better?" the doctor asked.

"Much," I said.

Sholto took the cup from me, and put it on a tray on the small table beside the chair. There was even a lamp beside the chair, curved up over the back of it. It was a modern lamp, which meant that this room at least was wired for electricity. As much as I had missed faerie in my exile on the West Coast, seeing the lamp, and knowing that I could turn it on with the flip of a switch, was very comforting. There were moments lately when magic seemed so plentiful that a little technology was not at all a bad thing.

"Do you feel well enough to join us at the bed?" the doctor asked.

I thought about it before answering, then nodded. "Yes, I do."

"Bring her, My King, for I need your help."

Sholto helped me stand. I had a moment of dizziness. His hand was very solid in mine, his other hand on my waist. The room stopped moving, and I wasn't certain if that was because of the wine, the magic in the wine, the night, or something about carrying two lives inside my body. I knew that if I was human, truly human, twins were supposed to be hard on the body. But it was very early in the pregnancy, wasn't it?

Sholto led me to the bed, and there was a ramp up to it so that it was on a dais, but with no steps. I wondered if the last king of the sluagh hadn't found steps to his liking. The pure-blooded nightflyers didn't have feet to use steps, so a ramp would work better. Of course, they could fly, so maybe the ramp had been meant for some even older king.

Someone snapped their fingers in my face. It startled me, made me see the doctor's face close to mine. "The wine should have taken care of this distraction. I am not certain she is well enough to help us, My King." The doctor, Henry, looked worried, and I could feel his concern. I realized that he could project his emotions. If he could choose what emotions to share with his patients, it must have made his bedside manner amazing.

"What do you need us to do, Henry?" Sholto asked.

"I have put a poultice on each wound, and it will draw some of the poison out, but all the denizens of faerie are magic. They need it to survive the way humans need air or water. I've long maintained that the reason cold iron is so deadly to faerie is that it negates magic. In effect, the iron in his body is destroying the magic that makes him live. We need to give him other magic to replace it."

"How do we do that?" Sholto asked.

"This is magic of a higher order than I have in my poor repertoire. It needs the magic of the sidhe, and I will never be that." There was a taste of regret to his words, but no bitterness. He had made peace with who and what he was long ago.

"I am not a healer," Sholto said.

The smell of roses and herbs returned. "It isn't healers who are needed, Sholto," I said. "Your doctor is a great healer."

Henry bowed to me. His twisted spine made it a shallow bow, but it was as graceful as any I'd been given. "You are most generous with your praise, Princess Meredith."

"I am honest." The perfume of roses was growing stronger. It was not the heavy, cloying scent of modern roses, but the light, sweet scent of the wild. The herbs added a warm, thick undertone to the scent, as if we were standing in the middle of an herb garden with a hedge of wild roses around it to guard it and keep it safe.

The wall beside the large bed stretched inward, like the skin of some great beast being pushed farther away. When the Seelie or Unseelie sithen moved, it was almost invisible. One moment this size, the next bigger or smaller, or just different. But this was the sluagh sithen, and apparently here we'd get to see the process.

The dark stone stretched like rubber into a darkness more complete than any night. It was cave darkness, but more than that, it was the darkness at the beginning of time before the word and the light had found it, before there was anything else but the dark. People forget that the darkness came first, not the light, not the word of Deity, but the dark. Perfect, complete, needing nothing, asking nothing, simply all there was was the dark.

The scent of roses and herbs was so real that I could taste it on my tongue, like drinking in a summer's day.

Dawn broke in the darkness. A sun that had nothing to do with the sky outside the sithen rose in the distant curve of sky, and as the soft light brightened, it revealed a garden. I would have said it was a knot garden, that time-consuming art of grooming herbs into clean, curved, Victorian lines, but my eyes couldn't quite make out the herbs' shape. It was almost as if the longer you tried to see the plants, and the stone walkway between them, the more your eye couldn't make sense of them. It was like a knot garden based on non-euclidean geometry. The kind of shapes that are impossible with physics the way it's supposed to work, but then there was a sun underground, and a garden that hadn't been there moments before. What was a little nonstandard geometry compared to that?

A hedge bordered the entire garden. Had it been there a second before? I could neither remember it; nor not remember it. It simply was. It was the circle of wild roses, like the one I'd seen in a vision once. That had been a mixed vision, part wonderment and part near-death experience. I fought not to remember the great boar that had nearly killed me before I'd spattered its blood on the snow, because with creation magic what you thought could become all too real.

I thought about healing Mistral. I thought about my babies. I thought about the man standing beside me. I reached for Sholto's hand. He actually startled, looking at me with eyes too wide, but he smiled when I smiled.

"Let us take him to the garden," I said.

Sholto nodded, and bent to pick up the still-unconscious Mistral. I looked back at the doctor. "Are you coming, Henry?"

He shook his head. "This magic is not for me. Take him, save him. I will explain where you are."

Sholto said, "I think the garden will remain here, Henry."

"We'll see, won't we?" Henry said with a smile, but there was regret in his eyes. I'd seen that look in other humans inside faerie. That look that says that no matter how long they stay, they know they can never truly be one of us. We can prolong their life, their youth, but they are still human in a land where no one else is.

I knew what it was to be mortal in a land of immortals. I knew what it was to know that I was aging and the others were not. I was part human, and it was moments like this that made me remember what that meant. Even with the most powerful magic in all of faerie coming to my hand, I still knew regret and mortality.

I went on tiptoe and laid a gentle kiss on Henry's cheek. He looked surprised, then pleased. "Thank you, Henry."

"It is my honor to serve the royals of this court," he said, in a voice that almost held tears. He touched where I had kissed him as I moved away, as if he could feel it still.

I went to Sholto, who stood there holding Mistral as if he weighed nothing and he could have held him all night. I took Sholto's arm, laid my other hand on Mistral's bare skin, and we walked into the garden.

CHAPTER THIRTEEN

THE STONES OF THE GARDEN PATH MOVED under my bare feet. I was suddenly aware that I had small cuts on my feet. The stones seemed to be touching the cuts.

I clutched Sholto's arm more tightly, and looked down at what we walked upon. The stones were shades of black, but there were images in them. It was as if pieces of the formless part of the wild hunt were inside the stones, but it wasn't just visuals. They reached out to the surface of the stones with tentacles and too many limbs, and they could touch us. The miniature pieces of the wild magic seemed particularly interested in anywhere that I was scraped or bleeding.

I jumped, nearly pulling Sholto off the path. "What is wrong?" he asked.

"I think the stones are feeding on the cuts on my feet."

"Then I need a place to lay the Storm Lord

down, so I can carry you." At his words, the center of the knot garden spread wide like a mouth, or a piece of cloth that you open to make room for a sleeve.

There was the sound of plants moving at speeds that no natural plant was ever meant to move, a dry, slithering rustling that made me look around. Sometimes when plants moved like that it was to simply make a new piece of faerie, but sometimes it was to attack. I'd been bled by the roses in the Unseelie antechamber. My blood had awoken them, but it had still hurt, and it had still been frightening. Plants don't think like people, and making them able to move doesn't change that. Plants don't understand how animals think and feel. I suppose the same is true in reverse, but I wasn't going to hurt the plants by accident, and I wasn't so sure that the whispering, hurrying plants would grant me the same safety.

Normally I felt safe when the magic of the Goddess was moving this strongly, but there was just something about this garden that made me nervous. Maybe it was the feel of the stones moving under my feet, using small mouths to lick and drink from the minute cuts in my feet. Maybe it was the knotted herbs that made it almost dizzying if you looked at their patterns too long.

I looked behind us and found that the rose hedge had knitted itself completely around the garden. No, there was a gate in the hedge. It looked like a white picket fence gate with a wooden arch that curved gracefully over it. Then I realized that there were images in the pale wood. Then I knew it wasn't wood. The gate was formed of bone.

There were four small trees in the center of the garden now, where the herbs and stones had moved aside. Vines curved up them, and the wood formed to the curving lines of the vines, the way that trees will when they've had the vines shaping them their entire lives. The vines interlaced above the trees, and the limbs and leaves of the trees interwove into a canopy. The vines formed a lacework lower down, and new herbs grew under the vines, forming a cushion of vegetation under them. The garden was growing a bed for Mistral.

Flower petals began to rain down upon the bed. Not just the rose petals that sometimes fell around me, but flowers of all colors and kinds. They formed four pillows that went across the width of the bed's head. They formed a blanket, which pulled itself down to the foot of the bed, turning itself down for the night.

Sholto looked at me. His look was a question. I answered it as best as I could. "Your sithen has prepared a place for us to sleep and to heal Mistral."

"And to heal you, Meredith."

I squeezed his arm. "To heal us all."

Sholto walked to the bed on a spill of green grasses so bright that it looked too green to be grass. The moment I stepped from the stone to the grass, I realized that it was small stones too. I gazed down at what we walked upon, and knew

that it was formed of emeralds. It crunched underfoot, but it wasn't sharp or hurtful. I had no words
for the texture of the emeralds. It was almost as
if they were real grass, but just happened to be
formed of precious stones.

Sholto laid Mistral in the center of the bed. It
was as if he knew what needed to be done to heal
him. Deity wasn't talking just to me tonight.

The bed was tall enough that I had to climb,
rather than step, onto it. Vines in the bed frame
curled around me, lifting me. It was actually a little
more help than was comforting. The bed was a
marvelous thing, but the thought of vines that
could move that much curling around me while I
slept wasn't a completely good thought.

Sholto knelt on the other side of Mistral from
where I was crawling up beside him. "Who is the
fourth pillow for?" he asked.

I knelt in the surprising softness of herbs,
vines, and petals, and stared at the pillow. I started
to say, "I don't know," but in the middle of the
breath to say it, another word came. "Doyle."

Sholto looked at me. "He is in the human
hospital miles away, surrounded by metal and
technology."

I said, "You are right," but the moment I said
it, I knew we had to get Doyle. We had to rescue
him. Rescue him? I said it out loud. "We have to
rescue him."

Sholto frowned at me. "Rescue him from what?"

I had that moment of panic that I'd felt before. It wasn't words but a feeling. It was fear. I'd only felt it twice before: once when Galen had been attacked by assassins, and the other time when Barinthus, our strongest ally in the Unseelie Court, had been at the wrong end of a magical plot in which our enemies had maneuvered the queen to kill him.

I gripped Sholto's arm tightly. "There is no time to explain. Mistral can rest here in the magic of faerie. We will return and give our magic to him, but for now, Doyle's life hangs in the balance. I feel it, and this feeling has never been wrong before, Sholto."

He didn't argue again, which was one of the qualities I valued about Sholto. The petal blanket slid over Mistral where Sholto had laid him without the aid of any hands we could see or sense. Magic touched every wound that the iron had made; it was the best we could do until we returned to him.

Sholto turned to me. Without Mistral's body to block the view, the tentacles looked like some sort of clothing, and they were the only thing he was wearing above the waist. "How do we reach Doyle in time?" he asked.

"You are the Lord of That Which Passes Between, Sholto. You took us where a field met woods, and where the shore met ocean. Isn't there anything in a hospital that is a place between?"

He thought for a second, then nodded. "Life and death. A hospital is full of people who hover between. But there is too much metal and technology for me, Meredith. I have no human blood in me to help me work major magic around such things."

I took one of his hands and wrapped my much smaller fingers around his. "I do."

He frowned at me. "But this is not your magic. It is mine."

I prayed. "Goddess guide me. Show me the way."

"Your hair," Sholto whispered. "There is mistletoe in your hair again."

I turned my head and could feel the waxy green leaves. A touch found the white berries. I gazed up at Sholto, and he had a crown of woven herbs. They bloomed with tiny stars of lavender, white, and blue. He raised his free hand and there again was a tendril of green like a living ring on his finger. It burst into white bloom, like the most delicate of gemstones.

I felt movement around one ankle, and raised my gown to find an anklet of green and yellow leaves, lemon thyme wrapped around me. Except for the mistletoe in my hair, this was what we had gained the night that Sholto and I had first made love. The mistletoe had been from a night when I was with other of my men.

A vine rose from the bed like a thorny green serpent. It moved toward our clasped hands. "Why is it always thorns?" I asked, but this was one moment when my wishes would not change faerie.

Sholto said it, "Because everything worth having hurts." His hand tensed against mine, then the vine found our hands and began to wind around us. Thorns bit into our skin with small biting pains. Blood began to trickle down our hands, mingling our blood as our hands were pressed more and more tightly by the thorns. It should have simply hurt, but the summer sunshine fell upon us, and the perfume of herbs and roses, warmed by the life-giving sun, was all around us.

The vine around our hands burst into flowers. Pink roses covered the vine, hiding the pain, and giving us a bouquet more intimate than any ever made by man.

I felt my hair move, and as Sholto leaned in to kiss me, he said, "You wear a crown of mistletoe and white roses."

We kissed, and his free hand with its ring of flowers cradled my face. We drew apart just enough to speak. "By our mingled blood," I whispered.

"By the power of the Goddess," he said.

"Let us join our power," I said.

"And our kingdoms," he replied.

"Let it be so," I said, and there was a sound like some great bell being rung, as if the universe had been waiting for us to say those words. I should have been afraid of what it meant. I should have had doubts, but in that moment, there was no room for such things. There were only Sholto's eyes gazing into mine, his hand on my face, our hands tied together by the very magic of faerie itself.

"So mote it be," he answered. "Now let us save our Darkness."

I'd traveled with Sholto to the between places, but I'd never been able to feel his power stretching outward. It was surprisingly similar to a hand reaching outward in the dark until it finds what it needs and draws it near.

One moment we were in the heart of faerie, the next we were in an emergency room surrounded by doctors, nurses, and screaming monitors. There was a strange man on the gurney, and a doctor was trying to restart his heart.

They stared at us for a moment, then we simply walked away, leaving them to save the man if they could. "Where is he, Meredith?" Sholto asked.

Sholto had gotten us here. Now it was up to me to find Doyle in time.

CHAPTER FOURTEEN

I HAD A MOMENT OF PANIC AS WE WALKED down a corridor. How did I find Doyle? I thought about him, and the mark on my stomach pulsed. It had begun as a real moth but had thankfully become a tattoo. If I ever made a flag or a shield to represent me, it would hold that small moth with its bright hind wings. It was called the beloved underwing, an Ilia Underwing. It was my mark, and some of my guards bore it on their bodies. Doyle was one of those. The mark pulsed as we moved, like a game of hot and cold. If Doyle had been well, I could have simply called him to me, but I was afraid to call him. If his injuries were life threatening, then getting out of his sickbed to come to me might kill him.

I could not take that chance. We paced through the hospital guided by the mark on my body. I kept waiting for people to scream and point, but they didn't. They acted as if they could not see us. I asked, "You're hiding us?"

"I am."

"I can never make people walk around me without making them think too hard."

"I am the King of the sluagh, Meredith. I can hide a small army in plain sight. An army that would blast the minds of the humans we pass."

I glanced down at the pristine floor and realized we were leaving a trail of blood drops. My hand didn't hurt anymore, wound with his. It was as if the pain had already become familiar, but we were still bleeding. I could see the blood drops clearly, but the humans walked in it and left tracks, as if they could not see it.

The hospital was no longer a sterile environment. Was our blood a problem? Magic was often like this. It worked, but it could have unforeseen consequences. Were we contaminating everywhere we walked?

What was supposed to be a tattoo fluttered against my gown. It was a moth with wings again, stuck in my body, as if my flesh were ice that had captured it but left its wings to struggle vainly to free itself. The sensation was a little stomach-churning, or maybe the way I thought of it. But the frantic wings let me know that he was above us, and that we needed the elevator. The pulsing had been harder to interpret, but the frantic wings were easier to judge. We were running out of time. If I'd been inside faerie I could have moved the fabric of reality like a curtain and found him much sooner, but reality was harsher here, even for me with my human blood in my veins, and on the floor behind us.

The elevator went to the floor that someone had pushed, but the doctor there seemed unwilling to get inside with us, though he didn't see us. Sholto was keeping our way clear. The doors closed and we went up again.

The elevator opened, but when Sholto tried to get off, the moth was so frantic it hurt, as if it were trying to fly free of my body. I pulled him back, and we waited for the doors to close. I hovered over the buttons, and hit the floor that the wings seemed most excited about.

I'd never navigated like this, and being inside so much metal and technology, I think I had assumed that the moth would not work very well here, but it was part of my body, and that meant that man-made things did not weaken its magic. I had to trust that all the magic I possessed would work here, and work well.

The elevator opened and the moth flew forward. I stepped in the direction that it wanted to go. Its frantic movements made me begin to run. We were close. Were we running into a trap, or were Doyle's injuries stealing him away from me?

Sholto trotted at my side. He spoke as if he'd heard some of my thoughts. "I can hide us from other denizens of faerie as long as we do not interact with them."

"I know only that he is in danger, not what that danger is," I said.

"I have no weapon," he said.

"Our magic works here. Not all of theirs will."

"The hand of power that injured Doyle and me worked just fine," he said.

He had a point but I said, "Brownies have always been able to work magic around men and machinery. It was one of the reasons that Cair used Gran. You need mortal and brownie blood to work major magic here."

Pain doubled me over. It felt as if the moth were trying to tear its way out of my skin. Only Sholto's hand on me kept me upright. I pointed at the door to our left. "In there."

He didn't argue with me, simply made sure I could stand, then reached for the door handle. He was using glamour to hide us, but a door opening on its own was almost impossible to hide. You had to wait for others to open things for you if you wanted to remain hidden, but there was no time. The panic was screaming in my head, the moth frantic against my body.

A doctor, a nurse, and a uniformed policeman sitting in the corner all looked up as the door opened. I started to rush forward, but Sholto held me back. He was right. If we wanted to remain unseen, we had to move slowly and let the door close behind us. If we drew any more attention to the magically opening door, someone might see us.

But it took everything I had not to simply run

across the room to Doyle. He lay terribly still against the white sheets. There were tubes and monitors everywhere. Needles pierced his body, and tape held them in place. Liquids ran down tubes into him.

I'd been prepared for an attack, a spell, but I had forgotten. Doyle was a creature of faerie. There was no mortal blood in him. Nor brownie. There was nothing in him but some of the wildest magics that faerie could offer.

"His vitals just keep going down, Doctor," the nurse said.

The doctor had turned from the now-closed door and was looking at Doyle's chart. "We've treated the burns. He should be improving."

"But he's not," the nurse said.

The doctor snapped at her. "I can see that."

The uniformed policeman was still looking at the door. "Are you saying that someone's using magic to kill Captain Doyle?"

"I don't know," the doctor said, "and I don't say that often."

"I know," I said.

They all turned toward my voice, frowning but still seeing nothing. If it had been my glamour hiding us, my speaking would have been enough to break the spell and reveal us, but Sholto's power was stouter stuff.

"Did you hear that, Doctor?" the nurse asked.

"I'm not sure."

"I heard it," the cop said.

"I can save him," I said.

"Who's there?" the cop asked, and he was standing, with his hand going for his gun.

"I am Princess Meredith NicEssus, and I have come to save the captain of my guard."

"Show yourself," the cop said.

Sholto did two things: he made his tentacles back into their lifelike tattoo, and he dropped the glamour. To the humans in the room, we simply appeared.

The cop started to raise his gun, then stopped in mid-motion. He blinked and shook his head, as if to clear his vision.

"So beautiful," the nurse said, and she looked at us with wonderment on her face.

The doctor looked frightened. He backed away from us until the bed was against him. He clutched Doyle's chart as if it were a shield.

I tried to think how we must look to them, crowned with living flowers, covered in the magic of the Goddess, but in the end, I couldn't imagine. I would never be able to see what they saw.

We moved toward the bed, and the policeman recovered himself enough to try to point his gun again. But the gun eased toward the floor once more. "I can't," he said in a strangled voice.

"Take the needles and tubes out of Doyle. You're using man-made medicine on him, and it's killing him," I said.

"Why?" the doctor managed to ask.

"He is a creature of faerie, and there is no mortal blood in him to help ease him around such modern wonders." I touched Doyle's arm, and his skin was cool to the touch. "We must hurry, Doctor, and remove him from this artificial place, or he will die." I reached for the IV in Doyle's arm. "Help me."

The doctor looked at me like I'd sprouted a second head, a frightening one. But the nurse moved to help me. "What do you want me to do?" she asked.

"Disconnect him from all of it. We need to take him back to faerie with us."

"I can't let you take an injured man out of my hospital," the doctor said, his voice regaining the ring of authority it had started with, as if now that he had a concrete fact, he felt better. Sick people didn't get taken from the hospital; it was a rule.

I looked at the policeman. "Can you please help the nurse free Captain Doyle of these machines?"

He holstered his gun, and moved to the other side of the bed to help.

"You're a cop," the doctor said. "You're not qualified to disconnect him from anything."

The cop looked at the doctor. "You just said that he wasn't improving, and that you didn't know why. Look at them, Doc, they're dripping magic all over the place. If the captain is used to living like that, then what is all the machinery doing to him?"

"There are channels to go through. You can't just walk in here and take my patient." He was looking at us.

"He is the captain of my guard, my lover, and the father of my children. Do you truly believe I would do anything to endanger him?"

The nurse and the cop were already ignoring the doctor. The nurse directed the cop, and between the two of them they turned everything off and left Doyle lying in the bed free of it all.

Now we could touch him; it was as if the magic knew that he needed to be free of all that was hurting him before we could heal him.

I touched his shoulder, and Sholto touched his leg. His body reacted as if we had shocked him, spine bowing, eyes wide, breath coming in a gasp. He reacted to pain a second later, but he looked at me. He saw me.

He smiled, and whispered, "My Merry."

I smiled back and felt the bite of happy tears. "Yes," I said. "Yes, I am."

His eyes lost focus, then fluttered closed. The doctor checked his pulse from his side of the bed. He was afraid of us, but not so afraid that he wouldn't do his job. I liked him better for that.

"His pulse is stronger." He looked at Sholto and me on the other side of the bed. "What did you do to him?"

"We shared some of the magic of faerie," I said.

"Would it work on humans?" he asked.

I shook my head, and the crown of roses and mistletoe moved in my hair, like some serpentine pet settling more comfortably. "Your medicine would have helped a human with the same injuries."

"Did your crown just move?" the nurse asked.

I ignored the question, because the sidhe are not allowed to lie, but the truth would not help her. She was already staring at us like we were amazing. The look on her face and to a lesser extent the policeman's reminded me why President Thomas Jefferson had made certain that we agreed to never be worshipped as deities on American soil. Neither of us wanted to be worshipped, Sholto and I, but how do you keep that look off someone's face when you stand before them crowned by the Goddess herself?

I expected the roses that bound our hands to uncurl so we could pick Doyle up, but they seemed perfectly happy where they were.

"Let us pick him up from the other side of the bed," Sholto said. "That way you will be carrying his legs, which are lighter."

I didn't argue; we simply moved to the other side of the bed. The doctor moved back from us as if he didn't want us to touch him. I couldn't really blame him. It had been so long since the Goddess had blessed us to this degree that I wasn't certain what would happen to a human who touched us in this moment.

Sholto bent over, putting his arms under Doyle's shoulders. I did the same at his legs, though I didn't have to bend nearly as far. It took some maneuvering, like an arm version of a three-legged race, but we picked Doyle up. He seemed to fill our arms as if he were meant to be there, or maybe that was just how I felt about touching him. As if he filled my arms, filled my body and my heart. How could I have left him to human medicine without another guard watching over him?

Where **were** the other guards? That policeman shouldn't have been on his own.

"Meredith," Sholto said, "you are thinking too hard, and we must move together to get him home."

I nodded. "Sorry, I was just wondering where the other guards are. Someone should have stayed with him."

The policeman answered. "They went with Rhys, and the one who's called Falen, no, Galen. They took the body of your—" and he looked hesitant, as if he'd already said too much.

"My grandmother," I finished for him.

"There were horses with them," the cop said. "Horses in the hospital, and no one cared."

"They were shining and white," the nurse said. "So beautiful."

"Every guard who they passed seemed to have a horse, and they rode out of the hospital," the cop said.

"The magic took them," Sholto said, "and they forgot their other duties."

I hugged Doyle to me, and gazed at his face cuddled against Sholto's body. "I'd heard that a faerie radhe could make the sidhe forget themselves, but I didn't know what it meant."

"It is a type of wild hunt, Meredith, except it is gentle, or even joyous. This one was for grief, and taking your grandmother home, but if it had been one of singing and celebration, they might have carried the entire hospital with them."

"They were too solemn in their grief," the nurse said.

"Yes," Sholto said, "and good for your sakes."

I looked at the nurse, gazing up at Sholto. She looked damn near elfstruck, a term for when mortals become so enamored of one of us that they will do anything to be near their obsession. It can happen about faerie in general, but we didn't have glorious underground places to give the mortals now. So that wasn't such a problem, but Sholto's face was as fair as any in faerie, and, crowned with the blooming herbs, in their haze of colored blossoms, he was like something out of the old fairy stories. I supposed we both were.

"We need to go, Sholto."

He nodded, as if he knew that it wasn't just Doyle's health we were attending to. We needed to get away from the humans before they became any more bemused by us.

We started for the door, having to use our bound hands to steady Doyle's body in our arms. The thin gown moved, and we were suddenly touching the bareness of his body. The thorns must have pierced his body because he made a small sound, moving in our arms like a child disturbed by a dream.

"You're bleeding," the nurse said. She was staring at the floor. Blood drops had formed a pattern beneath us. What was it about touching Doyle with the roses that had made her see the blood? I left the thought for later; we needed to get back to faerie. I suddenly felt like Cinderella hearing the clock begin to strike midnight.

"We must get back to the garden and the bed now."

Sholto didn't argue, only moved us toward the door. He asked the policeman to get the door for us, and he did without complaint.

The doctor called from the open door, "You melted the walls in the room you were in, Princess Meredith."

Did I say I was sorry? I was, but I'd had no control over what the wild magic did to the room I'd woken in earlier this night. It seemed like days ago that I'd woken in the maternity ward.

The doctor's call to us had made others turn. We walked through a world of stares and gasps. It was too late to hide now.

"Find us another patient who is betwixt and between," I said.

He led us to a patient who was housed in an oxygen tent. A woman beside the bed looked up at us with a tearstained face. "Are you angels?"

"Not exactly," I said.

"Please, can you help him?"

I exchanged a glance with Sholto. I started to say no, but one of the white roses fell from my crown onto the bed. It lay there, shining and terribly alive. The woman took the rose in her shaking hands. She started to cry again. "Thank you," she said.

"Take us home," I whispered to Sholto. He led us around the bed, and the next moment we were back in the edge of the garden, outside the gate of bone. We were back, and we had saved Mistral and Doyle, but the woman's face haunted me. Why had the rose fallen onto her bed, and why had it seemed to make her feel better? Why had she thanked us?

It was the humpbacked doctor, Henry, who opened the bone gate. We had to turn sideways to ease through with Doyle in our arms. The gate closed behind us without Henry touching it. The message was clear: none but we were allowed inside.

I was suddenly tired, very tired. We laid Doyle beside the still-sleeping Mistral. We took off Doyle's hospital gown, and crawled up on the bed. Our hands were still bound tightly, so it was awkward, but we seemed to know that we needed to be on either side of the two men. I expected to be unable to sleep with the thorns still in our hands and the bulky crown on my head, but sleep came over me in a wave. I had a moment to see Sholto on the far side of Mistral, still wearing his blooming crown. I snuggled in tightly against Doyle's body, and sleep washed over me. One moment awake, the next asleep. Asleep and dreaming.

CHAPTER FIFTEEN

THE DREAM BEGAN AS MANY DREAMS IN-
side faerie began for me, on a hill. I knew it wasn't
a real hill. It was more the idea of a green gently
sloping hill. I was never certain whether the hill
had never existed outside of dream and vision, or
whether it was the first hill from which all others
were copied. The plain that stretched below the hill
was green and full of cultivated fields. I'd stood on
this hill and watched war come to faerie, and seen
the plain dry and dead. Now it was so alive. Its
wheat was golden, as if autumn harvest was just
about to begin. But there were other fields with
vegetables, where the plants were small, just breaking above the surface of the rich earth. The plain,
like the hill, represented an ideal. The fact that it
was solid underfoot—and I knew that if I walked
down I'd be able to touch the plants, rub the grain
between my hands, and see the kernels free of the

dry husks, all of it real—didn't change the fact that it was both real and not.

There was a tree beside me on top of the hill, a huge spreading oak. Part of the tree had the first green leaves of spring, another had bigger leaves with the tiny green beginnings of acorns, then the leaves of late summer with the acorns green but much larger, then the brilliance of autumn and the brown acorns ready to be picked, all the way to a section that was winter-bare with only a few acorns and a few dried brown leaves clinging to the branches. I stared up at the dark lace of branches and knew they were not dead, but only resting. When I'd first seen the tree it had been dead and lifeless; now it was what it was meant to be.

I touched the bark of the tree, and it had that deep, thrumming energy that old trees have. It was as if if you listened hard enough you could hear it, but not with your ears. You heard it with your hands, or your face where you pressed it against the cool roughness of the bark. You felt the life of the tree beating against your body as you pressed yourself to its hard sides. It was like a slow, deep heartbeat that started as the tree, then you realized that it was the earth itself, as if the planet had a heartbeat of its own.

For a moment I felt the turn of the planet, and held on to the tree as if it were my anchor to so much reality. Then I was back on the hilltop, and I could no longer feel the pulse of the earth. It had been an amazing gift to sense the hum and flow of the planet itself, but I was mortal, and we are not meant to hear planets' heartbeats. We can have glimpses of the divine, but to live with such knowledge every moment takes holy men or mad men, or both.

I smelled roses before I turned to find the cloaked figure of the Goddess. She hid her face from me always, so that I got only glimpses of her hands, or a line of mouth, and every glimpse was different, as if she went back and forth in age, color, everything. She was the Goddess, she was every woman, the ideal of what it is to be female. Looking at that tall cloaked figure, I realized that **she** was like the heartbeat of the planet. You couldn't see her too clearly, or hold her too starkly in your mind, not without becoming too holy to live, or too mad to function. The touch of Deity is a wondrous thing, but it carries weight.

"If this place had died it would not have been just faerie that died, Meredith." Her voice was like the glimpses of her body, many voices melding into one another so you would never be able to tell what Her voice was, not exactly.

"You mean reality is tied to this place too?" I asked.

"And is this not real?" She asked.

"Yes, it is real, but it is not reality. It is neither faerie nor the mortal world."

She nodded, and I got a glimpse of a smile, as if I'd said something smart. It made me smile to see

Her smile. It was as if your mother had smiled at you when you were very small, and you smile back because her smile is everything to you, and all is right with the world when she smiles at you. For me as a child, it had been my father's smile and Gran's.

The sorrow hit me like a blow through my heart. Revenge and the wild hunt had put the grief aside, but it was there, waiting for me. You cannot hide from grief, only postpone when it will find you.

"I cannot stop my people from choosing to do harm."

"You helped me save Doyle and Mistral. Why couldn't we save Gran?"

"That is a child's question, Meredith."

"No, Goddess, it is a human question. Once I wanted to be sidhe more than anything else, but it is my human blood, my brownie blood, that gives me strength."

"Do you believe that I would be able to come to you like this if you were not the daughter of Essus?"

"No, but if I was not also the granddaughter of Hettie, and the great-granddaughter of Donald, then I could not walk through the human hospital to save Doyle. It is not just my sidhe blood that makes me the tool you need."

She stood there, Her hands drawn back into Her cloak, so that all of Her was in shadow. "You are angry with me."

I started to deny it, then realized She was right. "So much death, Goddess, so many plots. Doyle has nearly been killed twice in just a few days. Frost is lost to me. I would protect my people and myself." I touched my stomach, but it was flat, and I did not feel that first swelling of pregnancy. I had a moment of fear.

"No fear, Meredith. You do not see yourself as pregnant yet, so your dream image is how you see yourself."

I tried to quiet the sudden racing of my pulse. "Thank you."

"Yes, there is death and danger, but there are also children. You will know joy."

"I have too many enemies, Mother."

"Your allies grow in number with each magic you perform."

"Are you certain that I will survive to sit the dark throne?"

Her silence was like the wind, howling across the plain. It had an edge of coldness to it that made me shiver in the light of that sun.

"You are not certain."

"I can see many paths, and many choices being made. Some of those choices lead you to the throne. Some do not. Your own heart has debated whether the throne is even what you want."

I remembered moments when I would have traded all of faerie for a lifetime with Doyle and Frost. But that dream was already gone. "If I was willing to leave all of faerie behind and go with

Doyle and my men, Cel would hunt me down and slaughter us. I have no choice but to take the throne or die."

She stood with aged hands on a cane now. "I am sorry, Meredith. I thought better of my sidhe. I thought they would rally around you when they saw my grace return. They are more lost than even I could have imagined." Sorrow was thick in Her voice so that it made me want to cry with Her.

She continued. "Perhaps it is time to take my blessings to the humans."

"What do you mean?"

"When you wake, you will all be healed, but there are too many in faerie who would do you and yours harm. Go back to the Western lands, Meredith. Go back to your other people, for you are right, you are not just sidhe. Perhaps if they see that my blessings can pass them by and be given to others, it will make them more careful of them."

"Are you saying you would use me to give magic to mortals?"

"I am saying that if the sidhe turn away from me and mine, then we should see if there are other more grateful hearts and minds."

"The sidhe are magic, Mother; humans are not."

"The very workings of their bodies are magic, Meredith. It is all miracles. Now sleep, and wake rested, and know that I will do what I can for you. I will speak loudly to those who still listen. To those who have shut their hearts and minds to me, I can only put obstacles in their paths." She gestured toward me, and Her hand was young again. "Rest now, and when you wake you will go back to the mortal world."

The vision began to fade, and I was once more aware that I was in bed with my men. My hand no longer ached from the thorns, and I could move it so Sholto and I were free of our hand-binding. The thought was solid enough to wake me, but the blanket of flower petals tucked itself under my chin, like a mother tucking you in when you are very small, and again I had that feeling that nothing could harm me. Mother was there, and all was right with the world. I had a moment to find it strange that this abstract feeling of the Goddess was more comforting than she herself had been on the hillside. I felt the brush of a kiss on my forehead, and heard her voice, Gran's voice. "Sleep, Merry-girl. I will keep watch." And as I had when I was small, I believed, and slept.

CHAPTER SIXTEEN

I WOKE TO THE BRUSH OF FLOWERS, AND the spill of hair as warm as fur across my face. Doyle's face was the first thing I saw when I opened my eyes, and I couldn't have thought of anything better to wake up to. I reached up to touch his face. His smile widened, a flash of white in his dark face. His eyes filled with a look that was only for me. A look that once, not so long ago, I hadn't believed would ever be in those black eyes for anyone, let alone for me. Had he ever looked at anyone like that before? He was more than a thousand years old, so the answer had to be yes, didn't it? But for this moment, in my bed, the look was only for me, and that was enough.

"Doyle . . ." But whatever I was going to say was lost to a kiss. His lips on mine made me press into his body for more of a kiss. It grew into hands and arms, as if our bodies had been starving for each other.

I began to kiss my way down the smooth muscles of his chest, while he stayed above me and finally went to all fours. I wanted to celebrate that the burns on his torso were healed by touching every inch of him. I found his nipple ring and played with it, using my lips and teeth, and finally setting my mouth past the ring, and into the nipple beneath, to suck and play and tease, until he cried out "Enough" in a strangled voice.

That voice made me smile, because I had worked long and hard to get my Darkness to tell me when he'd had enough of anything. The queen had taught him, and the rest, to simply take what she gave them, for any touch was a blessing. I wanted to know what my men wanted, and to give it to them.

I laid down underneath him. His body was like a roof above me, so that I could gaze down the line of him and see all that he had to offer. His hair was a black richness that he'd thrown to one side of his body, like a living cloak. I was sheltered and content under the covering of his body.

I caressed my fingers down his body, wiggling lower so that I could cup the hard, swelling richness of his body in my hands. I wrapped one hand around that hardness, and put my other hand on the softness below so that I could cup him gently as I began to stroke him with my first hand.

"Meredith . . ." he said.

"I thought I'd lost you," I said, and wiggled down between his legs while he still held himself above me on his hands and knees. With my hand wrapped around him, there was still much of him bare, and I lowered that nakedness to my mouth. I licked the tip of him, peeking out from the circle of his foreskin, then slipped my mouth over him, tongue playing with the extra bit, rolling it, and sucking on it seperately from the rest of him, until I felt his body spasm above me. Only then did I take the meat of him more firmly in the center of my mouth, and suck him down, until I met my hand where it gripped the base of him. With this much of him in my mouth, I could no longer trust myself to be gentle enough to play on those softer bits, so I put my other hand on the smoothness of his hip to steady myself as I rose off the bed to take more of him inside me.

He moved one hand to touch my shoulder. "Meredith, if you do not stop, I will go."

I drew myself off him so I could talk, but kept my hands playing with him, and began to gently work that soft extra bit downward, so that when I put him back in my mouth, there would be only naked shaft to suck. I liked the sensation of the foreskin to play with, but I was sometimes too enthusiastic not to move something so delicate away from my teeth. I had wanted to do this with Doyle for so long, and been denied. He would not waste his seed in any way that would not gain him a child with me, but now . . .

"I want you to go into my mouth," I said.

"Meredith," he said, and he had to swallow

hard, and finally put his hand on mine. "I cannot think with you doing that."

"I don't want you to think."

He held my hands still, coming to his knees so he could hold both my hands, which were still around his body. "We have had this talk."

"But I'm pregnant," I said. "We can make love just for pleasure, and my pleasure is you in my mouth for the first time."

He stared down at me, then a strange look came over his face. I couldn't decipher it at first, then he smiled. He smiled down at me, shaking his head.

"Where in faerie are we?" he asked.

"We are safe. You are healed. I am with your child. I want to drown in your body. Let all the questions wait, Doyle, please."

He gazed down the line of his body to where I lay back against the bed, my hands still wrapped around him. My hands were hidden where his much larger one had closed around them, from hand to past my wrists, so that my pale skin was very white against all his darkness.

He glanced to both sides. "I'm not sure the others wish to wait."

I glanced to one side, then the other. Sholto lay on his side of the bed, on his stomach, which meant he'd turned his tentacles back to the tattoo, or he couldn't have lain that flat. He was watching us, with careful, hungry eyes. "I'll wait, for my turn."

"I will leave," Mistral said, and stood beside

the bed. The wounds on his body had vanished, as if the arrows had never touched all that muscled beauty. His gray hair covered his body, almost as if he hid from me with it.

Doyle was going a little softer in the nest our hands had made, but I had to concentrate on Mistral's mood for a moment. One of the hardest things about all the men was tending everyone's emotions. I knew Mistral less well than any of the other fathers, so here was my first moment to quiet that hurt look in the way he held his body, as if something had hurt him that had nothing to do with iron arrows.

"I want to celebrate that Doyle is alive and with me, Mistral."

He shook his head, not looking at us, and moved toward the path leading out. "I understand."

It was Doyle who helped. "But once we have," and he smiled at me, "celebrated, then you are one of us, and not to be exiled from the bed."

Mistral looked out through that veil of gray. His eyes had gone the green of a sky before a serious storm hits. I knew just enough of him to know that it showed great anxiety. I wasn't sure why, but our Storm Lord was worried.

"We are safe, Mistral, I swear," I said.

"You would truly let me join you?"

"If Merry wills it, then we share," Sholto said, not like he was entirely happy, but as if it were true.

Mistral moved back toward the bed, sweeping his hair back so more of his face showed, and his body was revealed in all its lovely potential. "I am not to be exiled?"

"You are my Storm Lord, Mistral. We risked much to save you. Why would we cast you out?" I asked.

Doyle squeezed my hands gently, and I released him so he could talk to the other man without being distracted. "You think Meredith is like the queen, but she is not." He held his hand out to the other man. "None of us have to leave. None of us have to watch while others satisfy their lust and know that we will go wanting. Meredith does not play such games."

Sholto spoke from the other side of the bed, on his knees now. "He speaks truly, Mistral. She is not Andais. She is not the other sidhe bitches who tease and torment. She is Merry, and she would not invite you to join her unless she meant it."

I looked at Sholto then, because it was a speech that I wouldn't have thought he knew me well enough to make. He answered the unasked question in my eyes. "You are honorable, Meredith, and just, and beautiful, and a goddess of lust and love." He looked past me to Mistral. "She is a warmer thing than we have had in any court of faerie in a very long time."

"I didn't know I still had hope," Mistral said. "To find it gone was more than I could bear."

I didn't completely understand his mood or his words, but I wanted to chase them all away. I held my hand out to him. "Come to me," I said.

"Come to us," Doyle said. "There is no cruelty here, no hidden tricks, I swear."

He came at last and took my hand, as Doyle touched his shoulder in that very male greeting when you would not dream of hugging. I'd noticed that when nude, the men were less open to hugs from one another.

Mistral looked down at me with eyes that were still anxious green. "Why would you want me now?"

"Why would I not?" I asked.

"I thought you would have no use for me."

I went to my knees and drew him down into a kiss that started soft and ended fierce and nearly bruising. His body was already happier than it had been just moments ago. I caressed him gently, and his face showed a pleasure so intense it was almost pain. He had truly thought I would not let him touch me again. I might have asked why or what, or even who had lied to him, but Doyle's hands came at my back, pulling me a little back from the other man.

"I would finish what we started."

"You are our Captain," Mistral said. "It is your right."

"It's not because of rank," I said. "It's because I thought I lost him, and I want the taste of him in my mouth to remind me that I have not lost everything I love."

Mistral kissed me more gently, then let Doyle pull me away. "To be third in your bed is more than I had hoped for, Princess. I am content."

"Meredith. I am simply Meredith here and like this," I said.

He smiled. "Meredith in the bedroom, then."

Doyle pulled me back to the center of the bed, and into his arms and his body. Sholto went back to lying on his side of the bed. Mistral climbed on it, but stayed sitting in one corner, his legs drawn up. Neither of them turned away, but I didn't mind an audience of my choosing, and neither did Doyle.

CHAPTER SEVENTEEN

DOYLE LAY BACK ON THE BLANKET OF petals, all that rich, black skin against the soft pastel of it. I admitted to myself that he looked like the devil slipped into some springtime heaven, but he was my devil, and all I wanted in that moment. There had been nights with Frost when I had had them both touching me at the same time, but tonight I wanted to concentrate just on Doyle. I didn't mind the audience, but I didn't want to be distracted either.

He let me crawl over his body until I could put my hands and mouth back where I wanted them. He'd accepted my logic, and I could finally taste him in my mouth. I played with that loose skin one more time, then teased it back, until he lay long and hard, exposed to my hands, my lips, my mouth, and, ever so gently, my teeth. I was using less pressure than a bite, but you have to be careful not to scrape, or what is an added pleasure becomes pain. I wanted no pain tonight for my Darkness. I wanted only pleasure for him and for me.

He protested, "But it will not be enjoyable for you."

"I can fix that," Sholto said.

We all looked at him. He smiled, and motioned at the tattoo on his body. "If you will allow, I can return the favor you are doing our captain so that you are equally pleasured."

It seemed like another lifetime ago when Sholto and I had managed to have our first encounter in Los Angeles. He had proven to me that the extra bits had more uses than the obvious. "You mean the little tentacles with the suction on them."

"Yes," he said, and there was a weight to his gaze. It wasn't an idle offer. He wanted to know how I truly felt about his extra bits, and he was wasting no time finding out. We'd had sex, but he had been terribly wounded, and no extra bits had been used.

I studied his face, then looked down at Doyle. He watched me patiently, almost passive in his waiting. He would abide by whatever I said, in that moment. Centuries of service to the queen had taken men who might have been more dominant and accustomed them to taking orders both in bed and out of it. Doyle could be a very dominant lover, but when it came to choices and preferences, he was like most of the queen's guard; he waited for my lead. It was up to me to make this moment what it was to be: good, ill, hurt feelings, or simply pleasure.

I said the only thing I could think of when a man offers me oral sex. I held my hand out toward him and said "Yes."

He gave me that smile that I had only recently known was possible for him, a smile that made all that handsomeness a little more human, a little more vulnerable. I valued that smile, and it made the yes worth it. I shoved my small doubts down, and watched his body go from an exotic tattoo to the reality of the image. I didn't know if it had been the magic of the wild hunt, or the times he had used the extra bits to comfort me this past night, but I could no longer see him in all his glory as anything but beautiful.

The tentacles were the same moonlight white as the rest of him; the thickest ones were just at the point where chest gave in to stomach. They were as thick as a good-sized python, but white with a marbling of gold on the skin. I knew from my nightflyer tutor, Bhátar, that those were for heavy lifting. They were what the nightflyers picked you up with, and carried you away. Under them was a line of longer, thinner tentacles, the equivalent of fingers, but a hundred times more flexible and sensitive. Then just above the belly button was a fringe of shorter tentacles with darker tips. I knew that those were secondary sexual organs like breasts because there was no human male equivalent. If I'd been a female nightflyer they would have had other tasks to do, but he had proven in our one brief moment in Los Angeles that there were uses for me too. Inches below all that was something as straight and thick and lovely as any man in court could boast. Without the extras in between, Sholto would have been welcome in any bed.

Once I had been horrified at the thought of having to embrace him with all the extras revealed, but as he knelt beside us and reached for me, all I could think of was how many uses we might find for so many of his extra bits. Was it the magic of faerie? Was it part of the magic that made me queen to his king that I could think of nothing but pleasure when reaching for him? If it was magic, it was good magic.

He took me in his arms, wrapped me against his body so that all of him touched me, but he did not try and embrace me with all of it. He simply laid it against my body as his two strong arms held me, and he kissed me. He kissed me, gently but firmly, but there was part of him that held back, like a tension in his body. I thought I understood; he was waiting for me to recoil from his touch. Instead I moved into that kiss, ground myself against all those extra bits, and let one hand caress one of those thick, muscular tentacles. He pressed himself harder against me, responding to my passion and my lack of fear. With most men I'd have been very aware that his erection was pressed against the front of my body, and I might have shuddered at the promise of it, but there were so many sensations with Sholto that it was almost as if my body couldn't pick and choose. The thicker parts streatched around me like extra arms. The thinner pieces caressed and tickled along my skin, and the lowest pieces eased their way between our bodies, between my legs, and I felt those searching "fingers" seeking that most intimate of spots. One of the long, stretching fingers found the spot, and proved to me once more that they had suction on the end, like small mouths that seemed designed to fit around that part of a woman's body, so that it was like some perfect key to fit the lock of my body. The sensations began to build almost immediately.

I felt the hum of energy from Sholto before I opened my eyes to see that his skin glowed with power. The white of his skin was all moonlight, but the tentacles had other colors. The bigger arms had bands and shapes that moved like colored lightning around me. Some were marbled with gold to match the yellow and gold of his eyes. The lower ones glowed white, their tips like red embers. I knelt embraced in color and magic humming against my skin, so that I made a small sound just from that.

"I take it the tentacles do other things than just glow," said Doyle, still lying next to me.

I nodded wordlessly.

"It is a combination of sidhe and nightflyer," Sholto said.

"It looks like colored lightning," Mistral said. He reached out, as if to touch one of the tentacles, then drew his hand back.

Sholto reached a thick limb and touched the other man's fingertips. A tiny jolt of colored light jumped between them. The air smelled of ozone, and every hair on my body stood to attention.

Doyle sat up. "What was that?"

Mistral was rubbing his fingers together as if still feeling the sensation. Sholto had drawn his limb back, a considering look on his face. His limbs had pulled away from the more intimate part of my body.

"I'm not certain," Mistral said.

"Once," Sholto said, "the nightflyers answered to the gods of the sky. We flew for them, and rode the lightning that they could call. Some say the nightflyers were created by a god of the sky and a goddess of the dead."

Mistral looked at his hand, then across at the King of the sluagh. The look on Mistral's face was one of pain. His eyes were the black of the sky before it shatters to earth. "I had forgotten," he said, almost as if to himself. "I had made myself forget."

Doyle said, "I did not know that you were . . ."

Mistral put a hand across his mouth. I think they were both startled. "Forgive me, Darkness, but do not say that name out loud. I am not that name anymore." He took his hand from Doyle's mouth.

"Your power calls to mine," Sholto said. "Perhaps you are he again."

Mistral shook his head. "I did terrible things back then. I had no mercy, and my queen, my love,

had less mercy than I did. We were . . . We killed."
He shook his head. "It began in magic and love,
but she fell in love with our creations in every sense
of the word."

"You **are** he, then," Sholto said.

Mistral gave him a look of utter despair. "I
would beg you to tell no one, King Sholto."

"It's not every night that a man meets his cre-
ator," Sholto said. He was watching the other man
with an edge of anger on his face, or maybe defiance.

"I am not that. The being who acted in such
arrogance was punished for it, and is no more.
Whatever I was once, the true Gods took it
from me."

"But our dark goddess," Sholto said. "It is said
that the gods tore her to pieces and fed her to us."

Mistral nodded. "She would not give up control over you. She would not give you the independence to be your own people. She wanted to keep
you as . . . pets and lovers."

Perhaps I looked surprised, because he spoke
to me. "Yes, Princess, I know well that there are
many uses for all those parts. She who was once my
love and I fashioned them for pleasure as well as
terror."

"You kept your secret well," Doyle said.

"When the gods themselves humble you,
Darkness, wouldn't you hide yourself in shame?"

"But your magic calls to mine," Sholto said.

"I never dreamed that the return of magic to

faerie would waken that in me." Mistral looked frightened.

"This is a legend so old my father never told it to me," I said.

"It is part of our lost creation myths," Doyle said, "before the Christians came and sanitized them."

Mistral crawled off the bed. He was shaking his head. "I cannot afford to be near when Sholto glows."

"Don't you want to know what would happen?" Sholto asked.

"No," Mistral said. "I don't."

"Leave him," Doyle said. "Nothing we do with Meredith is about force. We will not force Mistral now."

Sholto looked at Doyle, and there was that moment of arrogance that was all sidhe, and no amount of tentacled extras could disguise where it came from. I watched the thought cross his face and travel all the way through his eyes that he wanted to try. He wanted to know what would happen if he and Mistral joined their magic.

"No," I said, and touched Sholto's face. I brought him down to meet my gaze.

That arrogant defiance stayed for a second, then he blinked and was simply arrogant. "As my queen wills it."

I smiled at him because even I didn't believe it. He would remember this moment, and he would not forget the feel of power. Sholto was a very nice guy for a king, but in the end all kings seek power; it is the nature of who they are, and this king would not forget that the "god" who created his race was awake again.

I did the only thing I could think of to break the terribly serious atmosphere. I looked down at Doyle and said, "All my good work is undone with this serious talk. I'll have to start all over again."

He smiled at me. "How could I forget that nothing dissuades you from your goal?"

I put into my eyes all that I felt for him. "When my goal is such as this, why would anything dissuade me?"

He came to me, with Sholto still wrapped loosely around me. But when he touched the other side of us, there was no jump of power. For Doyle, Sholto, and me, it was just flesh and the magic of any sidhe when pleasure is in the air. Mistral found a seat on the edge of the garden that surrounded us, and did his best to ignore us. I hated for him to feel left out or sad, but it seemed important for us to make love in this place. It needed love, and so did I.

Mistral's deep voice said, "I was dying in the field. How did I get here, and where in faerie is here?"

"They rescued me from the hospital," Doyle said, then he frowned. "You were crowned and . . ." He raised my left hand, and for a moment it didn't look like my hand. There was a new tattoo on it, one of thorny vines and blooming roses.

He rose to his knees, but he wasn't looking at me now. He reached across to Sholto.

The other man hesitated, then offered him his right hand. Doyle held the paler hand in his black one, and the same tattoo curled around Sholto's hand and wrist.

Mistral walked back to us, and we saw that the marks of the arrows seemed to have vanished as had Doyle's burns. Neither of them looked happy to be healed, but instead were very serious.

Doyle drew our hands together so the tattoos were touching. "I did not dream it, then. You were handfasted and crowned by faerie itself."

"By the Goddess," Sholto said, and he sounded way too satisfied. The three men were acting oddly, and I had one of those moments when I knew I was missing something. That happened sometimes when you are barely more than thirty and everyone else in your bed is hundreds of years old. Everyone was young once, but sometimes I wished I had a cheat sheet so I wouldn't need all the explanations.

"What's wrong?" I asked.

"Nothing," Sholto said, again all too smug.

Doyle pulled Sholto's hand down so I could see our two hands together. "You see the mark?"

"The tattoo, yes," I said. "It's a shadow of the roses that bound our hands."

"You have been handfasted with Sholto, Merry," Doyle said, and he said each word slowly, carefully, giving me the intensity of those dark eyes.

"Handfasted. You mean . . ." I frowned at him. "You mean married?"

"Yes," he said, and there was rage in that one word.

"It took both our magics to save you, Doyle."

"The sidhe do not marry more than one spouse, Meredith."

"I bear children by all of you, so by our laws you are all my kings, or will be."

Sholto raised his hand, gazing at it. "I'm too young to remember when faerie married us to each other. Was it always like this?"

"The roses are more a Seelie mark," Doyle said, "but yes, handfasted and marked as a couple."

I stared at the pretty roses on my skin and was suddenly afraid.

"Am I within my rights to refuse to share Meredith?" Sholto asked.

I gave him a look. "I would be careful what you say, King of the sluagh."

"Faerie has married us, Meredith."

I shook my head. "It helped us save Doyle."

"We are marked as a couple." He held his hand out to me.

"When the Goddess makes me choose, she lets me know ahead of time. There was no choice offered, no warning of loss."

"By our laws—" Sholto started to say.

I interrupted him. "Don't start."

"He's right, Merry," Doyle said.

"Don't complicate this, Doyle. We did what we had to do last night to save you both."

"It is the law," Mistral said.

"Only if I am with his child and no one else's, which is not true. The goddess Clothra, who got pregnant from three different lovers, wasn't forced to marry just one of them."

"They were her brothers," Mistral said.

"Were they really, or is that just what legend made of them?" I was asking someone who might actually know.

Mistral and Doyle exchanged a look. Sholto wasn't old enough to know the answer. "Clothra lived in a time when gods and goddesses were allowed to marry whom they would," Doyle said.

"She wouldn't have been the first goddess to marry a close relative," Mistral said.

"But the point is, she didn't marry any of them, and the sovereign goddesses, the ones whom humans had to marry to rule, had many lovers."

"Are you saying that you're a sovereign goddess, a living embodiment of the land itself?" Sholto asked with a raised eyebrow.

"No, but I **am** saying that you wouldn't like what would happen if you tried to make me be monogamous with just you."

Sholto's handsome face set in petulant lines, and it was close enough to one of Frost's favorite emotions to make my chest tight. "I know you do not love me, Princess."

"Don't make this about hurt feelings, Sholto.

Don't be ordinary. In the old days there were different kings, but only one goddess to marry to rule, right?"

They exchanged looks. "But they were human kings, so the goddess outlasted them," Doyle said.

"From what I heard, the sovereign goddess didn't give up her lovers just because she had a king," Sholto said.

Doyle looked down at me. I couldn't read the expression on his face. "Are you saying you will change a thousand years of tradition among us?" he asked.

"If that is what it takes, then yes."

He looked down at me, the expressions on his face all mixed together. A frown, a half-smile, amusement in his eyes; but what I valued the most was the fear leaving them. For it had been fear when he saw the marks on Sholto and me.

"I will ask again," Mistral said. "Where are we? I do not recognize this bower we rest in."

"We are in my kingdom," Sholto said.

"The sluagh have no place so fair inside their faerie mound," Mistral said, his voice thick with certainty and sarcasm.

"How would any of the Unseelie nobles know what is inside my kingdom? Once Meredith's father, Prince Essus, died none of you darkened my door again. We were good enough to fight for you, but not to visit." Sholto's voice held that anger that he'd come to me with, an anger forged of years of being told he wasn't quite good enough to be truly

Unseelie. There had been years of the sluagh being used as a weapon. And like all weapons, you use it, but you do not ask a nuclear bomb if it wants to blow things up. You simply push a button, and it does its job.

"I have been inside your mound," Doyle said. His deep voice held an edge of something. Was it anger? Warning? Whatever it was, it wasn't good.

"Yes, and the sluagh would not follow the hound when they already had a huntsman." The two men glared across the bed at each other.

I'd known there was bad blood between them when they first came to me in L.A., but this was the first hint I had at what might lay behind it.

"Are you saying the queen tried to put Doyle in charge of the sluagh?" I asked. I sat up in the bed, the petals spilling around, as if the blanket had fallen back to being just flower petals.

The men looked up at the trees and vines that held the canopy aloft. "Perhaps we should finish this discussion in a more solid part of faerie?" Mistral asked.

"I agree," Doyle said.

"What do you mean 'more solid part'?" Sholto asked, laying a hand on the tree that formed one post.

"The blanket has gone back to what it began as. Some faerie magic does that," Doyle said.

"You mean like in the fairy tales, it only lasts a while," I asked.

He nodded.

A voice called from a distance, "My King, Princess, it is Henry. Can you hear me?"

Sholto answered, "We hear you."

"The opening to your new room is beginning to grow narrow, My King. Should you come away before it closes into a wall again?" He tried for neutral, but the worry was plain in his voice.

"Yes," Doyle said. "I think we should."

"I am king here, Darkness, and I say what we will and will not do."

"Gentlemen," I said, "as princess and future queen of all, I'll break the tie. We go before the wall grows solid."

"I will agree with our princess," Mistral said. He crossed to us and held his hand out to me.

I took the offered hand. He smiled at that one touch, wrapping his much larger hand around my small one, but the smile was full of something softer than anything I'd seen before. He started leading me down the path toward the bone gate. The herbs on the path were no longer trying to touch me. In fact, the stones that had been held together by the herbs were a little lose underfoot, as if whatever had formed them was letting go. We left Doyle and Sholto kneeling on the bed still glaring at each other. When we were back in Sholto's original bedroom, I would ask more questions about their mutual dislike.

The bone gate collapsed at Mistral's touch so that it was only a pile of debris. "Whatever held this place together is failing," he called back to them. "We need to get the princess to safety before it collapses completely."

Mistral picked me up, and carried me through the wreck of bones. Beyond the gate we could glimpse Sholto's bedroom, and Henry's worried face peering at us. The wall that had been as large as a cavern mouth was much smaller. I could actually see the stones knitting together like something alive, remaking themselves. They were strangely fluid; it was like watching flowers bloom, if you could catch them at it.

Mistral carried me through the opening, and we were back in Sholto's wine and purple bedroom. Henry bowed to us, then went back to peering behind us for his king. The opening continued to grow smaller, and neither of them was hurrying. Was it some kind of ego contest? All I knew was that with all that had happened my nerves couldn't stand watching them stroll toward the rapidly diminishing opening.

I called after them, "I will be really cross if you both get trapped behind the wall. We leave for Los Angeles tonight."

The two men exchanged a glance, then they began to jog toward us. Under other circumstances I might have enjoyed the view of both of them running toward me, nude, but the wall was closing. If it closed completely, I wasn't certain that we could reopen it. There were hands of power among the sidhe that could blast through stone, but neither Sholto nor Doyle possessed such a hand.

I called, "Hurry!"

Doyle broke into a run, spilling forward like some black, sleek animal, as if running were the purpose all that muscle and flesh had been designed for. I didn't get to see him from a distance much. He was always at my side. Now, I was reminded that without my human movement to hold him back, he could simply move. Like wind, rain, something elemental and more than flesh. I had a moment such as I had not had in months. A moment to watch him and marvel that all that potential would love me. I was, in the end, so terribly human.

Sholto followed behind him like a pale shadow. For a moment I could only see my Frost. He was the one who was supposed to be at Doyle's side. My light and dark; my men. Sholto was handsome and moved well at Doyle's side, but he couldn't keep up. He was a little behind, a little . . . more human.

Mistral said, "Ask the wall to stay open."

"What?" I asked, and was almost startled to find myself still in his arms, still in Sholto's bedroom.

He sat me down on the floor. "Stop staring at Doyle like a lovesick girl and tell the wall to stop closing."

I wasn't certain that the sluagh's sithen would obey me, but I had nothing to lose. "Wall, please stop closing."

The wall seemed to hesitate, as if thinking about obeying, then it went back to closing the opening. It was slower, but it had not stopped.

Doyle dived through the opening, doing a wonderful roll across the carpet, ending on his feet in a whirl of black hair and dark muscle.

Sholto dived through too, but ended up flat on the carpet in a spill of pale hair and breathlessness. Doyle was breathing heavily too, but he seemed ready to find a weapon and defend. Sholto seemed content to lie on the carpet for a time.

He gasped out, "Did the path get longer as we ran?"

Doyle nodded. "Yes."

"Why would it get longer?" I asked.

Sholto got to his feet, and looked up at the ceiling of his bedroom. I gazed upward, but saw nothing but the stone.

"Someone, or something, is here." He went to a wardrobe on the far side of the room, and got out a robe. It was gold and white, and didn't match the room at all, but it did match his eyes and hair to perfection. He suddenly looked all Seelie Court, and if not for one bit of genetics that had given him those extra bits he'd have been terribly welcome at the Unseelie Court. In the far past, even the Seelie Court would have been happy to have him. But Sholto, like me, could not hide his mixed blood. There was no illusion deep enough to make us one of them.

Doyle gazed up and around. Did he see something too? What was I not sensing? "What is it?"

"Magic, sluagh magic, but not . . . mine," Sholto said. He started for the door.

"My King," Henry said, and we all looked at him. It wasn't that I had forgotten he was there, but I guess in a way I had. "You were locked in the magical sleep for several days. There are those among the sluagh who feared you might be enchanted for centuries."

"Like Sleeping Beauty, you mean," I said.

Henry nodded. His handsome face was very worried, and I didn't know him long enough to read him that well. "They came and saw the garden, and it was very Seelie, my lord. More than that, none of us could pass its gate or walls. It held us back, and protected you from all who would come close."

"What has happened while we slept, Henry?" Sholto asked. He went to the man, gripping his shoulder.

"My King, the Seelie are encamped outside our sithen. They asked for parlay, and we had no king to speak for us. You know the rules—without a ruler, we cease to be sluagh, cease to be free people. We would be absorbed into the Unseelie Court, but before that happens, we would have to deal with the Seelie on our own without a king."

"They've chosen another king," Sholto said.

"A proxy ruler only."

"But it has divided the power of kingship, and whoever has part of the power did not want us— me—to escape the wall."

"Why are the Seelie outside?" Doyle asked.

Henry looked to Sholto, who nodded. "They say that the sluagh have stolen Princess Meredith away, and are holding her against her will."

"I am not their princess. Why should they be at the gates to rescue me?"

"They want both you and the chalice. They say both have been stolen," Henry said.

Ah, I thought. "They want my magic, not me. But under what right do they make siege upon the sluagh?"

"By right of kinship, your mother came to demand the return of her sweet daughter, and the grandchildren that she carries." Henry looked even more uncomfortable.

"One of the children I carry is Sholto's own. The right of the father supersedes that of a grandmother."

"The Seelie claim that the children belong to King Taranis."

Sholto went for the door. "Wait here. I must talk to my people before we confront the insanity of the Seelie."

"Might I suggest that you wear something else, Sholto?" I called.

He hesitated, then frowned at me. "Why?"

"You look too Seelie in the robe, and one of the things that seems to panic your people is the idea that you and I together will change them from the dark and terrible sluagh to a light and airy beauty."

He looked as if he would argue, then he went back to the wardrobe. He drew out black pants and boots, but he didn't bother with a shirt. And with a wavering of air in front of him, the tentacles came to life again.

"I will remind them that I am part nightflyer and not just sidhe."

"Would me by your side hurt you or help you?" I asked.

"Hurt, I think. I will talk to my people, then return for you all. Taranis has gone mad to besiege us."

"Why has not the Unseelie Court aided the sluagh?" Doyle asked.

"I will find out," Sholto said, and had his hand on the door when Mistral called out.

"My congratulations to you, King Sholto, on being king to Meredith's queen." His voice was almost neutral when he said it—almost.

"Congratulations to you, too, Storm Lord, though with so many kings around, I am not certain what kingdom you will share." With that Sholto was gone, with Henry at his side.

"What did he mean, wishing me congratulations?" Mistral asked. "I know that the princess carries Sholto's child and yours, Doyle. I heard that from the conversation in the bed when we woke."

"Mistral, didn't the queen tell you?" I asked.

"I was told that you had finally gotten with child by some of the others. I have had little news of anything but pain." He would not look at me as he said the next. "She was so angry when you left, Princess. Your green knight destroyed her hall of torture, so she took me as a guest to her room to be chained against her wall. There I have been at her mercy since you left."

I touched his arm, but he pulled away.

"I feared she would hurt you for being with me," I said. "I am so sorry."

"I knew it was the price I would pay." He almost looked at me, but finally let his long gray hair fall between us like a curtain to hide behind. "I was content to pay, because I had hoped . . ." he shook his head. "I hoped too late." He turned to Doyle and held out his hand. "I envy you, Captain."

Doyle came to take his hand, dark to light, clasping forearms together. "I cannot believe the queen did not tell her court the truth."

"I have only been released from the chains this night, so whatever she told her court, I do not know. I am too far out of favor to be told anything. I was released and lured to my death by one of our own. Onilwyn needs killing, my captain."

"He betrayed you?"

"He led me into an ambush of Seelie archers, armed with cold iron arrows."

"This is the first I have heard of it. He will be punished."

"He's already been punished," I said.

They both looked at me. "What do you mean, Merry?" Doyle asked.

"Onilwyn is dead."

"By whose hand?" Mistral asked.

"Mine."

"What?" Mistral asked.

Doyle touched my arm, and studied my face. "What has happened while I was in the human hospital?"

I told them as quick a version as I could. They were full of questions about the wild hunt, and Doyle held me while I confirmed that Gran was dead.

"The Seelie being at the gates here is partly my fault. I sent the Seelie sidhe who were forced to join the hunt back to Taranis with a message—that I had killed Onilwyn by my own hand, and that the chalice had chosen to come to my hand."

"Why did you show them the chalice when the queen has forbidden it?" Mistral asked.

"To save your life."

"You used the chalice to save me?" Mistral asked.

"Yes."

"You should not have wasted its magic on me. Doyle you had to save, and Sholto, but I was not worth such a risk."

Doyle looked at me.

"He doesn't know," I said.

"I do not think he does."

Mistral looked from one to the other of us. "What do I not know?"

"I did not mention Clothra's name without purpose, Mistral. Just as she had one son with three fathers, so I will have two babes with three fathers each."

"So many kings; what will you do with all of them, Princess?"

"Meredith, Mistral. Call me Meredith. If I am to bear your child, we should at least be on a first-name basis."

Mistral stared at me for a moment, then shook his head. He turned back to Doyle. "She speaks in riddles. If I had been one of the fathers, the queen would have released me and let me go to the Western lands."

"We found out only moments before the king abducted Meredith. So there was not time for you to come to us in the Western lands because we were here in faerie, and in St. Louis."

"Did she not know that I was one of the fathers?" Mistral asked.

"I informed her that Meredith was with child and who the fathers were personally," Doyle said.

"She unchained me, but she told me nothing." He turned to me, his eyes full of different colors, as if tiny slices of the sky, or clouds of different colors, were blowing through them. He didn't seem to know what to think or feel, and his uncertainty was bare in his eyes.

I went to him, touched his arm, and gazed into those uncertain eyes. "You are to be a father, Mistral."

"But I was only with you twice."

I smiled. "You know what they say; once is enough."

He smiled then, a little uncertainly. He glanced at Doyle. "Is it true?"

"It is. I was there when the visions spoke loudly to more than just Meredith. We are both to be fathers." Doyle flashed that white smile in his dark face.

Mistral's face filled with light. His eyes were suddenly the blue of a clear, summer sky. He touched my face very gently, as if afraid I would break. "Pregnant, with my child?" He made it a question.

"Yes," I said.

I watched clouds slide across his eyes, like a reflection. His eyes were the color of a rainy sky. That sky began to rain down his strong, pale cheeks. I watched him cry, and of all the possible reactions; that was not what I'd expected from the Storm Lord. He was always so fierce in the bedroom and in battle, and now he, of all the fathers, was the only one who wept when he found out. Every time I think I understand men, I'm wrong again.

His voice came a little broken around the edges. "Why did she not tell me? Why did she hurt me when I had done what she said she wanted most in all the world? To have an heir of her own bloodline to sit on her throne was her wish, and she tortured me for it. Why?"

I knew who "she" was. I'd noticed that many

of the guards spoke of Queen Andais as "she." She was their queen, and the absolute ruler of their fates. The only woman they had had hope of touching for so very long.

I said the only truth I had to offer. "I don't know."

Doyle came and gripped the other man's shoulder. "Logic has not ruled the queen for many years."

It was a polite way of saying that Andais was mad. She was, but to say it out loud was not always wise.

I touched Mistral's other arm. He jerked as if the touch had hurt. "If she finds out that faerie has handfasted you to Sholto, she could use it as an excuse to take the rest of us back into her guard."

"She cannot take the fathers of my children," I said, but I sounded more sure than I felt.

Mistral voiced my fears. "She is the queen, and she can do as she likes."

"She swore to give you all to me if you would come to my bed. She would be forsworn. The wild hunt is real again, and oathbreakers, even royal ones, can be hunted again."

Mistral grabbed my arm hard enough that it hurt immediately. "Do not threaten her, Meredith. For the love of the Goddess herself, do not give her reason to see you as a danger."

"You're hurting me, Mistral," I said softly.

He eased his grip, but did not let me go. "Do not think that being with her brother's grandchildren will keep you safe from her."

"I am not safe inside faerie. I know that. That

is why we must leave as soon as possible for Los Angeles. We must bring charges against the king and drag him before the human media. We must get away from faerie. The very magic that allows us to do great things is also a weapon to be used against us all." I turned to Doyle, and laid my other hand on his arm. "The Goddess has warned me that the sidhe have not come round to her way of thinking. There are too many enemies here. We must go back to the city and surround ourselves with metal and technology. It will limit the other's power."

"It will limit ours," Mistral said.

"Yes, but without the magic of faerie, I trust my guards to keep me safe with gun and blade."

"Faerie has come to us in Los Angeles, Merry," Doyle said.

I nodded. "Yes, but the closer we are to the faerie mounds, the more our enemies can gather round us. I'm not even certain that the Seelie are my enemies, but they are not my friends. They seek to control me and the magic I represent."

"Then we must go to Los Angeles," Doyle said.

"Sholto cannot leave his people besieged by the Seelie," Mistral said.

"Nor can we," I said.

"What do you mean to do, Meredith?" Doyle asked.

I shook my head. "I'm not certain, but I know that I need to convince them that the sluagh did not steal me away. I need to convince them that they cannot steal the chalice from me."

"They are asking for you and the chalice," Mistral said. "I think they understand that it is your hand it comes to."

"True," I said. I thought, "What do I do?" Goddess, what do I do to fix this? Then I had an idea, a very human idea. "There's a room in the sluagh mound just like in the Unseelie mound. There's a phone and computer, an office."

"How do you know that?" Mistral asked.

"My father had to make a phone call from here once when I was with him."

"Why did he not use the phone at the Unseelie mound?" Mistral asked.

I looked at Doyle. "He didn't trust the Unseelie," Doyle said.

"Not in that moment. It was only weeks before he died."

"What was the phone call about?" Mistral asked.

"He made me go with Sholto to see another part of the mound."

"I thought you were afraid of the King of the sluagh," Doyle said.

"I was, but my father told me to go, and to remember that the sluagh had never harmed me. That the sluagh and goblin mounds were the only faerie mounds where I had never been beaten or abused. He was right. Now the sluagh are afraid that my being Sholto's queen will destroy them as a people, but then I was just the daughter of Essus and they liked my father."

"We all did," Mistral said.

"Not all," Doyle said.

"Who did not?" Mistral asked.

"Whoever killed him. It had to be another sidhe warrior. No other could have stood against Prince Essus." It was the first time I'd heard Doyle say out loud what I'd always known, that somewhere in the faces of those around me at court was my father's murderer.

Doyle turned to me. "Who will you call?"

"I'll call for help. I'll say the truth, that the Seelie are trying to take me back to the king's hands. That they do not believe his guilt, and I need help."

"They cannot defeat the Seelie," Doyle said.

"No, but neither can the Seelie defend themselves against human authority. If they do, they lose their right to live on American soil. They will be banished from the last country that will have them."

The two men looked at me, then Mistral nodded. "Clever."

"You put the Seelie in a situation that they cannot win," Doyle said. "If they fail their king, he could have them killed."

"They have the ability to bring him down as king, Doyle. If they are too weak-willed to do it, then their fate is their own."

"Harsh words," he said softly.

"I thought being pregnant would make me softer, but when I stood alone in the snow and realized that Onilwyn meant to kill me, knowing that I was with child," I shook my head, trying to put it into words, "some terrible resolve took hold of me. Or perhaps it was Gran dying in my arms that finally made me realize."

"Realize what, Meredith?"

"That I cannot afford to be weak, or even too terribly kind anymore. The time for such things must be over, Doyle. I will save faerie if I can, but I will protect my children and the men I love above all else."

"Even above taking the throne?" Doyle asked.

I nodded. "You saw the noble houses when the queen presented me, Doyle. We have less than half the houses supporting me. I thought Andais was strong enough to push whatever heir she chose upon the nobles, but if the nobles of her court are conspiring with the nobles of the Seelie Court, she's lost too much power over them. There is no way to be safe on this throne, unless we can find more allies here."

"Are you giving up the crown?" Doyle asked, words very careful.

"No, but I am saying that I cannot take it unless my safety and the safety of my kings and children can be guaranteed. I will not lose another person to assassins, and I will not die at their hands as my father did." I put my hands on my stomach. Still so flat, but I had seen their tiny figures on the ultrasound. I would not lose them. "We go to the Western Lands, and we stay there until the babies are born, or until we are certain that we are safe."

"We will never be safe, Meredith," Doyle said.

"So be it, then," I said.

"Be careful what you say, Princess," Mistral said.

"I say the truth, Mistral. There are too many schemes, plots, enemies, or simply people who want to use me. My own cousin used our grand-mother as a weapon, and set her up to be killed. So many of the sidhe care nothing for the lesser fey, and that's wrong too. If I am to be queen here, then I will be queen of all, not just of the sidhe."

"Merry . . . ," Doyle said.

"No, Doyle, the lesser fey haven't tried to kill me and mine yet. Why should I keep being loyal to the very people who keep trying to hurt me?"

"Because you are part sidhe."

"I am also part human and part brownie. We'll need a guide to the phone room. It's been too long since I was there. But we will call the police and they will come and get us out. We will be on a plane to Los Angeles, and the plane itself will be enough metal and technology to protect us."

"It is not a happy thing for me to fly, Mere-dith," Doyle said.

I smiled at him. "I know that much metal is a problem for most of you, but it is the safest way for us to travel, and it will guarantee that we have human media on the other end waiting for us. We are going to embrace the media, because this is war, Doyle. Not a war of weapons, but of public opinion. Faerie grows stronger on the belief of mortals, so we will give them ourselves to believe in."

"Have you been planning this all along?" he asked.

"No, no, but it's time to embrace my own strengths. I was raised human, Doyle. I realize now that my father took me out of faerie as a child for the same reason I'm going now, because it was safer."

"You are exiling all of us, including our children, from faerie."

I went to him, wrapping my arms around him so that we were pressed together. "Only you lost to me would be exile."

He searched my face. "Meredith, do not give up a throne for me."

"I admit that the fact that they keep trying to kill you hardest of all affects my decisions, but it's not just that, Doyle. The magic around me grows wilder, and I cannot control it. I no longer know how much and what is returning. There are things that were driven from faerie long ago, not at the humans' request, but at our own. What if I bring back things that could truly destroy us all, human and fey alike? I am too dangerous to be this close to the faerie mounds."

"Faerie has come to Los Angeles, Merry, or had you forgotten?"

"That new bit of faerie cost us Frost, so no, I hadn't forgotten. If I had not been in the new part of faerie Taranis could not have taken me. We will put guards on the doors and I at least will stay in the human world, until the Goddess or God tell me otherwise."

"What dream did the Goddess give you, to make you so resolved?" he asked.

"It is the dream and the Seelie outside the sluagh's home. I bring danger to all who would shelter me inside faerie. It is time to go home."

"Faerie is home," he said.

I shook my head. "I saw Los Angeles as a punishment, but no longer. I will treat it as a refuge, and I will make it our home."

"I have never been to the city before," Mistral said. "I am not sure I will thrive there."

I held my hand out to the other man. "You will be by my side, Mistral. You will watch my body grow ripe, and you will hold our children in your hands. What more is home than that?"

He came to me then, to us, and they wrapped me in the strength of their arms. I buried my face in the scent of Doyle's chest, and hid against his body. My resolve would have been firmer if the other arms holding me had been Frost's. By returning to the human world and cutting myself off from faerie, I was cutting myself off from the last piece of him. The white stag was a fey creature, and it would not come to a metal city. I pushed the thought away. I was right in this choice. I felt it, like a firm yes in my mind. It was time to embrace the other part of my culture. It was time to go to Los Angeles and make it my home.

CHAPTER EIGHTEEN

CHATTAN, SHOLTO'S COUSIN, WAS ON THE door as guard again. His brother was not with him. A nightflyer stood on the other side of the door, flat upon the floor, its great wings pulled tight around it so that it looked like a black cloak. Standing, the nightflyer was a little shorter than I. I looked into its huge, lidless eyes, and a glance at Chattan's own eyes showed plainly where the genetics for those large liquid dark eyes had come from.

He was Sholto's cousin on his father's side.

Chattan came to attention, saying, "Princess Meredith, it is good to see you up and well. This is Tarlach. He is our uncle."

I knew what he meant by the "our." "Greetings, Uncle Tarlach. It is good to meet another of my king's relatives."

Tarlach bowed in that liquid way that the nightflyers had, as if their spines worked in ways that human spines never would. His voice had some of the sibilance of a snake goblin, but there was also a sound of wind and open sky in his words, as if the sound that wild geese make in the autumn could be mingled with the edge of a storm and become human speech.

"It has been long since a sidhe called me uncle."

"I bear the child of your nephew and your king. By sluagh law that makes us family. The sluagh have never stood on ceremony to make their family larger. Blood calls to blood." In the Unseelie Court that would have been a threatening line, blood to blood, but among the sluagh it simply meant that I carried Tarlach's genetics in my body.

"You know our ways; that is good. You are your father's daughter."

"Everywhere I go outside the Unseelie Court I find people who respected my father. I am beginning to wish that he was a tenth less likeable and a tenth more ruthless."

Tarlach moved what would have passed for shoulders if he'd had more of them, but I knew from my nightflyer tutor, Bhátar, that it was their nod.

"You think it would have kept him alive?" Tarlach asked.

"I plan to find out."

"You plan to be more ruthless than your father?" Chattan asked.

I looked at the taller sluagh and nodded. "Take me to the office so that I can make a phone call, and I will try to be both practical and surprising."

"What help is there from a phone against the Seelie?" Tarlach asked, in his wind and storm voice. Not all the nightflyers had such voices. It was a mark of royal blood among them, but more than that, it was a mark of great power. Even among the royal not all had the voice of storm.

"I will call the police and tell them that my uncle seeks to kidnap me again. They will come and rescue me, and once I am gone the Seelie danger to you all will go with me."

"If the sluagh cannot stand against the Seelie, then the humans cannot," Chattan said.

"But if the Seelie dare to attack human police, it is a breach of the treaty they signed when they first came to this country. It is war on American soil, and war on humans. They can be exiled from this country for that."

"You seek not to fight, but to make it impossible for them to fight," Tarlach said.

"Exactly."

His slit of a mouth smiled enough that it crinkled his lidless eyes into happy smiles, or that's how I'd always thought of it as a child when I'd made Bhátar smile that broadly. "We will take you to the office, but our king and nephew is fighting a different fight, which the human police cannot help with."

"Let us walk as you explain," Mistral said.

Tarlach looked up and gave the tall sidhe a look that was not friendly, though I wasn't certain that Mistral would be able to read it. I'd grown up staring into the face of a nightflyer, so I could.

"The sidhe do not rule here." Then he looked at Doyle.

"Once the queen ordered me to come and try to be your king, but you rejected me, and the sluagh's vote is final. I did as I was ordered, nothing more."

"It left a bad taste on our skin," Tarlach said.

"The queen orders, and the ravens obey," Doyle said, an old saying among the Unseelie that I hadn't heard in a long time.

"Some say the princess is only a puppet for the Darkness, but you have remained silent."

"The princess does well enough on her own."

"Yes, she does." Tarlach seemed to decide something, because he began to walk down the hallway. As graceful as they are in the air, they are less so on the ground.

"We heard that the sluagh had voted a new proxy king because they feared Sholto would not wake in time to deal with the Seelie," I said as I fell in step beside him. Mistral and Doyle came in behind me, much as they would have for the queen herself. Chattan brought up the rear.

"It was more than that, Princess Meredith. The bower you had created was terribly Seelie, though the bone gate was a nice touch."

"It was made of magic from Sholto and myself."

"But it was mostly flowers and sunshine. That is not very Unseelie, and most definitely not very sluagh."

"I cannot always choose how the magic will come."

"It is wild magic, and it chooses its own way like water finding a cleft in a rock," he said.

I simply agreed. "Is there a chance that they will try to dispossess Sholto?"

"Some fear that in joining with you he will destroy the sluagh. They have chosen a full-blooded nightflyer in his place as proxy. Only the fact that Sholto has been the best and fairest of kings saved him from waking to a kingdom that was his no more."

"Forgive me," Doyle said, "but could the sluagh simply vote their king out of office?"

Tarlach spoke without trying to look back at Doyle. "It has been done before."

We walked in silence for a few minutes. The sluagh's sithen looked much like the Unseelie's, with dark stone walls, and floors of cold, worn stone. But the energy was different. That thrumming, pulsing energy that was always present inside a fairie mound, unless you blocked it out, was slightly different. It was like the difference between a Porsche and a Mustang. They were both high-performance cars, but one purred and the other roared. The sluagh's sithen roared, the power calling to me louder and louder as we walked.

I stopped so abruptly that Doyle had to touch my shoulder to keep from walking into me. "What is wrong?" he asked.

"We will call, but Sholto needs me now, right now."

"You at his side will not comfort them," Tarlach said.

"I know I look too sidhe for them, but it is the power that they need to see. The sithen is talking. Don't you hear it?"

Tarlach gazed up at me. "I hear it, but I am nightflyer."

"It is roaring at me, getting louder, like the rain and wind of some great storm coming ever closer. I need to be at Sholto's side while he faces his people."

"You are too sidhe to help him," Chattan said.

I shook my head. "Your sithen doesn't think so."

The sound pulsed against my skin, as if I were leaning against some great engine, so that it vibrated along my body. "There is no time. The sithen chose Sholto as its king, as all the sithens once did. It will not take another, and your people are not listening to it."

"If you are truly his queen, and the sithen truly speaks, then ask it to open the way from here to the chamber of decision. It may speak to you, but does it listen to you?"

I remembered the wall trying to close against my wish, but that had been my desire, and the new king had been working against me. Now the sithen wanted something, and I wanted the same thing. We wanted to help our king.

I spoke. "Sithen, open the way to your king and the chamber of decision."

The vibrating energy grew so loud that I could hear nothing but the roar and pulse of it. It staggered me for a moment so that I reached out to Tarlach's slick muscled form for steadiness. Maybe it was the fact that I reached to a nightflyer and not a sidhe, but whatever the reason, the corridor in front of us ended, and became something else. It was suddenly the opening of a great cavern. I could see seats full of sluagh going up and up in a great amphitheater.

Sholto stood on the sand-covered floor facing a huge nightflyer almost as tall as himself. It unfurled its wings, and shrieked at us. Sholto turned a startled face to us. He only had time to say "Meredith" before the nightflyer launched itself at us. Tarlach threw himself skyward and met the larger form in a twisting fight that went upward.

"You should not have come," Sholto said, but he took my hand in his as the benches began to broil into a riot. The sluagh were fighting among themselves.

CHAPTER NINETEEN

THE TATTOOS ON OUR HANDS FLARED TO life, not as real roses, but as glowing, pulsing works of art. The smell of herbs and roses was thick on the air. I felt the weight of the crown as it curled through my hair, and I knew I was crowned once more with white roses and mistletoe. I did not need to look at Sholto to know that his crown was in place, a mist of herbs blooming above his pale hair.

Rose petals began to fall like rain, but they were not the pink and lavender that they had been before. White petals fell around the two of us.

It slowed the riot, stopped most of the fighting. It turned their faces to us, wide with astonishment. For a second I hoped that the fight would end, and we could talk, then the yelling began.

There were screams. "Sidhe! They are sidhe!" Others screamed "Betrayed! We are betrayed!"

Doyle was at my back, and I think he was talking to Sholto. "We need weapons."

I raised my face to the fall of white petals, felt them hit my face like soft blows. I spoke to the air. "We need weapons."

Sholto had the spear of bone and the dagger in his hand. I stood separate from him, unarmed. The ground underfoot shuddered, then began to split open. Doyle and Mistral grabbed me, pulled me back, but I wasn't afraid. I could feel the power of the sithen revving like the great magical engine that it was.

The opening widened, then stopped. It was a spiral staircase as white and shining as any in the Seelie Court, leading down into the ground. The banister was formed of human bones, and larger bones of things that had never been humanoid.

When the sound of the ground opening stopped there was no sound from the sluagh. It was so quiet that the sound of the rose petals hitting the sand made a noise like snow falling.

Then into that silence came the sound of cloth and footsteps. The sound was coming from the stairs. The first figure came, clothed all in white, hidden behind a cloak and robes that hadn't been worn in faerie for centuries. Hands as white as the cloth held a sword by its hilt. I thought at first that the hands were moonlight skin like Sholto's and mine, but then as the figure came farther up the stairs, I saw that the hands were bones. Skeletal hands held the white handle of the sword. The blade was white too, though it gleamed like metal and not bone.

The figure was tall, as tall as any sidhe. It looked at us with a skull for a face, hidden behind a gauzy veil. Empty eye sockets stared at me. It turned to Sholto, and offered the sword.

He hesitated for a second, then reached for the hilt. He brushed the skeletal hands, but did not seem to mind. The figure walked through the growing puddle of petals, the long trailing gown like some macabre wedding dress. She, for it was she, stood to one side and waited.

The next figure looked like a duplicate of the first: all white, all bone, that gauzy veil in front of the skull face. This one offered a woven white belt and scabbard. Sholto took them, fastening the belt around his waist and sheathing the sword.

A third skeletal figure came, but this one held a shield, as white as the sword. The shield was carved with figures of skeletons and tentacled beasts. If I hadn't seen the sluagh in their wildest form, I'd have mistaken the animals for great sea beasts, but I knew better now.

The skeleton bride offered the shield to Sholto. He took it, and once it was on his arm, the sithen roared around us. It was a sound, not just inside the head for magic, but as if the sithen were some great beast.

I would have thought that the parade of weapons was over, but I could see more of the figures on the stairs. The curve kept me from seeing how many, but I knew there were more.

The next figure came to me. She held a pale

sword, not white, but almost flesh-colored in its hilt. I reached for it, but Doyle stopped me with a hand on my arm. "Touch it only with the hand that contains the hand of flesh, Meredith. It is the blade Aben-dul. Anyone who touches it who does not wield the hand of flesh will be consumed in the same way the hand of flesh destroys."

My pulse was suddenly so hard in my throat that it hurt to breathe past it. The hand of flesh was by far my most terrible magic. I could turn someone inside out, and even meld two people together into one screaming mass. But the sidhe do not die from it. No, they live and scream.

I'd been reaching with my right hand, and it was the hand of flesh for me, but it was still good to know how terribly dangerous something was before you touched it. Always good to know that the same power that will help you will also trap you, but power is often like that, a two-edged sword.

I took the weapon, and a collective gasp went up from the sluagh. They had known what it was too, but they had shouted no warning. The hilt that had been plain moved under my hand so strongly that I had to grip it tightly to hold it. It felt alive. Images formed on the hilt of people and fey writhing and being welded together. Then it was suddenly carved with images of what the sword could do. In that moment, I knew that I could cut someone with it, as a normal sword, but I also knew that with it in my hand I could also project the hand of flesh over a distance in battle. It was the only object that I'd ever heard of in legend that was formed to be the perfect match for my hand of power. It had been lost to the sidhe long enough ago that it wasn't even in any of the stories.

How did I know about it? My father had made certain that I memorized the list of lost objects of power. It was a litany of what we had lost as a people, but now I realized that it was also a list of what we could recover.

The next figure held a spear that sparkled silver and white, almost as if it were made of some light-reflecting jewel. There were several spears of legend, and it wasn't until she moved around us and offered it to Mistral that I was certain of its name. It was simply Lightning. It had never been Mistral's spear. Once it had belonged to Taranis, the Thunderer, before he tried to be too human, and turned from what he was meant to be.

Mistral hesitated, then he wrapped his big hand around the spear's shaft. It could only be wielded by a storm deity. To touch it without the ability to call lightning meant it would burn your hand, or burn you up. I'd forgotten that about the old weapons. Most of them had only one hand that could wield them safely. To all others, they were destruction.

The spear flared in an eye-searing whiteness that left me blinking with ruined vision. Then the spear was a silver shaft, less brilliant, less otherworldly. Mistral gazed at it as if it were something wondrous, which it was. He could call lightning to his hand, and with the spear, legend had it, he could call and direct storms.

The next skeletal bride went to Doyle. He had a sword of power, and two magical daggers that had been his for many years. But I had asked for us to be armed, not just to pick and choose. Of course, what lay in the figure's hands didn't look like a weapon. It was a curved instrument formed of the horn of some animal I was not familiar with. It was black, and I could feel the weight of ages spilling off of it. It had a strap so it could be worn across the body.

There was a yell, and the huge nightflyer that had been fighting Tarlach landed beside us. I had a moment to wonder where Tarlach was, but then the nightflyer, the would-be king of the sluagh, reached for what lay in the skeletal hands.

Doyle did not try to stop him. None of us did.

CHAPTER TWENTY

THE NIGHTFLYER'S FOUR-FINGERED HAND wrapped around the ancient horn. He smiled, a wide, fierce grin, and held it aloft. There were some shouts of approval, but most were silent, watching. They knew what it was. Did he?

He turned to us, still smiling, still triumphant, then his expression changed. Doubt went across those flattened features, then his eyes widened and he whispered, "No."

Then he started to scream. He screamed, and shrieked, and the sound echoed in the chamber. He collapsed to the sand, the horn still in his grasp, as if he couldn't let it go. He rolled on the ground, writhing and screaming. It destroyed his mind while we watched.

When he was still except for a few twitches, Doyle walked to him. He knelt and took the black horn out of the would-be king's hand. The hand was limp, and did not fight to hold it now.

Doyle took the horn, and slipped the strap across his bare chest. He looked around at the assembled sluagh and spoke, his deep voice carrying. "It is the horn of the dark moon. The horn of the hunter. The horn of madness. It was mine once long ago. Only the huntsman of the wild hunt may touch it, and only when the magic of the hunt is upon him."

Someone actually called out, "Then how do you hold it?"

"I am the huntsman. I am always the huntsman." I wasn't entirely certain that I understood what Doyle meant by that, but it seemed to satisfy the crowd. I could ask for more details later or not. He may have given the only answer he had.

There was one more skeletal lady on the stairs. She carried a cloak of feathers across her arms. She walked, not to us, but across the sand to where Tarlach lay in a heap on the ground. I started to go to him, but Sholto grabbed my arm. Wait, he seemed to say, and he was right. Though knowing that I could call the chalice and possibly save Tarlach made it hard to watch the slow, stately progress of the skeleton in her graceful dress.

She knelt beside the fallen nightflyer and covered him with the cloak. She stood, and walked slowly back to join the others in their silent, waiting line.

For a moment I thought that he was too far gone to be helped by any legendary item, then he moved underneath the feathers. He staggered to his feet with the feathered cloak fastened around him. For a moment he stood there, the blood shining on the white of his belly where he'd been hurt. Then he launched himself skyward, and he was a goose. The other nightflyers launched skyward too, and suddenly the huge domed ceiling was full of geese, calling out. Then they landed on the sand, by the dozens, and were nightflyers when they touched ground.

Tarlach said, "We will not need the glamour of the king to hide us when we hunt. We can hide ourselves." He bowed in his liquid way, and the other nightflyers followed him. They knelt like a hundred giant manta rays kneeling without knees, but somehow all the more graceful for it.

There was movement in the benches around us, then I realized that everyone was bowing. They were dropping to their knees, or their equivalent, in a mass of devotion.

Tarlach began it. "King Sholto. Queen Meredith!" The other throats took it up, until we stood in the midst of the sound of it. "King Sholto, Queen Meredith!"

I stood in the only kingdom in all of faerie where you could be voted queen, and the sluagh had spoken. I was queen in faerie at last, just not the kingdom I'd planned on running.

CHAPTER TWENTY-ONE

SHOLTO'S OFFICE WAS FULL OF RICH, POL-
ished wood, stained as dark a brown as it was possible to do and not ruin the wood. The walls were
even paneled wood. There was a wall hanging behind the main desk. It was faded, but the threads
still showed a scene of the sky boiling with clouds
that held tentacles and sights best left to horror
movies. There were tiny figures on the ground of
people running in terror. One figure, a woman
with long yellow hair, gazed up at the clouds while
everyone else ran or hid their eyes. As a child I had
gazed at the hanging while my father and Sholto
did business. I knew from asking that the hanging
was almost as old as the Bayeux tapestry, and that
the blond woman was Glenna the Mad. She had
made a series of tapestries of what she'd seen when
the wild hunt had come through her countryside.
The tapestries gradually became more bizarre as her
senses left her.

I'd stared into what had driven Glenna insane, and I hadn't flinched. Had it been shock? Had it been the blessing of the God and Goddesses? Or had all the losses finally caught up with me?

Doyle was standing behind me, his arms around my waist, holding me against the front of his body. The weight and reality of him were like a lifeline. I was fleeing faerie for good reasons, the right reasons, but I could admit in my head that one of the main reasons was this man. Maybe it was Gran's death, but I think I'd decided that for Doyle and the children inside me I'd trade a throne.

A man's voice on the other end of the phone made me jump. I'd been waiting on hold for a long time. I think they hadn't believed that I was who I said I was.

Doyle hugged me a little more tightly, while my pulse calmed a little.

"This is Major Walters. Is that really you, Princess?"

"It's me."

"They're telling me you need a police escort out of faerie." A tendril of the roses in my crown curled downward to touch the phone receiver.

"I do."

"You do know that the walls of your hospital room melted. Witnesses say you and King Sholto flew out of the room on flying horses, but somehow the Mobile Reserve Team that was watching the outside of your room didn't see any of this until you were far enough away, then the holes in the walls just appeared to them." He didn't sound happy.

"Major Walters, I am sorry that I upset your Mobile Reserve and anyone else, but I've had a hell of a night myself, okay?" There was the tiniest catch in my voice. I took a few deep, even breaths. I would not break down. Queens didn't do that.

Doyle kissed the top of my head, laying his cheek between the roses and the mistletoe of the crown.

The rose tendril wrapped tightly around the phone, and tugged.

"Are you hurt?"

"Not physically."

"What happened, Princess?" His voice was gentler now.

"It's time for me to get out of faerie, Major Walters. It's time for me to get out of your jurisdiction. I'm too close to my relatives in St. Louis." The tendril pulled harder, as if it were trying to pull the phone out of my hand. Faerie had crowned me the queen of this mound. It didn't want to lose me to the human world.

I whispered, "Stop it."

"What was that, Princess?"

"Nothing, sorry."

"What do you need from us?"

Doyle touched the tendril and began to uncurl it from the phone. He tried to take both of his hands away to do it, but I put one arm back around my waist, so he was forced to do it one-handed.

I explained that my uncle's people were outside my refuge and were threatening war on the sluagh unless they handed me over. "My uncle is absolute ruler of the Seelie Court. He's convinced them that the twins I carry are somehow his, and he's their king. He claims that the sluagh stole me away, and the Seelies want me back." I didn't try to fight the catch in my voice now. "They want to give me back to my uncle. Do you understand?"

Doyle finally had the tendril unwrapped. I felt it move back up with the rest of the living crown.

"I heard what he's accused of, and I am sorrier than I know how to say, Princess Meredith."

"Accused of, Walters? Nice that you don't admit that you believe me."

Doyle held me more tightly.

Major Walters started to protest.

I cut him off. "It's okay, Walters. Just escort me back to reality. Get us all on a plane and back to L.A."

The tendril slid back toward the phone.

"You should have a doctor look at you before you get on a plane."

I put a hand over the receiver and hissed, "Stop!" The vine stopped in mid-motion like a child caught with its hand going for cookies.

"Princess, we'll come and get you, but on the condition that you let a doctor look you over before we put you on the plane."

"We melted the walls of the room I was in. Do you really think the hospital wants me back?"

"They're a hospital, and they want you safe. We all want you safe."

"You don't want me dying on your watch is what you mean."

Doyle sighed, and kissed my cheek. I wasn't sure if he was warning me not to be too harsh with the humans, or if he was simply comforting me.

"Princess, that is not what I mean," he said and he sounded like he meant it.

"Fine, I'm sorry. Please, come get us."

"It will take a little while to get things round, but we'll get there."

"Why a while?" I asked.

"After what happened last time, Princess, we've been given permission, or orders, depending on how you want to look at it, to have the National Guard with us. Just in case the sky boils and monsters come out again. I know your man Abeloec healed the ones who went mad, but enough of them remember some of what happened that this is more than a straight police matter."

"Mobile Reserve can't handle it?" I asked.

"The National Guard has witches and wizards assigned to their units now. The police don't."

"Oh," I said. "I'd forgotten that. That horrible thing that happened in Persia." It had been on the news for days, in horrible living color.

"It's not called Persia anymore, Princess Meredith, and hasn't been for a very long time."

"But the creatures that attacked our soldiers were Persian bogey beasts. They had nothing to do with Islam, and everything to do with the original religion of the region."

"That may be, but the National Guard will bring magic workers, and after what's been happening, I think I agree that we need them."

What was I supposed to say to that? The tendril curled around the phone and tugged again, and this time I hit it gently with my finger. It curled away as if I'd hurt its feelings. I appreciated being crowned by faerie itself. I appreciated the honor, but a crown wasn't going to protect me from my relatives. Once I'd thought it would, but I realized that that had been naive.

"I'll make the calls. How long can you hold out in the sluagh mound?"

"If we just stay inside, awhile. But I don't know how long the Seelie will wait to press the matter."

"Do they actually believe that your uncle is the father of your children?"

"My mother is out there with them, agreeing with it. I can't even blame them for believing her. She's my mother. Why would she lie?"

Sholto pushed away from the wall where he and Mistral had been waiting. I think they were giving me alone time with Doyle. But now, Sholto came and took my free hand in his, and laid a gentle kiss on it. I wasn't sure what I'd done to deserve such comfort.

"Why **would** she lie?" Major Walters asked.

"Because her greatest goal in life was always to

be part of the inner circle of the Seelie Court, and if she can make me Taranis's queen, then she's suddenly the mother of the queen of the Seelie Court. She'd love it."

"She'd trade your freedom for a little social climbing?"

"She'd trade my life for a little social climbing."

Doyle stood at my back, and held me. Sholto knelt at my feet and wrapped his arms around my legs, gazing up at me. The flowers on his crown were like a mist of lavender, pink, and white. He looked terribly Seelie kneeling there and staring up with those tri-gold eyes.

"No, Princess, she's your mom."

"She let my uncle beat me nearly to death when I was young. She watched him do it. My grandmother was the one who intervened and saved my life."

I touched Sholto's face, and knew in that instant that here was another man who would risk everything for me. He'd already proven that when he came to fetch me from the Seelie Court, but the look in his eyes now said more.

"There's a rumor that your grandmother was injured. My staff saw some of your men carrying her on horseback out of the hospital."

"She's not injured. She's dead." My voice was oddly flat when I said it.

Sholto's eyes showed pain, because he was the one who had struck the fatal blow. It was his hand that had killed Gran, even though he had had no choice.

"What?" Major Walters asked.

"I don't have time to explain, Major Walters. I need help. I need a human escort out of here."

"Why can't your Unseelie guard get you out?"

"I'm not certain what the Seelie would do if they saw Unseelie warriors right now. But they won't attack humans, especially human soldiers. It would break the peace, and they would risk being kicked out of America for waging war on your soil."

"They're trying to give you back to the man you've accused of raping you. That's not very rational. Do you really think that they'll let soldiers come in and take you without a fight?"

"If not, then kick their asses out of America."

"Are you setting us up to help you get rid of your enemies, Princess?"

"No, I'm doing the only thing I can think of that might, just might, avoid any more bloodshed or violence. I've seen enough for one night. I'm part human, and I'm going to embrace that part, Major Walters. They keep saying I'm too mortal to be sidhe, well, I'll go be mortal. Because it is too dangerous to be sidhe right now. Get me out of here, Major Walters. I am pregnant with twins, and I have some of the fathers of my children with me. Get us out of here before something fatal happens. Please, Major Walters, please help me."

The tendril curled back away from the phone. Doyle held me against his body. Sholto still had his ams wrapped around my legs, putting his arms between Doyle's body and mine, but it was all right in that instant, it wasn't competitive. Sholto laid his cheek against my legs, hiding his eyes.

"I am so sorry, Meredith, about your grandmother. Please forgive me."

"We punished the person who killed Gran. You know, we all know, that it wasn't your hand that did it."

He gazed up at me, his handsome face anguished. "But it was my hand that struck the blow."

"If you had not done it, and I could have," Doyle said, "it would have been my hand."

Mistral spoke from near the door. "What all has been happening while I was being tortured?"

"There is much to tell," Doyle said, "but let it wait for a later time."

Mistral came to stand near us, but there wasn't much of me left to touch. I offered him a hand, and after a moment's hesitation, he took it. "I will follow you into exile, Princess."

"I cannot leave my people," Sholto said, still on his knees.

"You will be in danger if you stay in faerie," I said. "They've already proven that the three of you are marked for assassination."

"You must come with us, Sholto, or never leave the safety of the sluagh mound again," Doyle said.

Sholto hugged my legs, rubbing his cheek along my thighs. "I cannot leave my people without both king and queen."

"A dead king is not worth anything to them," Mistral said.

"How long will this exile last?" Sholto asked.

"Until the babies are born, at least," I said.

"I can travel from Los Angeles to parts of the sluagh mound, for thanks to our magic there is a beach edge inside the mound. So I can visit my people without making myself a target to the sidhe."

"You say sidhe, not Seelie," I said. "Why?"

"Onilwyn is not Seelie, but he helped your cousin and her Seelie allies try to kill Mistral. We have enemies on all sides, Meredith. Isn't that why you are leaving faerie?"

I thought about what he'd said, then could only nod. "Yes, Sholto, that is exactly why we must leave faerie. There are more enemies than even the Goddess herself could have foreseen."

"Then we go into exile," Doyle said at my back, his voice rumbling through my body like a purr to ease my nerves.

"We go into exile," Mistral said.

"Exile," Sholto said.

We were agreed. Now we just had to find Rhys and Galen and tell them we were leaving.

CHAPTER TWENTY-TWO

DOYLE BORROWED A NONMAGICAL DAGGER from Sholto, who had several weapons stashed around the office. I wondered if his bedroom was similarly armed, and figured that it probably was. It showed a lack of arrogance and a caution that I found commendable in a sidhe warrior, and outrageously attractive in a king. Tonight, we were trying to survive and flee, and extra weapons that weren't major artifacts of power seemed like a very good idea.

Doyle used the dagger to contact Rhys. Most of faerie used mirrors, but some of the first reflection magic had been with one of the few reflected surfaces that all of us had carried. Even nonwarriors had carried a blade to cut food or do chores. A knife was useful for many things besides killing. You just needed a body fluid to paint across the blade. For whatever reason, mirrors didn't need that extra personal touch, which was probably why we'd gone to mirrors.

Doyle made a small cut on his finger and painted his blood across the side of the dagger. Then he leaned close and called for Rhys.

I sat in Sholto's big office chair, my feet curled up underneath me. The living crown had unraveled and gone to wherever it went. Sholto's hair was also bare once more. Apparently, the power had made its point.

I wasn't certain if it was the retreat of such major magic, or the events finally catching up with me, but I was cold. It was a cold that had little to do with the constant temperature of the faerie mound. Some types of cold have nothing to do with skin and blankets, but are a cold of heart and soul.

The sword Aben-dul lay on the clean surface of Sholto's big desk. The images that had appeared on its hilt were still there, frozen in whatever the hilt was made of. It felt like bone, but not quite. There was a woman's nude body frozen in a miniature attitude of pain and horror, her face melting into the leg of the man above her.

The hand of flesh was one of the most terrible magics that the sidhe possessed. I'd used it only twice, and each time haunted me. If I'd used it on humans it might have been less awful, for they would have died if you turned them inside out. The sidhe did not die. You had to find another way to bring them death while they screamed, and their internal organs glistened in the lights. Their heart beat in the open air, still attached by blood vessels and other bits and pieces.

The last person to wield the hand of flesh had been my father. But the sword on the desk had not reappeared to him. It had come to me. Why?

Mistral stepped between me and the desk, pushing the chair back with his hands on its arms. The chair rolled smoothly back, and I looked up at him where he bent over me.

"Princess Meredith, you look haunted."

I opened my mouth, closed it, then finally said, "I'm cold."

He smiled, but his eyes were serious as he turned to Sholto. "The princess is cold."

Sholto simply nodded, and opened the door to speak to the guards waiting outside. He was a king, and simply assumed that the guards would be there, and that one of them would be all too happy to fetch a servant, who would in turn fetch a blanket or a coat. It was the arrogance of the nobility. I'd never had enough servants who listened to me to acquire the habit. Though maybe my father had planned it that way. He'd been a man who thought far ahead. Maybe he'd understood that without that arrogance I would be more fair. Faerie was overdue for a little fairness.

Mistral knelt in front of me, and he was tall enough that he still blocked my view of the desk. The sword was not the only thing on the desk. His spear lay there too. It was no longer a shining, silver-white thing, but looked like some pale wood, though it was carved with runes and language so old that I could not read it all. I wondered if Mistral could, but I did not wonder enough to ask. There were other things that I needed to know more.

"Why did the sword not come to my father's hand? He held the hand of flesh."

Doyle answered from behind us. "He also held the hand of fire."

I did not look behind, but answered. "And I have the hand of blood. What does one thing have to do with another? Aben-dul is made for anyone who holds the hand of flesh. Why me, and not my father?"

"The artifacts of power had not begun to return when Prince Essus was alive," Doyle said.

Mistral asked, "Did you reach Rhys?"

"Yes." Doyle came to stand on my right side. He took my hand in his, the hand that had allowed me to touch a sword that without a matching magic would have turned me inside out, and I would have died, just like that.

He kissed the palm of my hand, and I tried to pull away from him, but he held me. "You carry a great power, Meredith. There is nothing wrong or evil in it."

I pulled harder on my hand, and he finally let me go rather than fight about it. "I know that a magic is not evil in and of itself, but because of what it does, Doyle. You've seen what it does. It is the most horrible magic I have ever seen."

"Did the prince never demonstrate the power for you?" Mistral asked.

"I saw the enemy who the queen keeps in a

trunk in her bedroom. I know my father made him into the . . . ball of flesh that he is."

"Prince Essus did not agree with what the queen chose to do with . . . it," Doyle said.

"Not it," Sholto said. "Him. If it hadn't been a him do you really think the queen would have gotten him out of his trunk?"

We all looked at him. Mistral's look was not a happy one. "We're trying to make her feel better, not worse."

"The queen took pride in letting Meredith see just how terrible she could be."

I nodded. "He's right. I saw the . . . what was left of the prisoner. I saw him in her bed, and was told to put him back in his trunk."

"I did not know," Doyle said.

"Nor I," Mistral said.

"Did you really think the queen spared the princess anything?"

"Andais spared her the worst of our humiliations," Mistral said, "because Meredith had never seen her torture us as she did the night the princess saved us." He took one of my hands in his, and gave me the look that I had earned at last. It was a look of respect, gratitude, and hope. It had been Mistral's eyes that night, his glance at me, that had given me the courage to risk death to save them all from the queen. His eyes that night had said clearly that I was just another useless royal. I had done my best to prove him wrong.

I wondered if he knew that, and something

moved me to tell him. "It was your eyes that night, Mistral, that made me risk death at the queen's hands."

He frowned. "You barely knew me then."

"True, but you looked at me while she bled some of you and made the others watch. Your eyes told me what you thought of me, that I was just another useless royal."

He studied my face. "You nearly died that night because I looked at you?"

"I had to prove you wrong, Mistral. I had to risk everything to save you all, because it was the right thing to do. It was the dutiful thing to do."

He held my hand in both of his, though his hands were so big, and mine so small, that he was holding more of his own skin than mine. He was still studying my face, as if judging the weight of my words.

"She does not lie," Doyle said from the other side of me.

"It's not that. It's that I have not had a woman care so much what I thought in longer than I can remember. That she reacted so, from just that glance. . . ." He frowned at me, then asked, "Were we always destined to be together? Is that why one glance from me did so much?"

I hadn't thought about it that way. "I do not know. I only know that it is what happened. You make me have to be more than I planned on being, Storm Lord."

He smiled then. It was a smile that any man

might have given a woman. A smile that said how pleased he was, and how much my words had meant to him. Everyone thinks that the magic of being with all the men is about the otherworldliness of them and me, but some of the most precious moments are the most ordinary. Moments that any man and woman could share, if they loved, and spoke the truth.

Did I love Mistral? In that moment, as he gazed up at me, I had only one answer: Not yet.

CHAPTER TWENTY-THREE

THE SERVANT CAME IN WITH A COAT. IT was leather pieced together with heavy Frankenstein stitches. The leather was shades of black, different sections having different textures, and some pieces of gray and white among the blackness, as if the coat had been made from different kinds of animals. The stitches and differences in skin should have made it an ugly coat, but it didn't. Somehow it all worked like a club kid meets Goth, with a little motorcycle thrown in.

The really surprising thing to me was that it fit, not just closely, but perfectly. It was so tight through the arms and upper body that I had to take the bloody hospital gown off to fasten the buttons. I knew the feel of the buttons; they were carved bone. The coat fit tightly enough that my cleavage was framed nicely in its V-neck. The tightest part of the coat was under my breasts, so it was almost an empire waist. Then the coat spilled out and down like a ballgown. It buttoned all the way to the floor.

Sholto actually knelt in front of me to finish the buttoning. He smiled up at me. "You look lovely."

Was it shallow to feel better just because I had a coat that fit me well? Maybe, but as bad as I was feeling, I'd take anything that made me feel better.

"It fits perfectly," I said. "Whose clothes am I borrowing?"

"It was made for the queen of the sluagh," he said, standing.

"What does that mean?" I asked.

"It means that the court seamstress had a dream some months back. She was told that I would take a queen and that she should sew accordingly."

I rubbed my fingertips down the leather. It was so soft. The seamstress had lined the inside of the coat so that the stitching didn't rub my skin.

"You're saying your seamstress knew Meredith would be queen before anyone else?" Mistral asked.

"Not Meredith, not by name, but the measurements, yes."

"And you let her sew for some phantom queen?" Doyle said.

"Mirabella has sewn for this court for centuries. She has earned the right to be indulged a little. But many of the clothes were made of scraps and pieces, like this coat, so it wasn't a loss." He gave me an appreciative smile. "Seeing Meredith in it lets me know that nothing was lost."

"Why would it be that important that I have clothes here? Important enough for a prophetic dream?" I asked.

"We are under siege," Doyle said. "Perhaps we will be here longer than we think. There are probably clothes to borrow for Mistral and myself, but you would be harder to fit."

"But why would nice clothes be that important?" I asked.

"Mirabella told everyone who would listen that I would take a queen and that she would be only this big." He made a gesture like you would measure a fish. "It forced the remaining hags and our female nightflyers to rethink their pursuit of me."

"You mean women of your court stopped pressuring you because this Mirabella was sewing clothes that would not fit them?" I asked.

"Yes," he said.

"Had you seen the clothes before this moment?" Doyle asked.

"No," Sholto said. "The women of my court were much interested but I stayed out of it. Honestly, I thought Mirabella might be doing it to help me keep the women from pestering me so hard." He ran his hand down my leather-clad arm. "But it was a true dream, this."

"I hope it doesn't mean we'll be trapped here," Mistral said. "Nothing personal, King Sholto, but that would mean that the humans were not able to get us out."

"I do not wish for anything to go wrong with Meredith's plan, but I can't say that having her with me longer wouldn't be a pleasure."

There was a soft, respectful knock at the door. I knew without really being told that it was a servant. It's as if they are taught that knock with the job description—a way of drawing attention to themselves, but not interrupting.

Sholto called, "Enter."

The woman who had brought the coat bowed as she came through the door. "King Sholto, I am sorry, but there is a matter that requires your attention."

"Speak plainly, Bebe. What matter?"

All three of her eyes flicked a look at Mistral and Doyle, maybe just a little more to Doyle, before she asked, "Are you certain you wish court matters to be spoken of before strangers?" She went to her knees immediately, "I do not mean Queen Meredith, but the two sidhe."

I thought it was an interesting distinction that they were sidhe but Sholto and I were not. Was it simply that you could not be sidhe and rule the sluagh, or was it an acknowledgment that we both looked too unsidhe-like? I didn't know Bebe well enough to ask her thoughts, but it was still interesting.

Sholto sighed, then turned to us. "I'm sorry, but it is true that you are not sluagh. I'll be right back, hopefully." He didn't look happy leaving us, but he went out into the hallway with the servant.

"Interesting that they do not consider their king to be sidhe," Mistral said.

"Or me," I said.

Doyle came to me, running his hands down the arms of my new garment. "You do look lovely in the coat. It becomes you."

"Yes," Mistral said. "I do not mean to ignore your beauty, Princess. Forgive me." He actually went down on one knee as I'd seen the guards do for Queen Andais when they feared that they'd displeased her.

"Get up," I said, "and never do that again."

He looked puzzled, but he stood, though the uncertainty on his face was almost painful. "I upset you. I am sorry."

"It was the dropping to the ground like you would for the queen," Doyle said.

I nodded. "I've had to do my own groveling on the floor all my life. I don't want to see it in my kings, or the fathers of my children. You can apologize, Mistral, but never drop to the ground as if you are afraid of what I will do. That is not my way."

He looked at Doyle, who gave one nod. Mistral came to stand by us. He smiled a little uncertainly at me. "It may take me a little while to understand this new way of doing things, but I am eager to learn things that keep me off my knees."

I had to smile at that. "Oh, I don't know. I like a man on his knees if it's for a good cause."

Mistral frowned.

Doyle explained. "She means that if you are giving her pleasure, you can kneel to reach."

Mistral actually blushed, something I had never seen him do before. He looked away, but answered, "I would be happy to do that again with you, Princess."

"Meredith, Mistral. My name is Meredith, or even Merry, when we are alone."

The door opened with no knock, and I knew by that that it would be Sholto. He came in, his face very obviously not happy.

"What has happened?" Doyle asked.

"Your mother has sent a message. She demands proof that you are well, or the Seelie are prepared to do more than just camp outside the sluagh's mound."

"Are they truly willing to attack you?" I asked.

"Whether they would do it, I cannot say, but that they threaten it is true enough."

"Do they not understand what they risk?" Doyle asked.

"I think they see no humans to tattle on them, and we have all made small battles one against the other where the humans have not seen them. We do not bear tales to the humans."

"Taranis changed that when he went to the human authorities and accused my men of rape."

"That was . . . odd," Sholto said.

"And if we can get to the human authorities,

we will return the favor, but with a true crime," I said, and even to me I sounded grim.

Doyle hugged me, and I slid my arms around the warm bareness of him.

"We can speak on the court mirror to your mother." Sholto got a strange look on his face.

"What is it?" Mistral asked.

"I just realized that this will be the first time I've spoken to my mother-in-law."

Doyle startled in my arms. "I have thought of Besaba as an enemy for so long, but you are right. She is Meredith's mother."

"No, she only gave birth to me," I said. "You have seen the death of the only woman who earned the right to be called my mother. Gran raised me with my father. My mother wants me now only because she thinks it may make her the mother of the queen of the Seelie. Before Taranis began to show interest in me, she cared nothing for me."

"She is your mother," Sholto said.

I shook my head, still wrapped in Doyle's arms. "I believe that you must earn that title. It's another by-product of being raised among the humans. I don't believe that just giving birth earns you anything."

"The Christians believe that you must honor your father and mother," Doyle said.

"True, but ask most Americans and they'll tell you you have to earn that respect."

"Do you wish to ignore Besaba's request then?" Sholto asked.

"No. She's pretending to be the aggrieved party. We must show her that there's no reason to be aggrieved." I gazed up at Doyle. "Would it be good or bad to have Doyle and Mistral at my side? Would you prefer that it be just you and me, Sholto?"

"I think a show of force is called for," he said. He looked at the other two men. "If you have no objection, I think Meredith and myself in front as king and queen with you at our sides, and some of my other guards behind us. Let us remind them what they would fight."

That seemed to meet with everyone's approval. Sholto said, smiling, "I think I have some clothes that will fit you both, though Mistral's a little bigger through the shoulders. Maybe an open jacket with no shirt, a very barbarian king."

"I will wear what you like," Mistral said. "I appreciate you letting us stay at Meredith's side in this moment."

"Those of the Seelie who are not afraid of the sluagh will fear the Queen's Darkness and Mistral, Lord of Storms."

"It is long since I have had the power to do what my name says."

"You hold the spear that once belonged to the Thunderer. Taranis's mark of power is in your hands, Storm Lord."

"I think," Doyle said, "that that is information best not shared with the Seelie. They are already here for the chalice. If Taranis knew that one of his objects of power had chosen another hand to guide it. . . ." Doyle shook his head and put his hands out, as if grasping for a word.

I finished the thought for him. "Taranis would go apeshit."

"Apeshit?" Doyle made it a question, then nodded. "I was going to say that he would kill us all, but yes, that term will do."

CHAPTER TWENTY-FOUR

DOYLE AND MISTRAL FIT NICELY IN SHOLTO'S clothes, but then except for Rhys and myself, all the sidhe I knew were around six feet tall. The men were all broad of shoulder, narrow of waist, and well built. The guards were muscled and hardened from weapons practice or actual battle. But Sholto was right about Mistral's shoulders. They were just a touch broader than either his, or Doyle's. Not by much, but it was enough that the shirts didn't fit, straining so badly that they didn't look right. Better to wear less clothing and look good than to wear more and look bad. We were about to deal with the Seelie Court, and they were all about appearances. If it looked good, it **was** good. So dysfunctional a family, that.

Mirabella, the court seamstress, walked around Mistral tugging at the coat she'd found for those broad shoulders. She pulled one side with a pale, slender hand, then smoothed a fold in the rich blue cloth with her black-and-white tentacle.

Her right arm was the tentacle of a nightflyer. She seemed perfectly human, except for that bit of extra. The tentacle was very dexterous, as I knew the nightflyers could be. She used both limbs without thought. It was the effortlessness of years of having both. Was she part nightflyer? The child of some attack, or even a willing roll in the hay? I wanted to ask, but it would have been rude.

Mistral looked amazing in the coat. The rich blue color seemed to make his eyes blue too, like a summer sky. The wide collar was lined with gray fur so that his own cloud-gray hair seemed to meld with it, and it was hard to see where fur ended and hair began.

Mirabella had him turn so she could see the long coat billow around him. There was more gray fur in a wide line down the back of the coat, so that the free spill of his ankle-length hair continued that mingling illusion—not an illusion of magic, but of skill and choice of clothing.

"It looks like it was made for him," Doyle said dryly.

The seamstress smoothed her brown hair in its neat bun with the tentacle, then looked at him with the full force of her olive-green eyes with their hint of brown and gray, and even almost gold around the irises. They were the closest a human could get to having multiple-colored eyes like a sidhe. She was tall and lovely, and moved with that stiff, strangely graceful, perfect posture that said that she was wearing a corset under her dress. The dress looked very 1800s, and was a deep, almost blackish green, which brought out the green in her eyes. The sleeves did not match the historical accuracy of the everyday dress. They were puffed at the top, and belled wide at the bottom so that they spilled back when she raised her limbs, and you got glimpses of the tentacle which went at least to where her elbow might have been.

Sholto said, "Mirabella, did you make this for Mistral?"

She didn't look at her king, but continued to fuss with the coat, which was almost more of a robe.

"I told you of my dream, Your Highness."

"Mirabella." He said her name with more force to it.

She turned, and gave him a nervous flick of eyes, then turned Mistral toward us, as if for inspection. He'd taken all her fussing without complaint. Queen Andais liked dressing up her guards for dinners, dances, or her own amusement. Mistral was used to being treated as if his opinion did not matter when it came to dressing. Mirabella had been utterly professional compared to Andais. Not a single grope.

Mistral was wearing a pair of black trousers, tucked into knee-high boots. Mirabella had tied a wide blue sash at his waist, and the color looked good against the moonlight-white of his bare stomach. The deep, deep blue of the coat framed his chest, all that pale muscled flesh. When Sholto had said that Mistral would be a very barbarian king, he'd been right.

"That coat was never made for my shoulders, Mirabella," Sholto said, giving her a look.

She shrugged her shoulders, and something about the movement made me certain that there was a human shoulder under the sleeve, or something harder, and with more bone than the tentacle.

She finally looked at her king. There was anger, no rage in those fine eyes. She dropped to her knees in a spill of heavy skirts and a glimpse of black petticoats. "Forgive me, My King, but hubris has gotten the better of me. If the Seelie are to see my work after so many years on other than you, King Sholto, then I want them to be impressed. I want them to see what clothes they might have had from my two good hands if Taranis hadn't taken one of them."

That answered one question. Once upon a time, Mirabella had had two good hands.

"You must have stayed up all night to sew this coat, and the outfit for Doyle."

"Don't you remember, Your Highness? I made the red for you, but the queen did not care for it at court, so you never wore it again."

Sholto frowned, then smiled and shook his head. "She thought it was too much color in her court. She called it too Seelie. I had forgotten."

Doyle was dressed in red, a beautiful clear

crimson that looked spectacular against the darkness of his skin. The contrast was almost painfully beautiful. The coat looked like a modern business suit jacket, except for the color and the fit. The fit flattered his broad shoulders and narrow waist—an athletic cut, they called it in the stores. There were pants to match, which she'd had to make small darts in so that they fit more closely at the waist, but the crimson cloth fit like a glove through the hips and thighs and spilled a little wide, so that the hem fell nicely over a pair of shiny black loafers.

She'd chosen a silk shirt in an icy gray, which complemented both the red of the suit and Doyle's skin. She'd even had the nightflyer who had accompanied her do his hair in a long braid. The nightflyer had used her tentacles to weave red ribbons through all that black hair so that it trailed to his ankles with the line of red tracing back and forth.

"And Una helped me sew the coat. She has become quite skilled, and I envy her all those limbs to sew with." She gestured at the nightflyer who had braided Doyle's hair.

The nightflyer who had been standing so quietly against the wall, gave a bow. "You are too kind, mistress."

"I give credit where credit is due, Una."

Una actually blushed a little across the paleness of her underbelly.

"I'm impressed that you made boots for Mistral in such quick order," I said.

Mirabella looked at me, a little startled. "The

sizes are almost the same. How did you know that they were new just by looking?"

"I've had to take the guards in Los Angeles shoe shopping. I've gotten pretty good at judging sizes."

She smiled, almost shyly. "You have a good eye."

I started to say thank you, but wasn't sure how long Mirabella had been inside faerie. "Thank you" can be an insult to some of the older denizens.

Instead I said, "I do my best, and the coat you made for me is perfect."

She smiled, truly pleased.

"You didn't make the boots," Sholto said.

She shook her head. "I made a bargain."

"The leprechaun," he said, and he said it as if there was only one of them, which wasn't true. There weren't many in the New World, but we had a few.

She nodded.

"Are you really going to date him?" Sholto asked.

She actually blushed. "He enjoys his work as I enjoy mine."

"You like him," I said.

She gave me that nervous eye flick again. "I think I do."

"You know that there are no rules among the sluagh for who you sleep with," Sholto said, "but the leprechaun has been pressing you for a hundred years, Mirabella. I thought you found him unpleasant."

"I did, but. . . ." she spread her hand and tentacle wide. "I just don't seem to find him unpleasant anymore. We talk of clothes, and he has a television in his home. He brings me fashion magazines and we discuss them."

"He's found the way to your heart," Doyle said.

She gave a little giggle and a smile. That alone let me know that the leprechaun had gotten some of his bargain already. "I suppose he has."

"Then you have my blessing. You know that," Sholto said. He was smiling.

Then her face went serious and grim. "Tully has courted me for a hundred years. He has been gentle, and he's never gotten above himself with me, unlike some I could name."

"Taranis," I said. I said the name without feeling anything. Parts of me were still a little numb, and that was probably a good thing.

She glared at me, then her face softened. "If I am not too presumptuous, Queen Meredith, I heard what he did to you, and I am most heartily sorry. He should have been stopped years ago."

"I take it he tried his version of courting with you."

"Courting." She almost spat the word. "No, in the midst of a fitting he tried to take me by force. I had been invited into faerie with promises of safety and honor. He had to drop all the illusions on his person for fittings, so his magic that made all the women see him as beautiful did not work on me. I knew that he was getting a little soft around the middle. I knew all the flaws in his illusions. I had truth on my side, and he could not seduce me with magic."

"You were probably also holding pins and needles made of cold steel," Doyle said.

She looked at him, then nodded. "You are correct. The very tools of my trade kept me from falling into his trap. In his rage, he cut off my right arm." She held up the tentacled limb. It moved gracefully in the air, like some underwater creature found on land. "Then he had me driven out of his sithen, because a one-armed seamstress was useless to him."

"How long had you been in faerie by then?" Doyle asked.

"Fifty years, I think."

"To drive you outside the sithen means that all those years would have come upon you all at once," Mistral said.

She nodded. "Once I had touched ground, yes. But not all in his court agreed with what he had done to me. Some of the court women carried me to the Unseelie Court. They petitioned the queen for me, and she said almost the same thing Taranis had said: 'What use is a one-armed seamstress to me?' " Tears glistened in her eyes, unshed.

Sholto went to her in the beautiful black and silver tunic, and pants, and shiny boots that she had made, or had had made for him. He raised her from her knees, with one hand on her hand and one on the end of her tentacle.

"I remember that night," he said.

She looked up at him. "So do I, My King. I remember what you said. 'She is welcome among the sluagh. We will tend her.' You never asked what I was good for, or if you had a use for me. The court ladies made you promise that you would not abuse me, for they were sore afraid of the sluagh."

Sholto smiled. "I want the Seelie afraid of us; it is our shield."

She nodded. "You took me in with only one good arm, not knowing that Henry could find a way to make me useful again. I have never asked, My King. What would you have done with me if I had had no skill to give you?"

"We would have found you some task that you could do with the one hand you had, Mirabella. We are the sluagh. There are those among us with only one limb, and those with hundreds. We are an adaptable lot."

She nodded, and turned away so he couldn't see that the tears had finally decided to fall down her face. "You are the kindest of rulers, King Sholto."

"Don't tell anyone outside this court that," he said with a laugh.

"It will be our secret, My King."

I said, "Did you say that Dr. Henry gave you your new limb?"

"He did," she said.

"How?"

"One of the nightflyers was kind enough to let

him take a limb from her. You know they can grow back their tentacles?"

"Yes," I said.

"Well, Henry had been working on the . . . concept that he might be able to put a limb from a nightflyer, who could replace it, onto one of the sluagh, who could not. He had not done it successfully, but he offered to try on me, if I was willing." She gave a small gesture with both her limbs. "I was willing."

"Humans have to get donors who are genetically compatible for any kind of organ donation. They're only just beginning to try with hands and things, but most of the time the bodies reject the new limb. How did Henry get past the rejection problem?"

"I do not understand everything you just said, My Queen, but Henry would be better able to answer your questions. If you want to know how I sew his jackets to flatter his body, I can tell you, but how he made the wonder of this new limb, I do not completely understand even now. I have had it for many, many years, and I marvel at it still."

She began to gather up her basket and sewing. Una helped her. When they were done, they turned back to survey us. "You all look suitable, as I'd hoped, if I do say so myself."

"Shall we find a reason to mention who did our clothes?" Doyle asked.

She gave him that flick of eyes again. "He knows I am here, Lord Doyle. Taranis might not have valued me, but there were those at his court who mourned my swift fingers and my needlework. There are still a few women of the court who come to me with commissions from time to time. Those who carried me on a cloak from sithen to sithen, trying to save me that dark night, have come to pay me for my work. King Sholto graciously allows it."

I looked at Sholto, and he looked a little embarrassed. "One king cannot keep a designer of your skills busy. The sluagh are not a court where clothes matter so terribly much."

She laughed. "The fact that most of your court goes nude is a disappointment to me." She looked at me, and the others. "Though I think that may be changing." She dropped a curtsey, Una bowed, and out they went.

"Taranis needs killing," Mistral said.

"Agreed," Doyle said.

"We will not start a war over what happened to me, or what he did to Mirabella."

"It's a history of such things, Meredith," Doyle said.

"Ah," Mistral said. "He was once a ladies' man, but when that failed him he was never above force."

"Was he always so cruel—taking her arm, I mean?"

"No, not always," Doyle said.

I kept hearing stories that Taranis had once been a hard-drinking, hard-loving, manly man, but

I'd never seen it. There wasn't enough reality left to my uncle for that now. Once he would have trusted his powers of seduction to get me into his bed. In fact, before he used magic to rape me, I would have said that he would never have believed that I would refuse him. His self-confidence was legendary. What had I done to make him think that his illusions could not win me?

"Why did Taranis use a spell to rape me, rather than trust his own attractiveness? I mean, his ego is huge. Why would he not believe that I would say yes eventually?"

"Maybe he didn't feel that there was time," Sholto said.

"He meant to keep me, Sholto. He **should have** felt that there was time enough."

"What are you asking, Meredith?" Doyle asked.

"I just find it curious that he used a spell so much different than his usual ones on me. He's nearly rolled over me with his attractive illusions all the way to Los Angeles in a mirror call. But this time he raped me almost as any man might. It doesn't seem like him."

"You've told us that you saw through his illusion when he first found you in faerie," Doyle said.

"Yes, he looked like Amatheon but I touched him and he didn't feel like him. Amatheon is clean-shaven, and I felt beard."

"But you shouldn't have felt it," Mistral said. "Taranis is the King of Light and Illusion. It means that his glamour stands up to almost anything. He should have been able to bed you without you ever knowing that he was not who he pretended to be."

"I had not thought," Doyle said.

"Thought what?" I asked.

"That his illusion was not as good as it should have been."

We all thought about that. "His magic is fading," Sholto said at last.

"And he knows it," I said.

"That would make the old ego-hound completely desperate," Mistral said.

"And completely dangerous," Sholto said.

We could only agree with him, unfortunately. We did the last-minute preparations for the mirror call with my mother and the other Seelie outside our gates.

CHAPTER TWENTY-FIVE

BESABA WAS TALL, SLENDER, AND VERY sidhe in her body build. But her hair was only a thick, wavy brown, bound on her head in a complicated hairdo that left her thin face too bare for my taste. She had her mother's hair, and brown eyes, very human eyes. It had only been in the last few months that I'd realized one of the reasons she had always hated me. I might be short, and too curvy, but I couldn't have passed for human with my hair, eyes, and skin. She could have.

She was wearing a dress of deep orange, decorated with gold embroidery. It was a dress to please Taranis, who was very fond of fire colors.

She was in a tent that they had set up on the ground outside. She looked to be alone, but I knew better. Taranis's allies would never have trusted her to make the call without watchers to "guide" her.

I was sitting in Sholto's official calling room, which meant it was richly appointed, and had a throne for a chair. It wasn't "the" throne of the sluagh court. That was made of bone and ancient wood. This one was a gold and purple throne, probably found in some human court long, long ago. But it served its purpose. It looked impressive, though not as impressive as the men around me, or the writhing mass of nightflyers who clung to the wall behind us like a living tapestry from some nightmare you'd rather forget.

Sholto sat on the throne, as befitted the king. I sat on his lap, which lacked a certain dignity, but we thought it might get the point across that I was having a good time. Of course, when someone doesn't want to understand, nothing you can do will make them see the truth. My mother had always been excellent at seeing only what she wished to see.

Doyle was on one side of the throne, Mistral on the other. If we hadn't had the nightflyers behind us, we'd have looked very sidhe. But we wanted whoever was with my mother, just out of sight of the mirror, to understand that they would not be fighting only the four of us, if they pressed. They needed to understand that above all else.

I had settled myself comfortably on Sholto's lap. His arm curved around my waist, putting his hand on my thigh in a very familiar way. He hadn't actually earned such a familiar gesture. Of the three men with me, he had been with me the least, but we were putting on a show, and one point of that show was to prove that I was their lover. When trying to prove something like that, a little hand on the thigh can say volumes.

"I do not need rescuing, Mother, as you well know."

"How can you say that? You are Seelie sidhe, and they have taken you from us."

"They have taken nothing that the Seelie valued. If you speak of the chalice, then all who can hear my voice know that chalice goes where the Goddess wills it, and she has willed it to me."

"It is a sign of great favor among the Seelie, Meredith. You must come home and bring the chalice, and you will be queen."

"Taranis's queen, you mean?" I asked.

She smiled happily. "Of course."

"He raped me, Mother." Doyle moved a little closer to me, though he was quite close to begin with. I reached out to him without thinking so that he held my hand, even while I sat in Sholto's lap.

"How can you say such things? You bear his twins."

"They are not his children. I am with the fathers of my twins."

Mistral moved nearer the chair. He did not reach out for me, because I was out of hands, one in Doyle's hand, and one on Sholto's arm. He simply moved closer, to help me emphasize my point, I think.

"Lies. Unseelie lies."

"I am not queen of the Unseelie yet, Mother. I am queen of the sluagh."

She settled the stiff, rich sleeves of her gown, and harrumphed at me. "Again, false-hoods," she said.

I had a moment when I wished I could conjure the crowns of faerie to me, but such magic came and went when it would. Though, frankly, seeing Sholto and me in the crowns might just make her more convinced that we were Seelie. It was all flowers and herbs, after all.

"Call it what you will, but I am content in the company I keep. Can you say as much?"

"I love my court and my king," she said, and I knew she meant it.

"Even after some of that court conspired to kill your mother, my grandmother, just days ago?"

Her face clouded for a moment, then she stood straight again and faced me. "It was not Cair who slew my mother. I am told that it was one of your guards who struck the blow."

"To save my life, yes."

She looked shocked then, and I think it was real. "Our mother would never have harmed you. She loved you."

"She did, and I her, but Cair's magic turned her against me, and my people. It was an evil spell, Mother, and the fact that she used her own grand-mother to carry it was worse."

"You lie."

"I led the wild hunt to get my revenge. If it had not been the absolute truth, the hunt would either have not answered my call, or when it arrived the hounds of the hunt would have torn me limb from limb. They did not. They helped me hunt Cair down. They helped me kill her, and save the fathers of my children, who were still being attacked."

She shook her head, but looked a little less sure of herself. A bit, but I knew her. Her certainty would return. It always did. She would get a glimpse of how wrong she was, or how evil her allies were, then she'd shake off that flitting insight and embrace her ignorance like a well-worn cloak.

I leaned forward in Sholto's lap, my hand finding his hand so that I held both his and Doyle's hands. I leaned toward the mirror on the wall and spoke quickly, trying to get through this small chink in my mother's willful ignorance.

"Mother, the wild hunt does not do the bidding of liars or traitors. Taranis did rape me, but he was too late. I am to have twins, and the Goddess has shown me who the fathers are."

"You have two babies, but three men. Who is to be left out?" She was retreating from the harshest truths to concentrate on smaller things. Not a question about the rape, or the traitors whom the wild hunt had helped us destroy, but the math of fathers and babies.

"The history of the sidhe is full of goddesses who had children by more than just one man, Mother. Clothra is the one most oft named, but there have been others. Apparently, I will need many kings, not just one."

"You have been bespelled, Meredith. All know that the King of the sluagh is a great one for glamour." She was back to her certainties. Sometimes I wondered why I tried with her. Oh, she was my mother. I suppose we never quite give up on parents. Maybe they feel the same way about us.

"Faerie itself has made us a couple, Mother." I unbuttoned my tight-fitting cuff, and rolled it back as much as the coat would allow, which was not much. Sholto's sleeve was looser, so that more of his rose and thorn tattoo showed, but enough showed to prove that the tattoos were a pair.

She shook her head. "You can get a tattoo at any human shop."

I laughed then. I couldn't help it.

She looked startled. "There is nothing funny here, Meredith."

"No, Mother, there is not." But my face was alight with humor. "But it is either laugh or start screaming at you, and I don't think that would be helpful."

I pushed my sleeve back down and closed the bone button once more. Sholto followed my lead. I stood and walked out of sight of the mirror, just long enough to fetch something from the table near the far wall.

Mistral said, "Do you think that wise?"

I looked at the table that held all the ancient weapons that had come to us. Was it a good idea? I wasn't entirely certain, but I was tired. I was tired of people trying to kill us. I was tired of people assuming that if they could strip me of my men I would be a pawn to be used as they saw fit. I'd had enough.

I hesitated with my hand over the sword Abendul. I prayed. "Goddess, do I show them what I am? Do I make them afraid of me?" I waited for some sign, and thought at first that she would not answer me, then a faint perfume of roses came. I felt the tattoo on my arm flare to life, and the moth on my stomach flutter. The weight of the rose and mistletoe crown wove itself to life on my head.

I wrapped my hand around the hilt of the sword. I was afraid of it. Afraid of what it could do in my hands. The hand of flesh was a terrible power. With this sword I could use that power from a distance, and no one could take it from my hand without risking the very horror that they were trying to avoid.

I walked back to the mirror with the sword held in one hand like you would hold a flag. I stood in front of Sholto, and held the sword before me.

"Do you know this sword, Mother? Does anyone within sight of this mirror know this sword?"

She frowned, and I was willing to bet that she wouldn't know it. Mother never cared for Unseelie power. But someone in the tent would know it, of that I was almost certain.

It was Lord Hugh who walked into view. He actually gave a little bow before he peered more closely at the mirror. He paled. That was answer enough; he knew it.

He spoke, hoarsely. "Aben-dul. So the sluagh stole that away as well." But he didn't believe it.

I reached my free hand back to Sholto. He took my hand and came to stand beside me. The moment his tattooed arm touched mine, the magic flexed, as if the air itself took a breath. The herb crown wove itself to life while the Seelie watched. The herb ring on his finger bloomed white, and his crown bloomed into a haze of pastel flowers. We stood crowned by faerie itself before them.

"This is King Sholto of the sluagh, crowned by faerie itself to rule. I am Queen Meredith of the sluagh, and I bear his child, his heir."

I let the hand holding Aben-dul drop to my side. "Hear me, Mother Besaba, and all the Seelie listening to my voice. The old magic is returning. The Goddess moves among us once more. You can either move with her power, or be left out of it. It is your choice. But it is truth that is needed, no more lies, no more illusions. Think well upon that before you decide to try to take me back by force."

"Are you threatening me?" she asked, and it was so like her to concentrate on the smaller issue. Though I suppose for her it might have been the large issue.

"I am saying that it would be unwise to force me to use all the power I have been given by the Goddess to defend myself. And I will use every ounce of power I have to keep from being forced back to Taranis. I will not be his victim again. I will not be raped again, not even by the King of the Seelie."

Lord Hugh had stepped back a little from the mirror. "We hear your words, Princess Meredith."

"Queen Meredith," I said.

He gave a little bow of his head. "Queen Meredith."

"Then disband this ill-conceived and un-needed rescue attempt. Go back to your faerie mound and your deluded king, and leave us in peace."

"His orders were very specific, Queen Meredith. We are to come back with you and the chalice, or not return at all."

"He has exiled you, unless you succeed?" I asked.

"Not in those words, but we are left few choices."

"You must kidnap me for him, or be kicked out," I said.

Lord Hugh spread his hands wide. "Blunter than I would have put it, but not inaccurate, unfortunately, for all concerned."

There was movement in the tent wall, and Lord Hugh said, "Please, forgive me, Queen Meredith, but I have a message." He bowed again and left me looking at my mother.

She said, "You look lovely in a crown, Meredith, just as I always knew you would." She even looked pleased, as if what she said were true.

I could have said a lot of things in that moment. Like "If you thought I would ever rule, why did you let Taranis nearly beat me to death as a child?" Or, "If you thought I would ever be queen, why did you give me away, and never wish to see me?" What I said out loud was "I knew you would like the crown, Mother."

Lord Hugh came back into sight. He bowed lower. "I am told that human police and soldiers are coming. You called the humans for help."

"I did."

"Now if we attack, the Seelie Court could be banished from this new land, which would leave the Unseelie and the sluagh in place, and in control of the last remnants of faerie."

I smiled sweetly at him.

"You would win all that Queen Andais has sought to win for centuries without the Unseelie, or the sluagh, striking a blow."

"The point is to not strike the blow," I said.

He gave the lowest bow yet, a real one, causing him to partially vanish from the view of the mirror. When he stood up, he had a look of naked admiration on his face. "It seems as if the Goddess and faerie have not chosen ill in their new queen. You have won. We will retreat, and you have given us a reason that even King Taranis will understand. He would never risk our entire court being cast from these shores."

"I am very glad that your king will take you back, and understand that to do anything but retreat would be extremely unfortunate," I said.

He bowed again. "I thank you for finding a

way out of our dilemma, Queen Meredith. I had not heard that you played politics well."

"I have my moments," I said.

He smiled, bowed once more, and said, "We will leave you to be rescued by the humans then."

"We aren't going to leave her with the sluagh," my mother said, as if horrified at her daughter's fate.

"Give it a rest, Mother," I said, and blanked the mirror.

She was still arguing with Lord Hugh, as if she believed what Taranis had told her. It was clear that Lord Hugh did not. But then if I went back as Taranis's queen, Besada wouldn't be the mother of the new queen of the Seelie. She had more to gain politically, if Taranis was telling the truth.

Sholto kissed my hand, smiling. "That was very well done, My Queen."

I grinned at him. "It helps when faerie itself crowns you, and major relics keep popping up."

"No, Meredith," Doyle said, "that was well played. Your father would have been very proud."

"Indeed," Mistral said.

And in that moment, holding a weapon that only myself and my father could have safely wielded, covered in faerie's blessing, and knowing that my father would have been proud of me meant more than all the rest. I guess in the end you never outgrow wanting to please your parents. Since I'd never please my mother, my father was all I had left. He always had been. He and Gran.

My parents were dead now, both of them. The woman in the mirror was just the person whose body spit me out. It takes much more than that to be a mother. I prayed that I would be a good mother, and for help to keep all of us safe. There was a shower of white rose petals from nowhere, coming down like perfumed snow. I guess that was answer enough. The Goddess was with me. As help went, it didn't get much better than that. As the Christians said, if God is with me, who can be against me? The answer, unfortunately, was almost everyone.

CHAPTER TWENTY-SIX

WE BUCKLED ON OUR NEW WEAPONS. I was very serious about putting the lock loops on my sword. As long as it was sheathed, someone could bump it without harm. If it was unsheathed, even a little, there was a chance that it would turn some poor soldier's arm inside out.

Doyle had put the horn of madness across his body on its leather strap.

"Shouldn't you put that in a sack or something?" Sholto asked.

"As long as I wear the horn across my body, it will not react to anyone bumping against it. It is only out of my hands that it becomes a danger."

"How do I carry the spear so that the Seelie do not see what it is?" Mistral asked.

"I don't think even Taranis will attack you for the spear today, in front of the humans," I said.

"But there will be other days," Mistral said. "He came to the Western Lands to find you,

Meredith. I think for one of his items of power he might travel again." He hefted the spear as he talked, as if judging the weight of it. It was a slender weapon, longer than Sholto's spear of bone that I'd used to slay Cair. I realized that Mistral's spear was almost too slender to stab or thrust with.

"Is it meant to be an actual spear, or is it like some huge lightning rod?"

Mistral gazed up at the shining spear, then smiled down at me. "You are correct. It is not meant to hack at men's bodies. It is more a great magic wand, or staff. With this in my hand, and a little practice, I could call lightning from a clear sky miles away to strike down an enemy."

"You mean you could use it as a tool of assassination?"

He seemed to think about it, then nodded.

"Let go of that thought," Sholto said.

Mistral and I looked at him. "What thought?" I asked.

He smiled and shook his head. "Don't be coy, Meredith. I see your faces. You're thinking you could use the lightning to rid us of a few enemies and no one would know. But it is too late for secrecy."

"Why?" I asked, then realized. "Oh, the entire sluagh saw."

"And some of them are as old as the oldest of the sidhe. They will have seen the spear in the hand of a king before, and they will know what it can do. My people are loyal, and would not betray us on purpose, I don't believe, but they will talk. The skeletal brides, the relics of power returning; it is all too good a story not to share it."

I sighed. "Well, that's disappointing."

Doyle came to me. "We need to go outside and welcome our human rescuers, but Merry, are you truly thinking of assassination as a cure for our problems?" There was no judgment on his face, just that patient waiting. That look that said that he simply wanted to know.

"Let us just say that I am no longer ruling out any solution to our problems," I said.

He cupped my chin in his fingers, and looked deeply into my eyes. "You mean that. What is it that has made you suddenly so much harder?" Then his fingers dropped away, and his face looked uncertain. "I am a fool. You watched your grandmother die."

I grabbed his arm, made him look at me. "I also had to watch you carried out by doctors, and thought you might die again. Taranis and the rest seemed very determined that you had to die first."

"They fear him the most," Sholto said.

"They tried to kill you too," Doyle said, looking at the other man.

Sholto nodded. "But it is not me personally they fear, it is the sluagh, and my command of them."

"Why did I get singled out then?" Mistral asked. "I have no army to command. I have never been the queen's right or left hand. Why did they go to such lengths to kill me as well?"

"There are those who are old enough to remember you in battle, my friend," Doyle said.

Mistral looked down, his hair falling around his face like gray clouds covering the sky. "That was very long ago."

"But much of the old power is returning. Perhaps the oldest among both courts feared what you would do if you were your old self again," Doyle said.

I had a thought. "Mistral is also the only storm deity we have in the Unseelie Court. The others either stayed in Europe or are Seelie."

"That is true," Doyle said, "but that is not your point."

"My point is," I said, "what if Taranis feared exactly what has happened? He knew that if his spear came back to a Seelie Storm Lord, he could command and they would give it over. But he cannot command Mistral. He cannot demand anything from the Unseelie."

"Do you truly think that he believed this would return?" Mistral asked, holding the spear ceilingward.

I shrugged. "I don't know, but it was a thought."

"I think it is simpler than that," Doyle said.

"What then?" I asked.

"Magic powers, hands of power, follow bloodlines. You are proof of that with your father's hand of flesh, and a hand of blood that is similar to your cousin Cel's."

"His is the hand of old blood, so he can open old wounds but not make fresh ones," I said.

"No, yours is a more complete power, but dealing with blood and body magic runs in your father's bloodline. The children you carry may inherit the ability to deal with storms and weather. If they do, and Mistral is alive, then it is clear who gave them that blood trait. But if Mistral were dead long before the babes were born, by the time they were old enough to exhibit such power, Taranis could make another plea that they were indeed his."

I shook my head. "But he is my uncle already. His brother is my grandfather, so I could carry the gene for storm magic in me already."

Doyle nodded. "True, but I think the king grows desperate. He has convinced half his court that the twins could be his, including your mother. Her belief in it, and her lack of belief that he . . . took you, will go far to convince doubters. They will think 'her mother would not believe lies.' "

"Do they not know her by now?" I asked.

"The Seelie, like most humans, do not want to believe such evil of a mother to her daughter."

"But the Unseelie know better," Mistral said.

Doyle and Sholto both nodded.

I sighed again. "My cousin actually thought that they could convince Rhys to join the Seelie Court again, and that Galen would be no threat. It's why they didn't attack the two of them."

"Then why did Taranis include Rhys and Galen in the false rape charges?"

"And Abeloec too," I said. That made me wonder. "Is Abe in danger too?"

"If Rhys comes back into his full power, he will be incredibly dangerous," Mistral said. "Why didn't they try to kill him? Why think they could persuade him to join them?"

"I don't know. I'm repeating what Cair said."

"Did she lie?" Doyle asked.

That hadn't occurred to me. "I think she was too afraid to lie, but. . . ." I stared at them. "Have I been a fool? Have we all been? No, the Goddess did not warn me of danger to Rhys or Galen. She warned me the last time Galen was nearly assassinated."

"I think they are safe enough, for now," Doyle said.

"But Doyle, don't you see? There are too many different plots, too many factions in faerie right now. Some want you dead, but there are those Unseelie who want Galen dead. They are convinced he is the Greenman who will put me on the throne. I believe the Greenman in the prophecy is simply the God, the Consort."

"I agree," Doyle said.

"Taranis may have believed his rape allegations against Rhys and the others. He's crazy enough to be manipulated by his courtiers. Maybe someone else wanted those three out of the way for some other reason, and used the king to do it," Sholto said.

"We are at the center of a spiderweb of plots. Some threads we may touch and travel on, but others are sticky and will alert the spider," Doyle said.

"And then it will come and eat us," I said. "We get out of faerie tonight, and we go back to L.A., and we try to make a life. There is no way to guarantee our safety here."

The three men exchanged looks. Sholto said, "I would trust that I am safe inside the sluagh, but outside of it. . . ." He shrugged. He was wearing his own white sword; the carved bone shield was leaning against his big chair. He picked up the shield, and settled it on his arm. It covered his body from neck to mid-thigh.

"Why don't these things of power come and go like the chalice and the spear of bone and the white knife?" I asked.

"Things that come from the hands of the gods themselves, that are given in vision or dream, will come to the hand like magic, but things that are given by the guardians of the earth, or water, or air, or fire are more like mortal weapons. They can be lost, and if you do not carry them, they are not with you," Doyle said.

"Good to know the difference," I said.

The phone rang in the office. Sholto picked it up, murmured something, then handed it to me. "It's for you—Major Walters."

I took the receiver and said, "Hello, Major Walters."

"We're outside, and the siege is breaking up. Your uncle's people are packing up and going home."

"Thank you for that, Major."

"My duty," he said. "Now, if you'll just come outside. We'd like to get home."

"We'll be right out. Oh, and Major, I have two more men I need to find who will be going back to the Western Lands, I mean Los Angeles."

"Would that be Galen Greenhair and Rhys Knight?"

I hadn't heard their names from their driver's licenses in a while. "Yes, that would be them. Are they with you?"

"They are."

"I'm impressed. Even in faerie people don't anticipate my wishes quite that well."

"They found us. Mr. Knight said that when he saw all of us he figured he'd better tag along to see what trouble you and Captain Doyle had gotten into."

"Tell him the trouble just went back to the Seelie Court."

"I'll pass it along. Now, if you could just join us, and tell us how many seats we need to find in the vehicles."

"Myself and three others."

"We'll find room."

"Thank you again, Major, and we'll see you all in moments." I put the phone back in its cradle and turned to the men.

"Rhys and Galen are already with them," I said.

"Rhys would have known that there was only one person that the National Guard would come to faerie to rescue," Doyle said.

"I'd be flattered, if my life wasn't in danger so constantly."

Doyle came to me, smiling. "I will give my life to keep you safe."

I shook my head and didn't smile back. I took his hand in mine. "Silly man. I want you alive and at my side, not dead and heroic. Bear that in mind when you're making choices, all right?"

His smile had faded, and he was studying my face, as if he could read things in the back of my mind that even I didn't know. Once that look would have made me squirm, or be afraid, but not now. Now I didn't want secrets from Doyle. He could have them all, even the ones I kept from myself.

"I will do my best never to disappoint you, Merry."

It was the best I was going to get from him. He would never promise not to lay his life down to protect me, because that was exactly what he would do, if it came to it. I'd made the choice for him, in a way. I'd decided to give up all of faerie, any throne offered, to keep us all safe. I wanted the fathers of my children alive by the time they were born.

He touched my face. "You look sad. I do not want to make you sad."

I leaned my cheek against his hand, feeling the

warmth and reality of him. "It makes me nervous that all our enemies seem so determined to kill you first, my Darkness."

"He's hard to kill," Mistral said.

"I am," he said.

I patted his hand and stepped away, looking at all three of them. "You better **all** be hard to kill, because leaving faerie won't stop all of it. It will give us some breathing room, and charging Taranis with rape will make the media our friends, and cut down on the attacks, unless they want pictures of it on the news."

"Are you saying the paparazzi will be our safety?" Doyle sounded incredulous.

"The Seelie pride themselves on being the good guys. They won't want pictures of them being bad."

Doyle looked thoughtful. "An evil turned to a good."

"What are paparazzi?" Mistral asked.

All of us, including Sholto, looked at Mistral. Then I swear that an almost evil grin crossed Doyle and Sholto's faces. "If we have to make another bargain with the devil for posed pictures, Mistral, you can be with Merry," Sholto said.

"What are you talking about?" Mistral asked.

Sholto said, "I saw those pictures, Darkness. You, Rhys, and Meredith, nude by the pool doing the nasty."

"We were not having sex," I said.

"Some of the tabloids in Europe used pictures that left that to doubt," Sholto said.

"When were you in Europe?" I asked.

"I have a clip service that cuts out anything worldwide about the fey."

"That's an excellent idea," Doyle said. "I would suggest it to the queen, except. . . ." He turned to me. "I no longer serve that queen."

I had a moment to wonder if I should apologize for that. Then the look on his face made an apology unnecessary. He loved me. It was there in his face, his eyes. Doyle loved me, and you should never apologize for that.

CHAPTER TWENTY-SEVEN

MY BREATH FOGGED IN THE WINTER NIGHT as we walked across the frosted grass. Mirabella had found me a cloak made of cream-colored fur. It was a hooded cloak out of some fairy tale, all white and gold and cream, over the black leather of the coat. Sholto had had enough winter cloaks and coats to fit the men. My hands were on the arms of King Sholto and Captain Doyle, which would be the titles they would use with the soldiers. Mistral came behind us, with his spear wrapped in soft cloth to hide it from prying eyes. There would be spies watching. It was faerie; there was always someone watching. Not necessarily spies for either court, but the fey are a curious lot. Anything unusual will bring them out to hide, and cling to the leaves and trees, and watch.

The sight that met our eyes was unusual enough to bring out an audience. If the fey had been human, we'd have had a crowd of gawkers that the soldiers would have had to hold back, but our people could watch and never be seen. We weren't called the Hidden Folk for nothing.

Major Walters was there at the front of the group of men, but at his side was a man who had his own air of authority. And to either side of them were more police and more soldiers. But mostly soldiers.

Sholto leaned over and whispered, "More soldiers than we've ever seen since we came to America."

Doyle must have heard, because he whispered, "I think the Major was preparing for trouble."

"A good leader always does," I said.

"We do," he said. I felt a push of magic from him.

Mistral spoke low from behind us. "There are too many curiosity seekers to discern any ill intent."

Doyle nodded.

Sholto said, "I'm not sure what you mean."

"Cannot you sense our hidden audience?" Doyle asked.

"Obviously not," he said.

"Neither can I, though I knew they would be there," I said softly.

A voice called out, "Just give yourselves a few more hundred years of practice." Rhys walked out of the mass of soldiers and police. He was grinning at me. Someone had loaned him a uniform, so he was all in camouflage. His white waist-length curls looked out of place against the military look.

Someone had even loaned him an eye patch, in basic black.

I let go of the men on either side of me and held my arms out to him. He wrapped me in a hug, and laid a kiss on my forehead. Then he moved our faces back, just enough so he could study me.

"You look good," he said.

I gave him a look. "Was I supposed to look bad?"

He grinned again. "No, but. . . ." He shook his head. "Later."

"Where is Galen?" Doyle asked.

"He is talking to their wizard. I made her nervous."

I frowned up at him, still with my arms around his solid, muscled realness. I wanted all my men out of faerie and safe in Los Angeles tonight. "What did you do to make her nervous?"

"Answered too many questions truthfully. Some humans—even wizards, or in this case witch, though the military term is wizard—some humans are freaked at the idea that I lost my eye hundreds of years before they were born."

"Oh," I said, and hugged him again.

Major Walters came forward with the man in camouflage who seemed to be in charge. There was almost no rank to see on his uniform to my uninformed eyes, but the way the other soliders treated him made any gaudy ribbons unnecessary. He was simply in charge.

"Princess Meredith, this is Captain Page. Captain, may I introduce Princess Meredith NicEssus, daughter of Prince Essus, heir to the throne of the Unseelie Court, and from what I hear, maybe the Seelie Court, as well."

Walters gave me a look. "You've been a busy princess," he said.

I wasn't sure if he really knew about the Seelie offer, or if he was pretending to know to fish for information. Police can be tricky, sometimes because it's their job, and sometimes because it's become habit.

The Captain held out his hand, and I took it. He had a good handshake, especially for a man with a hand as big as his shaking a hand as small as mine. Some big men never get the hang of it. I was close enough now to see his name on his uniform, and to notice the two district bars on the front and neck of it.

"The Illinois National Guard is honored to escort you to safety, Princess Meredith."

"I am honored that I have such brave men and women to call for help."

Page studied my face as if wondering if I was being sarcastic. He finally frowned at me. "You don't know my people well enough to say that they're brave."

"They came to the faerie mounds thinking they might have to go up against the Seelie Court itself. There have been human armies that refused to do that, Captain Page."

"Not this one," he said.

I smiled at him, putting some effort into it. "My point exactly."

He smiled, then looked flustered.

Rhys leaned in and whispered, "Tone it down."

"What?"

"The glamour, tone it down," he said without moving his smiling lips.

"I didn't. . . ."

"Trust me," he said.

I took a deep breath and concentrated. I did my best to swallow back the glamour that Rhys said was getting away from me. I'd never had enough of this kind of glamour to worry about it before.

Captain Page shook his head, frowning hard.

"You okay?" Walters asked him.

He nodded. "I think I need more . . . preventive."

Rhys said, "They've actually got essence of four-leaf clover smeared on them."

"Did you give it to them?" I asked.

"Nope, they came up with it all on their own. Apparently, they have contingencies in place in case the fey get nasty."

"We would never presume," Page began.

Doyle interrupted. "It's all right, Captain. We are pleased that you have protection. We will not purposefully bespell any of you, but there are others among the fey who are not so scrupulous."

The humans looked around them nervously, though Page and Walters kept looking at us.

"I do not mean an overt attack," Doyle said. "I just mean our people's sense of . . . humor."

"Humor," Walters said. "What does that mean?"

"It means that the fey enjoy poking at any-thing new. This many of our good men and women of the military would be almost irresistible to a certain number of our populace."

"What he means," Rhys said, "is that we have a lot of gawkers, but they're fey so you won't see them. But we know they're there. They might have a hard time resisting luring some of your sol-diers off the beaten track, just to see if they could do it."

"Your people came as close to war on Ameri-can soil as they've ever come tonight. I would think you all risking getting kicked out might make them more serious."

I shook my head. "The sidhe, perhaps, but there are a lot more people here than the sidhe. Be-sides, Captain, it was the Seelie who were threaten-ing to make war, not the sluagh, not the Unseelie. The only court that was in danger of breaking the treaty was the Seelie."

"Yeah, and the last time we all had a little bat-tle, it wasn't a war because they were monsters of faerie, and not any of the other courts," Walters said, but his voice was a little dry.

I shivered. Strangely, I wasn't really chilled from the cold. Apparently, my growing power, or perhaps my men's, was keeping me warm. But Wal-ters didn't know that, and if I acted cold, we might speed things up, and get us to a plane and the hell out of here.

Captain Page said, "Let's get the princess inside where it's warmer."

Walters nodded and said, "Fine." But he looked at me, suspicion plain on his face. What had I done to earn that look? Oh, wait, kept more secrets from him than I'd shared, and endangered his men the last time. I hadn't meant the endangering part, but I **had** kept secrets from him. I was hiding a lot, and still asking them all to risk themselves for me and my men. Was that fair? No, not in the least. But if it would get us out safely, I'd endanger them all.

I admitted that to myself, but I didn't like myself very much for it.

CHAPTER TWENTY-EIGHT

RHYS CURLED MY ARM THROUGH HIS, and leaned in to talk to me as we walked. Doyle had my other arm, so he could hear. Though, frankly, with the superior hearing of the sidhe, Mistral and Sholto could probably hear too. The point was that the soldiers we walked through did not hear.

I'd expected Sholto to fight to keep my arm, but he had graciously and uncomplainingly let Rhys take his place. Then he'd dropped back like a good bodyguard beside Mistral. Sholto was most agreeable for a king.

Most of the soldiers gave us eye flicks and tried not to stare, but some didn't bother being subtle. They stared as we walked past. Most of us looked like something out of a movie. Doyle's more modern suit was hidden under a gray cloak that looked like something out of a Dickens novel. Mistral had simply fastened the neck of his blue and fur cloak so that one got glimpses of his bare chest as he moved. Sholto had chosen a white coat that looked like a cross between a trench coat and an officer's coat from World War II. It hid the very unmodern clothes, so that he, of all of us, could have walked out into a crowd and been the least noticeable.

I realized that Sholto usually dressed to blend in, wherever he was. He dressed appropriately, if he could. I guess when you spend your life with your body so out of the ordinary, you don't want clothes to set you apart.

"Why are you wearing a uniform?" I asked.

Rhys asked, "Don't you remember what duty you gave me?" He looked far too serious.

"You had Gran's blood on your clothes," I said. He nodded.

Doyle leaned across and asked, "But why did you not get clothes from the Unseelie Court, or your own house?"

Rhys was one of the few sidhe who had his own house away from faerie. He'd said that the magic interfered with television reception, and he liked his movies. Frankly, I think it was to get some privacy. Though he did love movies.

"How much time do you think has passed?" he asked.

"The sluagh said we were in the enchanted sleep for days," I said.

"Maybe inside the sluagh's mound, but out here, and at the other courts, it's only been hours."

"Time moves differently around Merry, but

not in all of faerie," Doyle said, almost like he was speculating out loud.

Sholto moved up beside us, or rather leaned over me. I was short enough to make that possible. "Are you saying that my court is a few days ahead of the rest of faerie now?"

"So it would seem," Doyle said.

Mistral added, "The time inside the Unseelie Court changed when the princess was inside last too. Not by days, but hours' difference in the few clocks that we had, and those outside."

"I don't think it's me, exactly. I think it's the magic of the Goddess."

"But it is you who is the nexus for it," Doyle said.

That I couldn't argue with.

Captain Page simply stopped walking ahead of us. He turned with Walters at his side. "What are you all whispering about?"

"Don't bother," Walters said. "They'll just lie."

"We never lie," I said.

"Then you'll hide so much that you might as well lie," he said.

"Why are you so unhappy with me, Major?" I asked.

He gave me a look, as if I should know.

"I am sorry that I endangered your men and the other police and federal agents last time. I would change the level of danger around me if I could, Major. Please believe that I am not having a good time either."

His face softened, and he nodded. "I'm sorry. I know that you are in real danger, and that awful things keep happening to you. I know it's not just us mere humans who are in the way of it all."

It was the way he said "mere humans" that gave me a clue. "Has something been happening on your end of the problems that I don't know about, Major?"

"Your uncle, the King of Light and Illusion, is demanding that we turn you over to him. He says that he will protect you from your kidnappers." He motioned to the men around me.

"Let me take the next one," Page said.

Walters motioned for him to go ahead.

"Your aunt, the Queen of Air and Darkness, is demanding that you return to her court, and she says that she will protect you."

"Did she really?" I asked.

"You seem more surprised by that one," Page said.

"The last time she spoke to me she admitted that she could not keep me safe inside faerie and bid me flee to Los Angeles."

The two men exchanged glances. "Her court has been very adamant," Page said.

"Her court," Doyle said. "Not the queen herself?"

"No, but then we haven't spoken directly to either of them. We've been talking to subordinates."

Page gave a laugh. "You don't talk to the president to find out what he wants you to do, not without more brass on your shoulders than I've got."

"Who has made the demands on behalf of the queen?" Doyle asked.

"Her son, Prince Cel," Page said.

"Yeah," Walters said, "he seems very worried about his cousin." Walters watched my face as he said it.

I fought to keep a blank face and give nothing away. But I knew Cel didn't want me well. He wanted me dead. Me pregnant meant that the queen could give me her throne now. She'd vowed in open court that she would give the throne to whoever got with child first. Technically, I could have pushed the matter, and demanded a crown now, before the babies were even born. But I knew better. I knew that if I went back to the Unseelie Court pregnant, I would never live to see them born. Cel had to kill us all now.

"Our queen is different from most leaders," I said. "Trust nothing that doesn't come from her personally. Taranis is fond of flunkies delivering his messages, but Queen Andais likes the personal touch."

"Are you saying that your cousin is lying?" Page asked.

"I'm saying that until a few weeks ago he was the sole heir to his mother's throne. How would you feel if your birthright was suddenly up for grabs, Captain?"

"You're saying he's a danger to you," Page said.

I looked at Doyle. Did I tell the truth? He nodded.

"Yes, Captain, Prince Cel is a danger to me."

"If he makes an appearance," Doyle said, "we will have to treat him as a very dangerous person."

"We would have to attack the prince?" Page asked.

"At the very least make certain he does not come near the princess," Doyle said.

"Damnit," Walters said. "Who else who's supposed to be on your side is actually a danger to the princess?"

I laughed. "You don't have time to hear the list, Major. Which is why I need to get away from here. Faerie is no longer safe for me or mine."

The two men looked even more serious. Page began yelling orders, and people in uniforms started moving like they had a purpose. Actually, it looked like they were simply running about, but things started getting done, and we were taken to our very own Humvee, what the Hummer was before the idle rich all wanted one. Which meant that it was painted for camouflage, and was just scarier looking, like the difference between guns for Olympic shooting and guns for killing things. They both shoot, but just by looking at them you know that they can't do each other's jobs.

Galen was standing beside the Humvee, talking to a woman with short dark hair. Her face was raised to his, and she was studying his face as if trying to memorize it. He was simply being his usual charming self, but her body language was much more intimate than that. They both looked at us as we came up. Galen with a glad smile, but the woman . . . I swear it wasn't a friendly look.

He was in uniform too. The new digital camo was mostly browns and grays and eye-tricking shapes, though oddly, I hadn't had any trouble seeing anyone in the new camo. Weren't the uniforms supposed to be invisible in the wilderness? Maybe it didn't work on the fey. Interesting. The dull colors seemed to bring out the green undertone of his pale skin. His father had been a pixie, and it showed in his skin color and his green hair. He hugged me so thoroughly that my feet came off the ground and I was left a little breathless. He finally put me down, then studied my face. His usual smile faded to something far more serious.

"Merry," he said, "I thought I'd lost you."

"What has been happening while we slept?"

"We found Onilwyn's body, and the marks of your magic on him."

I nodded. "He tried to help the Seelie assassins kill Mistral, then he tried to kill me."

Galen hugged me tightly again, burying my face in his chest. "When we didn't find any marks from any of the other guards on him, we thought you were alone. Alone and without me or Rhys to protect you."

I pushed back so I could breathe better. "Sholto got there."

"Before?" he asked.

I shook my head.

Sholto said, "We were killing the archers at the time, but I will never forgive myself for leaving her alone in the snow."

Galen looked at him. "She is our priority. Her safety. Nothing else really matters."

"I know that," Sholto said.

"You left her alone in the snow. You said it yourself."

Sholto opened his mouth to argue, then closed it. He nodded. "You are right. I was derelict in my duty. It will not happen again."

"See that it doesn't," Galen said.

Doyle and Rhys were looking from one man to the other. "Is that our little Galen talking, or have you learned to throw your voice?" Rhys asked.

"I think our little Galen is growing up," Doyle said.

Galen scowled at them both.

Mistral said, "It must have been very dangerous where you have been for Galen Greenhair to be talking like the Darkness."

The rest of us exchanged looks, then I said, "The Western Lands are safer, Mistral, but they are not safe."

"Nowhere will be safe for Merry, while our enemies live," Galen said.

I hugged him. He was saying the truth, but to hear him be so harsh hurt something inside me.

"We can't kill them all," Rhys said.

"The problem is not killing them all," Doyle said. "The problem is that we do not know who they all are."

And that was indeed the problem.

CHAPTER TWENTY-NINE

THE WOMAN TALKING WITH GALEN WAS one of their wizards. Specialist Paula Gregorio was only inches taller than me, with sleek black hair, a thin dark face, and huge brown eyes. Her eyes dominated her face so that she looked younger than she was, and much more delicate than the personality that burned out of them.

She shook my hand a little too hard, like some men will when they want to test another man. But our hands were the same size, and no matter how fit she was under that uniform, she didn't have the strength to hurt my hand. I might have looked as delicate as Specialist Gregorio, but comparatively, I was a lot harder to hurt. I was only part human, and she was all human.

But the fact that she didn't like me from the moment she saw me was not a good start, since, theoretically, she was here to keep me safe and alive; it would have been better if she'd liked me.

But one flick of those big dark eyes to Galen let me know exactly why she didn't like me. What had he been doing out here for the last few hours with Specialist Gregorio to make her look at him that way and me the other?

Knowing Galen, nothing he thought of as flirting. He was just being friendly. He'd have talked the same way to a male wizard, but Gregorio didn't know that, and explaining it would have sounded either insulting to her or like I was trying to keep her away from Galen. Neither was what I meant, so I let it go. Hopefully, my safety would not depend on her. If it did, we had other problems than the fact that she thought Galen liked her.

The second wizard was tall, though not as tall as most of the sidhe, which put him just shy of six feet. He was as blond and pale as Gregorio was black-haired and dark. Staff Sergeant Dawson had an easy smile and hair cut so short you could see scalp on either side of his cap. "Princess Meredith, it's an honor to escort you to safety." He shook my hand, and there was no physical challenge to it, but there was a flare of magic. Not on purpose, because his own face looked too startled for that, but just a very powerful human psychic touching the hand of the new queen of faerie.

He didn't drop my hand, but he jerked, as if it hadn't felt entirely good. I drew my hand out first, slowly, being polite, but as I gazed up at him in the light of flood lamps, I saw something I hadn't before. There was an uptilt to his blue eyes, and the fingers of his hand were just a little too long, a little too thin, a little too delicate for his height. There was a sound like bells, and the scent of flowers, though not roses.

"What was that?" he asked, in a voice gone just a little breathy.

"I didn't hear anything," Gregorio said, but she looked out into the dark, past the lights. She trusted Dawson's instincts. I bet he had a lot of odd hunches that proved to be right.

"Bells," Galen said, and he moved closer to Dawson and me. He looked at me over the wizard's shoulder. He and I shared a moment of knowledge.

Dawson noticed it. "What is it? I heard the bells too, but you both know what it is. Is it something dangerous?" He was rubbing his hands on his arms as if he were cold, but I knew he wasn't cold from the winter chill. Though I had no doubt that his skin ran with goose-flesh, as if someone had walked over his grave.

I started to say something ordinary to hide it all and not spook him more, but what came out of my mouth was the opposite. "Welcome home, Dawson."

"I don't know what. . . ." But the words died on his lips, and he simply gazed at me.

Gregorio turned back to us. She jerked Dawson by the arm hard, so that it broke our eye contact. "We were warned about her effect on men, Sergeant."

He looked embarrassed, and then stepped

away from me so that he addressed his next words to the night beyond us. "It's not that I'm not flattered, ma'am, but I've got a job to do."

"Do you both think that I just tried to seduce the sergeant?" I asked.

Gregorio glared at me. "You just can't seem to leave any men for the rest of us, can you?"

"Specialist Gregorio," Dawson said in a sharp voice, "you will not speak to the princess like that. You will treat her and her party with the utmost respect." But he still didn't look too closely at me when he said it.

"Yes, sir," she said, but even those two words held anger.

"It isn't my physicality that called to you just now, Sergeant Dawson."

He shook his head. "I'll be riding in the first truck with the male driver. We've got a female driver and the specialist to ride with you in the second vehicle."

"You have some faerie blood in your ancestry," Rhys said.

"That's not. . . ." But again Dawson's words failed him. His hands were balled into fists, and he was shaking his head.

"Don't make us have to put up wards against you, Princess," Gregorio said.

I laughed. I couldn't help it.

"What's so funny?"

In my head I thought, "You couldn't ward against me now if you tried." Out loud, I said, "I'm sorry, Specialist, I'm just tired, and it's been a rather difficult few days. It's just nervous tension, I think. Just get us out of here. Farther away from the faerie mounds will be better for all of us."

She looked like she wanted to argue but just nodded and went to check on her sergeant.

Rhys and Galen moved close to me. Rhys said, "Your power called to his blood."

"You mean his genetics?" I asked.

"I suppose so," Rhys said.

Doyle moved up behind me, putting his hands on my shoulders, drawing us all in close to talk. "Is this what it means to call someone's blood?" I asked.

Rhys nodded. "Yes, it's been so long since any of us could do it that I'd forgotten what it meant."

"I don't understand," I said, pressing myself back into the curve of Doyle's body. Sholto and Mistral were on either side of our group, but they were watching outward while they listened, as if Doyle had told them to do it. He probably had.

"You hold the hand of blood, Merry," Doyle said against my hair.

"The power to call blood isn't just calling it out of the body," Rhys said. "It's also being able to call to the magic in a person's body. It may be that now you'll be calling to any fey blood in the humans around us. That's good on one hand; it will up their power level, and maybe yours. But it's going to creep out the humans you do it to until you figure out how to do it a little more quietly."

"What does it mean, exactly, that my hand of blood calls to Dawson's blood?"

"It means that your magic calls to his."

"Like calls to like," Mistral said, his eyes still directed out into the night.

"The fey in Europe intermarried with a lot of humans whose families immigrated to the United States," I said.

"Yes," Rhys said.

"So this may happen a lot?" I asked.

He nodded and shrugged. "Maybe."

"But it means more than that," Mistral said. "It means that the princess may be able to call the part-fey to her cause."

I looked up, trying to see Doyle's face, but he laid his cheek on top of my head. Not to stop me from seeing his face, but just for comfort, I think. "What does that mean?"

Doyle spoke low, his chest and throat so close to me that his voice vibrated against me. "Once, to hold some hands of power, you could call the humans to be your army, or your servants. You could call them to your side, and they came willingly, lovingly. The hand of blood was one of the few that could make humans want to join you. Literally, if you have all the power that the hand of blood once held, you call to the magic in their blood, and they will answer."

"Do they have a choice?" I asked.

"When you master this power, they will not

want to have a choice. They will want to serve you, as we do."

"But. . . ."

Rhys put his fingertip on my lips. "It's a type of love, Merry. It's the way men were supposed to feel for their lord and master. Once it wasn't like it is now, or has been for so long." He lowered his finger, and looked utterly sad. "I could do it too, call men to me. I gave them safety, comfort, joy. I protected them, and I did love them. Then I lost my powers, and I couldn't protect them. I couldn't save them anymore." He hugged me, and because Doyle was so close, he hugged us both.

Rhys whispered, "I don't know whether to be happy that this kind of power is returning to us or sad. It's so wonderful when it works, but when it went away, it was like I died with my people, Merry. They died, and they were pieces of me dying. I prayed for true death then. I prayed to die with my people, but I was immortal. I couldn't die, and I couldn't save them."

I felt the liquid on my face. I pressed my face against his cheek, and felt tears from his one good eye. The goblin who took his other eye had taken its tears too. I felt Doyle's arms tighten around us both. Then I felt Galen come in behind Rhys and hold him too.

Sholto put a hand on Rhys's hair, and Mistral's deep voice came. "I do not know if I want to be responsible for so many again."

"Me, either," Rhys said, in a voice squeezed with tears.

"Me, either," I said.

Doyle spoke. "You may have no choice."

And that was the truth, the wonderful and horrible truth.

CHAPTER THIRTY

DOYLE HESITATED AT THE DOOR OF THE armored humvee. he peered into its depths as if looking into a cave that he wasn't sure was empty of a dragon. The moment I saw the line of his body, the set of his head, I realized that the army coming to our rescue was a mixed blessing.

"It's armored, and that's too much metal for you to ride inside," I said.

He turned and looked at me, face impassive. "I can ride inside with you."

"But it will hurt you," I said.

He seemed to think about his answer, then finally said, "It will not be pleasant, but it is doable."

I looked at the Humvee in front of us, and found the other men milling about at the door too. None of them wanted to be inside that much metal.

"None of you will be able to do magic once inside that much metal, will you?"

"No," Rhys said, beside me.

"We will be, what is the word you have used, head-blind. We will be as close to mortal senses as we can come encased in such as this."

"If someone left you inside this much metal, would you fade?"

They exchanged a look. "I do not know, but some might."

Rhys pulled me into a one-armed hug. "Don't look so serious, Merry-girl. We can do it for a short ride. Besides, this much metal doesn't just keep **us** from doing magic."

I looked at him, and thought I understood what he meant, but it was too important to leave to chance. "Do you mean that if we are attacked their magic won't work around the armored vehicles either?"

"I think this much man-made shielding will shatter any spell directed at it," Doyle said.

"Then let's get inside," Rhys said, "and get our princess out of here."

Doyle nodded firmly, and moved to slip inside. I took his arm, made him turn and look at me. I laid a kiss upon his lips. He looked startled.

"What was that for?"

"For being brave," I said.

His smile flashed bright in his dark face. "I would be brave forever for you, my Merry."

That earned him another kiss, this one with a little body language to it.

Specialist Gregorio cleared her throat loudly.

Then she seemed compelled to add, "We're running a little short on time, Princess." She made "Princess" sound like an insult.

I broke from the kiss, and looked at her.

She flinched.

"What's wrong?" I asked.

"Your eyes—they're glowing."

"That happens sometimes," I said.

"Is it magic?" she asked.

I shook my head. "It's the effect he has on me."

"Besides," Rhys said, "her eyes are barely glowing at all. You should see what our eyes look like in the middle of major magic, or actual sex. It's a show."

She scowled at Rhys. "TMI. Too much information."

Rhys took a step toward her. "Oh, I haven't begun to tease."

Doyle and I both drew him back with a hand on one arm and shoulder. "Enough," Doyle said.

"We have to get in the big, bad car and go," I said.

Rhys turned to me and there was no teasing on his face, but almost a sadness. "You don't know what it's going to be like for us inside there, Merry."

I squeezed his arm. "If it's that bad, Rhys, then you and the other men ride in something more open. I saw some Jeeps. I'll ride in here by myself."

He shook his head. "What kind of guards would we be if we did that?" He leaned in and whispered, "And what kind of future fathers would we be?"

I laid my face against his cheek. "Being my king may never be safe, or easy."

"Love isn't supposed to be easy, Merry, or everyone would do it."

I drew back enough to see his face. "Everyone falls in love."

"It's not the falling, Merry, it's the staying in love." He flashed me that grin of his, the one that Galen had a version of that made you have to smile back. I hadn't seen Rhys do his version in a while.

I smiled at him, and gave him a chaste kiss that wouldn't make our escort complain.

"For bravery?" he asked.

"Yes."

"Our captain has it right, Merry. You make us all want to be better than we are."

"What is this a late-night **Gidget** rerun?" Specialist Gregorio asked.

"I don't know what you mean," I said.

She frowned at me. "The moral of the original **Gidget** movie was that a real woman makes the men around her want to be better people. Which I hated, because then if the men around you are bastards, it implies that if you were woman enough, they'd straighten up. Which is bullshit."

I looked at the two men nearest me. Galen waved from the other truck they were getting inside. I blew him a kiss, and wished I could have done more.

"A good leader inspires her troops to do their best, Specialist Gregorio."

"Sure," she said.

Doyle spoke as he slipped into the Humvee. "Women are always the head of the household, if the house runs well," he said, and he slipped inside the great metal beast.

Specialist Gregorio looked at me, frowning. "Is he for real?"

I nodded. "Oh, yes, he's for real." I smiled at her. "Remember, we're Goddess worshippers. It makes us see things a little differently."

She looked thoughtful, and I left her with that thought. I climbed into the Humvee, and felt Rhys at my back.

CHAPTER THIRTY-ONE

THE HUMVEE WASN'T MADE FOR COMFORT. It was made for war, which meant it was armored and safe, but cramped and full of odd protrusions, straps, and just bits and pieces that would never have been in a civilian version.

Our driver had hair so short from behind that you thought "male," but when she'd turned and looked a question at Specialist Gregorio, there'd been no mistaking Corporal Lance for anything but female. She made me look not as well-endowed. Maybe that was why she did the very masculine haircut, to try to look more like one of the guys. I didn't say it, but I thought that nature had made being one of the guys impossible for her.

Specialist Gregorio got in the seat beside her. The wizard's eyes followed Galen as he got in the Humvee in front of us. We'd all decided that it would be better if they spent less time together, since his effect on her had been stronger than intended. We'd have also put the other wizard, Dawson, farther away from me for similar reasons, but we weren't given a choice. Dawson got in with the male driver in the Humvee that would hold Galen, Mistral, and Sholto. I'd thought the king of the sluagh might protest being separated from his queen, but he didn't. He simply kissed me gently, and did what he was told. He agreed that Rhys needed to fill me and Doyle in on what had been happening while we slept in faerie. Galen could do the same thing for Mistral and Sholto while we drove. It was a very logical arrangement, which was one of the reasons I expected someone to argue. The fey of any flavor are not always the most logical of people, but no one debated. We just all went to our vehicles and climbed in.

My clothes were made more for a ball than for climbing into military vehicles. I had to do some pulling, and Rhys did some picking up and pushing from behind. Doyle took my hand and helped me take my seat beside him. We settled my clothes and had to push all the cloth around to give Rhys room to fit into his seat.

Even though Doyle's coat was in a style from circa the 1800s, it still took up a lot less room than my clothes. I guess women's clothing is always the least practical, no matter what century you're in.

The engine roared to life, and I realized that we wouldn't need to do a damn thing to keep the two humans from hearing us talk. All we had to do was not yell.

Rhys took my hand in his, raising it so he could lay a kiss across my knuckles. He was so solemn it made me nervous. Then he grinned at me, and something tight in the center of my chest eased a little.

"What has happened in the rest of faerie while we had days inside the sluagh?" Doyle asked.

Rhys kept my hand in his, running his thumb over my knuckles repeatedly. He could grin all he wanted, but touching like that was a nervous gesture.

"Do you remember the task you gave Galen and me in the hospital?" he began.

I nodded. "I gave you Gran's body to take home."

"Yes, and you conjured sidhe horses for us to ride on that journey."

"Sholto and I called them into being, not just me," I said.

Rhys nodded, his eyes flicking past me to Doyle. "We heard rumors that you'd been crowned queen of the sluagh."

"It is true," Doyle said, "and married by faerie itself."

Rhys's face fell; such sorrow came over him that he suddenly looked old. Not old the way a human will, for he would always be boyishly handsome, but as if every day he had lived, every hard ounce of experience was suddenly etched into his face, spilling into his one blue eye.

He nodded again, biting his lower lip, and took his hand back from mine. "Then it is true."

I took his hand back into both of mine, cradling his in my lap. "I have already had this talk with Sholto. I am not monogamous, Rhys. All the fathers of my children are dear to me, and that is not going to change, no matter how many crowns I wear."

Rhys looked not at me but at Doyle. The big man nodded. "I was there for her talk with the king of the sluagh. He did make noises about her being his queen alone, but our Merry was very . . . firm with him." There was the faintest hint of humor to that last.

I glanced at Doyle, but his dark face was impassive, and gave nothing away.

"But once faerie has chosen a spouse, then. . . ." Rhys began.

"I think we are going back to very old rules," Doyle said, "not the human ones we adopted some centuries ago."

"The Seelie adopted human rules, but the Unseelie, it wasn't about human rules," Rhys said.

"No," Doyle said, "it was about our queen seeking an heir for her throne whom she did not think would destroy her kingdom. At some level I think she has always known that her son was flawed. I think that is one of the reasons she sought a second babe for herself so desperately."

Rhys held my hands back, squeezing. "There are those in our kingdom right now who want Merry on the throne."

"How did Prince Cel take that bit of news?" I asked.

"Calmly," Rhys said.

Doyle and I both stared at him. "He was mad as a hatter when we last saw him," Doyle said.

"He was ranting about killing me, or forcing me to have a child with him so we could rule together," I said.

"He was as calm as I've seen him in years," Rhys said.

"That is bad," Doyle said.

"Why is that bad?" I asked, trying to read his face in the dimness of the Humvee.

Rhys answered, "Cel may be crazy, Merry, but he's powerful, and he still has a lot of allies among the Unseelie. His serene demeanor pleased the queen, which is probably what he wanted. He doesn't want to be blamed if something happens to you."

"Onilwyn would not have tried to kill me or Mistral without orders from Cel," I said.

"The prince is blaming the Seelie traitors that you all killed. He says that they must have offered Onilwyn a return to the Golden Court."

"The prince lies," I said.

"Maybe, but it is plausible," Rhys said.

"It might even be true," Doyle said.

I looked at him. "Not you too?"

"Listen to me, Merry. Onilwyn knew that Cel was not going to live to see the throne. He also knew that you detested him personally. What would his life have been like in the Unseelie Court with you as queen?"

I thought about what he'd said. "I don't know what the Unseelie will be like after I'm on the throne. There are nights when I think I'll never live to see the throne."

Doyle hugged me one-armed; Rhys squeezed my hands. "We'll keep you safe, Merry," Rhys said.

"It is our job," Doyle said, with his mouth against my hair.

"Yes, but now my bodyguards are precious to me, and injury to you is like a wound to my heart."

"It is the downside to dating your body-guards," Rhys said.

I nodded, settling against the solid, muscled warmth of Doyle, and drew Rhys in closer. I wrapped them around me like a second cloak. "Cel has been requesting that you be sent to the Un-seelie Court for your own safety," Rhys said, his breath warm on my cheek.

"What does the queen want me to do?" I asked.

"I haven't been inside the court, Merry. Galen and I took Hettie back to her inn. But as we rode toward it, other sidhe and lesser fey joined us. They followed behind us, singing and dancing, and the white light of the horses flowed across all of them."

"It was a faerie radhe," Doyle said, and his voice held wonderment.

"Yes," Rhys said.

I pushed them both away enough so I could study their faces. "I know what a faerie radhe is—when the sidhe used to go riding across the land. Other sidhe would join with their horses and hounds, and lesser fey would be drawn to it, to march with us. Even humans could be drawn into it sometimes."

"Yes," Doyle said.

"But there has never been a faerie radhe on American soil," Rhys said. "We lost our horses and our ability to call the folk to us."

He laid his lips against my temple, almost a kiss, but not quite. "We rode along the highway, and cars passed us. People took pictures with their cell phones, and they're already up on the Internet. We made the news."

"Is that good or bad?" I asked, leaning in against him. Doyle moved with me so that I was still held securely by both. Touching was a way of feeling better, and the metal we rode in could not have felt good to them.

"The Seelie who joined us are eager for you to bring them into their power."

"We had Seelie who were forced to join the wild hunt, too," I said.

"The old powers return," Doyle said.

"Every brownie on American soil came out to receive Hettie. They took her from us, and keened for her."

"I should have been there," I said.

Rhys hugged me close. "Your aunt Meg asked

where you were. Galen told her that you were hunting down the people responsible for your Gran's death. Meg was content with that, and so were the other brownies. She asked only if the murderer was sidhe."

Rhys did kiss the side of my face then. "We said yes."

Doyle reached out and touched the other man, squeezing his arm, as if he too heard the pain in Rhys's voice. Rhys continued. "Another brownie who I don't know by name asked, 'The princess will kill a sidhe for the murder of a brownie?' Galen said yes. That really pleased them, Merry."

"She was my grandmother. She raised me. Brownie or sidhe or goblin, I would have sought vengeance for her."

He kissed my cheek ever so gently. "I know that, but the lesser folk are not used to being thought of as equal to the sidhe, not in any way."

"I think that is about to change," I said.

They held me more tightly, so tight that it was getting too warm in my fur cloak. I was about to ask them to give me some breathing room when the radio crackled to life, and Dawson's voice came. "We've got a group of sidhe standing in the middle of the road. We can't go forward without running them over."

Rhys whispered, "If we said run them over, would that be bad?"

"Until we know who it is, probably," Doyle said.

"Who is it?" I asked.

Specialist Gregorio relayed my question.

"Galen Greenhair says one is Prince Cel and the other is the captain of his guard, Siobhan."

"Not good," Rhys said.

"I don't know," Doyle said. "I've wanted to kill Siobhan for years."

I studied his face, and found a hint of a smile. "You're pleased," I said.

"I am the queen's assassin, and a warrior of many battles, Meredith. I did not become one of the greatest killers of our court because I didn't enjoy my job."

I thought about that as he held me in the curve of his body. I thought about him enjoying the killing. I didn't like the thought much, but if he was a sociopathic killer, then he was **my** sociopathic killer. And I'd let him slaughter them both if it would save us. No, more than that, I knew that eventually Cel and Siobhan had to die for me and mine to live. Tonight was as good a time as any, if he gave us enough excuse to justify it later to the queen.

I sat there, with my Darkness and my white knight, and thought, utterly calmly, that if we could kill Cel tonight, we should probably do it. Maybe I shouldn't be pointing fingers at Doyle's inner moral compass when mine seemed just fine with his.

CHAPTER THIRTY-TWO

SPECIALIST GREGORIO SPOKE INTO HER radio, and relayed the response to us. "The prince says he wants Princess Meredith to return with him to the Unseelie Court so they can protect her," she said. "Say again Sierra four."

She turned in her seat to look at me. "He says he wants to take you back to the court so they can crown you queen. Isn't he the competitor for that crown?"

"Yes," I said.

She raised an eyebrow at me. "Rumor says he tried to kill you."

"He did."

She gave me a look to go with the eyebrow. "And now he's just going to give up?"

"We don't believe it either," Rhys said.

Her eyes flicked to him, but came back to settle on me. The radio crackled, and she hit the switch again. Dawson's voice came tinny, but a few words were clear, "with child . . . conceding."

Specialist Gregorio turned back to me. "The prince says that now that you're with child, he'll concede the throne, because it's best for the kingdom." She didn't even try to keep her disbelief out of her voice.

"Tell him that I appreciate the offer, but I am returning to Los Angeles."

She relayed the information. Dawson's answer was quick. "Prince Cel says he can't allow you to leave faerie carrying the heirs to the Unseelie throne."

"I'll just bet he can't," Rhys said.

"He and his people are blocking the road. We can't run them down," Gregorio said.

"Can we drive past them?" Doyle asked.

She got back on the radio. The answer: "We can try."

"Let us try," Doyle said.

Gregorio said, "Princess, permission to speak freely?"

I smiled. "I didn't think you needed my permission, but if you do, you have it."

"How stupid does this Cel think you are? No one would believe this shit."

"I don't think he believes the princess is stupid," Doyle said. "I believe that the prince is deluding himself."

"You mean he honestly expects her to go

with him quietly, and us not to fight him?"

"I believe that is his plan," Doyle said.

"You'd have to be crazy to believe that," Gregorio said.

"You would," Doyle said.

The woman looked at all three of us. "Your faces have all gone blank. You're trying not to let me see what you're thinking, but your blank faces say it all. You think he's crazy, as in certifiable."

"I do not know what certifiable means," Doyle said.

"It means crazy enough to be committed to a hospital," Rhys said.

"He is a prince of faerie. Such personages are not committed to insane asylums," Doyle said.

"Then what do you do with them?" she asked.

"They tend to die," he said, and even in the darkened car I could see that hint of a smile again.

Gregorio didn't smile back. "We can't kill a prince of anything for you guys."

"I didn't call you in to do our killing for us," I said.

"Why **did** you call us in, Princess?"

"To get me the hell out of here, Gregorio. You saw the Seelie simply leave rather than try to fight you. I thought that no one would be willing to confront the American military."

"You thought wrong," she said.

"And for that, I am sorry."

The line of cars began to move to the far side

of the road, scraping against tree limbs, but since the Humvee was supposed to be able to stand up to artillery fire, a few branches wouldn't faze it. The trick was, would Cel and Siobhan simply let us drive away? How crazy was he, and where was Queen Andais, and why wasn't she keeping a better leash on her son?

CHAPTER THIRTY-THREE

THE HUMVEE CRAWLED ALONG THE EDGE of the road, the trees scraping the windows, sides, and roof. "The prince and his people must still be in the road," Rhys said, "or they'd be moving faster."

"Have Mistral tell us who else is with Cel besides the captain of the guard," Doyle said.

I conveyed the request to Gregorio. She looked like she would argue, but he gave her the full force of his gaze. His face must have been almost lost in the dimness of the night and the car, but something about what she saw made her pick up the radio and do what he asked.

The answer came back as a list of the people who had backed Cel for centuries. But the crowd wasn't as large as I'd thought. Important names were missing, which didn't mean that the missing Unseelie were on my side. It simply meant that they'd abandoned Cel. One important oversight was that Siobhan was almost the only guard he had left. We'd discovered that the guards, most of whom had begun their careers as my father's personal guard, had not been asked if they wished to serve Cel. They had been forced, and no oath of allegiance had been given by most of them. Which meant that their service, and their torment by Cel, were illegal by our laws.

To join the guard of our royalty, you had to choose, and bind yourself with oaths. That Cel had stolen their freedom without that was a grave abuse of authority.

Gregorio watched our faces as she relayed the names. If she'd thought she'd learn something from Doyle or Rhys, she'd been mistaken. I think I just looked tired.

"The Queen must have given his guard a choice," Doyle said.

"The choice they should have had from the beginning," Rhys said.

"Yes," he said.

"What do you mean 'a choice'?" Gregorio asked.

"Prince Cel took over the personal guard of Prince Essus, Princess Meredith's father, after his death. By our laws, the guard should have had a choice to either follow the new prince or leave the royal service, but Prince Cel gave them no choice. The princess found this out recently, and petitioned the queen to give the prince's guard that choice."

"So they all bailed on him?" Gregorio asked.

"So it would seem."

"Or maybe they're out in the woods waiting to ambush us," Rhys said.

"That too is very possible."

"Couldn't you sense if there were that many sidhe hiding in the woods?" I asked.

"Not inside this much metal and human-made technology."

"We're almost head-blind, Merry. It doesn't kill us to be inside this much metal, like some of the lesser fey, but it curtails our magic, a lot," Rhys said.

"If there are other guards hiding in the woods, would it explain why Cel isn't attacking?" I asked. I huddled in more tightly against Doyle. Rhys was gazing out the windows, trying to see what lay ahead.

"It might," Doyle said.

Gregorio took it upon herself to hit the radio again. "The prince has a lot more personal guards than those in the road. We might want to check the woods and see what's there."

A man's voice said, "Roger that."

"So it's either a trap," Rhys said, "or he's waiting for the truck with us in it. We're his targets, after all."

"He is most likely saving his attack for us," Doyle said, "but as we cannot work magic inside the trucks, neither can he work magic upon us while we are surrounded by this much metal."

Gregorio asked, "Are you saying that we should let them throw magic at us, and the trucks will take care of it?"

Doyle and Rhys exchanged a look, then Rhys nodded and shrugged. Doyle answered. "The magic should fall apart around the trucks, and as long as your people stay inside them, they should be untouchable."

I turned in Doyle's arms so I could see his face, though dark on dark, I could see little of his expression. Of course, when he didn't wish me to, bright light wouldn't have clued me in to his thoughts.

"Are you saying that we are completely safe inside here from their magic?" Gregorio asked.

Doyle stirred beside me, pulling me even more tightly against him. Rhys took my hand in his, playing with my knuckles again in that worry-stone way, over and over.

"Either they can work magic inside here or they cannot," I said.

"It is not that simple," Doyle said at last.

"Well, since the Humvee with Galen and the others in it is going to be close to them very soon, I suggest you make it simple."

He smiled. "Spoken in the tone of a queen."

"I'm with her," Gregorio said. "I've got people depending on Dawson and me to keep them safe."

I shook my head. "Take the tone any way you like, Doyle, but you're both hiding something from me. Tell me."

"As my lady asks," he said, "no magic from his

hand or the others can touch us in here. He may not know that, but we are safe inside the trucks."

"I hear a 'but' in your voice."

He smiled a little more. "But there are things that can pierce the metal."

"Remember, Merry, our people didn't use armor once, for obvious reasons, but we ran into enemies who did. Our metalsmiths came up with a few things that would go through metal."

"Such as?" I asked.

"There were spears forged long ago," Doyle said. "They are locked away with the few other magical weapons left us."

"The queen would have to give him permission to open the vault of weapons," I said.

"She would, which makes it unlikely that he would have such a thing, but I do not like the fact that he and his followers are in the middle of the road, demanding things from us."

Rhys said, "The queen would never permit him to appear weak or evil in front of the humans. She's worked too long and hard to make the Unseelie Court's reputation better to let Cel ruin it now. It's the one thing she's never allowed him to do, to abuse the humans, or be seen abusing anyone else in front of them."

"And now he's in the middle of the road, behaving badly," I said.

"Exactly," he said.

"Where is Queen Andais?" I asked.

"Where indeed," Doyle said, and he moved

again, as if the seat wasn't quite comfortable. It wasn't, but it wasn't the seat that was bothering him. Doyle could sleep on a marble floor and not flinch.

"You're afraid for her," I said.

"One thing she accused you of, my sweet Merry, is very true. You have stripped her of all the best and most feared of her personal guard. She retained her position, in part, because of. . . ."

"You," I finished for him.

"Not only me."

I nodded. "You can say his name, Doyle. The Queen's Darkness, and her Killing Frost."

"It upsets you to hear his name."

"It does, but that doesn't mean we don't say it."

"It would if you were Queen Andais," Rhys said.

"I am not her."

"But Doyle is being too modest," Rhys said. "Yes, Frost was feared by the queen's enemies, but it was fear of the Queen's Darkness that kept a lot of courtiers in line."

"You exaggerate," Doyle said.

I shook my head. "I'm not sure he does. I've heard people talk about you, Doyle. I know that the queen would say, 'Bring me my Darkness. Where is my Darkness?' and then someone would die. You were her greatest threat, next to the sluagh."

"Are you saying that Captain Doyle here is as feared as the host of the sluagh?" Gregorio asked.

We all looked at her. I said, "Yes."

"One man, against a host of nightmares," she said, and didn't try to keep her disbelief out of her voice.

"He can be pretty scary all on his own," Rhys said.

Gregorio stared at Doyle, as if trying to see more of him in the dim light.

"Shouldn't you tell Sergeant Dawson that the magic will be stopped by the trucks?" I asked.

"I'll tell him it will probably be stopped." She got on the radio.

Rhys said, "Some of them might be able to make illusions real enough to lure the soldiers outside the trucks."

"What kind of illusions?" I asked.

Voices came over the radio, frantic. "Sierra four to all Sierra, we have wounded soldiers in line of travel. Stopping to render aid."

"Those kind," Doyle said.

"Tell them it's not real," I said.

"Tell them not to get out of the trucks no matter what," Doyle said.

Gregorio tried, she really did, but one thing our soldiers are not trained to do is leave their wounded behind. It was a brilliant trap. The soldiers went to check the wounded, and once they left the trucks, the sidhe attacked, and no human magic could stop them.

CHAPTER THIRTY-FOUR

VOICES CAME IN SNATCHES OVER THE RADIO. "It's Morales, but he died in Iraq! It's Smitty . . . died in Afghanistan. . . ."

"It's Siobhan," Rhys said. "She can bring back the shadows of the dead whom you know. Shit, I thought she'd lost that power."

"The princess returns power to all of faerie, Rhys, not just us," Doyle said.

The real trick to the ambush was that the soldiers didn't realize yet that they were under attack. Gregorio twisted in the seat and turned to us. "It doesn't sound like they're doing anything to our people."

"The dead are not the only mind games the sidhe can play," Rhys said.

"What do you mean?" she asked.

Shots sounded.

"They're shooting at us!" Gregorio said, and went back to the radio, trying to get someone to talk to her.

We heard Dawson's voice. "Mercer just shot Jones. He's shooting at us!"

"He's shooting at nightmares," Doyle said.

"What?" Gregorio asked.

"They're using illusion to make your solider see monsters. He doesn't know he's shooting at you," I said.

"But we're all wearing anti-faerie stuff," she said.

"Are you sure that this Mercer is wearing his?" Doyle asked.

"They could persuade him to take it off," I said.

She cursed and got back on the radio with Dawson. There was more gunfire, and it sounded different this time. Gregorio got off the radio, her face grim.

"We had to kill Mercer, our own man. He thought he was back in an ambush in Iraq."

"Get the men back in the trucks," Doyle said. "Tell them to believe nothing that they see outside of them."

"It's too late, Doyle," Rhys said. They exchanged looks that were far too serious.

"We might be able to prevent the illusions," Doyle said.

"You're our protectees," Gregorio said. "My orders clearly state that you aren't getting out of the safety of these vehicles until I hand you off at the flight line."

I gripped Doyle's hand and Rhys's arm. This was a trap for us, for my men and me. I agreed with

Gregorio, but. . . . The yelling continued, then it became screams.

"Sergeant Dawson, talk to me!" Gregorio yelled into the radio.

"We've got men bleeding. Bleeding from old wounds, but they're fresh now. What the hell is going on?"

"Cel is the Prince of Old Blood. That does not mean he's from an old lineage," Doyle said.

"You mean the prince is doing this?" she asked.

"Yes."

I sat there in the Humvee with my death grip on them both, and couldn't think. Maybe the last several days, or months, were finally catching up with me. I was frozen with indecision. The human soldiers had no chance against this, but it was a trap for us, which meant that Cel and his allies had plans to stop anything we could do. I'd dueled enough of the people with him when Cel was trying to kill me legally. I knew their powers, and some were fierce.

"Shoot them," I said. "The sidhe are not proof against bullets."

"We can't shoot at a royal prince and his guard unless they attack us with something we can see and testify to in court," Gregorio said.

"Cel can bleed most of you to death without ever lifting a weapon," I said, leaning forward as far as the seat belt would allow.

"But we can't prove he's doing it," she said. "You've never tried to prove a magic attack in a military court. I have. It ain't pretty."

"Would you rather they all die?" I asked.

"We can help them, Meredith," Doyle said.

I turned to him. "That's what he wants, Doyle. You know that. He's hurting the soldiers to lure us out."

"Yes, Meredith," he said, cupping my face with his free hand, "and it is a good trap."

I shook my head, moving back from his touch. "The soldiers are supposed to protect us."

"They are dying to protect us," he said.

My throat was tight, and my eyes burned. "No," I whispered.

"You will stay inside this truck, no matter what happens, Meredith. You must not get out."

"Once you are dead, they will drag me out. They will drag me out and kill me and your unborn children."

He flinched, something I had never seen before. The Darkness did not flinch. "That was harsh, My Princess."

"Truth is often harsh," I said, and let him hear my anger.

"She's right, Captain," Rhys said.

"Would you let them die in our place?" Doyle asked.

Rhys sighed, then kissed me on the cheek. "I will follow where my captain leads, you know that."

"No," I said, louder.

"I can't allow any of you to leave the safety of the vehicle," Gregorio said.

"What will you do to stop us?" Doyle asked, his hand on the door handle.

"Shit," she said, and started to get on the radio.

Doyle touched her shoulder. "Do not give away what little surprise we will have."

She let go of the button and just stared at him. "The princess is right. This ambush is meant to lure you to your deaths."

"It is," he said. He turned back to me. "Kiss me, Meredith, my Merry."

I was shaking my head over and over. "No."

"You will not kiss me good-bye?"

I wanted to scream at him that I would not. I would not endorse his stupidity in any way, but in the end, I couldn't let him go without it.

I kissed him, or he kissed me. He kissed me gently, his hands on my face, then he drew me into his arms so that our bodies molded against each other. He drew back with a last chaste kiss on my lips.

Rhys said, "My turn."

I turned to him with tears glittering in my eyes. I would not cry, not yet. Rhys's face was so sad, gentle but so sad. He kissed me delicately, then he grabbed me fiercely, almost painfully, and kissed me as if my lips were food and water and air, and he would die without my kiss. I fell into the fierceness of his mouth, his hands, and his body, and when he finally broke away, we were both breathless.

"Wow," Gregorio said, then said, "sorry."

I didn't even look at her, only at Rhys. "Don't go."

The door opened behind me, and I turned in time to see Doyle sliding out. I whispered, "If I am your queen, then I can order you to stay."

Doyle leaned back in the doorway. "I vowed never again to listen to humans die screaming for my cause, Meredith."

"Doyle, please."

"You are now and always will be my Merry." Then he was gone.

A sound escaped my lips that was almost a cry, but it was not a sound that I ever wanted to hear from my own mouth.

The door opened on the other side of me, and I turned to see Rhys climbing out. "Rhys, no!"

He smiled at me. "Know that I would have stayed, but I cannot let him go without me. He is my captain, and has been for more than a thousand years. And he's right. I too vowed never to let humans die for me again. It was wrong then, and it's still wrong." He reached in, touched my face.

I held his hand against my cheek. "Don't go."

"Know that I love you more than honor, but Doyle wouldn't be Doyle if he felt the same way."

The first tear trailed, hot and painful, down my face as he drew his hand away. I held on to him with both hands on his one. "Rhys, please, for the love of the Goddess, please!"

"I love you, Merry. I've loved you since you were sixteen."

I thought I would choke on the next words, but I got them out, "I love you too. Don't you die on me."

He grinned, and it almost reached his eyes. "I'll do my best." Then he was gone into the night, and the sound of fighting.

CHAPTER THIRTY-FIVE

GREGORIO TURNED AROUND IN HER SEAT and grabbed my arm. She held on tightly. She thought she knew what I was thinking, but she didn't. I was mortal, and I knew it. But I was also part brownie and part human, which meant I could do magic inside the car. I could do every bit of magic I had, and not suffer. I didn't want to get out of the car. I needed to lure Cel to the car.

If I could get him close enough, I could kill him but be surrounded by metal, so that his magic could not harm me. We could turn the trap against him. If only we could figure out how to lure him to me. If I'd thought of it before Doyle and Rhys got out of the car, they would have done it, but I'd been too emotional. Goddess, help me think of something!

"Gregorio," I said, "I need to lure the prince to me, to this car."

"Are you crazy? He's making people bleed from a distance."

"We both have a version of the hand of blood. It runs in the family. But magic cannot touch us in the metal of this car. But my magic can go out."

"Why can your magic work in the car, and his can't?"

"I'm part human. My magic works here, just like yours and Dawson's."

She looked at her driver. The two women exchanged a long look.

"If we get her killed, the least that will happen to us is being given a dishonorable discharge," said Corporal Lance. "We'd be lucky not to be brought up on charges."

Gregorio turned back to me. "Lance is right."

"Listen to the screams. Your men are dying. My men are in danger. We can stop this, because once the prince is dead, his allies will melt away into the night, because if he can't take the throne, there's no point to this fight. They're fighting to kill me and win the throne for their choice. If we take away their choice, we take away their reason to fight."

The women exchanged another look. A particularly piteous scream rose in the silence between gunfire and magic. It was the sound of death. It was the sound of mortal life being ripped away.

"If I were willing to do this, how would I lure him?" Gregorio asked. The moment she said it, I knew she'd do it, if I could just think of a way to bring him to me.

I spoke, thinking aloud, because I had no clear

plan. "He wants to find me. He knows by now that my guards are not with me in the car. If I were him and his allies, I'd find me."

A mist formed on the other side of the road in the fringe of trees. It wasn't a wide road, and before I could even voice a warning, figures appeared out of a mist that shouldn't have been there, and hadn't been there just moments before. I should have remembered that I was still on faerie land, and wishes can come true. I'd wanted Cel to find me, not all of his warriors. Be specific when you wish in faerie, and be careful what you wish for.

CHAPTER THIRTY-SIX

SIOBHAN STEPPED OUT OF THE MIST, HER long white hair haloing around her like spider silk caught in the wind. She was close enough that I could see the runes carved on her white armor. I knew that the armor seemed to be carved of old bone, but I had seen her on the dueling sands, and knew that the "bone" was as hard as any metal. The sword she held in her hand was also white. The blade was a killing blade, even if I'd been immortal. It was overkill for me. Then she held her blade up so it caught the moonlight. Blood gleamed on the edge of the bone blade. It might have been the blood of human soldiers, but then again, it might not.

She meant me to think it was the blood of my men, my lovers, the fathers of my children. She meant the sight of that blood to be a blow that would soften me up for the real blow to come. But I would have known if Doyle's blood decorated her blade. I would have known if Rhys had been touched. As much as I valued Sholto and Mistral, my heart would survive their deaths.

"Shit," Gregorio said. I felt her start to cast a spell, a prickling build of power. It was a pale thing, but very real.

"Don't," I said. "I know what to do."

"Are you insane?" the driver asked. "Look at them."

I glanced at the other soldiers with Siobhan. In their armor, they looked more like Seelie sidhe. Their colors were silver and gold, but there was also armor that seemed to be made of leaves, bark, fur, and things that humans had no words for. The Unseelie had kept closer to their origins, and not traded everything for metal and jewels. I recognized some of the soldiers, but some I had never seen in full armor. But they all stood behind Siobhan, not in front of her. Kill her and the rest would be leaderless, a snake without a head.

"I grew up seeing them," I said finally.

I concentrated on Siobhan, she who had been Cel's right hand for longer than any remembered. She whom Doyle feared, and the Darkness feared almost nothing. But some magics are no respecter of power; they will kill a king as quickly as a beggar.

I lowered my window. She called out to me, "The blood of your Darkness decorates my blade."

I unbuckled my seat belt, and came to my knees, unsheathing Aben-dul as I moved. The odd hilt with its carved horrors fit my hand as if it had waited forever for my fingers to grip it. It came smoothly, like drawing silk across the skin. I pointed the blade at her.

She laughed. "You surprised me when you used the hand of flesh on Rozenwyn and Pascoe, but I know to stay out of reach now, Princess. I don't need to get within reach of that little hand of yours. I can kill you from a distance, and free faerie of your mortal taint. We will put a true prince on the throne this night, and your challenge will be forgotten."

Rozenwyn and Pascoe had been twins, and maybe that had caused the hand of flesh to combine them into one mass. It had been one of the most horrible things I'd ever seen. Horrible enough that Siobhan had offered up her sword, and surrendered to me and my guards.

"She's bluffing," I said aloud for the soldiers' benefit. "She would have to drag me from the car to work magic, and she won't touch me."

"Why not?" Gregorio asked.

"She fears the hand of flesh."

"What is that, the hand of flesh?"

I didn't bother to explain, because in moments, if all went well, it would explain itself.

Siobhan started to close the few yards that separated us. She would come closer, just not too close, so whatever she had planned needed less space between us. The others came at her back, gleaming in their armors of many colors and many shapes like an evil rainbow, combined with your brightest dream and worst nightmare. We were the Unseelie, terrible and wonderous.

"Whatever you're going to do," Gregorio said, "you better do it fast."

I opened the invisible mark on my hand that held the hand of flesh. That mark now touched the hilt of Aben-dul. It is an enchanted weapon, but when it finds its rightful wielder, there is no learning curve. There is only a sense of rightness, and knowledge, as if the use of the weapon were like breathing, or the beating of my heart. I did not have to think how to focus the hand of flesh down that blade. I simply had to will it.

Siobhan reached behind her and lifted a pack off her shoulder. She opened the flap, and began to fiddle with something.

Gregorio screamed, "Bomb!"

"It can't take out this vehicle," the driver said.

"What happens if she gets it through a window?" I asked in a careful voice, because if even my voice wavered, it would hurt my control. I had never used Aben-dul before, and it was like trying to walk up a steep flight of steps with something hot and dangerous in your hands. Careful, or it spills.

"No one can throw through this glass," the driver said, thumping her window with a knuckle, "so just roll up the window, Princess."

"You have no idea how strong Siobhan is," I said. "She could throw anything through any glass."

The driver turned in her seat and looked at Gregorio. "Are the sidhe that strong?"

"Intelligence says yes."

"Shit," the driver said, and she started scrabbling for something on the floorboards.

I kept my attention on Siobhan and her package. I'd meant to simply unleash the power, but now, suddenly, I had to focus it. I aimed the sword at the hand that held that innocent-looking pack. If a soldier told me it was a bomb, I believed her.

Siobhan stood and reared her arm back to throw. Then the arm wasn't quite as long as it had been. I thought, flow, twist, become. . . . The flesh of her hand flowed over the strap of the pack. I'd seen my father do this, concentrate on the part of the body he wanted to damage. He'd had to touch the body to do it, but the principle was the same. He'd been able to flow flesh to a degree, and stop it if he wished. I didn't have that control yet. No, being honest, at least to myself, I had a plan for the bomb, and it didn't include stopping short of the worst that the hand of flesh could do. The plan relied on doing my worst to Siobhan.

She screamed and shrieked. The darkly glittering throng at her back stepped away. She stood there with the pack melding to her body. But she moved in a circle of empty space. None of them would chance touching her. They knew the story of what had happened to Pascoe and Rozenwyn; no one would risk such a fate.

She began to run toward our Humvee. Even as I prepared to destroy her, I admired her bravery.

She knew what I was going to do, and she would, with her last effort, try to take me with her. Her determination was flawless.

A rifle shot rang out, so close I was deafened by it. Our driver, Corporal Lance, was shooting out her window, and had taken out one of Siobhan's legs at the knee. I hadn't even been aware that Lance had rolled her window down. But I had to focus, had to keep the spell where I needed it. Had to . . . Siobhan's flesh rolled, her face going under a wall of her own internal organs as if water were drowning her. But she was sidhe, and she could not die for lack of oxygen. You could drown me. It had been one of the proofs my aunt had used to call me worthless. But Siobhan would not die just because her mouth and nose were inside a ball of her own flesh. Sidhe do not die that easily.

Moonlight glittered on blood and shiny things that should never see the light of day. There was nothing left of her but a ball of flesh. Her heart was on the outside, pulsing, living, just like the last time I'd done this. I was too far away to hear her scream, but I had no doubt that she was screaming. Screaming or cursing me.

"What is that moving on her front?" Gregorio asked.

"Her heart," I said.

"She's not dead?"

"No."

"Jesus!"

"Yes," I said.

Some of the armored figures had dropped to their knees, but not all. I saw Conri, in his red and gold, he who had tried to kill Galen once. I aimed the sword at him, and he began to melt. It could have been anyone though, any who stood. If they knelt, they could live, but if they defied me, they would suffer. It was that simple.

As Conri screamed, and twisted inside out, the last standing warriors dropped to their knees. The ones who were already on their knees pressed their faces to the ground. It had bothered me when my guards had tried to do that, but this night, this moment, I was glad of it. They had come to kill me, and all whom I loved. If I could not destroy them all, then I needed them to fear me.

Corporal Lance yelled as she handed her rifle to Gregorio and rolled up her window. "Close your window, we gotta move!"

"Why?" Gregorio asked.

"Wizards. You don't think when you're doing spells." She started the engine and we started forward. "Raise your damn window!"

"If you raise the window, I can't do this spell," I said.

"The bomb is still going to go off."

"You said it couldn't hurt this car," I said.

"You're our protectee. I'd rather not take the chance."

She eased us forward, and started angling around the truck in front of us. The radio was asking why we were moving. The word "bomb" seemed to galvanize everyone. Engines roared to life, and unfortunately, there was confusion. Too many people had fallen to the illusions and tricks, so there were just a few moments of confusion while they sorted who would collect the people who were hurt or dead. Seconds only, but seconds count.

I don't know what I had thought would happen. I simply put the bomb inside Siobhan's body. Had I thought that her flesh would be enough to contain the explosion? I think I had, but I was no solider. I wasn't truly even a warrior. I made the mistake of someone whose main ability is magic. I didn't think of the physical, and suddenly the physical was all there was.

The concussion of the bomb rocked the Humvee, splattering it with bits of flesh, bone, and shrapnel. My window was open. Something smashed into my right shoulder and upper chest. I was rocked backward, thrown onto the seat, and ended on the floorboards.

I'd lost my grip on Aben-dul. I managed to yell out, "Don't touch the sword, whatever you do! Don't let anyone touch the sword!" I forced myself to get up and grope for the hilt. If Gregorio or Lance touched it, they'd be turned into what Conri and Siobhan had. . . .

Gregorio's face was over me. "You're hit!" She turned back to the driver. "She's hit. The princess is hit!"

I just kept trying to reach the sword. It was as

if the world had narrowed down to me getting the hilt back in my hand. I couldn't let them touch it. They wouldn't know. They wouldn't understand.

Gregorio ripped my cloak away. I crawled back up on the seat as Corporal Lance drove us over the uneven road. My hand closed on the hilt as I felt Gregorio behind me. "I have to see the wounds, Princess, please."

She'd climbed into the back with me. Her hands were bloody as she reached for me. I turned from her, and used every bit of concentration I had left to slide Aben-dul into its sheath and set the locks.

Gregorio turned me to face her as the Humvee bounced over the road. "Fuck! We need a medic, now!"

I looked down where she was looking, and saw nails sticking out of my body where the leather coat had left it bare. I stared down at the blood and the things sticking out of me, and thought, "Shouldn't it hurt more?"

"Her skin's cold. She's going into shock. Shit!"

I thought, "No, I can't go into shock. That might kill me. Wouldn't it?" I couldn't seem to think clearly. But the moment I decided not to go into shock, the pain hit me. It was like a smaller cut, when it doesn't hurt until you see the blood. But this was not small, and the pain was shearing, burning. Why did it burn? Was it my imagination, or could I really feel the nails embedded in my flesh?

I grabbed Gregorio with my left hand, because I couldn't raise the right one. Something was very wrong with my shoulder. "I need Doyle. I need Rhys. I need my men."

"We're getting you to safety, then we'll worry about your guards," the driver yelled back.

Corporal Lance kept us moving, and the other Humvees moved so that we could. We were moving past the car that had held Galen, Sholto, and Mistral. They weren't in it. Gregorio was trying to get me to lie down. I batted her hands away. Where were they?

I sent my magic seeking them, and felt a tug on that line of power. Someone who was attached to my power was hurt, very hurt. His life flickered like fire in a strong wind. Death was coming.

I couldn't think of anything else but that I had to get to him. Had to get to him. Had to. . . . I touched Gregorio on her face, and whispered, "I'm sorry," then smiled at her. I called my glamour and let her see not what I wanted her to see, but anything she wished to see. Anything if it would get me out of here, and to that flickering light I could feel out there in the dark.

Her face softened, and she whispered, "Kevin."

I smiled, and when she leaned in to kiss me, I kissed her back, ever so gently, and laid her down on the seat with a smile still curling her lips. She would dream of the man who had given her that kiss. It was a type of glamour that was completely illegal, under the same heading as a date-rape drug. But I had no interest in anything but getting out.

I opened the door. Lance slammed on the brakes, and yelled, "What are you doing, Princess?"

"He's dying. I have to help him." I stepped out into the road. I used my good arm to cradle the injured one, and began to move through the trees. I would have run, but that line of power was flickering too low. If I ran, I would lose it, as if my running were a stronger wind than his life could survive. I prayed, and wrapped glamour around me. Glamour to keep our driver from seeing me and dragging me back. Glamour to hide from the sidhe who wanted me dead. Glamour to make me look like whoever the person expected to see, and would be glad to see. It was a type of personal glamour that I had never tried before, but I just suddenly knew that I could do it. I hid by being whoever or whatever they needed to see, and I moved away from them all. I had to find him before he died. I wouldn't let myself think who it was that I chased in the dark. There would be time enough to see who I had lost when I got to his side.

CHAPTER THIRTY-SEVEN

OF EVERYONE I HAD EXPECTED TO FIND AT the end of that powerful drawing in, a soldier was not among them. The man lay on his stomach, hidden where he'd crawled into the woods. His uniform had done what my glamour did, hidden him.

I would have questioned whether I'd taken a wrong turn or followed the wrong scent, but the sense of urgency and rightness was too clear. This was the man who had drawn me, blind with magic, through the edges of battle.

I knelt in the leaves and weeds in the winter-locked forest. I had to turn him over with my left hand, for my right shoulder was still full of the nails. I could flex my hand, but I could not raise it high enough to do anything but steady the man's body as I pushed. The pain from just that small helping movement was excruciating. It left me breathless, and the bare trees swam in streamers of sickening black and white. I rested on the man's chest for a moment, eyes closed, not sure if I was going to throw up or pass out.

Then something fell against my cheek. The touch made me raise my head. A single pink rose petal slid onto the man's chest. The Goddess was with me. I would not fail.

I raised my eyes and found the face under the uniform. It was the wizard Dawson, with his pale hair and paler face. So terribly pale among the darkened trees. He looked like his own ghost.

I touched his face with my good hand. He was icy to the touch. I checked for the big pulse in the neck. My chest tightened, because there was nothing. Then . . . a tenuous, hesitating pulse. He was near death, but not dead.

I whispered, "Goddess, help me help him."

The pink petal blew or rolled onto his lips. His eyes flew wide, and he grabbed my injured arm. The pain took my vision, filled the world with white starbursts and nausea.

My vision cleared, and someone was holding me in their arms. It was Dawson, sitting up, looking down at me. "Princess Meredith, are you all right?"

I laughed. I couldn't help it. He'd been the one who was almost dead, and he wanted to know if I was all right. His hand hovered above my shoulders and arm where the nails were still embedded. He held up a bloody hand, and showed me a nail.

"I woke up with you and this on me. I was dying. I know I was dying. You saved me. How?"

I had no idea how to explain. I opened my mouth to say "I have no idea," but what came out was, "Remember when you felt the call of my touch?"

"Yes."

"I followed your call."

"But you're hurt."

"But you're not," I said. "Help me up."

He did what I asked, no arguing. Maybe it was shock, or maybe he couldn't refuse me. I neither knew nor cared. There was more need out there in the dark. I could feel it.

Dawson kept a steadying hand on my good arm, and let me lead us through the trees. The fighting was a distant sound of guns, the flashing of lightning, and green fire. The fire meant that Doyle was still alive. I wanted to go to him, but another single pink petal fell onto the front of my coat. In that moment, more than any other before it, I trusted in the Goddess. I trusted that she would not have me save the soldiers and lose the men I loved. I prayed for courage enough not to falter or question. My reward was another body on the ground.

The man lay on his back. Dark eyes stared up at the sky. His mouth opened and shut as if he couldn't figure out how to breathe. The front of his uniform was torn away from one side of his chest. It had been peeled away as if by something stronger than human hands. His chest steamed in the winter air. I'd never seen a wound steam in the cold, never thought, "The warmth of life is floating away."

Dawson helped me kneel. He said, "Brennan, this is Princess Meredith. She'll help you."

Brennan's mouth opened, but no words came out, only a trickle of blood that was too dark, too thick. I laid the pink petal on his face, but there was no miraculous waking. He was awake, and the terror in his eyes said that he knew he was dying. I did not know how I had healed Dawson, so I did not know how to repeat it.

I prayed, "Goddess, help me help him."

Brennan shuddered, his body convulsing, and there was a sound in his chest as he tried to breathe. Dawson said, "Help him, please."

I laid my hand on his wound and prayed, and then there was pain. Pain that stole the world, and then I found myself waking, collapsed across the soldier's chest.

A hand was stroking my hair. I opened my eyes to Brennan staring down at me. Dawson cradled Brennan's head in his arms, and they both looked at me. They looked at me as if I were the most wonderful thing in the world. They looked at me as if I'd walked on water. The thought filled me with no comfort, only a vague anxiety. I had never wanted any human being to look at me like that.

Brennan held a bloody nail up so I could see it.

Dawson said, "It fell out, just like mine did. Blood and the nail, and then he was healed."

I nodded as if that made sense to me. This time I had a solider on each arm, but when Brennan took my injured arm, it didn't hurt quite as much. I think I was healing each of my nail wounds every time I healed a solider. Did that mean that I could only heal as many as I had nails in my flesh? On the one hand, being healed would be good, but on the other hand, there were many more soldiers than the nails I had in my body. Would I lose the ability to heal the rest when I was healed myself? I didn't want to stay injured, but . . . I let the thought go. We would do what we could, then we'd see. I did my best not to think too hard about anything. I did my best to keep walking, and let the men I'd saved help me. If I thought too hard, I'd be like Peter walking across the sea to follow Jesus. He did fine until he thought too hard, then he fell beneath the waves. I could not afford to fall. I could feel the need of the injured in the dark. That need called to me, and I had to answer it.

We found two soldiers together. I didn't know what Cel and his people had done, but it was as if all of the wounded had crawled off to die. Where were the doctors, the medics? Where was everyone? I could hear the fighting in the distance, a little closer now as we moved, but whatever illusion had been used had made them crawl away to die, and not seek help.

Dawson and Brennan helped me kneel beside the fallen soldiers. It took me a moment to realize that one of the soldiers was a woman. She was hidden under a vest and some gear. Her skin was almost as dark as Doyle's in the night of the trees.

Dawson said, "It's Hayes."

Brennan was kneeling beside the other soldier, who was collapsed on one side. "It's Orlando, sir."

I laid my hand against Hayes's neck, and felt something sticky. I didn't bother to raise my hand to the faint light. I knew it was drying blood. It shouldn't be drying that fast, should it? Had I lost track of time?

I spoke out loud without really meaning to. "Was she ever wounded?"

"Yes," Brennan said. "We both got hit in the same ambush. She dragged my ass to safety, just like she did Orlando here."

"Was your chest wound an old wound?" I asked.

"Yes, ma'am. That prince, he pointed his hand at me and it was like the wound just came back. Then he ripped my vest back so he could see the wound. He seemed to enjoy seeing it."

"Was she wounded in the neck?" I asked.

"Yes, ma'am."

Cel was hurting my people. He was hurting people who had sworn to protect me. They were dying to protect me and mine. It wasn't right. We were supposed to protect them, not the other way around.

I prayed to the Goddess as I touched Hayes. She was brave, and had saved lives once with this wound in her body. It seemed wrong to make her live through it twice, but even in the midst of the horror, she had grabbed another solider and dragged him with her. So brave.

There was pain, and this time I didn't pass out. This time I saw the nail push its way out of my flesh in a spurt of blood. The blood spattered Hayes's face as her eyes flew wide, flashing white. She gasped, and grabbed my arm. The nail fell on to her chest, and her other hand closed on it automatically, as if she hadn't noticed.

"Who are you?"

"I am Princess Meredith NicEssus."

She clutched my arm, her fist clutching the bloody nail to her chest. She swallowed hard. "It doesn't hurt."

"You're healed," Dawson said, leaning over her.

"How?"

"Let her heal Orlando, and you'll see."

Dawson helped me stand, but I was feeling a little better, and didn't have to lean so heavily on his arm. I still let him and Brennan help me to my knees. I still couldn't move my shoulder, though my hand and lower arm now had more range of movement.

There was no visible wound on Orlando, but his skin was cool to the touch, and I couldn't find a pulse in his neck, not even that thready hesitation that Dawson had had. I tried not to think what that meant. I tried not to question this miracle, or to think too hard that I didn't really know what I was doing or how. I prayed harder, and laid my hands on the man's cooling skin.

A shower of rose petals blew across us, like pink snow. I felt the man shudder underneath my hands, and there was more pain, more blood, and another nail fell into his half-open hand. His hand convulsed around the nail, just like Hayes's had done.

"Dear God," Hayes said.

"I think you mean Goddess," Dawson said.

The man on the ground stared up at me, his face frightened. "Where am I?"

"Cahokia, Illinois," I said.

"I thought I was back in the desert. I thought. . . ."

Hayes gripped his shoulder, and turned him to look at her. "It's all right, Orlando. She saved us. We're safe."

I wasn't sure about that last part, but I let it go. I had only a few nails left, only a few more lives to save. When I was healed, would I lose the ability to save them? I wanted to be healed, but I didn't want to lose any of them. They had offered their lives to save us, and I wanted to repay that. They shouldn't die in our war.

I felt the call close by. There were more wounded. I would do what I could. I would do what the Goddess helped me do. I wanted to save them all. The question was, could I?

CHAPTER THIRTY-EIGHT

I HAD EIGHT SOLDIERS WITH ME, EACH clutching a bloody nail, each brought back from the brink of death. Once the last nail was out of my body, the call faded. There was something about the pain and the injury that had made the magic possible.

A sidhe warrior appeared out of the dark, dressed in crimson armor that gleamed in the moonlight, as if made of fire. His name was Aodán, and I knew that his hand of power matched his armor. I felt him call his hand of power, and I spoke without thinking. "Kill him."

They should have hesitated. They shouldn't have taken my orders. Dawson was the ranking officer, but they aimed their recovered guns at the figure and fired. The bullets did what bullets had been doing to faerie from the moment humans had made them. They tore through that brilliant armor, and into the flesh underneath. He died before he could send his hand of fire to scorch us. I could feel them calling their hands of power. If we could keep shooting them before they had time to unleash that power, we could win this. Such a simple solution, if you had soldiers who would follow unhesitatingly, and a complete willingness to kill everything in your path. Apparently, I had both.

Other soldiers joined us, not because of me, but because we had formed a unit on the field of battle. We seemed to know what we were doing, and we had an officer with us. They formed around us because we were moving with purpose, and you need purpose in the midst of battle. Purpose, and no hesitation.

I felt magic come our way. Some cried out in horror at whatever illusion one of the armored sidhe had created. I'd been able to share glamour with one or two other sidhe before. I spread that pool of protective glamour out and out. I spread it farther than I'd ever attempted before, spreading it over my people, the way you'd spill water over fevered skin.

As the screams of my men stopped and they began to murmur, I spoke low to Dawson. "Shoot the ones in armor." I had to concentrate on keeping all of us free of the illusions. Even shouting would make me stumble.

Dawson never questioned me. He simply yelled out my order, "Shoot the ones in armor! Fire!"

Immortal warriors who had seen more centuries than any of us would ever dream of fell before our weapons. They fell like dreams brought down to earth. They couldn't cloud the minds of the men, and without their illusions to stop the soldiers from firing, we mowed them down.

Dilys stood, all in yellow, glowing like she had swallowed flame, and it had filled her skin and her hair, and blazed out of her eyes. She wore no armor of any kind. Her dress looked as if she were expecting to walk down some marble staircase to a ball. But where the warriors fell, their magical armor pierced by human ingenuity, she stood. The bullets seemed to hit a wavering glow, like heat off a summer road. The bullets hit, hesitated, then melted, in little spurts of orangey light.

"What is she?" Dawson said, beside me.

"Magic," I said. "She is magic."

"What kind of magic?" Hayes asked.

"Heat, light, sun. She's a goddess of the summer heat." I'd always wondered what she'd been before she fell from grace. Most of the really powerful ones hid their pasts, some out of shame for power lost, others for fear of enemies who had retained more power settling old scores. But as I had returned Siobhan's illusions to her, so apparently I had given Dilys, or whatever her real name was, back her heat.

Others of the armored warriors had hidden behind her wavering shield. They huddled around her as they were supposed to huddle around me, but I would never burn like that. I was not sun, but moon.

In that moment, I didn't want to kill her. I wanted her to come back to me. I wanted her to be one of my court. I wanted the summer's heat to warm us all.

I called, "Dilys, we are all Unseelie. We should not be killing each other."

She spoke in a voice that held an edge of roar, and I realized it was the sound of some great fire, as if her very words burned. "You say that because your human weapons cannot harm me."

Hayes flinched beside me. She whispered, "It hurts to hear her speak."

"Not as much as it would if the princess wasn't shielding us all," Dawson said.

He was right. The glamour that protected them from the illusions was also saving them from the full force of that burning voice. She wasn't fire, she was the heat of sun. It fills the fields with life, but too much of it and the fields wither, die, and become lifeless dust.

You needed water and heat for life. Where was her mate? Where was her balance? The ring on my hand pulsed once. It had been known as the Queen's Ring for centuries. Andais had given it to me to show her favor. But she was a thing of destruction and war only. I was life as well as death; I was balance. The ring had once belonged to a goddess of love and fertility. Andais had taken it from the Goddess's dead finger.

Death should never take the tools of life, because it won't know how to use them. But I knew.

There was a rain of pink petals around me and my soldiers. The ring pulsed harder, hot against my finger. Something moved at the edge of the clearing. A white figure limped out from among the trees. It was Crystall. The last time I'd seen him, he'd been in the queen's bed, being tortured to a red ruin. One of the serious downsides to being immortal and being able to heal from almost anything was that if you fell into the hands of a sexual sadist, the "fun" could last a very long time.

She'd picked him as her victim because he'd been one of her guards who had tried to answer my call. He would have come to L.A. with me, but Andais declared that she could not lose all her guard to me. So she punished those who had to stay but did not wish to stay. She wasn't getting volunteers to take the place of the guards who had come to me. She'd been too harsh a mistress for too long. The men knew what to expect, and they just weren't signing up. That had made her even worse to the men she still had. Crystall showed that as he moved into the clearing.

When he could no longer lean on the trees, he fell to the ground on all fours and began to crawl toward us. The soldiers aimed their guns around him, as if they expected to see what had injured him coming out of the trees. It was a thought. Where was the queen? Why was she letting Cel and so many of her nobles go against her express orders? It wasn't like her to sit idly by if she could punish people. But watching Crystall crawl, seeing the bloody wounds on his body, I thought that she might be busy. Sometimes she fell so far into her bloodlust that she forgot everything but the pain and flesh under her hands. Was she somewhere intoxicated with sadistic pleasure while her son imploded her kingdom? Had she lost control to that degree?

I started moving toward Crystall. The soldiers moved with me, guns trained on Dilys, on the trees, on the dark, but I wasn't sure there was anything to shoot right now. Later. There would be things to shoot later.

Dilys called across the field in her voice with its edge of fire sound. "Your bloodline is corrupt, Meredith. Your aunt has tortured her guards until they are useless for anything but slaves."

I looked at the golden figure, and called back. "Then why are you helping Cel? Isn't he just as corrupt?"

"Yes," Dilys said.

"You'll help him kill me, then you'll kill him," I said.

She said nothing, but her light flared a little brighter. It was the magical equivalent of that little smile that you can't always keep from your face. That satisfied, things-are-going-my-way smile.

Crystall collapsed, and I thought for a moment that he wouldn't get back up, but he did. He began to crawl, painfully, slowly, toward that golden glow.

I started to go forward and help him, but the

ring pulsed harder, and I took that as a sign. I stayed where I was. I let him do that slow, piteous crawl. His white hair, which I knew in the right light wasn't white but almost clear, like crystal or water, dragged on the ground, like a rich cloak fallen on hard times.

Dawson said, "Do you want us to help him?"

"No," I said in a low voice. "I want her to help him."

He gave me a look, then when my look didn't make any sense to him, he did the look with Brennan and Mercer. Mercer said, "But won't she kill him?"

"Not if she wants to be saved," I said.

"I don't think she's the one who needs saving," Mercer said.

Dilys yelled at me. "Aren't you going to help him, Princess?"

"He's not here for me."

"You speak in riddles," she said.

Crystall continued his agonizingly slow crawl across the field with its dead and wounded. But it was clear now that he wasn't aiming for me. He was crawling inexorably toward that golden glow.

"Do not let him throw his life away, Meredith. If he tries to harm me in this condition, I will destroy him."

"He's not here to harm you, Dilys," I said.

"Why else is he here but to save you and your humans?"

Crystall had reached the edge of the golden

light, but had not quite touched it. The light, like sunlight will, sparkled through his skin and hair as if he were made of his namesake, crystal. Her light caught rainbows along his body. Small, winking colored lights, to chase back the dark.

He put out his hand, and the moment it entered the circle of her light, he knelt and looked at her. The blood on his body gleamed as if formed of rubies.

"What magic is this?" Dilys asked, but her voice was not the burning thing it had been.

Crystall stood, and walked into that light. His body began to glow, like sunlight on water, or the reflected light on diamonds. He moved into her sunlight, and reflected it, making it a thing of beauty.

"What are you doing to him, Meredith?"

"It is not me who is doing it."

Crystall was almost within touching distance of her golden, glowing form. He stood there, tall and lithe, his body lined with muscles, but lean like a runner. He had always had a delicate strength. He was like a jewel thrown into the sun, gleaming with rainbows from the tips of his hair to every inch of bare skin. The wounds had closed, as if just being near her power had healed him.

She looked . . . frightened. "I am no healer, but he is healed. How is this possible?"

Crystall held his hand out to her.

"What does he want?" she yelled, and the fear was plain in her voice.

"Take his hand, and you'll know."

"It's a trap," she said.

"I wear the queen's ring, Dilys. I saw you burning with the heat of the summer sun, and thought, 'Where is her balance?' Where is her coolness to keep her from burning everything to death?"

"**No!**" She shouted it at him.

Crystall simply held his hand out to her, as if he could hold that shining hand out forever.

Then her golden hand began to move, as if of its own accord. Her fingertips brushed his, and the golden heat became half silver, and I saw the waver of heat meet the sparkle of water in front of them, like the sun on the surface of a summer lake.

Then they were in each other's arms. They kissed as if they had always kissed, though I knew they had not. He had never been her lover, her god to goddess, but he was what was left. He was the coolness she needed, and I had called what I could find.

Her glow banked to a hard, yellow light as if she were carved of it. Crystall glowed as if he were formed of rainbow light.

"Oh, my god," Hayes whispered.

"Yes," I said.

"What did you do?" Dawson said.

"They will be a couple, and there will be children. Two children."

"How do you know that?" Brennan asked.

I smiled at him, and knew that my eyes had begun to glow, green and gold.

He swallowed hard, as if the sight disturbed him. "Oh, yeah, magic."

"Make love, not war," another solider said.

"Exactly," I said.

Then there was a shriek from the far edge of the field. Cel stood there, screaming wordlessly at me in his gray and black armor, surrounded by followers in every color of armor and some that looked like bark and leaves or animal pelts, but they would stand up to anything but steel and iron. Those dreamlike warriors carried a figure between them, and from the moment I recognized him, my heart failed me. His hair fell loose around him, blacker than the moon-fed night. Their white sidhe hands seemed an insult against all his dark perfection.

Cel screamed across the field at me. "He still lives, barely! Is this mongrel worth your life, cousin? Will you walk to me across this field to save him?"

I could not take my gaze from him, dark and so terribly still. Was he even still alive? Only death would make him so still. The thought that I had lost them both, my Darkness and my Killing Frost, was too much. Too much pain, too much loss, just too much.

I whispered his name. "Doyle." I willed him to look up, to move, to let me know that if I walked to him, there would be something to save. My hand went to my stomach, still flat, still so unmoved by the pregnancy, and I knew that I could not trade myself for my Darkness. He would never forgive me if I made such a bargain. A wave of nausea washed over me, and the night swam, but I couldn't faint. I couldn't be weak; there was no time for weakness. I pushed the feelings away that would unman me, and clung to the ones that would help me: hatred, fear, rage, and a coldness that I didn't know I had inside me.

"It's war, then," I whispered.

"What?" Dawson asked.

"We will give Cel what he wants," I said.

"You can't give yourself to him," Hayes said.

"No, I cannot," I said, and my voice sounded like someone else's, as if I didn't recognize myself anymore.

"If we don't give him you, what do we give him?" Mercer asked.

"War," I said simply, and began to walk across the field. My soldiers came with me. Either Cel would die this moment or I would. Seeing Doyle thrown onto the ground like so much motionless garbage, I was content with that.

CHAPTER THIRTY-NINE

I ORDERED MY SOLDIERS TO SHOOT THE unseelie nobles who were standing. Cel was a prince of faerie. He was heir to a throne. He had diplomatic immunity. They shouldn't have taken my order, but we had crossed a battlefield together. I had saved their lives. My orders through their sergeant had kept us alive and unharmed. We were a unit, and as a unit they fired on my order.

I watched the nobles' bodies jerk and dance to the explosion of the bullets. The noise was deafening. They were wounded in a sort of silence, because the guns were so loud, and seemed to have nothing to do with the movement at the other end of the barrel. It was as if we fired, but they fell because of something else. But not all of them fell; most remained standing. I had to do something before they unleashed their hands of power on us all.

Blood leaked black in the moonlight, but it wasn't enough blood. I needed more, so much more. For the first time I felt no dread of my power, no pain at the call of it, just a fierceness that was almost joy. That fierceness poured over my skin in a wash of heat. It hit my left hand and poured out my palm.

Dawson yelled next to my ear. "What are you doing?"

I had no time to explain. I said, "The hand of blood." I pointed that hand, palm out, toward our enemies. I should have worried that I would hit Doyle, but in that moment I knew, simply knew, that I could do it. I could control it. It was mine, this power, it was me.

Blood fountained in black sheets from their wounds. They screamed, then Cel raised his hand. I knew what he meant to do. Without thinking, I stepped out from between my men, my soldiers, my people. Dawson grabbed for me to pull me back behind the shield of their bodies, but then Cel's hand of old blood hit us all, and Dawson's hand fell away. There were yells behind me, but I had no time to look.

I screamed "Mine!" There was pain. I could feel the nails in my arm and shoulder again; the knife wound I'd taken in a duel; claw marks in one arm and thigh from an old attack. It hurt, and I bled for him, but he could only make the wound as bad as it had been, and I had never had a blood injury that was near fatal.

"What did you do?" Dawson asked. "One minute we were bleeding, now we're not."

I had no space in my concentration to explain. Cel's hand might not kill us, but there were others at his side who could. It was a race now to see if I could bleed them to death faster than they could recover themselves.

I screamed, "Bleed for me!"

Blood geysered from them, and I could feel their flesh tearing under my power, their wounds like a doorway that my power could rip apart. The blood arched, black and shining liquid. The sound of it was like rain on the grass and trees around them.

The brilliant armor in all its rainbow colors began to turn black with blood and gore. They were screaming now, but what they screamed was "Mercy!" They called for mercy, but as I watched Doyle lay motionless at their feet, covered in black blood, I discovered that I had no mercy to give them.

I had never meant them to die for me. The thought came, "What did you think would happen if you sent soldiers against the Unseelie?" But even Cel wasn't supposed to be mad enough to fight the United States Army. I hadn't foreseen this, hadn't dreamed that he would be so out of control. But my lack of foresight didn't matter. I had asked for help, and my help was dying around me.

I stood there bleeding, staring across the yards of the frosted grass at my cousin's mad eyes. His helmet left his face bare save for a crosspiece down the line of his nose. His eyes burned with the color of his magic. He had called all his power, and I realized that it wasn't enough. It had never been enough.

The wind picked up the long blackness of his hair where it spilled free around his armor. He'd always worn it loose in battle. Too vain to hide his beauty, too bad a warrior to be willing to hide the hair that marked him as high court Unseelie. He would never braid it or put it back as Doyle did.

Cel was weak, evil-minded, and petty. Faerie would never accept him. I was going back to L.A. but I could not leave my people to him. I could not leave faerie in his inadequate hands.

I whispered onto the wind, "Bleed for me." The wind carried my voice, my magic, and where it moved it began to form into a whirlwind. A tornado formed of ice and blood and power. Faerie was the land, the land was faerie, and I had been crowned its queen. It rose to my word, my power, and my desire.

The nobles around him who could move, ran. Those who could crawl did so. They picked up their wounded and fled. Cel screamed at them, "Come back, cowards!"

His concentration had slipped away from me, and my old wounds were closed, as if by . . . magic.

Cel lashed out at his followers. Some fell in the winter-kissed grass, brought low by ancient wounds reopened by the man they would have made their king.

A wave of blackness moved across the field, as if a different night moved in a line above the frost. This night was moonless, and darker than dark. I knew, before she materialized completely, who would be standing in the way of my cold wind and blood.

Andais, Queen of Air and Darkness, stood in front of her son, as she had always stood in front of him. She wore her black armor, carried her raven blade. Her cloak spilled out behind her, and it was darkness itself spun into cloth, and more. She held darkness around her, and I felt her power of air push back at my own.

The twister I had conjured with faerie's help stopped moving forward. It did not die or fade, but it stopped, as if its twisting front had hit an invisible wall.

I pushed at that wall, willed my power to move forward, and for a moment the wall softened. I felt the whirlwind move forward; then it was as if the air was drawn away from it, sucked out and sent whirling into the moonlight. She pulled the air from my whirlwind as she could pull the air from your lungs.

Lieutenant Dawson barked orders and the soldiers formed two lines, one standing, one kneeling, both pointing at her. Would I have fired on my queen? I had a moment of hesitation, and that was my undoing. Darkness poured over us, and we were blind. The next moment the air was heavy, so heavy. We could not breathe. We had no air even to call for help. I collapsed to my knees, my hands on the cold grass. Someone fell against me, and I knew it had to be Dawson, but I could not see him. She was the Queen of Air and Darkness, a goddess of battle, and we would die at her feet.

CHAPTER FORTY

I WAS LOST IN THE DARK. HER BLACKNESS had taken the sky. Only two things remained, the ground under my cheek, and the body next to me in the choking dark. I no longer knew right from left, and only the frozen ground let me know up from down, so I did not know who lay pressed against me in the blackness. A hand found mine, a hand to hold while we died.

The frost crunched under my free hand, and I clung to the warmth of that other hand. The frost began to melt against my hand, and I wished for Frost, my Killing Frost. He had let faerie take him away because he thought I loved him less than Doyle. It broke my heart to think that he would never know that I had loved him too.

I tried to say his name, but there was no air left to spare for words. I clung to the melting frost and the human hand, and let my tears speak for me into the frozen ground.

I regretted the babies inside me, and I thought, "I'm sorry. I'm so sorry I couldn't save you." But part of me was content to die. If Doyle and Frost were both lost to me, then death was not the worst fate. In that moment, I stopped fighting, because without them I didn't want to go on. I let the dark and the choking wash over me. I gave myself to death. Then the hand in mine spasmed; it clung to me as it died, and it brought me back to myself. I could have died alone, but if I died there was no one left to save them, my men, my soldiers. I could not leave them to the airless dark, not if there was anything I could do to save them. It was not love that made me fight again, it was duty. But duty is its own kind of love; I would fight for them, fight until death took me silently screaming. The babes inside me, without their fathers to help raise them, were almost a bitter thing, but the soldiers who clung to me had lives of their own, and she had no right to steal them. How dare she, immortal that she was, take their few years away.

I prayed, "Goddess, help me save them. Help me fight for them." I had no power in me to fight the dark and the very air made too heavy to breathe, but I prayed all the same, because when all else is lost, there is always prayer.

At first, I thought nothing had changed, then I realized that the grass under my hand and cheek was colder. The frost crunched as my fingers flexed, as if the melting that my warmth had caused had never happened.

The air was bitingly cold, like breathing in the heart of winter when the air is so cold it burns going down. Then I realized that I was breathing a complete full breath of the frigid air. The hand in mine squeezed, and I heard voices saying, "I can breathe," or simply coughing as if they'd been fighting to draw a full breath all this time.

I whispered, "Thank you, Goddess."

I tried to lift my head from the grass, but the moment my face got more than a few inches from the ground, the air was gone again. Sounds in the dark let me know that I wasn't the only one who had discovered how narrow our line of air was, but it was there. We could breathe. Andais could not crush our lungs. She would have to come into the dark and find us if she wanted us dead.

The frost thickened under my hand until it was like touching a young snow. The air was so cold that each breath hurt, as if ice were stabbing me. Then the frost thickened more, and moved under my hand. Moved? Frost didn't move. There was fur under my hand, something alive, growing out of the very ground. I kept my hand on that furred side, and felt it go up and up, until my hand was stretched tall to follow the curve of something. I stroked my hand down that furred but strangely cold side, and found the curved haunches of something. It was only as my hand followed the curve of the leg to find a hoof that I thought I understood. The white stag had formed out of the frost. My Killing Frost was here, beside me. He was still a stag, still not my love, but it was still him in there somewhere. I stroked his side, felt him rise and fall with breath. The stag's head had to be far above mine, and if he could breathe, so could I. I rose slowly to my knees, keeping one hand on the stag's side and the other in the hand that still clung to mine. The hand moved with me, and its owner got to their knees.

It was Orlando, next to me, who said, "I can still breathe."

I didn't answer. I was afraid to talk, as if my words would frighten the stag, make it run like the animal it was. My hand found the rapid beat of its heart against my palm. I wanted to wrap my arm around its neck, hold it tightly, but I was afraid that it would climb to its feet and run. How much of my Frost was in there? I had seen him watching me, but did he understand, or had the Goddess just sent the stag to help us?

I whispered, "Oh, Frost, please, please hear me."

The stag shook, as if something that it didn't like had touched it, and it got to its feet. My hand was just on its leg as I struggled to my feet in my long coat, with no hand to help me hold the hem, but I was afraid to lose my grip on either warmth that my hand touched. The stag because it was the closest I'd been to Frost since he had vanished, and Orlando's hand because it had been that touch that had made me fight. A human hand that had made me realize that a queen does not despair as long as her people are in danger. You fight, you fight even if your heart is broken, because it's not just about your happiness anymore. It's about theirs, too.

I stumbled on the hem of my coat, and Orlando's hand steadied me as I righted myself by the stag's side. It shifted nervously, as if getting ready to bolt. I knew he was a stag, and I knew he wasn't really in there, but this was the closest I had come to him, and I wanted him to stay. This curve of fur and warmth was all I had left of him.

The stag began to walk. I kept my hand on its side, and pulled Orlando with me. I felt a tugging, and thought that Orlando had someone else by the hand. The stag pranced nervously, and I felt the presence of someone else on its other side. We touched the stag, and held hands like children, as it led us forward in the dark.

It was Sergeant Dawson who said, "Weapons off. Safe. When we can see again, fire. Don't give her a chance to use her magic again."

Andais was queen and my aunt. My father had refused to kill her and take her throne. That bit of mercy had probably cost him his life, because once the rebels offer you a throne, even if you don't take it, there are those who fear that you will. He had loved his sister, and even his nephew. I realized in that moment that I did not. They had both made certain that there was no love between us. Some would say I had a duty to my queen, but my duty was to the men crowded around me in the dark. My duty was to the stag who led us forward, and what was left of my Frost. My duty was to the children inside me, and anyone who would steal them away was my enemy. War in the abstract is a confusing thing. War on the ground, in the middle of a battle, is not. When someone shoots at you, they are your enemy, and you shoot back. When someone tries to kill you, they are your enemy, and you try to kill them first. War is complicated, battle is not. She was going to kill us, even knowing I held the grandchildren of her brother inside me. In that moment I had only one duty, for all of us to survive.

If she used her magic again there might not be a second miracle to save us. Goddess helps those who help themselves. We were armed with automatic weapons; we'd help ourselves.

I felt the soldiers around me shifting, and thought they were readying their guns. Orlando squeezed my hand one last time, then took his hand into the dark. He was getting ready to kill my queen. Would she still be where we'd left her? "The queen may not be standing where we last saw her," I said.

Dawson gave orders for the men to cover a circle around us, because there was no cover save the darkness that held us. Once free of that, we would be naked to the view of all.

We stepped into the moonlight, and it seemed unbearably bright, bright enough to make me blink. I was still blinking into the brightness when the first gunshots exploded around me. It made me jump, but the stag jerked so violently that for a moment I thought he had been hit. Then he bounded away, a blur of white, streaking away from the noise, the guns, the violence.

I yelled his name. I could not help it. "Frost!" But there was no one inside that body to answer the sound of human words. The stag vanished into the tree edge, and I was alone again.

Dawson yelled beside me, "Field of fire, the black area. Suppressive bursts with rifle, squad weapons, give me ten seconds of raking fire. She's hiding behind it."

I turned and looked at the battlefield. I turned and looked at my aunt and my cousin and the nobles from the court I was supposed to be fighting to rule, and I cared more about the stag leaving than about them dying.

Andais had called darkness, like a mist to hide herself and Cel and the other nobles. Dawson and the rest were firing into it. If they were still there, the bullets would find them, but there was no way to tell what lay in the dark. Had she fled?

I looked behind us, and found that the men who had been given the job of watching the back of the circle were doing just that. They were letting the others fire into the dark, but they watched to see whether the darkness was a trick, whether our enemies were trying to sneak up behind us.

What could I do to help them?

"They're behind us!" someone yelled, and I turned with that yell.

I had time to knock the rifle to point at the

ground, and move myself into the line of fire. I could have tried yelling, but watching the Red Caps move out of the darkness, I knew that words wouldn't have kept the men from firing on them. The Red Caps were small giants, seven to twelve feet tall, and all of them wore close-fitting caps on their heads that bled fresh blood down their faces and bodies. Before magic returned to faerie, their hats were dry, and only fresh death helped them wet them again. My hand of blood had given them back their own blood magic. But there was no time to explain all that in the middle of battle. I did the only thing I could think of; I stood between the two groups with my hands outspread. It kept the soldiers from firing and gave Dawson time to turn around and give orders.

I yelled, "They are allies, friends!"

"Fuck that," someone said.

I couldn't blame them for the fear in those words. It looked like every Red Cap the goblin kingdom could boast was coming toward us across the field. There were dozens of them, armed to the teeth, covered in blood, and coming for us. If I hadn't been certain they were on our side, I'd have shot them too. Shot them, and run for my life.

When I was sure that my people wouldn't shoot them, I walked to meet the Red Caps. Jonty was in the front. He was nearly ten feet tall, with scaly gray skin, and a face nearly as wide as my chest. His mouthful of jagged teeth and nearly lip-less mouth had become something more human, more . . . handsome. My magic had changed the Red Caps to something more Seelie, though I had not done it on purpose. Jonty wasn't the largest of them, but my eyes went to him first. Maybe it was because I knew him and he me, but the other Red Caps let him be ahead of them without arguing. Goblins are all about strength, the ultimate survival of the fittest, and Red Caps are the most violent, the most wedded to power and strength. For them all to fall back and let him lead them said that it wasn't just my eyes that saw the power in Jonty. Of course, I sensed it; the Red Caps had probably made him fight for those few feet of respect.

Dawson was beside me when Jonty and I met in the field. The wizard trusted me, but he had brought soldiers with guns, just in case. Jonty smiled down at me through his mask of blood. I tried to see that smile the way Dawson and the other humans must see it. Frightening, I supposed, but I could not see it that way. It was Jonty, and the blood flowing down him called to my hand of blood, so that I held that hand out to him. He put his large fingers against my palm, and magic jumped between us, tingling and rushing, like warm champagne with a little electricity in it.

"What was that?" Dawson asked, which meant he'd felt something, too.

"Magic," I said.

The blood ran faster, thicker, from Jonty's cap, so that he had to wipe his hand across his forehead to keep his eyes free of blood. He laughed, a great, rumbling, joyous sound. The other Red Caps began to crowd around, to touch the blood on him. Those who touched bled more.

"What is happening?" one of the other soldiers asked.

"I carry blood magic, and the Red Caps react to it."

"She is too modest," Jonty said. "She is our mistress. The first sidhe with a full Hand of Blood in centuries. We felt her call to our blood, and we came to join the battle." He frowned then. "The other goblins did not feel the call of blood."

"I have a treaty with Kurag. He should have still sent men."

"The goblin king knew who you fought, and he would not stand boldly against the queen."

"Coward," one of the other Red Caps muttered.

"You went against your king to come here," I said.

Jonty nodded. "We cannot go back to the goblin mound."

I looked at them, dozens of the most dangerous warriors that the goblins could boast. I tried to picture them permanently stationed in Los Angeles. I couldn't quite picture it. But I couldn't leave them homeless. They had shown more loyalty than most of the sidhe to me. I would reward that, not punish it.

Orlando called out. "The darkness is fading."

We turned, and found that he was right. The

darkness was fading like some polluted mist. Andais was gone, and so were Cel and several of the other armored figures, but not all. Had she left them as a punishment or because she could not transport all of them? She had gained in power like most of faerie, but not to the point that she had once been, when she could make entire armies of the Unseelie appear and disappear. Andais might try to make a reason for leaving some of Cel's allies behind, but in the end, I knew she had left them because she wasn't strong enough to save them. For she would be certain that any left behind would be killed. It's what she would do.

In truth, there was only one figure on that side of the field that I cared about. Whether the rest lived or died was nothing to me. Only Doyle mattered. If he lived, then it was all good; if he was . . . not alive, then I wasn't sure what I'd do. I couldn't think past the need to cross the field and see if his heart still beat.

Dawson stopped me from taking the lead, and put some of his men in a line of guns pointing at the wounded sidhe. Jonty stayed at my side, and the Red Caps came at our backs. I started to say that we should put the Red Caps in front. They were a lot harder to kill than humans, but we were almost there. I didn't want to do anything to delay touching Doyle. In that moment, I was not a leader of men, I was a woman who wanted the man she loved. In that moment, I understood that love is as dangerous as hate. It will make you forget, make you weak. I did not push the soldiers aside and run for Doyle. That took all the control I had left. Beyond that, there was nothing but the fear that crushed my chest tight, and the ache in my hands to touch his skin. If he were dead, I wanted to touch him while his skin still felt like him. A body doesn't feel like your loved one once it grows cold. It's like touching a doll. No, I have no words for what it feels like to touch someone you love once their body has given up its warmth. All the wonderful memories of my father, and the one that haunts is his skin under my hands, cold and unyielding with death. I did not want my last touch of Doyle to be like that. I prayed as we closed that distance. I prayed for him to be alive, but something made me pray for warmth too. Did that mean I already knew the truth? Did that mean he was already gone, and I was simply bargaining for what that last caress would be like?

There was a pressure building inside my head, pushing at my eyes. I would not cry, not yet. I would not shed tears when he might still live. Please, Goddess, please, Mother, let him be alive.

The wounded sidhe cried out, "Mercy, mercy on us, Princess. We followed our prince, as we would follow you."

I didn't answer, because I simply didn't care. I knew they had betrayed me, and they knew I knew it. They were painting the best picture they could because we had filled them with bullets, had injured them until they could not flee. Their queen and their prince had left them to my mercy. They had nothing else to count on but the possibility that I was my father's daughter. He would have spared them; such gestures of mercy were what made everyone love him. His mercy was also the thing his assassin had most likely used to lure him to his death. In that moment, for the first time, I saw my father's mercy as weakness.

"Move away from Doyle," I said, and my voice was choked with emotion. That I could not help. I wanted to run to him, to throw myself on him, but my enemies were too close. If Doyle were dead, then my death and the death of our children would not bring him back. If he still lived, then a few minutes of caution would not change that. Part of me screamed inside, hurry, hurry, but there was a larger part of me that was strangely calm. I felt icy, and somehow not quite myself. Something about tonight had stolen me away, and left a colder, wiser stranger in her place.

My father once said that as a ruler shapes a country, so the people of a country shape a ruler. The nobles on the ground, who were crawling, limping, and dragging their wounded away from Doyle's still form, had helped bring me to this cold stranger. We would see how cold my heart would stay.

Jonty said, "Princess Meredith, we would protect you from their magic."

I nodded.

"We are protecting the princess," Dawson said.

"They can put their bodies between me and the hands of power of the nobles here. They would kill or maim you, but Red Caps are a tougher lot, Sergeant. They can be our shields."

Dawson looked up at the towering figures. "You'll be our meat shields?"

Jonty seemed to think about it, then nodded.

Dawson glanced at me, then shrugged as if to say, "If they're willing to take the hit, better them than my men." "Okay" was what he said out loud.

The Red Caps moved around us so that they shielded both me and the soldiers. The humans were a little nervous, and several of them asked, "They're on our side, right?"

Dawson and I assured them that, yes, Jonty and the rest were on our side. I wasn't as reassuring as I might have been, because most of my attention was on the glimpses of Doyle that I kept getting as everyone moved around us. In that moment, I wasn't sure I cared about anything, or anyone else. My world had narrowed down to that spill of black hair on the frost-rimmed grass.

My hands tingled with the need to touch him, long before Dawson and Jonty felt that it was safe. Finally, the way was clear, and I was able to hold up the leather skirt and run to him. I collapsed beside him, the skirt protecting me from the winter-rough grass. I reached for him, then hesitated. It seemed ridiculous that a moment before all I had wanted was to touch him, and now that I could, I was afraid. I was so afraid I could barely breathe through the tightness in my throat. My heart couldn't decide if it was beating too fast, or forgetting to beat, so that my chest hurt with it. I knew that it was the beginning of a panic attack, not a heart attack, but a tiny part of me wasn't sure I cared which it was. If he was dead, and Frost was lost, then. . . .

I fought my breathing until it came more smoothly. I fought until my breath was deeper, more even. I would not lose control of myself. Not in front of the men. Later, in private, if. . . .

I cursed myself for a coward and made myself reach out those last few inches to that long, black hair. The hair was thick and rich and perfect as it moved under my hands, so I could find his neck, and check his pulse. My fingers brushed something hard. I moved back and stared at the smooth line of his neck, exposed to the moonlight. There was nothing there but the collar of the designer suit that Doyle had borrowed from Sholto.

I shook my head and reached for his neck again. My eyes told me I was touching skin, but my fingers told me there was something in the way. Something hard, but cloth-covered, something. . . . There was only one reason that my eyes and my fingers weren't telling me the same thing.

I fought down the first flutter of hope, squashed it flat, and had to calm myself for a very different reason. Positive emotions can blind you as surely as negative ones. I had to see the truth, had to touch the truth, whatever it might be.

I closed my eyes, for they were what was being

fooled. I reached for the side of his neck, and found that hard cloth again. With my eyes closed, I could feel it better, because my sight wasn't arguing with my sense of touch. I pushed past whatever piece of clothing it was, and found the neck. The moment I touched the skin, I knew it wasn't Doyle. The skin texture wasn't his. I searched for the big neck pulse, and found none. Whoever was under my fingertips was dead; still warm, but dead.

I kept my eyes closed and moved my hands upward, to find very short hair, and the roughness of the beginnings of stubble, and a face that was not the face I loved. It was illusion, really good illusion, but in the end, it was magic, not reality.

I had a moment of relief so complete that I half fell onto the body. It wasn't Doyle. He wasn't dead. I let myself collapse onto the body. I hugged it to me, my hands searching for the uniform, the weapons they hadn't even bothered to remove. Such disdain, such arrogance.

Dawson knelt on one side of me, and Jonty came to the other. "I am so sorry, Princess Meredith," Dawson said, touching my back.

"The Darkness was a great warrior," Jonty said in his deep voice.

I shook my head, pushing myself up from the body. "It's not him. It's not Doyle. It's an illusion."

"What?" Dawson said.

"Then why are you crying?" Jonty asked.

I hadn't even realized I was crying, but he was right. "Relief, I think," I said.

"Why are they holding the glamour in place to make it look like Darkness?" Jonty asked.

Until that moment I hadn't thought about it, but he was absolutely right. Why would they not drop an illusion guaranteed to make me angrier at them if they were truly giving up? Answer: they weren't giving up, and they hoped to gain something through the trick. But what?

Jonty helped me to my feet, his hand so large that it encircled my upper arm with his hand almost in a fist, as if he could have wrapped his hand around me over and over.

He kept moving me over the frozen ground away from the glamour-hidden body. "What's wrong?" Dawson asked.

"Mayhap nothing, but I do not like it."

I started to say "Jonty," but never got it out. It wasn't the sound of the bomb that hit first; it was the physical push of the explosion. The rush of energy hit us before the sound so that we had a moment of being hit. Then Jonty was cradling me, hiding me against his body, and only then did the sound hit, a sound that rocked the world and deafened me. It was like getting hit twice by something huge and angry. I'd heard stories that giants could be invisible, and this was like that. It seemed wrong that something so powerful could be so unseen. That something so destructive could be merely chemicals and metal. There was something so alive about it, as it drove us to the ground, and smashed the world around us.

CHAPTER FORTY-ONE

THERE WERE VOICES. SCREAMS, CRIES FOR help. I could see nothing, but I could hear them. There was something on top of me, something heavy. I found that I had hands, arms, and could push at the weight on top of me, but I could not move it. But the more I pushed at it, tried to turn my head against it, the more I began to realize what I was pushing at. Cloth, and under the cloth flesh; I was pushing at someone. Someone was on top of me, someone large and heavy, and . . . Jonty.

I whispered his name, still trapped in the darkness underneath him. His broad chest was so wide that I could see nothing but the dimness of his body. The ground underneath me was solid, and the frost on the grass was already beginning to melt, which meant that Jonty and I had lain here long enough for our body heat to begin to warm the ground. How long had we lain here? How much time had passed? Who was screaming for help? It wasn't the Red Caps. They would not scream. The soldiers, the human soldiers, it had to be them. Oh, Goddess, help me help them. Don't let them die like this. Don't let them die for me. It seemed so unfair.

I braced against the ground, and pushed with all my might. Jonty's weight moved a little higher, but that was it. I had a moment of hope, then the weight simply did not move anymore. But warm liquid ran down my hands, and began to soak into my sleeves. The blood was still warm. That was good. Either it was his blood, and he was still alive enough for it to be warm, or it was his magical blood from his hat, and the fact that it was flowing at all meant he was still alive. I could see a thin line of moonlight. It was still night. My arms began to tremble, then finally collapse. I tried to keep the weight from crushing me, but other than that, I was trapped. The blood began to trickle down the side of my face, like a warm creeping finger. The darkness seemed thicker for that bit of brightness I'd seen.

The blood trickled down the side of my neck. I fought the urge to wipe at it, since I couldn't reach it anyway. It was just blood. Blood wasn't bad, and it was warm, and that was good. I fought to calm my pulse; panicking would not help me. I used what little movement I had with my hands to search for Jonty's heartbeat. I was much lower than his heart, though. I could not reach high enough to touch his heart. Was there another pulse point close to my hands? Was there any way for me to tell if he was still alive?

If I couldn't reach higher, could I reach lower? There was a big pulse point on the inner groin. The femoral artery was as good as the carotid in the neck, it was just usually too intimate to use. But, under the circumstances, I didn't think Jonty would mind.

I inched my hand down the side of my body until I found the joint of his hip, then I traced inward, fighting against the weight and the sheer bulk of him. Since I couldn't see anything but the darkness of him above me, I closed my eyes and concentrated on my fingers, on what I was feeling.

My fingers found something softer than his thigh, which meant I was close to the artery. I moved my fingers down a little and to the side. As I pushed my way lower, his body reacted to my touch. What had been large and soft was becoming less soft. Did that mean that Jonty was alive? I tried to remember what I knew of the freshly dead. I knew that death sometimes made you have one last orgasm, but was this that, or was the quickening of his body against my wrist a sign that he was alive? I couldn't remember if any professor or book in college had ever talked about it; probably not, too much information for most human classrooms. In fact, you got in trouble for asking things like that, or I had. That embarrassed silence, the mortified look on the teacher's face.

My fingers slipped inside his thigh. I had to

squirm my fingers just a little more into that warm, close place. His body continued to be happier against my arm. I was going to take it for a good sign, a sign of life, but I wanted to feel the beat of his pulse. I wanted to know that the swelling of his groin was not the last beat of his heart, the last thing he would ever feel. "Please, Goddess, please don't let him be dead."

I was almost certain that my fingertips were where they needed to be to feel the pulse. Admittedly, trapped underneath him, it was harder to judge, but I was almost sure. I couldn't feel anything. I took a deep breath in and held it. I held my breath and put all my attention into my fingers, into feeling what there was to feel. I stilled my body so that I wouldn't mistake my own pulse for his. I pressed my fingers into his flesh through his clothes, and willed that pulse to beat against my fingers.

There, was that it? The pulse came again, slow and thick against my fingers. It was slower than it should have been, but it was there. If we could get him to a healer, he would live. If we could get help, Jonty would not have to die for me. If we could find anyone who wasn't my enemy tonight.

The bomb had worked. I could hear the muffled screams of the soldiers. If Jonty's damage was any indication, the Red Caps were badly hurt too. Why had the Unseelie nobles not hunted me down and finished me while I was unconscious? What had they been waiting for?

I felt the scream beginning to build, like a pressure that I couldn't fight. No, didn't want to fight. I couldn't move. I couldn't help Jonty. I couldn't see what was happening. I couldn't fight back, but I could scream. That I could do, and it was as if even that would be a release, a help to my awful growing panic. I took deep, even breaths, forced myself to slow my pulse, and that trembling sensation that was trying to steal me away from myself. If I started screaming from sheer panic, I wouldn't stop. I'd scream, and squirm under Jonty's body until my enemies found me. I had no illusions what would happen if Cel's people found me. Were there Seelie warriors on the field tonight too? If they found me, would they try to take me back to Taranis? Probably. Death, or more rape by my uncle. Please, Goddess, let there be other choices.

Where was Doyle? He hadn't been the body at their feet, but if he was able to come to my side, where was he? Galen, or Rhys, Mistral, Sholto, any of them, what could have kept them from my side this long? Were they . . . dead? Were all whom I had loved dead?

Jonty moved above me. "Jonty," I said.

He didn't answer, and I realized that I couldn't feel his muscles tensing at all. He was still unconscious above me, but he began to lift without his arms moving at all. Someone was lifting him. A few moments before I'd wanted him off of me so badly that I had had to fight down panic. Now, I wasn't so certain. Whether the Red Cap being lifted slowly off of me was a good thing or a bad thing depended entirely on who was doing the lifting.

My pulse sped up as Jonty's big chest rose upward. It was taking so long that I began to wonder if it was the humans, the soldiers. They would have trouble lifting him. Then he rose upward enough that I could see legs. The leg of a uniform, the torn leg of a designer suit. I said, "Doyle!"

He knelt, hands still on the big Red Cap, pushing like you'd shoulder press a weight. "I'm here," he said.

I reached out to touch his leg. My hand came back with blood on it. Was it Jonty's, or Doyle's? What had been happening while I lay unconscious? In that moment, I almost didn't care, because Doyle was here. I could touch him. It was all right, because he was there.

I could see more legs. Another was in black trousers and boots—Mistral. I remembered now that Galen and Rhys had been wearing soldiers' uniforms. They were all here, all of them. Thank you, Goddess.

"Are you hurt?" Doyle asked.

"I don't think so."

"Can you move out from under the Red Cap?"

I thought about it, and realized that I could. I began to push my way out from under Jonty's rising body. I had to do a sort of modified crab walk on my elbows and butt, but finally my face was in the clean, fresh air. I took a deep breath of winter air, and kept pushing. When I was clear enough, I turned and crawled on my hands and knees. A hand took my arm and helped me stand. It was Dawson. He looked unhurt.

"Princess," he said, "are you all right?"

I nodded. "I think so." I touched his hand. "I'm glad to see that you're okay. I heard screaming."

He got a strange look on his face. "I'm okay now."

I thought it was an odd way to phrase it. But Galen was beside me, taking me into his arms, and there was no time to question Dawson. Galen lifted me off my feet, holding me so tightly that I couldn't see his face clearly. But I could see Jonty's back over Galen's shoulder. The sight stole the smile from my face.

The Red Cap's back was a mass of wounds, a red ruin. Doyle and the others laid him gently down on the grass. I knew why they'd moved him slowly now. "Oh, my God, Jonty," I said.

Galen loosened his grip enough to see my face as he lowered me to the grass. "I'm sorry, Merry." Blood was drying on the side of his face from a gash near his temple.

"You're hurt."

He smiled. "Not as bad as some."

I looked back at Jonty with the other men grouped around him. They were too serious, too quiet. I didn't like it. "Jonty's heart is still beating. If we can get him to a healer he won't die."

Galen's face was stricken in the moonlight, so pain-filled. "But you would have died."

He was right. If the bomb had done that

much damage to a Red Cap, then I'd have been so much red ruin. Me, and our babies, would have been turned into so much raw meat.

"Cel's followers did this," I said.

"Dawson told us," Galen said.

I started toward Jonty and the others. Galen slid his hand in mine and we walked to him hand in hand.

Doyle laid his hand against my cheek, and I pressed my face against his hand. "The Red Caps did our duty for us," he said.

The comment made me raise my face from his hand and look past Jonty and the other guards. Soldiers were standing, helping wounded move across the field, but the Red Caps were still figures lying across the grass. Almost none of them were sitting up, and none were standing.

"How are the humans up and the Red Caps so hurt?"

"We were hurt," Dawson said, "but we healed."

"What?" I asked.

"Every solider who you healed earlier healed on their own. Then we healed the others."

"What?" I asked again, because it still didn't make sense.

"We healed them," Dawson said. "We used the nails. They were like some sort of magic wands."

"Can it heal the Red Caps?" Doyle asked.

"They're metal," I said.

"They are dying, Meredith. I don't think it will hurt them now," Rhys said. One of his arms was in a sling, and the sleeve of his uniform was blackened.

Mistral's coat was a blackened ruin across his back. Had Taranis himself attacked with his Seelie warriors? I realized that Sholto was still missing.

"Where's Sholto?"

Doyle dropped his hand from my face, and answered me while turning away. "Sholto is well. The sluagh came to his call. It is all that saved us from Taranis and his men. They fled from the sluagh."

I grabbed Doyle's arm with my free hand. The other was squeezed tightly in Galen's hand. There was too much happening, and I didn't know how to cope with it all. But I knew one thing; I didn't want Doyle's face to look like that.

He turned and looked at me, but his face was that old unreadable darkness, only his eyes flinching around the edges. Now I knew what that little flinch meant.

"I want to wrap you around me like a coat, and cover you in kisses, but we have wounded to save. But do not doubt what I feel for you, even in the midst of this." The first hard tear slid down my cheek. "I thought you were dead, and. . . ."

Galen's hand dropped away, and Doyle wrapped me in his arms. I clung to him as if his hands on my body were air and food, and everything I needed to live.

I heard Rhys say, "Come on, Dawson, let's see if those little nails will help Jonty."

I wanted to melt into Doyle's kiss and never come up for air, but there was duty. There was always duty, and some horror that had to be fought, or healed, or. . . . Everyone thinks they want an extraordinary life, but you don't. When standing knee-deep in yet another disaster, ordinary begins to look very good.

We broke apart, and he led me to Jonty's side. Dawson was already kneeling on the ground. He held the nail that had come out of me when I healed him. He held it point down above one of the wounds.

"We'll have to get the shrapnel out of his body first," Rhys said.

"It didn't work that way for us," Dawson said.

"How did it work?" I asked, my arm wrapped around Doyle's lean waist, the strength of him beside me almost too good to be real.

Galen was carefully not looking at Doyle and me. I realized that he had come to me first. That he had swept me off my feet, and though I had been glad to see him, it hadn't been the feelings I had had for Doyle. It simply hadn't. I couldn't change how my heart felt, not even to save the feelings of one of my best friends.

"Like this," Dawson said, and he began to pass the nail over Jonty's wounds, point down, as if he were invisibly carving something. My hand tingled. The mark of blood on my palm tingled.

I stepped away from Doyle. He tried to catch my hand, but I drew it away before he could touch it. Somehow I wasn't sure that him touching the hand of blood while it was itching to be used would be a good thing. I didn't entirely understand what was happening, but I didn't question the urge to step up and drop to my knees beside Dawson.

I spoke words without willing them, as if the universe had been waiting for me to speak them, and with each word, it was as if time itself let out a breath that it had been holding. "You call me with blood and metal. What would you have of me?"

Dawson looked at me, and his lips moved, but it was as if he too wasn't in complete control of what he said. "Heal him, Meredith. I ask this with blood and metal and the magic you have given to this flesh."

"So be it," I said, and I spread my hand over Jonty's back. My skin ran with heat, as if the blood in my body was turning to molten metal. There was a moment of almost unbearable pain, then blood fountained upward from Jonty's body. Metal rained upward, expelled from the body with the blood.

Jonty came to with a gasp. But the blood kept pouring out. I scrambled back from him, and Dawson came with me. The blood slowed, but though the metal was out, the wounds were not healing.

Jonty turned his head with obvious effort, and said, "You call my blood, My Queen. You cleanse me of the human metal. I die for you, and I am content."

I shook my head. "I don't want you to die for me, Jonty. I want you to live."

"Some things are not meant to be, Princess," he said.

"It looks like it's a good thing we didn't come when the call first hit us, or we might be dying too," said a voice from the dark. I turned and found the goblin twins, Ash and Holly. In the dark you could have mistaken them for full-blooded sidhe, so tall and straight, only a little more bulky in the muscles, but hitting the gym a little harder could explain that away. Their yellow hair was a little short, just touching their shoulders. If it had been longer, they could have indeed passed for sidhe.

It was too dark to see that Ash's eyes were a solid green like the leaf of the tree he was named after, and Holly's eyes were the scarlet of winter berries. Only the solid color of their eyes with no whites truly betrayed their goblin blood.

"I did not call to you," I said.

"Your magic calls to the Red Caps, and our father's blood is in us," Ash said.

"I hate that your white-fleshed magic calls to us," Holly said.

They nodded in unison. "We hate that your hand of blood calls to us as if we were Red Caps. We are Seelie, and you have helped us understand that there is more to us than goblin blood, but yet your power calls to us as if we are lesser things," Ash said.

"For me, it was enough that your magic in Los Angeles made me a more powerful goblin, but I thought it would make me what the goblins had once been," Holly said. "But, even I, even we, are still less, or your magic would not pull at us like a dog to its master's whistle." His voice was bitter.

"Would you let them die for pride's sake?" I asked.

"We are goblins," Holly said. "We do not heal anything. We slaughter and destroy. It is what we are, and the treaty that brought us to America so long ago stole us away from ourselves. There is no room for goblins anymore."

I stumbled as I got to my feet, stepping on the hem of my coat. Holly laughed at me, but I didn't care. I knew something. I got it. Knew it; understood it. I wasn't even certain in that moment what "it" was, but the compulsion of it moved me toward the twins. It kept me walking across the winter grass, the frosted weeds making a dry sound against the leather of my coat.

Doyle came to my side. "Have a care, my Merry."

He was right to be cautious, but the feeling inside me was right, too. The scent of flowers rode the air, as if a breath of summer's heat trickled across the cold moonlight.

Rhys came to our side and touched Doyle's arm. "The Goddess is near, Doyle. It will be all right."

I kissed Doyle first, and he had to bend down

to help me do it, then I kissed Rhys. He looked at me, and there was sadness on his face. But it was not a sadness that I could fix. I could only kiss him gently on the lips, and let him know that I saw him and appreciated him, but nothing that either of us could do would make me love him the way I loved Doyle or Frost. That it pained him pained me, but not enough to change it.

I walked the rest of the way alone. Ash and Holly stood in front of me. They tried to look arrogant or hostile—their handsome faces were made for both—but under all of it was uncertainty. I made them rethink themselves, and neither sidhe nobles nor goblin warriors are accustomed to rethinking anything. Their sense of rightness is absolute in most things. I gazed into their eyes, and wasn't sure what was about to happen, but as the scent of roses grew stronger on the cold air, I knew the Goddess was coming. The scent of roses mingled with the rich scent of herbs and leaves, as if we stood on the edge of some forest glade.

"Do you smell flowers?" Holly asked.

"I smell forest," Ash said. "A forest like nothing in this land."

"What are you doing to us?" Holly asked.

"You wanted to be sidhe." I held my hands out to them.

"Yes," Ash said.

"No," Holly said.

I smiled at Holly. "You both want power, don't you?"

"Yes," Holly said, his voice a little reluctant.

"Then each of you take my hands."

"What happens if we do?" Ash asked.

I smiled, then I laughed, and the scent of roses and the sensation of summer sun on my skin was so real that it was almost dizzying to have my eyes see the winter's dark.

"I don't know what will happen," I said, and that was the truth.

"Then why should we do it?" Ash asked.

"Because if you let the smell of summer and autumn fade, if you miss this moment of power, you will always wonder what would have happened if you took my hands."

The brothers looked at each other. They had a moment between them made up of years of scheming, fighting, surviving, all come to this second, this choice.

"She's right," Ash said.

"It is a sidhe trick," Holly said.

"Probably," he said, then he smiled.

Holly grinned back at him. "This is a bad idea, brother."

"Yes."

Holly reached out, and Ash echoed him. They reached out for my hands as if they'd practiced the movement. Their fingers tingled power down my skin, and it must have felt the same for them, because Holly started to draw back.

Ash said, "Don't stop, Holly."

"This is a bad idea, brother," he repeated.

"This is power," Ash said, "and I want it."

Holly hesitated a heartbeat longer, then his hand moved with his brother's so that they took my hands in theirs in echoing moves. "I've followed you all my life," he said. "I won't stop now."

Then the field and the winter's cold were gone, and we stood in a circle of standing stones on a wide plain under a full moon and a summer's spill of stars.

CHAPTER FORTY-TWO

ASH SWUNG ME AROUND SO THAT I FACED away from him, one hand on my throat, the other around my waist, pinning my sword to my body. Holly drew his own sword, and faced the outside of the circle. His sword gleamed like cold moonlight made solid.

"Take us back," Ash hissed in my ear.

"I didn't bring us here."

"Liar," he whispered, and his fingers tightened just a little around my neck. That one flex of fingers, the firmness of his palm against my throat, made my pulse speed.

I spoke carefully, not wanting to do anything to make his fingers tighten any more. "I cannot change winter to summer, or transport us to a different country."

His fingers squeezed just a little more, until swallowing was uncomfortable. "What do you mean, 'a different country'?"

I spoke even more carefully. "There are no standing stones in America, not like this."

His hand tightened until my breath wheezed under his grip.

"Then where are we?" he asked.

"A place between," a woman's voice answered.

Ash went very still beside me. His fingers didn't tighten, for which I was glad, but they didn't loosen either. My breath still wheezed out from between his fingers as he turned slowly toward that voice.

Holly said, "Who are you?"

The woman's voice said, "You know who I am."

Ash turned so that he saw her before I could, but I knew what we would see, or what I would see. She wore a hooded cloak that hid most of her face, but for an edge of chin or a glimpse of lips. She held a staff, and her hand would be pale one moment, dark the next; old and young; slender and not. She was **the** Goddess. She was all that was female, all that was woman, and all at once.

It was Ash who said, "Why have you brought us here?" Holly was still facing the figure with his sword out, as if he meant at any moment to attack.

She wasn't flesh and blood, I knew that. I didn't think his sword could hurt her, but it seemed wrong to be threatening her. I might have protested except that Ash's hand squeezed too tightly for words.

"Take us back or your chosen one dies."

"Harm her and you will never have the power you seek, Ash."

His hand eased a little so that I could breathe without fighting for it. "So if I let her go you'll give me power?"

"She is the key to your power. Without her there is nothing."

"I do not understand."

Holly lunged toward the figure. A sword clanged down the length of his blade, pushing it against the grass, and a body was on the other end of that sword. He was tall and short, muscled and not, dark and light, all men and none. He had thrown off the cloak that they wore to save our minds so that you simply had to see all the many forms at once. He stood bare in all his beauty and terror, for a long, muscled body can be just for pleasure, but that same muscled weight can thrust a sword and spill blood. He was the greatest of tenderness and the greatest of destruction all at once. The potential was all there in that swirl of images, shapes, scents, and sights.

He disarmed Holly, but he had to cut the goblin's hand to do it. It spoke of Holly's skill or the God's impatience. His voice was deep and rumbling as gravel, and the next light and airy as any, all men echoed in his voice. "Who am I?"

Holly went to his knees with the sword point at his neck. "You are the God."

"Who is my consort?"

"The Goddess," Holly answered.

The God stepped back to the cloaked Goddess, but the moment they touched hands her cloak was gone, and they stood side by side. I don't know what the goblins saw, but I saw a dizzying swirl of faces and bodies. They were all these beings at once, but my mind could not hold it all. I finally closed my eyes, for I could not take it all in.

Ash began to move, and I opened my eyes as I realized that he was moving us both to kneel on the summer grass. He'd stopped choking me somewhere during the revelation. In fact, now the arm that had been choking me was around my shoulders. What had been hurting me was holding me almost tenderly now.

"It has been long since the goblins saw the face of God," Ash said.

"And Goddess," the Goddess said, and there was chiding in her voice. It was the voice of every mother, every big sister, every aunt, every teacher, all rolled into one echo.

"And longer still since the goblins saw the face of the Goddess," Ash said. If he resented the chiding, it didn't show in his voice.

"Are you goblins?" the God asked.

"Yes," Holly answered.

Ash was a little slower with "Yes."

"Are you sidhe?" the Goddess asked.

"No," Holly answered.

"We have no magic," Ash answered, as if that answered the question, and perhaps it did.

"What would you give to possess the magic of the sidhe?" she asked.

"Nothing," Holly said. "I am goblin, and that is enough."

"She did not say we had to become sidhe, brother," Ash said. "She spoke of the magic of the sidhe."

"Magic of the sidhe, but still goblin," Holly said. "That would be worth much."

"Once there were many courts, even among the goblins," the Goddess said.

"Once," the God said, "there was magic in every court of faerie."

"The sidhe stole our magic from us," Ash said, and his hand that had been tender tightened against my shoulder. He didn't hurt me, but his body was suddenly tense as it knelt beside me.

"Daughter," the Goddess said, "what say you to this?"

"The sidhe stripped the goblins of their magic to win the last Great War between our peoples."

"Do you think this was well done?" She asked.

I thought before I answered, because I could feel the magic beginning to gather around us. You would think that in the presence of Deities there would be no room for magic to build, that their presence would mask everything, but whatever was building in this summer night in this place between pressed against the air like the weight of invisible rock, as if a mountain were building above us one thought at a time.

Ash's arm across my shoulders was almost trembling with tension. I had a moment to glance up at him, and he was staring as hard as he could straight ahead. I think he was afraid of what I might see in his eyes.

"I've been told that if we hadn't taken the magic from the goblins they would have won the war."

"But your two peoples are no longer at war, are they?" She asked.

"No," I said. Ash had gone utterly still beside me. I could feel the tension along his muscles, as if he fought himself to be still.

"If you could undo the wrong done the goblins, would you?"

"Was it wrong?" I asked.

"What do you think?" She asked.

I thought again. Had we been wrong? I had seen what the sidhe had done with their magic. They had used the fact that only we had major offensive magic to be tyrants. We had won the wars, but in the end, it was the humans with their technology who had truly won.

"I think we won a battle, but not a war, by taking the goblins' magic."

Ash's hand spasmed against my shoulder.

"But was it right, the right thing to do?" the God asked.

I started to say yes, then said, "I don't know. I was told that our magic came from You. That would mean that we stole magic from the goblins that You had both given to them. Did you agree with what we did?"

"No one asked us," the Goddess said.

Ash startled beside me, and I just gaped at them. They had hooded themselves again, so my eyes and my mortal mind would be able to deal with them better. When had they hooded? Just now? Minutes ago? I couldn't remember.

"Taking the goblins' magic was the beginning of You turning from us," I said.

"What if you, daughter, could undo that injustice?" the God asked.

"You mean give magic back to the goblins," I said. It was always good to be clear.

"Yes," they said together.

"You mean give Holly and Ash hands of power," I said. Ash had actually dropped his hand, as if it were all too much.

"Yes," they answered again. Were they beginning to fade?

"They are sidhe as well as goblin," I said.

"Would you give them their sidhe-side powers, daughter?" Now I was answering voices.

If I said no, would the Goddess retreat from me, from all my people again? I looked at Ash, and he would not look at me. I glanced in front of us at Holly. He was glaring at me. His face showed plainly that he thought I would deny them. But it wasn't his anger that I saw, it was the reason behind the anger. Years of looking in the mirror, and seeing all that sidhe blood looking back at you, and knowing that you would forever be denied. It didn't matter how sidhe you looked. If you had no magic, then you weren't real to the sidhe. You were simply not one of them. I knew what that felt like, to be among them but not one of them. I looked less sidhe than the brothers did. At least they were tall, and until you saw their eyes they could have passed. I would never pass for pure-blooded sidhe, not with a thousand crowns on my head.

"Will you give them their birthright back?" the voices asked.

For politics, I should have said no. For the safety of my world, no. For the safety of everything we'd signed treaties for, no. But in the end, I gave the only answer that felt right. "I will."

CHAPTER FORTY-THREE

WE WERE LEFT ALONE IN THE CIRCLE OF stones under the round, white glow of midsummer's moon. It rose above us, unnaturally close, a harvest moon close enough that it seemed as if we had only to reach out to caress the surface of it. In that moment, I wasn't certain whether it was illusion or reality. Could I have touched the moon? Perhaps, but the two men with me weren't interested in celestial bodies, and they convinced me that the moon was for gazing at, and that their bodies were the world.

Their skin was as pale and perfect as that of any sidhe. Only the scars that decorated their skin said that they didn't have enough magic to heal their wounds cleanly. But I was Unseelie, not Seelie, and scars were just another texture to run my fingers over, lick my tongue across, and worry at with my teeth.

I made Holly cry out with pleasure with my

teeth around a scar on the hard, muscled expanse of his stomach. Ash's back was crisscrossed with claw marks, white and shiny with age. I traced my fingertips across all of it, and said, "What happened?"

Ash lay on the grass in the nest we had made of our clothes. He let my fingers play across his bare back, but he drew no breath to answer me. It was Holly who answered. "Cathmore found Ash alone when we were young. Cathmore was a great warrior, but he hunted the younger warriors whom he thought might be a threat to him someday. A lot of the warriors bear scars from him."

I traced the claw marks down and down, until I found the firm smoothness of his ass. He shivered under the gentleness of it. I didn't know if it was the magic of this place or the fact that there were no goblins to impress, but they both showed that gentleness, and not just pain, worked for them as pleasure.

"Cathmore. I do not know the name."

Holly gazed at me across his brother's body, then he touched the scars and smiled. A close, tight smile. "When Ash was healed, we hunted Cathmore down. We killed him and took his head so everyone would know that we had slain him."

He showed me the arm that lay across his brother's back, flexing the muscle to show a curve of hard white scar tissue. The scar looked as if his arm had nearly been cut off. "Cathmore did that, with his sword, Cathmore's Arm." I knew it was not unusual for a goblin to name his sword after himself. I'd always found it a little odd, but it wasn't my custom, it was theirs.

I touched the scar, tracing my fingertips down the line of it. "A fearsome wound," I said.

He grinned at me. "Ash carries his sword."

"Because he gave the killing blow," I said.

That made Ash rise enough to gaze over his shoulder at me. "How did you know that?"

"It's goblin law. The one who strikes the killing blow gets first pick of the weapons."

"I had forgotten that your father used to bring you to visit the goblins," Ash said, propping himself up on his elbows.

"The goblins are the foot soldiers of the faerie court. No war has been won since the goblins joined us that would not have been lost without you."

"Now that we are forbidden to make war, the nobles of both courts forget that," Ash said. "We are an embarrassment even to the Unseelie."

"We don't clean up well enough for the press to please the queen," Holly said. He was sitting up now, his knees drawn to his chest, his arms encircling them. It made him seem younger, more vulnerable. I had a moment of seeing what he might have been when he was young enough for Cathmore to think them prey.

I crawled over the clothes and the movement of the grass underneath until I was in front of Holly. His gaze did not even pretend to look away from my breasts. It didn't bother me. We were naked, and I wanted them to want me.

I rose, coming off of all fours, letting his gaze stay on the heavy roundness of my breasts. "I think you look amazing."

He looked at my face then, and there was anger in the crimson of his eyes. I hesitated in the midst of the kiss I'd been seeking, not understanding the anger.

"Good enough to fuck, but not to be seen in public with," he said.

I leaned back on my heels. "I don't understand."

Ash sat up, one knee bent, the other leg out straight so he framed his swell nicely. Neither of them had anything to be ashamed of in that area. I had trouble raising my gaze from between his legs to his face.

He laughed, and it was that masculine sound, pleased and sure of itself. "You're not the first sidhe woman to want to sample forbidden fruit."

"You've said that I was."

"In public," he said. "In front of the other goblins, yes. If a goblin lays with a sidhe, then they must show marks of violence. To do less in our kingdom is to be seen as weak. To be seen as weak is to invite challengers. We are already half sidhe, Meredith. If the goblins knew we could take our sex gentle and enjoy it, we would be challenged until even we were killed."

Holly traced my shoulder with the edge of his hand. "Gentleness has no reward for goblins, only punishment."

I glanced at Holly, then back to Ash as he said, "We have lived by that rule. We have punished others who were gentle. Your own pet goblin, Kitto, suffered at our hands."

"Did you enjoy his suffering?" I asked.

He smiled. "No one but you would ask that, blunt as a goblin, with that pretty sidhe face."

"Human too," I said.

He nodded, but reached out to touch my cheek. "And brownie in there somewhere, though it does not show."

I looked away from his face, out into the night. "My cousin, Cair, hated her brownie looks enough to kill our grandmother in a bid for power."

"We heard you hunted her down with the wild hunt. Named her kinslayer."

I nodded. "Yes."

Holly wrapped his arms around me, all that scarred muscled strength so gentle. He held me, and whispered in my hair, "When we are alone we can say how terrible for you. That we're sorry for the loss of your grandmother."

Ash moved closer to us, moving my face with his fingers so he'd be sure of my gaze being on his face. "But in the world, in front of anyone, Meredith, and I mean anyone else, we are goblins. We will have to behave as goblins."

"I understand," I said.

"The other is not an act, Meredith. It is us, too."

Holly pressed his face into my hair. "You smell clean and sweet, like everything good. Good enough to eat."

I tensed a little in his arms. "Goblins would mean that as a threat."

"Never be fooled, Meredith," Ash said. "We are goblins, but we are also ourselves." He frowned at his brother.

"I'm a little more goblin than my brother," Holly said.

"If you were sidhe, I'd say that you don't get to give me oral sex, but I know the goblins see giving oral sex as an insult. I can perform on you, but you won't perform on me."

"True," Holly said, "but my brother's a pervert."

It took me a second to understand, and it made me smile. Ash actually looked embarrassed. "There's no one to see, no one to tell," he said. "I can do what I want."

I spoke from the circle of his brother's arms. "And what do you want?"

"I want to taste you until your pleasure makes you shine for me."

"Then can we fuck?" Holly asked.

Ash frowned at him, but I laughed. "Yes, eventually we'll fuck."

"I'd rather make love," Ash said, and there was a longing in his face that I never thought to see. A longing for things he didn't get a chance to do much. There was almost no privacy in goblin society for sex. To hide away meant you were embarrassed, or bad at it in some way.

I leaned toward Ash. Holly let me go, enough so I could put a gentle kiss on his brother's lips. "Taste me, make love to me, Ash, please."

He kissed me back, his hand sliding down to cup my breast and play with the nipple until it hardened and I made a small sound into his mouth. He drew back enough to whisper, "On your back, Princess."

I gave the only answer there was to give. "Yes."

CHAPTER FORTY-FOUR

ASH MOUNDED THE CLOTHES UNDER ME so that my lower body was angled higher for him as he lay flat on the ground between my legs. The moon loomed over us, white and shining, so close I could see the gray shapes of craters, and the black marks of deeper holes. I reached a hand upward, but as close as it looked, it was beyond my reach.

Ash curved his fingers around my legs, opening them wider. He kissed along my thighs, putting a gentle touch of lips on first one leg, then the other, until he came to the inside of my thigh, and there he lingered. He kissed and nuzzled, just short of the spot I was wanting him to find. He laid a kiss in that hollow at the very innermost part of the thigh that is still thigh and not groin. He laid a second kiss in the hollow of the other side. He breathed along my flesh so that it was warm and close, and all of it made me more and more eager for him to touch me in that most intimate of places.

Holly made a small noise. It made me look at him. He was hugging his knees tightly to his chest again, watching us. He looked eager, true, but there was more than that. Again, I got that glimpse of how lonely he and Ash must be. They were fierce goblin warriors, but part of them was not. Part of them craved different meat than the bloody raw stuff they got at their court. And here, in this place between time, between space, where no time would pass, might be their only chance to be sidhe and not goblin. Holly could say he wanted to be goblin rather than sidhe, but the longing was there on his face in the moonlight.

Ash came to my edges at last, and it brought me back to gaze down my body at him. I could see only part of his face, the lower half of him hidden against my own body as if it were a mask. He rolled his eyes upward, and they were huge and almond shaped, the green turned to darkness by the moonlight. His hair was almost white with contrast, but his gold-kissed skin looked almost highly tanned in the dimness. He licked around my edges, gazing at my face as he did it. Whatever he saw there pleased him, because he moved to my center, and licked from my opening, to the top in one quick, wide, wet line. It made me shudder, and that seemed to please him too, because he licked me over and over until my hands found his hair and held on. My skin began to glow softly, paled by the glow of the moon, but rising under my skin, as if I were reflecting the great shining orb above us.

Ash pressed his mouth against that most intimate part, and began to suck. It made me press myself against his mouth, eager for more. He responded by giving me more, pressing his mouth around me in a tight seal so that the sucking became more intense. That sweet pressure began to build between my legs. It grew with each movement of his mouth, each caress of his lips, his tongue, and the press of his teeth, not biting, but helping raise the sensation level. He brought me to that trembling edge, as the weight grew and grew between my legs until, with one last kiss, one last suck, one last flick of his tongue, he spilled me over the edge and brought me screaming, hands reaching up toward the moon, as if I would claw my pleasure on the very surface of it.

Holly was suddenly there, taking my hands and putting them against his chest. Ash kept sucking, kept the orgasm rolling over and over, and I marked Holly's flesh with the pleasure of it, tracing my nail marks among the scars of battle, fresh red to join all that white.

There were crimson lights, green and gold shadows, and I realized it was me, my hair, my eyes glowing so bright that they challenged the glow of that huge moon.

Ash moved away from me, and I started to protest, to call him back, but then I felt him above me. I looked down from Holly's body to find Ash hard and ready, as he pushed his way inside me. Just him entering me made me cry out again. I was still spasming inside from the orgasm he'd given me so that my body squeezed and writhed around him as he shoved himself in.

Holly pinned my wrists to the clothes and grass beneath us, using one big hand for both of mine. Ash stayed up on his arms so that almost all that was touching me was that part of him that thrust in and out, his skin glowing in the white light. It took me a few heartbeats to realize that Ash's skin was glowing on its own. He was beginning to glow like a sidhe.

I gazed up at Holly to see if he had noticed to find that the blood I had drawn from his chest was glowing in crimson lines. I might have remarked on it, but he angled his body, and I knew what he wanted. I moved my mouth so that he could slide himself into it as his brother slid himself between my legs.

They both found their rhythm, and worked as if they'd done this before, or as if something helped them know just where the other would be, and what they would be doing, so that they mirrored each other, one in my mouth, one between my legs.

I raised my hips for Ash, and moved my mouth eagerly toward Holly, but both of them controlled what I did, Ash with his hands on my hips, holding me still so he could find the spot he wanted, Holly with his free hand in my hair, holding me a little away from him so he could stare down at me as he drove himself in and out of me.

I made small whimpering noises around Ash's

body as he found that spot inside me, and began to work over and over it. The orgasm began to build again. Holly's hand jerked my hair, hard and fast enough for pain. It made me cry out, and press my mouth eagerly against him, trying to take all that long hard length into my mouth at once.

Ash began to lose his rhythm, shoving more deeply at the end of each thrust. I felt him fight his body to keep going inside me until I came first. That wasn't just being sidhe; goblins prided themselves on their stamina, and how many orgasms they could bring their partners. He fought his body, fought to keep some rhythm as he began to thrust more and more deeply, losing his concentration, but he didn't need it, not anymore. He'd done his work well, and from one thrust to another, he brought me. He brought me screaming my orgasm around his brother's body. Holly cried out above me and thrust into my mouth so far and deeply that during anything but full-blown orgasm it would have been too much, but in that moment, at that second, it was exactly right. The sensation of both of them inside me at once brought me screaming again, bucking around both their bodies.

Holly spilled down my throat in a rush of heat, crying out again. Ash thrust one more time, deep inside me, hitting the end of me with the end of himself, like a battering ram, but it felt so good. It brought me again, screaming and writhing around them both.

Holly pulled himself out of my mouth, and let me scream my pleasure at the moon. He knelt above me on all fours, head down, one hand still pinning my wrists. His hair glowed like yellow fire around his face, and he blinked eyes that glowed with the same crimson fire of the blood that still dripped down his chest.

Ash drew himself out, and collapsed beside me. He threw one hand over my waist, and lay there panting. He blinked eyes at me that glowed like emerald fire. His hair was a halo of gold and yellow fire against the ground.

Our glows began to fade, like fire banked for the night. Holly collapsed on the other side of me, a little more of him curving around my head so that I was cradled against his chest.

Ash took one of my hands in his and raised it for us all to see. Our skins glowed together, mine white like the moon, theirs as if they'd swallowed the gold of the sun. Holly reached down and laid one of his hands over both of ours, and it was like we'd all swallowed the lights of the sky into our veins.

CHAPTER FORTY-FIVE

WE REAPPEARED IN THE WINTER FIELD hand in hand. we'd dressed ourselves, and tied our weapons back on, and left that place of peace and magic, to step back into the aftermath of battle. No, worse than battle: bomb. There were no enemies to fight, just physics gone horribly wrong.

There were moans from the Red Caps, and for them to make noises of pain meant they were dying. But I knew what to do. I knew it as surely as you know your name, or your favorite color. I simply knew, because the air still smelled of summer, and our skin still held the dim glow of the moon and sun.

We stood in the center of the wounded, and we pushed our magic outward; as the queen had pushed darkness, we pushed blood and flesh. Blood to wash the metal bits from their bodies. There were cries of pain, clouds of blood in the dimness. Flesh to heal the wounds. Then the cries stopped, and the Red Caps got to their feet, a little shaky perhaps, but healed and whole. They stood to a man, and turned to us.

I held Holly and Ash's hands upward in mine. I called out, "The hand of blood!" and Holly stepped forth, his hand held high, his skin and hair and eyes shining with the healing that we had done.

"The hand of flesh!" and Ash stepped away from me, glowing with magic, and smiling.

I held my hands up to the sky and said, "I hold the hands of flesh and blood, and now I can make whole what is torn apart."

The Red Caps gathered around us, then dropped to their knees, their faces covered in blood from the caps that gave them their names. I went to Jonty, and touched his face. The moment I touched him, his cap ran with blood as if I'd dumped a bucket over his head. The other Red Caps clustered around me, touching, and where they touched, they bled. Then one of them grabbed Holly's wrist. Holly snarled at him, but stopped in the middle of drawing his blade because blood was pouring down the Red Cap's face.

Holly stared over his shoulder at me. "I truly have the hand of blood." He made it almost a question.

"Yes," I said, and nodded in case he was too far away to hear my voice.

A look of wonder crossed his face, and he turned back to the Red Cap at his feet and touched him gently with his free hand. The blood flowed faster, and the Red Caps began to cluster around him too.

One of them tried to grab Ash, but they did not bleed faster. "The hand of flesh," Ash said, and it wasn't a question.

I nodded.

The Red Caps clustered around Holly and me, but Ash didn't seem to mind. He just stared at his hand, as if he could feel which one held the power.

Doyle came to me, wading between the Red Caps, like walking through small, kneeling mountains. He went to his knees in front of me.

I shook my head and reached down, taking his hands in mine. I raised him to his feet. He took my hands in his, but he was staring at me in a way that I'd never seen before. "What's wrong?" I asked.

"Look at yourself," he said, his voice soft.

I didn't understand what he meant; then I caught the soft glow on the edge of my vision. There was something on my head, and it was glowing, but the glow was so faint that I hadn't noticed it.

One of the Red Caps unsheathed his great sword, and held it up for Doyle. He took it, and held the flat of the blade so I could see myself. The image was distorted, but I could see something black and silver on my head, though silver was too strong a word. I turned my head, and the moonlight caught the dew, and outlined the spiderweb that formed the crown.

"Oh, my God," I whispered.

"It is the Crown of Moonlight and Shadows," he said.

I stared at him. "But that's the crown of the Unseelie Court."

"Yes," he said.

"And it's mine!" Cel screamed it, from the edge of the field. He held a spear in his hand. The runes glowed across the field, and I knew it was the spear known only as Shrieker. The queen had indeed opened the weapons vault to her son. Shrieker had once been able to slay armies, not with its blade, but with the screaming it made in the air when it was thrown.

I saw a flash of white on the edge of the field. Cel's arm pulled back, and he made a small running start to cover us all with its deadly scream. The white stag leaped. It made a graceful arc, and put itself in the way of the spear. Cel couldn't stop the blow, so the spear buried itself in the white stag's side, and was jerked from Cel's hands as the stag tried to run.

Doyle and the rest were running, closing on Cel. I had eyes only for the stag as it collapsed to its knees. The Red Caps and the brothers ran for the fight, except for Jonty. He scooped me into his arms, as he had that one night when he'd run across the fields to get me to a different battle in time. Now he ran like the wind was at his back to get me to the stag. To get me to Frost's side before he breathed his last.

CHAPTER FORTY-SIX

THE FIGHT WAS BETWEEN US AND THE dying stag. As always, Cel was between me and what I loved. Jonty sat me on the ground. My body was splattered with the warm blood of the Red Caps' magic. He looked carved of blood from holding me so close. He drew his own sword to wade into the fight, but I realized that the reason the fight was taking so long was that they were trying not to kill Cel. He wanted them dead, and even as I watched he opened a wound in Galen's arm that sprayed blood, and made him retreat.

There was blood on Rhys's face and a wound in Mistral's side that he was favoring, which meant he was hurt. Cel was no match for them, but if they only wanted to disarm him and he was willing to kill them, it put even the best warrior at a disadvantage. Holly and Ash were actually not fighting, because a goblin does not fight except to kill. It raised again the idea that the Red Caps had once been their own kingdom with its own customs.

Doyle sprang backward just in time to avoid a sword thrust. He had not drawn his sword. I think he didn't trust what he would do to Cel with a blade in his hand. It had been ingrained in them for centuries that they were not allowed to harm Cel, no matter what he did. The queen would have killed them for it. But Andais was no longer queen.

I yelled, "Kill him! Do not die to protect him!"

Galen looked my way, and got a cut across his chest that made him stumble. Cel came in for the kill, and only Doyle's sword kept the blow from falling. He'd drawn his sword at last. He drove Cel back with whirring swordwork so that his blade moved too fast to follow with the eye, like the blade of some handheld electric thing. No one was that fast, no one but Doyle.

Cel actually kept the blade at bay, his own swordwork an answering blur. In that moment, I saw for the first time that Cel wasn't just a mamma's boy. There was a warrior in all that spoiled prince. Few could have withstood Doyle, even for a few moments, but Cel managed. He made no progress, but he kept the blade from touching him or disarming him.

The field had gone utterly silent; there was nothing but the ring of blade on blade, and the grunts of effort from Cel. Doyle worked in silence, except for the slither of his feet on the ground as he moved, and the hiss of his blade along Cel's.

It was too fast for me to follow, but Andais was a goddess of war, and she saw more. She yelled out across the cold air, "Darkness, please, spare him!"

I saw a hesitation, a moment in Doyle's whirring movements. Cel tried to press the advantage, but suddenly his blade was spinning through the air, and Doyle's blade was at his throat, as he lay on the ground, panting up at the other man.

Cel was breathing hard, but he was smiling. He was smiling up at Doyle with that same arrogance I'd seen him wear all his life. His mother had saved him again. The Queen of Air and Darkness had that power.

Doyle stood with Black Madness pressed to Cel's throat, but did not drive it home. Andais was walking across the field toward us. "No, not again" was all I thought.

I looked at Mistral on his knees, clutching his side, leaning on his shining spear, his sword still naked in his hand. Galen was down to one useable arm. He stood breathing hard, his sword in his hand, rage plain on his usually smiling face. Rhys's face bled freely, and I realized that Cel had tried to cut out his only good eye. He had missed, but the fact that he'd tried meant he hadn't taken the fight seriously. He had wanted to hurt us, not necessarily kill us. He had wanted to maim.

Ash and Holly bore wounds, for they had

joined the fight after I called for Cel's death. That Cel could wound them so quickly said just how much I'd underestimated him as a warrior.

I said "No." The crown glowed like a dark halo as I moved forward. I looked at Sholto on the edge of the field with his sluagh, and I yelled out, "Why did you not join the fight?"

"The queen forbade it," he called back.

I stared across the field at Andais. She wasn't quite to us. I called out, "Andais, do you see the crown upon my head?"

She hesitated, then said "Yes." The one word sighed and seemed to touch everyone on the field.

"What crown is it?"

Her hand tightened on the pommel of her sword, Mortal Dread, which could bring true death to anyone. "It is the Crown of Moonlight and Shadows. It was once my crown." There was bitterness to that last.

"Now it's mine."

"So it seems," she said.

"You vowed in open court that whichever of us became pregnant first would be your heir. You may not have intended to keep your word, but faerie kept it for you. Goddess and Consort have crowned me."

"You wear the Crown of Moonlight and Shadows," she said.

Cel screamed out, "And it is mine! You promised it to me!" Doyle's sword tip pushed a little harder, and a drop of blood welled black in the moonlight.

Andais stood there with her cloak of darkness and shadows swirling around her. Her helmet was tucked under one arm. We looked at each other over that cold ground.

"Did you promise him your crown?" I asked.

"Yes," she said.

"After promising me the chance to be queen," I said.

"Before," she said.

"You are an oathbreaker, my aunt. The wild hunt lives."

"I know you and my Perverse Creature can summon the wild hunt. I know you slew your cousin and the other conspirators of the Seelie Court."

"Would you have us hunt you?" I asked.

"Would it save my son's life?"

"No," I said.

"But still, I am an oathbreaker. I deserve to be hunted."

Andais was the ultimate survivor. There was only one reason she would choose to die.

"Before Sholto and I give chase, I will order Cel's death," I said. "Our chase will not give him time to escape, and I don't think he has enough friends left in court to save him."

"I have allies," Cel yelled from the ground.

I looked only at my aunt, not at him, as I said,

"Siobhan is dead, and your so-called allies fled when they could. The only one who came to save you is your mother. If she is dead, then I think, cousin, you will find that you have no allies left. They don't follow you. They follow her."

"They will not follow you, Meredith," Cel said. "Crown, or no crown, if it is not me on the throne, then they will kill you and choose their own ruler. My spies have heard them plot this."

I laughed, and finally looked down at Cel. Whatever he saw on my face widened his eyes, and made him catch his breath, as if he saw something that frightened him. "You never understood me, cousin, or you, my aunt," I said. "I never wanted to rule. I know they hate me, and no matter how much power I show them, they will always see me as the future of the sidhe. They see me as the diminished them. They see in me what they see in Sholto, that the sidhe grow weak. They would rather hide in their hollow hills and waste away than change and go outside to meet the world. I had hope for our people. My father had hope for our people."

"His hope is what killed him," Cel said.

I looked down at him where he lay on the ground, Doyle's sword at his throat, but he didn't look frightened. He believed that Andais would save him. Even now, he was confident in her power to protect him.

"How do you know that hope killed my father?" I asked.

Something crossed through his eyes, some thought or emotion. I smiled at him.

"It's just an expression," he said, but his voice wasn't so confident now.

"No," I said, "it's not." I knelt beside him.

"Cel," Andais said, "Cel, don't. . . ."

My smile stayed. I couldn't seem to stop smiling, though I wasn't happy. "I hadn't seen you fight before. I didn't understand how good you were."

Cel tried to sit up, but Doyle's sword point pushed him back down. "I am glad you finally understand that I could lead our people."

"You killed him. You killed Prince Essus. You yourself. It's why we couldn't find an assassin. It's why no matter how many people Andais tortured they had nothing to tell us about my father's death."

He yelled, "She's mad, Mother. You ordered me not to plot against my uncle. I obey you in all things."

"But you didn't plot," I said. "You did it yourself. Because you were good enough with a blade, and because you knew he would hesitate. You knew my father loved you. You counted on it."

Andais's voice was almost a wail, "Cel, tell me she's wrong."

"She's wrong," he yelled.

"Swear by the Darkness that Eats all Things. Swear by the wild hunt. Swear, and I'll believe you," she said. "Swear those oaths and I will fight to the end for you."

He tried. "I swear by the Darkness That Eats All Things. . . ." and for a moment I thought I'd been wrong, then he stopped. He tried again. "I swear by the wild hunt . . . I swear." He screamed it. "I swear!"

"What do you swear, Cel? Son, tell me you did not kill my brother. For the love of Goddess, tell me you did not kill Essus."

He lay on the ground, staring from Doyle to me, to the circle of my other guards who had gathered around us. He stared up at us, his eyes wide, shifting back and forth as if seeking a way out. Rhys stood beside Doyle, his face a mask of blood. Galen came to kneel by me. He had no good arm left to both hug me and keep his blade. He leaned his head against my cheek, and whispered, "I'm sorry, Merry."

Mistral was still kneeling where he'd been left, which meant he was hurt indeed. But he called out, "Essus was the best of us."

Cel yelled, "So good, my uncle, that they wanted him to be king. They wanted him to kill my mother and be king."

"Essus would never have done that," Doyle said.

"My brother loved us!" Andais screamed it at him. She looked at me, and there was real pain in her eyes. In all the years of seeking, it had never occurred to her that it was her own son.

"Yes," Cel said. He grabbed my arm, and Doyle's sword brought another drop of blood from his throat. "Do you know what your father's last words were, Meredith?"

I could only shake my head.

"He said he loved me." Then I felt his power spill up and over us all. One moment he was helpless, the next he was the wielder of old blood, and everyone around him had wounds to be reborn.

CHAPTER FORTY-SEVEN

I WAITED FOR THE PAIN OF THE SHRAPNEL wounds, but it was nothing compared to the pain of my men. Two thousand years of war. A thousand years of being tortured by my aunt. Every sword cut, every spear thrust, every whip mark, every claw was there on their bodies in one red ruin.

Galen writhed on the ground beside me clutching the bloody front of his pants. I knew what wound had reappeared. Rhys's missing eye was a bloody hole again. Doyle lay on his side, fighting to try to get to his knees, but he was too hurt. They were all too hurt. There were cries in the distance, and it was not just my men. The Red Caps were back to being damaged. I understood in that moment what a terrible hand of power Cel possessed. I hadn't understood until that moment. I hadn't understood so very much until that moment.

Cel jerked me to my feet by my wrist. He

pulled me in against his body, and turned me to gaze out at the field. Everyone was on the ground, everyone. Andais was just a dark heap on the frost-whitened grass. Her cloak of shadows had gone, which meant she was either unconscious or worse.

"Draw your sword," he hissed in my face. "Let me disarm you in front of them all, and drive it into that fertile womb of yours. Did you know that's why my mother turned against me? She made me take those human doctors' tests and found that I couldn't father children. That's when she called you home." He traced his free hand up the side of my neck, until he entwined his fingers in my hair. He stopped just short of where the crown still burned with its darkling flame on my head.

He let go of my wrist, and put his other hand on the other side of my face. He turned me to face him and cradled me oh so gently between his hands. "Draw your sword, Merry. Draw it, and let them see how weak you truly are." He whispered it against my face as he came in for a kiss.

I put my hands on his hands, bare skin to bare skin, as he kissed me. My arm that had been crippled by the original injury seemed a little less hurt. Was it the crown protecting me, or the fact that I was queen at last?

He laid a gentle kiss on my mouth, a good kiss, and not what I'd expected, but then he was full of surprises tonight.

He drew back from me, taking my hands in

his. He smiled, and his eyes were completely mad. "I'm going to kill you now."

"I know," I said, and I used the hands of blood and flesh together. Where Holly and Ash and I had used them to heal, now I used them to destroy. I drove the hand of blood into him, not in search of wounds, but in search of blood. I used the hand of flesh to cut and tear his body from the inside out. As the hands of power had flowed over the battle-field in a wave of cleansing blood and smoothing flesh, now they filled this one man.

Cel's eyes went wide. "You can't," he whispered.

"I can," I said, and I flexed that power, flexed it like a giant's fist that I'd shoved deep into his body, then I opened that fist. One moment Cel was there, eyes wide, hands in mine, the next he wasn't. Blood smacked into me, and thicker things hit my face. There was a sharp pain in my cheek, and I was left standing alone, covered in blood and thicker things. I scraped what was left of my cousin off my face so I could see, and found that it was his teeth in my cheek, blown there by the force of the magic. I pulled them out, and promised myself a tetanus shot, and antibiotics if I could have them while pregnant. I promised myself a lot of things as I stood there, shaking.

Doyle was suddenly at my side. Rhys was there too, wiping the blood from his face. His eye was back to its usual scar. Galen was with me too. His only injuries were the fresh ones from the fight.

"But how . . . ?" I asked.

"He died, and his hand of old blood died with him," Doyle said. I held my bloodstained hand out to Doyle. He took it, and I drew him over the red ruin that was all that was left of our enemy. I drew him down into a kiss, and the moment our lips met, our skin ran with light. I was moonlight, and he was black fire, bright enough that it cast shadows across the field.

There were gasps and whispers, and I finally came away from the kiss to find that there was a crown woven into Doyle's hair. Thin thorn branches formed a latticework above his head, but each thorn was tipped with silver. It was Jonty who whispered, "The Crown of Thorn and Silver."

Doyle reached up and touched the crown. He came away with a bright spot of crimson on his fingertip. "It is sharp."

"My king," I said.

He smiled. "One of them."

Then a sound, a horrible wet throaty sound, drove the answering smile from my face. "Frost," I said, and turned back to the stag. It lay on its side, the spear sticking up like a young tree stripped of its branches. Blood had drenched its white coat.

Doyle and I went to him. I knelt and touched the fur where it was clean of blood. He was warm to the touch, but there was no movement. "No," I said. "No."

"He was a willing sacrifice," Doyle said.

I shook my head. "I do not want this."

"He gave himself so you could rule the Unseelie."

I shook my head again. "I don't want to rule them without him at my side." I laid my head on the stag's still-warm side, and whispered, "Frost, come back to me. Please, please, don't go. Don't go."

I smelled roses, thick and warm as summer's kiss. I rose and there was a shower of rose petals falling from the winter sky.

It was Galen who wrapped his hands around the spear, and took it out of the stag's side to show the horrible wound. Galen stood above us, bathed in the rose petals, the spear in his hands, his face anguished, his clothes covered in blood.

Rhys knelt by the stag's head, hands gripping the smooth white horns. Tears trailed from his one good eye. Mistral came to stand with us, gripping his own more slender spear. I saw Sholto at the far edge of the field, his sluagh like a black cloud of nightmare shapes flying and creeping with him. He stopped to stare at us grouped around the white stag. He bowed his head, as if he knew.

Ash and Holly stood with the Red Caps. They had all lowered their weapons and pointed them at the ground as a sign of respect.

A voice came out of the sweet fall of petals. "What would you give for your Killing Frost?"

"Anything."

"Would you give the crown upon your head?" the voice asked.

"Yes," I said.

Mistral said "Meredith." But the other men said nothing. Mistral hadn't been with us from the beginning, so he didn't understand.

"And you, Darkness, would you give up your crown?"

Doyle took my hand in his, and said, "To have my right hand at my side again, I would."

"So be it," the voice said. There was a wind, and the scent of rain, and the dark light of the crowns was gone.

But a hand reached up through the hole in the stag's side. I touched that hand, and it wrapped around mine. "Goddess, help us," I said.

"She is," Doyle said, and he went to the hole in the stag's side. He tore at it with his hands. Rhys joined him. Mistral crawled to us, but he was too wounded to help. Galen gave the spear Shrieker to Mistral, and used his one unwounded arm to help tear at the hole. It was as if the stag's body had become a shell, something dry and un-real. It flaked and tore under their hands, and a second hand appeared along with the first, then arms. And then we were pulling him from the wreck of his other form.

That fall of silver hair fell over my lap, and then finally he turned and looked at me. Those gray eyes, that face that was almost too handsome for words, but there was no arrogance in my Frost now. There was only pain, and so much emotion trapped in those eyes.

He fell into our arms, mine and Doyle's. We held him while he shook. He clung to us while we cried. The Darkness and the Killing Frost clung to each other, and to me, and wept.

CHAPTER FORTY-EIGHT

ANDAIS IS STILL QUEEN OF AIR AND DARK-ness, but the crown did not appear above her head. Taranis is still King of Light and Illusion, but our lawyers are trying to get someone to sign off on forcing him to submit a DNA sample to compare to the sperm they found in me. It got leaked to the press somehow that my uncle might be my rapist. The tabloids are finally picking on the Seelie Court, and the mainstream press is following their lead. It's too juicy a story to ignore, no matter how charming a king he may be.

Lord Hugh and some of the nobles of the Seelie Court are still trying to get me declared queen of their court, but I've sent word that I'm not interested.

Andais has offered to do what she vowed, and step down for me to take her throne even if the Crown of Moonlight and Shadows never reappears. I've refused.

Cel was insane, but he was right about one thing. Too many of the nobles of both courts see me as the mongrel who proved that even their highest nobles were losing their magic. I was mortal, and it's a sin they won't forgive. Cel is dead, and Andais's days are numbered. Too many of her nobles want her throne and see her as weak. We're staying in Los Angeles, far away from the infighting. We'll see who survives.

The only thing we did before we left faerie was to free the prisoners. Barinthus, my father's closest advisor and once the sea god Manannan Mac Lir, had been imprisoned by Andais simply because he was my most powerful ally.

He's in Los Angeles with us now, and watching the former sea god swim in a real sea after so long being landlocked is a wonderful thing.

I'm back at Gray Detective Agency, and so are my guards. We're all useless for undercover work, but people are paying through the nose to consult with Princess Meredith and her "bodyguards." People are actually offering our boss, Jeremy Gray, more money for us to grace their Hollywood parties than they'd pay for us to detect anything. Though we still try to do some real work now and then.

Sholto visits, but he can't bring the sluagh to Los Angeles, not permanently. Mistral is homesick for faerie, and doesn't like this modern world. Galen and Rhys both have enough glamour to do actual work for Gray Detective Agency. Rhys loves being a real detective at last. Kitto was happy to have us home, and had already cleaned out a room to be turned into a nursery.

Nights are spent sleeping between Doyle and Frost, or Sholto and Mistral, or Galen and Rhys. The sharing is fair for the sex, but the sleeping arrangements are not. My Darkness and my Killing Frost find their way to me more often than not. No one seems to argue about it, as if they've worked it out among them all.

In the interest of getting good press, and in some cases getting more money into the house, I've taken some interviews. Because we had the soldiers there at the end, they've talked to the press. They saw wonders, and they said so. I don't blame them. We even get visits from Dawson, Orlando, Hayes, Brennan, and some of the others.

There's one television interview that got a lot of showing, and once it hit the Internet, well, it seems everyone downloaded it. It's me, sitting be-tween Doyle and Frost, them in their tailored suits, and me in the designer coat, still not showing yet. Frost's hand is in mine. Doyle sits beside me, more at ease than our Frost, who hasn't completely shaken his phobia of public speaking.

The interviewer asked, "So, Captain Doyle, is it really true that you gave up a chance to be king of the Unseelie Court to save Lt. Frost's life?"

Doyle didn't even glance around, but just nodded and said, "It is."

"You gave up a kingdom to save your friend."

"Yes."

"That's quite a friendship," the interviewer said.

"He has been my right hand for more than a thousand years."

"Some people are saying that perhaps he's more than just a friend to you, Captain."

"A thousand years makes for a very close friendship."

You'd think that the interviewer might ask about the whole thousand years thing, but she didn't. She chased something else. "Some people are saying that you gave up the throne because you love Frost."

This was the moment when Doyle didn't catch the double entendre. He answered honestly. "Of course I love Frost. He's my friend."

She turned to me then, and said, "Meredith, how do you feel knowing that Doyle loves Frost too?"

I reached over and took Doyle's hand so that I was holding both their hands at once. "It makes it easier for all of us to sleep together."

Which was a little too bold for that particular interviewer, but she recovered. "Frost, how do you feel knowing that your lovers gave up being king and queen to save you?"

The camera went in for a close-up that showed the closed arrogance that he used to hide his nerves behind. But nothing the camera could do made him any less than amazing to look at. "I would have told them not to save me."

"You'd have rather died?"

"I thought Meredith wanted to be queen, and I knew that Doyle would make the best of kings."

"It's been a few weeks. How do you feel now? Are you glad they made the sacrifice?"

He turned and looked at us both as the camera drew back so that it showed us looking at him. Our faces softened, and there were smiles, even from the men. "Yes, I am."

"And Meredith, princess, but never queen, how do you feel about that decision?"

"Better every day," I said.

"So no regrets?"

I raised their hands in mine and said, "If you had this waiting at home, would you regret?"

She'd laughed, and just agreed with me. The interview got a lot of attention, mostly for the whole love-between-the-men thing. None of us are bothered by it. In the end, if the rumors don't bother us, what do they matter?

People seemed amazed that we gave up being queen and king for love. Milton said, "Better to reign in hell than serve in heaven." I say, let heaven and hell fight their own battles, and rule themselves.

I go to sleep pressed between the warmth of their bodies. I wake in the night to the sound of their breathing. I got to watch their faces at the doctor's office, all of their faces, as we heard the heartbeats of our babies, so fast, like frightened birds. I saw their faces as we watched those shadows on the screen move and flex, and found out that one of them was very much a boy. They are debating names now, and I'm enjoying how happy they all are, we all are.

The question that no interviewer has asked was this: If you had let Frost die, and taken the throne, how would you have felt? We had missed our Killing Frost, and found that no throne, no crown, no power, no gift of Goddess made up for the loss of him. We'd already felt the sorrow of that loss, and neither Doyle nor I had ever been king or queen. You cannot miss what you never had, but you can miss forever the man you loved and lost.

I don't want to miss anyone else, ever again.

I am Princess Meredith NicEssus and I finally have my happy-ever-after ending in the City of Angels on the Shores of the Western Sea. Sometimes Fairyland is where you make it.

ABOUT THE AUTHOR

LAURELL K. HAMILTON is the **New York Times** bestselling author of the Meredith Gentry novels: **A Kiss of Shadows, A Caress of Twilight, Seduced by Moonlight, A Stroke of Midnight, Mistral's Kiss,** and **A Lick of Frost,** as well as sixteen acclaimed Anita Blake, Vampire Hunter novels. She lives in St. Louis, Missouri. Visit her website at www.laurellkhamilton.org.